WHIT~~E CHRISTMAS~~
FOR THE ~~SINGLE MU~~M

BY
SUSANNE HAMPTON

A ROYAL BABY
FOR CHRISTMAS

BY
SCARLET WILSON

MILLS
& BOON

Christmas Miracles in Maternity

*Hope, magic and precious new beginnings
at Teddy's!*

Welcome to Teddy's Centre for Babies and Birth,
where the brightest stars of neonatal and obstetric
medicine work tirelessly to save tiny lives and
deliver bundles of joy all year round—but there's
never a time quite as magical as Christmas!

Although the temperature might be
dropping outside, unexpected surprises
are heating up for these dedicated pros! And as
Christmas Day draws near secrets are revealed,
hope is ignited and love takes over.

Cuddle up this Christmas
with the heart-warming stories of the doctors,
nurses, midwives and surgeons at Teddy's in the
Christmas Miracles in Maternity miniseries:

The Nurse's Christmas Gift
by Tina Beckett

The Midwife's Pregnancy Miracle
by Kate Hardy

White Christmas for the Single Mum
by Susanne Hampton

A Royal Baby for Christmas
by Scarlet Wilson

All available now!

WHITE CHRISTMAS FOR THE SINGLE MUM

BY
SUSANNE HAMPTON

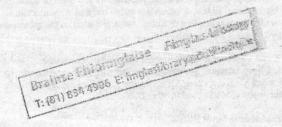

MILLS & BOON

Published in Great Britain 2016
By Mills & Boon, an imprint of HarperCollins*Publishers*
1 London Bridge Street, London, SE1 9GF

© 2016 Harlequin Books S.A.

Special thanks and acknowledgement are given to Susanne Hampton for her contribution to the Christmas Miracles in Maternity *series*

ISBN: 978-0-263-91527-3

Our policy is to use papers that are natural, renewable and recyclable products and made from wood grown in sustainable forests.
The logging and manufacturing processes conform to the legal environmental regulations of the country of origin.

Printed and bound in Spain
by CPI, Barcelona

Dear Reader,

In this Christmas story my heroine, Dr Juliet Turner, is seconded from a hot Australian summer to the snow-covered Cotswolds. Ordinarily this wouldn't be an issue for her, a young, single, world-renowned specialist, but while Juliet has no man to hold her back she *does* have a four-year-old daughter, Bea, to consider. Despite her reservations, it appears that Juliet is the only one concerned about her taking Bea on this adventure that will include their first white Christmas alone on the other side of the world.

But *will* it be a Christmas alone? Pretty quickly Bea thinks that her mother's nemesis, handsome OB/GYN Dr Charlie Warren, might just be a suitable daddy. Although widower Charlie finds moments of joy with the little girl and her mother, he is still burdened with overwhelming guilt over his wife's death. Can Charlie step from behind the cloud that darkens his life? And can Juliet learn to trust again after being left after only one night with Bea's biological father? Love has healing properties like nothing else, and that is just what Charlie and Juliet need to leave their pain behind. Will a white Christmas bring this single mum the happiness she deserves?

I hope you enjoy Juliet and Charlie's journey to happily-ever-after, and I wish you all a very Merry Christmas filled with love!

Warmest regards,

Susanne

Thank you to the wonderfully talented and incredibly witty Mills & Boon authors who shared this writing journey with me… Scarlet Wilson, Kate Hardy and Tina Beckett. You have made writing this book like a road trip with new friends. You all helped to make it a joyful experience and one I will never forget.

And to my amazing editor, Nicola…thank you again for your guidance and unending patience as we brought this book to life.

Married to the man she met at eighteen, **Susanne Hampton** is the mother of two adult daughters, Orianthi and Tina. She has enjoyed a varied career path, but finally found her way to her favourite role of all: Medical Romance author. Susanne has always read romance novels and says, 'I love a happy-ever-after, so writing for Mills & Boon is a dream come true.'

Books by Susanne Hampton

Mills & Boon Medical Romance

The Monticello Baby Miracles
Twin Surprise for the Single Doc

Midwives On-Call
Midwife's Baby Bump

Unlocking the Doctor's Heart
Back in Her Husband's Arms
Falling for Dr December
A Baby to Bind Them
A Mummy to Make Christmas

Visit the Author Profile page
at millsandboon.co.uk for more titles.

Praise for
Susanne Hampton

'A stunning read about new beginnings that is guaranteed to melt any reader's heart.'

—*Goodreads* on
Falling for Dr December

CHAPTER ONE

IT WAS FOUR in the morning and snow was gently falling in the darkness like tiny stars floating to the ground when Charlie Warren awoke from a nightmare that was all too familiar. Beads of perspiration trailed over his half-naked body. The nights it happened were less in number than the year before but they still came with a regularity he found strangely comforting. Feeling the pain was better than feeling nothing. Or facing the fear of letting go completely. That was something he could still not bring himself to contemplate.

For the few hours that sleep claimed him during those nights, Charlie would relive the moments of impact. Sounds echoed in his mind, each as haunting as the one before. The buckling metal and splintering glass as his car skidded out of his control and slammed into the old oak tree. It was the crash that had claimed his wife and had come close to claiming Charlie's sanity. He would wake and in the deafening silence lie motionless in his bed thinking over and over about the conversation they should have shared that fateful night. The one when he told his wife it was too dangerous to venture out. The one when he firmly and resolutely refused to take the risk on the treacherous road. The conversation he would regret for the rest of his life that they'd never had.

Some nights were worse than others and on the very worst the nightmares began the moment his head hit the pillow and ended as he sat bolt upright woken by either the ringing of the telephone or his alarm clock. Both signalling he should head in to the hospital, the only place that gave him purpose.

But this night he'd been woken from his tortured sleep by the sound of a falling branch outside his window. The weight of the snowfall had been too much for the narrow branch and it had snapped, crushing against the leadlight window. It had not broken the glass, merely scratched down the panes as it fell, making a noise not unlike a dying animal's scream.

Still damp with sweat, Charlie rushed to the window believing an injured deer might have roamed into his property, but he quickly saw the silhouette of the damaged tree lit by the moon. There were no streetlights as Charlie's home was on a large estate. The seven-bedroom, seventeenth-century, run-down and previously unloved manor home was undergoing much-needed renovations so he was sleeping downstairs on the leather chesterfield in the sitting room while work was being completed on the upstairs part of the house.

The stone slate roof had been in a state of disrepair for too long and the ceilings had been damaged in most of the upstairs rooms. The master bedroom was due to be finished within a few days. The rooms were all empty and waiting to be filled with new furniture although Charlie had no burning desire to see any of it, let alone choose it, so he had left those decisions up to the decorator. He wasn't rushing to move back into the master bedroom. He had not shared it with anyone for two years and he had no plans of sharing it again. His wife, Alice, had begun the renovations and he was seeing them through to completion in her honour. After that he did not know what he would do with the home.

Or himself, for that matter. Other than work, he had no plans for the future.

As always, once Charlie had been woken he found it hard to fall back into a sound sleep again. He read for a while and then tried once again to sleep. But slumber evaded him so he slipped on his heavy winter dressing gown, tied it loosely around his hips, headed into his kitchen and made himself a coffee. While memories of the accident monopolised his dreams, it was the impending arrival of the Australian *in-utero* surgeon that dominated his waking thoughts, leaving him both anxious and irritated about her potential interference.

The hospital's decision, or more precisely Assistant Head of Obstetrics, Oliver Darrington's decision, to fly the specialist over to consult infuriated him. In Charlie's opinion there was nothing to be gained and everything to lose. The quadruplets were only weeks away from being big enough to deliver and, as the attending OBGYN, Charlie thought any deviation from the treatment plan should be his decision. *In-utero* surgery carried risks that he did not consider warranted. And he wouldn't readily agree with the procedure without proof it was the best way forward.

As he looked out over what many would call a joy of the Cotswolds at Christmas, the majestic sight of dawn breaking over the snow-capped hillside, Charlie barely noticed any of the landscape. With his blood pressure beginning to rise, he sat down at the large oak kitchen table, sipping the coffee that was warming his fingers.

Dr Charlie Warren was unable to appreciate anything because he was preparing himself for a professional battle.

This time his words of caution would be heard. And heard loudly.

* * *

'What on earth do you mean, *there's no need for me to scrub in*?'

Juliet Turner spun around with confusion dressing her brow and a surgical gown covering her petite frame. 'My patient's on the operating table, prepped for an open foetal repair of a neural tube defect. I *have* to scrub in. This can't be postponed.'

'It hasn't been postponed, Dr Turner,' the theatre nurse told her. 'The surgery's going ahead today. It's just that you're not the surgeon operating.'

Juliet's nostrils flared behind the operating mask. 'That's even more ridiculous. There has to be a mistake.'

'No mistake, Dr Turner. Another *in-utero* specialist has been brought in to take over,' the nurse replied firmly. 'He's already arrived, and in gowning now. Orders came from further up the food chain than me, so don't go shooting the messenger.'

'*He's* in gowning! I'm sorry, Angie, but this is absolute nonsense,' Juliet said as she returned her focus to lathering her hands and forearms as a visible protest. She wasn't backing down and had no intention of relinquishing her role. Kelly Lester would have her surgery and her baby would have the best chance of a normal life. And she was operating as scheduled.

Being a female in a male-dominated profession had taught her to stand up for herself very early on. She had known entering the profession that women were at least twice as likely to drop out of surgical training programmes as men, making her well aware that it would not be an easy path and a shrinking violet would not succeed. During her studies her father, also a surgeon in the same field, often told her that, while half of the medical students in Australia and New Zealand were female, women made up less than ten per cent of fully qualified surgeons. It was a harsh reminder that she would have to be strong, focused and have a voice to survive. And she was going to use her voice whenever needed. Loud and clear.

It appeared that day was going to be one of those occasions.

'I will not allow another surgeon to just step in now without a damned good reason. I know this is not at the patient's request. I spoke to her only an hour ago.'

'No, it wasn't the patient who has requested the change, Dr Turner, and I understand you're taken aback but I'm just passing on the message, not making the decision. However, I'm telling you the decision's final. You really do need to stop scrubbing. Having sterile hands won't change the outcome.'

Not hiding her irritation, Juliet turned off the flow of water with the foot control. 'Well, we'll just see about that.'

'On the bright side, your replacement will no doubt meet with your approval. You've worked together more than a few times.'

Juliet was doubly confused with the smirk on Angie's face. None of it made any sense but if she was to believe the nurse, and she had no reason to doubt her, she was being replaced without notice or reason. 'I don't care who's been brought in to take over, it's still madness,' Juliet replied as she pulled her surgical cap free and the mass of brown curls dropped around her face. At that moment, the replacement doctor entered the scrub room.

'Really,' she announced, shaking her head in disbelief. 'This is becoming more and more ludicrous by the minute. They call you back here two days after you retire. What is this craziness? I've a patient about to be anaesthetised and I'm told I'm not operating. Will someone please explain the absurd rationale behind all of this? And who made the call to replace me as Kelly's surgeon?'

'The hospital director…but with good reason,' he replied.

'I can't think of one.'

'You have to prepare for your trip.'

Juliet paused for a moment with a perplexed stare. 'For goodness' sake has everyone gone completely mad? My trip's not until the middle of next week. I've got five days to prepare for the lectures and board the plane, but Kelly's baby needs this operation now if he's to ever walk.'

'That's where you're wrong…not about Kelly and her baby—you're right on that one, I just finished reading the notes and the surgery's urgent—but your trip's not next week. It's tomorrow. You're leaving on an eight o'clock flight in the morning.'

'Tomorrow? But why?' Juliet dropped her head into her hands still damp from the antibacterial wash. 'The lecture is not until next Thursday.'

'You're not delivering the lecture in Auckland…you're off to the UK—'

'The lecture's been cancelled?' she cut in.

'No, the lecture is going ahead…'

'But without me?' she asked as she pulled free her surgical gown and dropped it unceremoniously in the bin alongside her discarded cap.

'Yes.'

'And the surgery's proceeding too, just without me?' They were framed as questions but Juliet's tone made it obvious they were statements that she was none too happy about.

'That's right.'

'And I'm off to the UK?' she continued with the volume of her voice escalating and increasing in speed with each word. 'Before I go completely loopy, just tell me why my schedule is changing before my eyes without my approval?'

'The call came through from Cheltenham just now.'

'Cheltenham? As in the Cotswolds?'

'One and the same.'

'And who over there's making decisions without consulting with me?'

'The decision was made by four babies.'

Juliet blinked and shook her head. 'Four? You're speaking in riddles and you know that frustrates me.'

'Apparently the Assistant Head of Obstetrics at Teddy's, which is the maternity wing of the Royal Cheltenham hospital, spoke with our Head of Obstetrics about the quads. Almost twenty-nine weeks' gestation, suffering twin-to-twin transfusion syndrome. Two sets of monozygotic twins. While the girls are fine at this stage, the boys have developed the TTTS. Oliver Darrington believes you're the best chance that the quads have of all surviving should the parents agree to the *in-utero* laser surgery. And Professor Le Messurier just approved your secondment.'

'That's all very flattering but why am I being called in at the eleventh hour? If there was a risk, I should've been consulted upon the initial diagnosis. Surely being quads they would have been having weekly scans and intense monitoring and they'd know at Teddy's that the earlier the intervention, the better the outcome.'

'Apparently the quads were being closely monitored throughout the pregnancy, but the TTTS diagnosis has only just been made,' her replacement continued as he began scrubbing in, and over the sound of the running water he continued his explanation. 'The girls have separate placentas while the boys have one shared placenta so they were being scrutinised for any signs of transfusion. Up until now there was no indication of anything being amiss. It was picked up when the patient presented in what she thought was premature labour.'

'Caused by the amniotic fluid imbalance affecting the recipient twin.'

'Again, apparently but you'll know more details when you get there.'

'But the lecture in Auckland?'

'Handled. I'm not sure who's your proxy but your focus needs to be on the quadruplets. Darrington's worried it could deteriorate quickly and there's an increased risk they could lose at least one of them if you don't get over to Teddy's immediately, and of course we know the risks if one dies to the remaining foetuses. The parents have been briefed and want to be fully informed so they can consider *all* options, in particular the *in-utero* surgery.'

'Anything else I need to know?'

'Just one thing…the attending OBGYN, Dr Charlie Warren, is averse to fetoscopic laser surgery. Believes the risks are too great so no doubt he'll be challenging you.'

Juliet took a deep breath. 'Looks like I'll be catching a plane tomorrow morning to meet Dr Warren's challenge and convince him otherwise.'

'I hope he knows what he's up against.'

'He soon will.' With her head tilted just slightly, and the remnants of bewilderment still lingering, she looked at her replacement. 'Okay, Dad, looks like Kelly and her baby are in your hands now.'

'Don't worry, honey. I'll do you proud.'

CHAPTER TWO

'DR TURNER, WE'RE about five minutes away from the Royal Cheltenham hospital.'

The voice of the immaculately suited driver made Juliet lift her tired eyes to meet his in the rear-view mirror. They were warm and smiling back at her but with a curiosity that she had been so very accustomed to over the years. She was well aware that she didn't look her thirty-three years and many apparently found it difficult to believe she was a doctor let alone a surgeon. Her curly brown hair and spattering of freckles along with her petite frame, she realised, didn't help her quest to be taken seriously. She had no time for make-up except for a natural lip gloss to prevent her lips from cracking, and that too added to her young appearance. It also helped her go under the radar and not gain the attention of the opposite sex and, although it wasn't her primary motivation, it was a welcome side effect.

But despite the general consensus, she was both a surgeon and a mother and she took both roles incredibly seriously. Her work, she loved with a passion, and her daughter, she loved more than anyone and anything in the world. And more than she had ever dreamed possible.

'Thank you,' she responded as she gently turned to stir the little girl fast asleep and leaning against her. Running her fingers down the child's ruddy cheeks, she softly kissed the top of her head. 'Wake up, Bea, my precious little sleepyhead.'

The little girl silently protested at being disturbed and nestled in tighter to the warmth of her mother's woollen overcoat. Her eyelashes flickered but her eyes were far too heavy to open.

'Well, I hope this part of your marathon travel's been pleasant,' the driver commented.

'Very pleasant, thank you.'

'So how many hours have you two been travelling to be here this morning?'

'I think it's about thirty five hours, but it feels like for ever,' she replied with a little sigh, thinking back over the logistical nightmare they had survived. 'We left Perth early yesterday, Australian time, had a layover in Singapore before we headed on to Heathrow, and then the sixty-mile trip to the Cotswolds with you,' Juliet added as she continued to try and wake her still-drowsy little girl as gently as possible. She wasn't sure just how coherent she was but didn't want to appear rude. She had a lot on her mind, including the impending *in-utero* surgery on the quadruplets within the week. The reason she had been seconded halfway around the world at a minute's notice.

Keeping all four babies viable was everyone's focus. And something everyone agreed could not be done with Juliet on the other side of the world. Well, almost everyone agreed. She knew she would have her work cut out convincing the quads' OBGYN, Dr Charlie Warren. She presumed he would be leaning towards bed rest, high-protein diet and medication for the quads' mother. It was conservative and Juliet was surprised that he was not encouraging the laser surgery. She'd had no time to research the man but assumed he might be perhaps closer to the driver's age and had managed previous TTTS cases in that manner. But once he heard her argument for the surgery, surely the traditional English physician would see that her method had clear benefit? Particularly once she stated her case and the supporting statistics. How could he not? With both hospitals agreeing that Juliet was best placed to undertake the procedure, all she needed was the parents' approval. She was not about to allow Teddy's overtly conservative OBGYN to question the validity of her surgical intervention. It was an argument she was more than prepared to have. And to win.

But that wasn't the issue that had weighed most heavily on her mind on the long flights over to the UK. It was her parenting. How responsible was it to drag her daughter with her? she had wondered incessantly. And with less than twenty-four hours' notice. The poor little girl barely knew what was happening. The only thing that she could really comprehend was a plane trip to see snow.

Up until that point Juliet and Bea's lives had been so settled and planned. Some might say overly so, and among those were Juliet's parents. They had openly encouraged her to take Bea with her and together enjoy the opportunity to travel. In her home town, Juliet's mother looked after Bea three days a week and the other two days Bea was in childcare only five minutes from Juliet's workplace at the Perth Women's and Children's Medical Centre. When the proposition of travelling to the UK had been forced upon her, Juliet's parents had quickly had to push her out of her comfort zone and into embracing the opportunity. Her mother had immediately brought the suitcases down from the attic and personally delivered them to Juliet's home and offered to help her pack. Juliet didn't doubt it would be better for the quads for her to be there but it was not just *her* any more. She had her daughter to consider in every decision she made.

'I just hope I'm doing the right thing in dragging Bea to the other side of the world for such a short time,' Juliet had muttered in the car on the way to the airport at five-thirty in the morning. Her father had been driving, her mother next to Bea in the back seat.

'That's just it, honey, it might not be a short time,' her father reminded her as he pulled up at traffic lights and turned to his daughter. 'You don't know when the quads will arrive and it's best you stay until they do. There could be post-operative or postnatal complications, so it's better to remain there up to the birth.'

'I know you're right, but this whole trip is so rushed, I've had no time to prepare mentally. I know it's too late, but I can't hide the fact I'm having second thoughts about everything.'

'It's an amazing opportunity to consult at Teddy's and no one can come close to your level of expertise,' he said with pride colouring his voice as the lights changed and he took off down the highway. 'It's part of a teaching hospital, and along with assisting those four babies, not to mention their mother, you can add value to the students', interns' and residents' learning experience. You're the best in your field, Juliet. And I should know since I've operated alongside you more than once. It's time you took your skills out to the world, not just in research papers and journals and lecture tours, but in person in an operating theatre.'

'Dad, you're completely biased.'

'Nonsense, your father's right. We're both proud of you and you need to take that knowledge and expertise where it's needed most. Those babies and their parents need you,' her mother argued from the back seat. Her voice was soft but her tone was firm. Gently she kissed the top of her granddaughter's head. 'While we'd love to have Bea stay with us if it was for your three-day trip to Auckland, this is not three days. Poor little thing, she would fret terribly without you for any longer than a few days and visiting the UK will be such a wonderful experience for her too. It will be her first white Christmas.'

'And mine,' Juliet said, but her tone lacked her mother's enthusiasm as she drummed her fingers nervously on the leather upholstered seat. There was an uneasiness stirring in the pit of her stomach.

'Exactly, so stop questioning your decision. It's made now, you're both going,' her father piped up as he took the turnoff to Perth International airport in the dawn light. 'You've been hiding away, Juliet. You're not the only professional woman who's going it alone as a single mother. It's not the eighteen hundreds, and you don't need a man to help you realise your dreams. You have your career and Bea.'

She was hardly *going it alone*, in her opinion, with all of the help her parents provided, she thought as she looked out of her window and up into the still-darkened sky. But her father was right, she mused. She didn't need a man to experience or enjoy life. She and Bea would be just fine on their own. The plane would be up in that same sky in less than two hours, the sun would be up and they would be heading off to the other side of the world. To see four babies…and snow.

Juliet tried to muster a smile for everyone's sake. Her parents were always forthcoming with their very modern wisdom and they were generally right about everything. The quads needed surgical intervention and Bea needed to be with her mother. And Juliet could hardly stand being away from her daughter for a day, let alone the possibility of three or four weeks. So if Juliet went, then so would Bea.

Initially she wasn't sure how she would manage but when the information had arrived via email the night before, providing the details of the onsite hospital crèche, it had given Juliet no valid reason not to say yes to everything. Besides which, the tickets had been arranged. There was no turning back. And so it was that, with less than a day's notice, Juliet and Bea had left their sunburnt homeland behind and were on their way to Teddy's.

'It's a beautiful part of the world,' the driver announced, bringing Juliet back to the present. 'I've lived here for almost thirty years. Raised my children and now my grandchildren. You'll be sure to love it too.'

Juliet smiled at the way the man praised his home town. 'I won't be here quite that long, but long enough to enjoy the stunning scenery.' She looked out from the car window across fields blanketed in snow and dotted with trees and bushes in variant shades of green, all dusted by a fresh layer of white drift along the fences. It was so picturesque and a very long way from the long hot summer days of home. Since she could not turn back she had decided that she needed to accept her decision and be excited to share her first white Christmas with Bea. While she knew it had the potential to be a stressful time for her, with the impending surgery she would be performing, she was glad the two of them were together. They were like two musketeers off on an adventure.

Juliet had long accepted there would never be a third musketeer in their lives and that suited her fine. She didn't need a man in her life. Apart from her father, the rest just brought grief. Even in a new country, a man she had not laid eyes upon, Dr Charlie Warren's objection to her surgical option was another piece of proof that men caused unnecessary anguish.

And she didn't need any more of that.

'So you're only here for a short visit, then?'

'I'm consulting at Teddy's for a few weeks. I agreed because it was a short term. I couldn't keep my daughter away from her grandparents for too long. They'd miss her terribly.'

'I can see why. She's a proper little sweetie,' the man added, clearly wanting to keep the conversation flowing.

Juliet guessed him to be in his mid-fifties. He looked a little like her father, quite distinguished, greying around his temples with a moustache and fine-rimmed gold glasses. Her father was a chatty man too, even in the operating theatre. Perhaps it was his age that made it easy for her to talk to this man. There was no hidden agenda. Just pleasant conversation.

'Thank you. She's my little angel and she's a real sweetie.'

'She's got your curls and pretty eyes. I don't think her father got much of a look-in there. My granddaughter's just the same, spitting image of her mother.'

Juliet felt her stomach sink a little, the way it always did at the mention of Bea's father. The man who had caused more anguish than she had ever thought possible. A man who didn't want *a look-in*. He was the one time she had let down her guard and the reason she would never do it again. After the one romantic night they had shared, he had walked away and never looked back. Married the fiancée he had forgotten to mention to Juliet while he was seducing her. And as quickly as he had swept into her life, he was gone. Well before she had discovered she was having his baby. Two months after the night they spent together, Juliet had caught sight of his wedding photo complete with huge bridal party in the society pages of the local newspaper.

She had instantly felt overwhelmingly sad for his new wife.

Heaved twice with morning sickness.

And sworn off men.

For ever.

Juliet paid the driver and asked him to take her bags to the boutique hotel where she was staying for a few nights. The hospital had contracted the car service and, after their conversation, she felt she could trust him to take her belongings, including Beatrice's pink fairy princess suitcase, and leave them with the hotel concierge. Being over fifty meant he fell in the trustworthy category. Men under forty had no hope in hell of being trusted with anything belonging to Juliet.

Not her suitcases…her medical decisions…or her heart.

With Juliet holding Bea's gloved hand tightly, the two of them stepped inside the warmth of the main entrance of the hospital to hear the heart-warming sound of piped Christmas carols. Juliet slipped off her coat and laid it over her arm and then unbuttoned Bea's as she watched her daughter's eyes widen at the sight of their surroundings. Teddy's, as the hospital was affectionately known, was certainly dressed in its Christmas best. Neither Juliet nor Bea had seen such a huge tree and certainly not one as magnificently decorated as the one that filled the glass atrium. It was overflowing with brightly coloured baubles, and tiny lights twinkled from behind the gold tinsel generously covering the branches. Their eyes both scanned around the foyer to see a Santa sleigh and carved wooden reindeers welcoming patrons to the hospital tea room and all the staff appeared as happy as both Juliet and Bea felt at that moment.

'Ith very beautiful, Mummy.'

'It is indeed.'

Taking hold again of her tiny daughter's hand, Juliet approached the information desk and introduced herself and mentioned her appointment with the OBGYN with whom she would be working.

'I'm sorry, Dr Turner, but Dr Warren hasn't arrived yet. He was due an hour ago but, to be honest, I haven't heard anything so I can't be sure what time we'll see him.'

Juliet's expression didn't mask her surprise. She had flown almost eight thousand miles and had arrived on time and Dr Charlie Warren, whom she assumed to be a resident of the Cotswolds and who therefore had a significantly shorter journey, was the one late for their meeting. She was not impressed and hoped he had a darned good explanation since she and Bea were each in need of a bath and some sleep and had gone without both to meet with him.

'Is Oliver Darrington available, then?'

'Mr Darrington's on surgical roster today so, I'm sorry, he won't be available until after four-thirty.'

Juliet was trying to think on her feet. And both her feet and her brain were tired. 'Then while we're waiting for Dr Warren perhaps I can take my daughter to the crèche.'

'Of course, that's on this floor but the other side of the building overlooking the visitor gardens,' the young woman told her. 'If you follow the corridor on your left to the end then turn right, you'll see it.' Then smiling, she added, 'And hear it. It's quite the noisy place with all the little ones.'

Juliet hesitated; she didn't want to walk away with

Bea and have Dr Warren arrive. She checked her mobile phone for messages. Perhaps Dr Warren had been delayed and sent the hospital a message that hadn't reached Reception but had been relayed to her in a text. It seemed logical and it would give her an indication of how much time she had to settle Bea into the crèche, but after quickly finding her phone she discovered there was no such message.

'I suppose I shouldn't be surprised,' she muttered under her breath. 'Another unreliable man.'

'Pardon, Mummy?'

Juliet looked down at the angelic face staring back at her. 'Nothing, sweetie, Mummy was just mumbling. Everything's just perfect.'

'Okay,' Bea replied as her eyes darted from one festive decoration to the next before she began pulling her mother back in the direction of the main doors.

Juliet knew everything in their lives was not perfect but she would make it as perfect as she could for her daughter. She would devote her life to ensuring that Bea never felt as if she was missing out on anything. Particularly not about the lack of a father in her life. Juliet often felt sad that, while she enjoyed a wonderful relationship with her own father, Bea would never experience that bond. Although, she conceded gratefully, while the special father-daughter relationship would never be a part of her daughter's life, an unbreakable grandfather-granddaughter relationship had already formed. Juliet's father and Bea were like two peas in a pod and seeing that closeness brought Juliet joy.

She was drawn back to the current situation, caused again by a man. Bea's grip was tight and she was clearly on a mission as she tried to pull Juliet along. Juliet tugged back. 'It's so cold outside, darling. Let's stay in here where it's nice and warm.'

'But, Mummy, it lookth like the top of my cake.'

'What looks like the top of your cake, sweetie?'

'Out there,' the excited little girl replied as she pointed to the snow-covered ground. The branches of the trees and even the cars that had been parked for a few hours had been blanketed.

Juliet had to agree that it did look like Bea's fourth birthday cake. Her grandmother had baked a triple-layer strawberry sponge cake with a generous covering of brilliant white icing and decorated with four different fairy tale princesses for her beloved granddaughter. But this was not a cake, it was their reality for the next few weeks, and, despite her reservations and her annoyance with Charlie Warren, it was very pretty. Postcard pretty. And it was the first time either of them had seen snow up close and she couldn't blame her daughter for wanting to go outside and enjoy it.

'But I need to stay inside and wait for the doctor. He'll be here any minute, *I hope*, and I don't want to miss him when he arrives because after my meeting with him you and I can go to the hotel and have a nice nap.'

'*Pleeease* can I play in the snow?'

Juliet felt the sleeve of her blouse being tugged by two tiny hands, still gloved, and Bea's eyes were wide with anticipation and excitement. Juliet looked out to the fenced area near the entrance doors. There was a park bench, see-saw and a small slide and the playground was secured with a child safety gate. It was clearly a designated area for children to play on a sunny day but it wasn't a sunny day. It was freezing cold, overcast and the ground was covered with snow, which she knew was the draw card for Bea but a cause for concern for Juliet.

Although she didn't want to impose a fear of almost everything onto her daughter, she couldn't help but worry.

After a moment she took a deep breath; she had made her decision. 'All right, you can play outside but only if we button up your coat again, put on your hat and keep your gloves on…and only for five minutes. And I mean five minutes—you'll catch a terrible cold if you stay out any longer.'

'Yeth! Yippee! Thank you, Mummy.'

With trepidation, Juliet buttoned up her daughter's heavy overcoat, pulled a knitted cap from her bag and popped it over Bea's mass of honey-blonde curls, pulling it down over her ears, and then slipped on her own coat again before walking the little girl outside into the wintry weather. She was still worried about leaving Bea for even five minutes, but common sense told her it would be safe. It was ten o'clock in the morning not the middle of the night and it was no longer snowing.

Her father's words rushed back into her head, 'You can't keep Bea in bubble wrap. Let her have some fun sometimes or she'll grow up scared of taking chances. Who knows what she can do in life if she's allowed to really live it? She might even become a surgeon like her mother…and grandfather.'

Although Juliet loved her work, she wasn't convinced medicine was the life she wanted for her daughter. Part of her wondered if the lack of a social life due to the years of heavy study load, and then the long shifts at the hospital as an intern, then as a resident didn't assist Bea's father to deceive her. She was far from streetwise about men. She'd had friends but never a love interest until she met him and he'd swept her off her feet and into his bed. Making her believe their night together was the beginning of something more. She wanted Bea to be wiser and not naive about the opposite sex.

But that was many years away and this was a playground. But it was still making Juliet very nervous.

She paused at the playground gate and looked down at her daughter, trying unsuccessfully to mask her concern.

'Mummy, I'll be good, I promith.'

Juliet realised she was being silly. It was only a children's playground and one she could see from inside and so too could all of the staff in the hospital foyer and the tea room. Juliet needed to meet with the now quite late Dr Warren. There might be a message from him any minute. She also wanted to meet the quadruplets' mother as soon as possible to discuss her treatment plan. Bending down and looking Bea in the eyes, she said, 'Mummy has to talk with the nice lady at the desk inside. I'll be back in five minutes. You know my rule—don't talk to strangers.'

Bea nodded. 'Okay.'

With that Juliet closed the childproof gate with Bea inside the playground wearing an ear-to-ear smile, already making small snowballs with her tiny gloved hands. Juliet tugged again on the gate to check it was closed properly before she headed back inside. She doubted she would leave Bea for five minutes, estimating it would only take two to check again on Dr Warren's whereabouts and see if there had been an update on his ETA. And she would be watching her the entire time through the large glass windows.

Charlie Warren pulled into the Royal Cheltenham hospital astride his black motorcycle. Both he and the bike were geared for riding in the harsh winter conditions of the southern English countryside. The sound of the powerful engine reverberated across the grounds as he cruised into the sheltered area of the car park. Charlie climbed from the huge bike that would have dwarfed most men, but, at six feet one, his muscular frame dressed in his leather riding gear stood tall against the bike. He removed his snow-splattered black helmet and heavy riding gloves and ran his still-warm fingers through his short but shaggy blond hair. It was cold riding to work every day, even brutal his colleagues would tell him some days in the middle of winter, but Charlie wouldn't consider for a moment taking a car. He couldn't; he didn't own one. Not any more and not ever again. He hadn't driven a car of any description in the two years since the crash.

Two years and three days to be exact. The anniversary was only a few days earlier, and, he assumed, was the reason the nightmares had returned. He knew he would never forget the date. It was the day the life he loved had ended.

After that, little brought him joy outside his work.

He had nothing to look forward to each night he rode away from the hospital. So he didn't stay away from Teddy's for too long.

Juliet watched Bea giggling as she climbed carefully up each rung of the tiny ladder on the slide. Her gloved hands gripped on tightly, her tiny feet, snug inside her laced-up leather boots, struggled a little not to slide, but she still smiled a toothy grin at her mother. Juliet loved seeing her daughter so happy and she smiled back but her smile was strained. Worry was building by the minute as she watched her only daughter take each slippery step, but her father's words resonated in her head, forcing her to stay put. Reminding her not to run to her daughter or call out, *Climb back down...it's dangerous.*

No, on this trip she would heed his instructions and let her daughter have a bit of fun after all and the slide was only a few feet tall.

What could possibly go wrong?

Bea looked down at each rung then back to her mother. Juliet could see that Bea thought she was such a big girl and seeing that reinforced that her father did know best. Juliet had to let Bea try new things. She had to unwrap the cotton wool that she had lovingly placed around her daughter…but only just a little.

Juliet gave a little sigh and resigned herself to her four-year-old's growing independence and her desire to encourage it but her fear at the same time. She wondered how she would cope when she turned sixteen and asked to get her driver's permit. Mentally she shook herself. *That's twelve years away…you have time to prepare for it.*

With any luck Dr Warren would arrive before then, she sniggered to herself.

At that moment, a smiling Bea lifted her right hand and waved at her mother. But Juliet didn't have time to smile back as she watched in horror as Bea lost her concentration and then her footing. She gasped out loud as her daughter's tiny hands lost their grip too. Helplessly Juliet watched from inside the building as Bea fell backwards to the ground.

CHAPTER THREE

CHARLIE SAW THE small child fall from the playground equipment. He was only too aware that while there was a thick blanket of freshly fallen snow in some places, in other areas there was only a thin covering. The shade the trees gave in summer when they were covered in lush green leaves was lovely but the branches had acted as natural canopies preventing the snow from building up to a level that would have broken her fall. He felt a knot in the pit of his stomach at seeing the child lying motionless on the ground and he rushed across the car park.

While it wasn't an overly tall slide, the child, he could see, was very tiny. As he drew closer he could see there was no one with her. Why would anyone leave a child out in the freezing weather unattended? He looked around and there was no one in sight. No one running to help. Fuelled by concern for the child and anger at the parent or parents, he raced to the gate.

'How damned irresponsible,' he muttered under his breath and shook his head. But his words were driven by something deeper. His dreams of being a father had ended the day his wife died and that made it even harder to see that this child had been left alone. If he were the father he would protect his child at any cost and he would never have left one so tiny out in the cold. Alone.

He undid the safety latch with a sense of urgency as he heard soft moans coming from the child he could then see was a little girl, lying still on her side. She was conscious. He quickly crossed to her and knelt down. 'You'll be okay, honey. I'm a doctor at this hospital. I just want to see if you've been hurt.' He kept his words to a minimum as he could see just how young she was.

'Where'th Mummy? I want Mummy.' Bea's eyes suddenly widened and began to fill with tears.

'We'll try and find Mummy,' he said as he wondered the very same question.

Where the hell was the little girl's mother? And her father?

As he began to check her vital signs he guessed she was between three and four years of age. 'Where does it hurt?'

'My arm hurths,' she said, abruptly sitting upright with tears running down her ruddy cheeks.

Charlie was surprised but relieved to see her level of mobility and suspected her tears were fuelled by fear and pain in equal amounts. 'Anywhere else?'

'No. It'th jutht my arm. Where'th Mummy?' Her chin was quivering and the tears were flowing freely.

Charlie reassured her again they would find her mother as he continued his medical assessment. As she awkwardly tried to climb to her feet, it was obvious to Charlie that she had only injured her arm so he scooped her up ready to take her to the emergency department. Neither a stretcher nor a paramedic team was needed and he wanted to get her out of the bitter cold air immediately and into the warmth of the hospital where she could be thoroughly assessed.

'Put my daughter down now!' Juliet's loud voice carried from the gate to where Charlie was standing.

Charlie's eyes narrowed on her. 'I'm a doctor, so please open the gate for me and step aside. This child's been hurt,' he told her as he approached with Bea still firmly in the grip of his strong arms. 'I'm taking her to have an X-ray.'

Juliet hurriedly opened the gate. 'She's my daughter. I can take her,' she said, reaching out for Bea, but Charlie ignored her request and moved swiftly, and in silence, in the direction of the emergency entrance with Juliet running alongside him.

'I said, I can carry her.'

'I heard you but I have her, so let's keep unnecessary movement to a minimum.'

Juliet nodded. It was logical but she still wished her injured daughter were in her arms, not those of the tall, leather-clad stranger who was supposedly a doctor. 'I saw her fall but I couldn't get to her in time.'

Charlie's eyebrow rose slightly. 'That's of no consequence now. I saw her. I'll get her seen immediately in A&E and then you can perhaps explain why she was left unattended out in this weather at such a young age.'

'Excuse me?' Juliet began in a tone that didn't mask her surprise at his accusatory attitude. While she thought it was unfair and unjust it also hit a raw nerve. 'I wasn't far away—'

'Far enough, it would seem, for me to get to her first,' Charlie cut in with no emotion in his voice. As the three of them entered the warmth of the emergency department, the feeling between them was as icy as the snow outside. 'I need her name and age.'

'Beatrice, but we call her Bea, and she's four years and two months.' Juliet answered but her voice was brimming with emotion. Overwhelming concern about Bea and equally overwhelming anger towards the man who was carrying her child. How dared he be so quick to judge her?

'Four-year-old girl by the name of Bea, suspected green stick fracture of the forearm,' he announced brusquely to the nursing staff as he took long, powerful strides inside with Juliet following quickly on his heels. Charlie carried Bea into one of the emergency cubicles and laid her gently on the examination bed. With the curtains still open, he continued. 'We need an X-ray *stat* to confirm radius or ulna fracture but either way, if I'm correct, we'll be prepping for a cast. And bring me some oral analgesia.'

'Ibuprofen, acetaminophen or codeine?' the nurse asked.

'One hundred milligrams of suspension ibuprofen,' Charlie replied, then, as it was a teaching hospital and he was aware that three final-year medical students had moved closer to observe, he continued. 'Generally paediatric fracture patients have significantly greater reduction in pain with ibuprofen than those in either the acetaminophen group or the codeine group and they suffer less negative side effects.'

'What'th happening, Mummy?'

'The doctor,' she began before she shot an angry glare over her shoulder in Charlie's direction. She was impressed with his knowledge but not his attitude towards her. 'Sweetie, the doctor thinks you may have broken your arm when you fell from the playground slide so he'll take a picture of your arm with a special machine.'

'Will it hurt?'

'The machine won't hurt you at all but they will have to very gently lift your arm to take off your coat and then take a picture. So the doctor will give you some medicine so it doesn't hurt.'

The nurse returned with the ibuprofen and Charlie asked Bea to swallow the liquid.

'Please do as the doctor asks because it will make the pain go away,' Juliet told her daughter with a smile that belied how worried she was. 'Don't worry, Bea, I'll be with you every minute. I'm not leaving your side.'

'That'd be a nice idea,' Charlie put in, with sarcasm evident in his voice just enough for Juliet alone to know the intent of his remark but no one else. Without looking up, he signed the radiograph request the A&E nurse had given him.

Juliet took a deep breath and counted silently to three. It was not the time to tell him just what she thought of his snide remarks, particularly not in the presence of her daughter and the medical students. But that time would come once everyone was out of earshot. And he would hear in no uncertain terms just what he could do with his unwarranted opinion.

'Can you please complete the paperwork?' the nurse asked of Juliet. 'We only need the signature of one parent.'

'Bea only has one parent,' Juliet said flatly before she accepted the clipboard from the nurse and hurriedly but accurately began to complete the details so she could expedite the process and allow Bea to have the X-ray. She wasn't sure if the doctor had heard and she didn't care as Bea's parental status wasn't his concern.

'Dr Warren,' another young nurse began as she neared the trio with a clipboard, 'would you like me to call for the paediatric resident so you can return to the OBGYN clinic?'

'No, I'm here now, I'll finish what I've started.'

'Of course,' the nurse replied. 'Then we can take the patient down as soon as the paperwork is completed.'

'Dr Warren? Dr Charlie Warren?' Juliet demanded as she fixed her eyes on Charlie for a moment. He was not the borderline elderly OBGYN she had pictured. Dr Charlie Warren, she surmised, was closer to his early thirties.

'Yes. Why do you ask?'

Juliet didn't answer immediately. Instead she ensured she had not missed any details on the admissions form before she signed and returned it to the nurse. It gave her a few moments to compose herself and reconcile that the man treating her daughter was the OBGYN who had stood her up for their meeting and the one who wanted to oppose her treatment plan for the quadruplets. He was already very much on the back foot but, with his obvious bad attitude, it did not augur well for them working together.

'Well, Dr Warren, it appears that you owe me an apology since you're the reason why my daughter is in here.' Juliet wore a self-satisfied look, one she felt she more than deserved to display.

'I hardly think so. I just pulled into the car park when your daughter fell. We both know that I had nothing to do with her accident so let's not waste time trying to shift blame. Leaving a child this young alone is something I am not sure I can fully understand...or want to.'

'That's where you're wrong. You have everything to do with the accident because if you'd been on time for our meeting my daughter would not have stepped outside to play.'

'Our meeting?'

'Yes, our ten o'clock meeting,' she began. 'I'm Dr Juliet Turner. The *in-utero* surgeon who has flown halfway around the world and managed to be here on time for a meeting about your quad pregnancy patient, and, I might add, we travelled straight from the airport. My daughter needed to stretch her legs for a minute after such a long journey, so I allowed her to play in the fenced area that I assumed would not be open unless it was in fact child-safe while I enquired further about your arrival. If heavy snowfall changes the safety status of the area then it should be closed. You may like to speak to the hospital board about looking into that matter.' Juliet had not taken a breath during the delivery. Adrenalin was pumping out the words. She was scared for Bea. And extremely angry with Charlie Warren.

'Dr Turner? I had no idea…'

'Clearly…and apparently no time management either.'

Charlie was momentarily speechless. Juliet felt momentarily vindicated.

She noticed a curious frown dress his brow. Then she also noticed, against her will, that his brow was very attractive, as was his entire face. She had been focusing on Bea and not noticed anything much about the man who had whisked her daughter unceremoniously into A&E. But now she noticed his chiselled jaw, deep blue eyes and soft, full mouth. In fact, each moment her eyes lingered on his face she realised he was in fact extremely handsome, even when he frowned. His powerful presence towered over her with long, lean legs and his leather riding gear accentuated his broad shoulders. She shook herself mentally. His manner was both judgmental and conceited. Alarm bells rang in her head. Why were her thoughts even teetering on noticing him past being her daughter's emergency physician? He was just another arrogant man and one she was going to be forced to work with in some capacity.

In a perfect world she would have nothing to do with him once he had finished treating Bea. But she also knew that they didn't live in a perfect world. And not seeing Charlie Warren again wasn't possible. They would be consulting on the high-risk patient until the birth of the four babies.

And she was well aware that, after challenging her parenting, he would shortly be challenging her treatment plan. There was no way this working relationship was going to run smoothly. And she doubted with his attitude he intended to play nicely.

'I had additional house calls this morning as I needed to cover another OBGYN's patients. He's down with the winter virus that swept through Teddy's. With both patient loads it look longer than I anticipated, but point taken. I should have called in.'

Juliet couldn't help but notice him staring at her. It was a curious stare, no longer angry or accusing.

'I understand covering for ill colleagues happens but a text would have been prudent,' she continued, ignoring his reaction, suspecting like everyone else he was looking at her as if she weren't old enough to be a surgical specialist. She had grown tired of that look and in Dr Warren's case she wasn't about to give him any leeway. Nor was she about to give her unexpected reaction to him any acknowledgement. Her tone was brittle but with his masculinity hovering around eleven out of ten he was making it difficult not to be a little self-conscious despite her ire.

'We can speak further about my delay later, Dr Turner, but let's get Bea into Radiography and ascertain the extent of the fracture,' Charlie announced, breaking her train of thought.

Juliet did not respond to Charlie as she wasn't sure what exactly she would say. Her equilibrium was beyond ruffled and she was struggling to keep her thoughts on track. She returned her attention to Bea, and stroked her daughter's brow. 'Mummy and the doctor will be taking you on this special bed to have that picture now. And then if the doctor is right and you have broken the bone in your arm then you will have a cast put on until it's all healed.'

'What'th that?'

'You know when Billy, the little boy from playgroup, fell over last year and he had a bright blue plaster on his arm? And everyone drew pictures on it with crayons? That's a cast.'

Bea nodded. 'I drew a star and a moon.'

'That's right, and it was a very beautiful star and moon.'

'Can I take it off? Billy couldn't take it off.'

'No, you won't be able to take it off but it won't be too uncomfortable,' Charlie chimed in with a voice that Juliet noticed had suddenly warmed. She wasn't sure if that warmth was directed at Bea alone or if he was attempting to be nice to Juliet as well. 'There's a soft bit inside and a hard layer outside that stops your arm from moving so that it can heal.'

Juliet turned back to face Charlie to ask another question and immediately wished she hadn't. He had moved closer and his face was only inches from her. His cologne was subtle and very masculine. She tried to keep the same professional demeanour but dropped her eyes, refusing to keep the courtesy of eye contact for two reasons. One, she was still fuming and waiting for an apology that she doubted she would ever receive, and, two, she didn't want to risk falling into the dark blue pools that were more blue than any she had ever seen before. She didn't want to forgive him for his appalling behaviour. Without all of the facts he had jumped to a conclusion that was unjust. But her hormones were overriding her good sense.

It was completely out of character for her. She was angry and she never paid attention to men, good-looking or not. And she would be damned if she would allow it to happen that day. Or any day in the future.

She quickly decided she didn't want to hear an apology from Charlie. If one was not offered it would mean that she could then remain furious with good reason, keep the man at arm's length and her mettle would not be tested. If he made amends, he might prove to be a distraction on some level that she didn't want. Although she knew her sensible side would win, she didn't want to waste any time on some ridiculous internal battle of hormones versus logic. Particularly when she had a very real battle to fight with the very same man.

Coughing, she cleared her throat in an attempt to gain some composure. Dr Warren's nearness was, for some inexplicable reason, threatening to awaken something in Juliet she had buried a long time ago. And it didn't need digging up now. That part of her life was over. Perhaps it was just sleep deprivation, she wondered. She had not travelled for so many hours straight before either. Nor had her daughter ever suffered an injury of that nature. It had to be the series of events stacked against her that was messing with her logic. Making her emotions a little unstable. It wasn't her. It definitely had to be the combination of factors, she decided, not Charlie Warren himself. Suddenly she had everything back in perspective, the way she liked it. Charlie Warren was her daughter's doctor and her potential nemesis.

'Will you be using fibreglass?' she asked, quieting any sign of emotion. Her heart was no longer beating madly and the butterflies were one by one exiting her stomach. She was proud of herself for so quickly once again gaining control of the situation. Although she was still disturbed the *situation* had presented in the first place.

Jet lag, she quickly told herself. Definitely jet lag.

'If Bea needs a cast we'll use fibreglass and, since it will be difficult to expect Bea to keep it dry, I'll use a waterproof lining too,' Charlie told her.

'Billy had blue but I don't like blue,' Bea said softly, looking down at her arm.

'We have pink and yellow and I think red too,' Charlie responded with his mouth curving to a half-smile and that did not go unnoticed by Juliet.

'I like red for Chrithmath…but pink ith pretty… I want pink,' Bea announced.

Juliet smiled at her daughter. As she lifted her head her eyes met Charlie's eyes staring back at her and her heart once again began to pick up speed. It was madness for certain. The intensity of his gaze wouldn't allow her to look away. It was as if there was something deeper, something hidden behind the outer arrogance. Warmth and kindness seemed almost trapped inside him.

And she couldn't ignore, no matter how much she didn't want it to be true, and how much she'd fought it over the years, that there was a tiny part of her craving warmth and kindness from a man like Charlie.

CHAPTER FOUR

'UNFORTUNATELY BEA HAS a distal radial fracture…but at least it's non-displaced so we should be grateful for that news.'

Charlie turned back from the radiographs on the illuminated viewer in the room to see Juliet holding her daughter closely. He could not help but notice the tenderness in her embrace and the obvious love Juliet had for her daughter. He had been wrong about her, he admitted to himself as he watched her gently kiss the mop of blonde curls on the top of her daughter's head. He had not accompanied them to the radiography department. Instead he had excused himself to change into street clothes he kept in his office and then met them back in the emergency department.

Their eyes met and he paused in silence for a moment. He hoped she had not noticed him staring longer than was necessary but he could not help himself. Despite their professional differences, there was something about Juliet that was making him curious. Making him want to know more about the single mother with the Australian accent; the very pretty face; the spitfire personality; and the adorable daughter. He had noted her mention Bea only had one parent. Whether she was widowed, divorced or had never married, he didn't know. And it was none of his business.

It was out of character for him to be distracted by anything or anyone. Least of all someone he had only just met. But he could not pretend even to himself that he had not been distracted by Juliet, and it was not just her appearance. She was a conundrum. A surgeon who looked closer in age to a first-year medical student while he knew she would have to be in her thirties, with an academic record that would come close to that of a professor and an attitude when provoked of a bull. Not to mention a love for her child that was palpable. He had not met anyone quite like Dr Juliet Turner before.

Charlie was never thrown by anyone or anything. Charlie Warren's life was organised and predictable. It was the only way he could function. He had few friends, save his colleagues during his work hours. Socialising was a thing of the past although he had been forced to attend the recent hospital fundraiser, escaping as soon as decently possible.

He spent any time away from the hospital alone and preferred it that way. In more than two years, Charlie had never experienced any interest in anything other than his work. Returning home only to sleep and prepare for the next day's surgery or consultations. His patients were his sole passion in life. And now the Australian *in-utero* expert, with whom he completely disagreed on a professional level, was rousing his curiosity in knowing more about her.

And it was unsettling.

The second anniversary of the accident had just passed and it was a day he wanted to do differently every night as he lay alone in his bed reliving the hell that had become his waking reality. One he couldn't change. One he had accepted a long time ago that he would live with for the rest of his life. And to be spending any time thinking about a woman other than his late wife was ridiculous.

But as much as he fought the distraction, he couldn't control his wandering thoughts.

He wondered for a moment what life had dealt Juliet. Just being a surgeon would have provided struggles along the way. He had found the study and workload gruelling and he was not raising a child alone. Whether or not her status as a single mother was recent he was unsure. She looked to him like a waif but she had the fire and fight of someone a foot taller and he assumed she would have faced life head-on. His wife had been similar in stature but very different in demeanour and profession. She was quietly spoken, and a local Cotswolds girl who managed a craft shop in town. She spent hours quilting and running the little store that doubled as a social hub for the local community.

Charlie doubted that Juliet would have any interest in quilting. But it bothered him greatly that questions about the woman holding her daughter had suddenly and unexplainably captured his thoughts.

He was grateful that Juliet had been distracted by the nurse coming back and looked away. For some unfathomable reason he was struggling to do just that. The woman before him was nothing close to the stoic surgical specialist he'd been expecting and he was shocked at just how much he had noticed about her in such a short space of time.

And he was angry and disappointed with himself for doing so.

Juliet forced herself to blink away her wandering thoughts. Charlie Warren was nothing close to what she'd been expecting. His white consulting coat covered black dress jeans and blue striped shirt. He was still wearing his black motorcycle boots. The combination of the leather and gunmetal hardware of his boots was both edgy and masculine. It had to stop. She had not flown to another hemisphere to find herself distracted by the first handsome man she met. First handsome, *arrogant* man who would be her work colleague for the next few weeks.

She felt butterflies slowly returning just knowing he was so close to her. Close enough to reach out and touch her. Not that he would…nor would she want that, she told herself sternly. But it was as if she could see there was something more to the man who had rudely stood her up and then berated her for inattention to her daughter. Was his brash exterior a shield? She wasn't sure as she tried in vain to analyse the ogre. Perhaps it was the way he had rushed to Bea. As a man and as a doctor, he had not hesitated to help Juliet's daughter. He had lifted her into the safety and strength of his arms the way a father would. The way Bea's own father never would and the way no man other than her grandfather up until that day had done.

But it was romantic nonsense. He was just the tall and not so dark—more dusty blond—handsome stranger of happily ever after stories that she knew didn't really exist.

There wasn't anything more to this man, her practical self was saying firmly and resolutely despite how her body was arguing. He wasn't even nice let alone the type to sweep her off her feet. He was far too brusque and cold. What was going on in her tired mind? she wondered. It had to be international time difference setting in. Most definitely. It couldn't be anything else stirring her thoughts into chaos. She needed a good night's sleep and all would be as it should be. And she would be looking at her colleague as just that, a colleague. And if his strong, borderline obstinate opinion about her plans on surgical intervention with the quadruplets' mother remained, they would in fact shift from colleagues to adversaries.

She took solace in the idea that their differing opinions would add another protective layer to the armour she wore very comfortably.

'Hmm-hmm…' Juliet coughed. 'I said I'm happy there's no need for a closed reduction.'

'That makes two of us,' he replied, turning back to the radiographic films.

'So there'll be no intervention to realign the bones, just a cast as we already discussed, then?' Juliet continued as she fought to keep her thoughts professional.

'It's standard practice to give the arm a few days in a sling to allow swelling to subside,' Charlie explained to everyone in the room. 'But I'm concerned at Bea's age she may cause further damage if we don't protect the fracture with a cast. There's a marginal amount of swelling around the fracture site but not enough to warrant risking further damage by allowing it to be without protection.' He then asked the nurse to prepare for the cast while three medical students, who had quickly become part of the furniture, continued listening intently. The nurse moved swiftly, while the medication still kept Bea's pain at bay. 'And we need pink. That is the colour you want, isn't it, Bea?'

Bea looked up and nodded.

'Then pink it is,' he told her. The nurse helped Juliet to carefully roll up Bea's long-sleeved top that she had worn underneath the woollen jacket that was still under Juliet's arm.

'You were all layered up, weren't you, young lady?'

the nurse commented with a smile. 'Rugged up for our chilly winter?'

Bea nodded and watched as her mother and the nurse worked gently to lift the clothing free so the cast could be applied.

'It's a nice loose top so it should roll down again afterwards, but the jacket will never fit so we'll have to just rest that over her shoulders and go shopping for a cape,' Juliet mentioned as she dropped the little coat on the nearest chair.

Charlie began the process of applying the cast, explaining to Bea in simple language every step, while also including a short tutorial for the students' benefit as they stood observing the process from the sidelines. Juliet listened to the way he spoke so tenderly to her daughter and she felt the flutter of the annoying butterflies emerging once again. She hated the feeling but she was unable to control it. His manner and tone to Bea made him appear almost fatherly. She sternly told herself it had to be his standard bedside manner...but she wasn't completely convinced.

'Applying a cast is quite a simple procedure,' he began as he turned his attention to the students. 'I'll begin by wrapping several layers of soft cotton around the injured area. Today I'll be applying a short cast that extends from the wrist to just below the elbow as the break is a distal radial fracture so extending further than that would cause unnecessary discomfort to the patient.' Charlie worked at wrapping Bea's tiny injured arm, and as he spoke the fibreglass outer layer was being soaked in water. Gently he wrapped the fibreglass around the soft first layer. 'While the outer layer is wet at the moment, it will dry to a hard, protective covering. I'll make some tiny incisions in the cast to allow for any potential swelling.'

In less than thirty minutes, Beatrice Turner was the proud owner of a pretty pink cast. And her mother could not help but be impressed with the way in which Dr Charlie Warren had attended to her daughter, executed the delicate procedure and managed to deliver a tutorial to the students. All the while continuing to look devastatingly handsome. She shook herself mentally and tried to remind herself of his initial overbearing attitude. But it was difficult when he was displaying such empathy to the little person she loved most in the world.

'Now you need to rest this arm quite still for about an hour, Bea,' Charlie said. 'The nurse will keep an eye on it and we'll leave your top rolled up for the time being.'

Bea just looked at the cast. Her eyes told the story. They were filled with confusion. It had been an overwhelming experience for her and she wasn't taking in much of what was being said at that moment.

'And we can give you a sling to hold it up because it might get heavy over the next few weeks.'

Still Bea just sat in silence. Juliet suspected it was a combination of jet lag and the pain beginning to resurface.

'Mummy will be here,' she told her softly as she stroked her hair.

Juliet waited for another snide remark, in fact she hoped for one, but Charlie made none. She didn't like not having a reason to dislike the man.

'It may get itchy, Bea, and if it does you can tap on the outside and that might help, but don't put anything inside like a pencil because it might scratch your skin and we don't want germs in there.'

Juliet watched as Bea tilted her head slightly with a curious expression on her beautiful face. She knew her daughter was still a little confused by everything that had happened so quickly. It was a lot for a four-year-old to take in such a short amount of time.

'Is there anything else we can do?' Juliet asked, holding Bea's free hand and quickly trying to recall her training in paediatric fractures during medical school. It had been so long since she had graduated from her general medical studies before specialising and she was stretching her memory.

'It would be best to sponge-bathe Bea so that the cast doesn't fill with water in the bath or shower. While the outside of the cast is waterproof, as you know, the inside isn't, even with the special lining. It needs to be kept dry, so no lotions or oils either.' He paused to recall the other instructions that once rolled off his tongue as an A&E resident. 'And if the itching starts to bother Bea, you can use a cool hairdryer to blow air in around the edge of the cast and check now and then that she hasn't hidden small toys or sweets inside the cast. Believe it or not, during my A&E rotation I had more than one child think of it as their secret *hideyhole*.'

'No doubt,' Juliet said with a smile that she hadn't thought previously she would ever display in Charlie's presence. Her defences were slowly melting as his bedside manner warmed the room. She began a mental inventory of Bea's belongings, wondering if she'd brought anything that small with her on the trip. She felt certain as she looked at the tiny gap that Bea's possessions would not fit inside.

'I'm sure you'll have it under control,' Charlie said to her before he turned his attention once again to the medical students. 'Along with asking the parents or caregivers to check the cast regularly for cracks, breaks, tears and soft spots, what else would you ask them to look out for and what would warrant medical attention?'

'Pain that doesn't get better with the prescribed pain relief,' one of the students offered.

'Yes, anything else?'

'If the child complains of feeling numb or tingly in the vicinity of the fracture,' another chimed in with a self-satisfied smile.

'Good.'

'Blisters inside the cast,' the third student said confidently, then continued, 'and fever, or any significant increase in temperature.'

While being a tutor was nothing new to Charlie, doing so back in A&E was a change of pace and very different subject content but he didn't want to exclude the students. 'Well done. You seem to have a good understanding of the basics of paediatric fractures.'

The A&E resident poked her head in at that moment and directed her conversation to the medical students. 'If you're finished here, there's suspected tetanus in bay three and gallstones in bay seven. Take your pick.'

Charlie grinned. 'It's been a while since I've heard a call for one of those conditions. It's usually onset of labour or unexplained abdominal cramps over in Teddy's.'

The three looked at Charlie for approval to leave, which he gave in a nod, and they left, as did the attending nurse, leaving Charlie and Juliet alone with Bea.

'Well, it looks as if we're all finished, then,' Juliet offered in a voice that did not give anything away about the effect Charlie was still having on her, being so near. His natural affinity with her daughter was thawing parts of her she wanted to remain frozen.

'I think we are.' His eyes once again locked on hers for just a minute but long enough to make her heart race just a little faster.

She swallowed nervously, growing more irritated with

herself by the minute. Behaving like a schoolgirl experiencing her first infatuation was not her usual demeanour, nor one she intended to entertain. Not for another second. Reinstating herself as the quads' surgeon, not Bea's mother who had a borderline crush on her daughter's doctor and her own soon-to-be colleague, was a priority.

Biting her lower lip, she tried to channel someone very different from herself. A detached, bumptious persona she had created over the years when people looked at her like a child and they needed reminding of her medical credentials. And it would work perfectly at that moment. 'It's best, then, that we reschedule the *in-utero* surgical consultation that you missed earlier. If you can provide me with overnight obs about both the mother and babies, we'll be off to the hotel so Bea can rest and I can brief myself on their progression and return this afternoon.'

Her voice had suddenly morphed from warm to officious. And as she stood her relaxed posture had become stiff. Her body language screamed confrontation. But Charlie didn't appear to take the bait as he helped Bea down from the examination table. Although his tone returned once again to something more formal and detached.

'I'll email you the updates, Dr Turner.'

She felt she had been successful. The atmosphere in the room had cooled and for that she was grateful. It was just the way she wanted it.

'I appreciate that, Dr Warren.'

'Great, I'll leave you both in the A&E's care and head up to visit with Georgina and Leo. They're waiting for my update on their babies' treatment plan, because since the diagnosis it appears the recipient twin is now struggling.'

Juliet froze on the spot. 'Georgina and Leo Abbiati? The quads' parents?'

'Yes.'

'But that's why I'm here. Why would you not include me in that consultation? And why would you not update me immediately?'

'Because you just excused yourself.'

'No, I didn't,' Juliet argued with her nostrils beginning to flare. 'I excused myself from *our* meeting. Not the meeting with the quads' parents. I thought that was scheduled for this afternoon.'

'It was, but yesterday I decided to bring it forward since the condition had deteriorated slightly. Which is what I just mentioned.'

'What exactly do you mean by "deteriorated slightly"?'

'There's more amniotic fluid so the uterus is almost at capacity. It might be a good idea to do an amniotic reduction.'

'I'll need to assess her immediately,' Juliet told him. 'And I wouldn't be considering the reduction if we are undertaking the laser surgery in a few days.'

'Whether the laser surgery will go ahead is still to be decided by the Abbiatis.'

'And without me, it would appear. Didn't you think that it would be nice to consult with me about treatment plans? I thought we would meet at *ten this morning*, you would brief me on the current viability of all four babies, the affected babies' condition and the mother's status and I would take that into consideration and then, with a consolidated treatment plan, meet with the parents late today.'

'I scheduled it for now as I thought you'd want to meet with the parents immediately.'

Juliet drew a deep breath. She needn't have worried she was warming to him because Charlie Warren had very quickly given her a cold shower when he'd returned to being a dictator with a medical degree. She wasn't sure if he had taken her cue or it was his intention all along but either way any attraction she had felt instantly disappeared.

Juliet had to think on her feet. She would not be made to appear less than professional by not attending the consultation. This was about the option of surgical intervention. Not Charlie Warren's conservative treatment plan. Waiting for the birth was not in her expert opinion the best way forward. The best chance was surgery to remove the offending artery and save all four babies and she wanted the Abbiatis to have all the facts before they made their decision.

'I want to meet with them as soon as possible.'

'Then let's go. I'm meeting with them in fifteen minutes.'

'What about Bea?'

Charlie looked down at Bea's little face and his heart began to melt. If life had been different he would have been looking at the face of his own child every night. He or she would have been younger than Bea but he and his wife had planned on children. Four of them if possible. Leaving the hospital every night to return to his wife and those much-loved children, to read them bedtime stories and tuck them in to sleep, was his dream but instead he returned to an empty house in the middle of renovations that he didn't care about. His life was as empty as his house.

And suddenly the daughter of the overbearing woman who shouldn't have any effect on him was doing just that. He wasn't able to define what made her special— perhaps it was because she was like a tiny angel with a broken wing. Although he did not feel her mother had fallen from heaven.

'I said, what do you propose I do with my daughter?' Her voice was firm but not much more than a whisper. She didn't want Bea to feel she was in the way or not wanted.

'Bring her along to my office and I'll ask one of the nurses to keep an eye on her,' he told Juliet as he patted Bea's hand.

'I don't feel comfortable with that.'

'Then go home…'

'Go home?'

'I meant go back to the hotel and we'll arrange a second consultation tomorrow.' Charlie walked over and opened the door. 'We're all finished in here,' he told the nurse as he left A&E.

'So you won't postpone the consultation until this afternoon, then?' she asked, exasperated with his attitude and following slowly on his heels with Bea in tow.

'No, definitely not. Postponing has the potential to make both parents extremely anxious, not to mention Leo's taken time away from the family business to be here.' Charlie pressed the elevator button for OBGYN on the second floor and turned back to face her.

Juliet's gaze swept the hospital corridor as she rubbed her forehead. In her mind, the Abbiatis needed to be provided with both treatment plan options to consider. Charlie would no doubt suggest a 'wait and see' treatment plan or next propose medication as an option. After sleeping on it, the second option of surgical intervention, she conceded, would be the scarier of the two to Georgina and Leo. The delivery gap between both might sway them to what was not in their best interests. Nor the interests of the babies.

She felt trapped.

'Fine, we'll do it your way. I'll attend,' she said as the

three of them stepped inside the empty elevator. 'But I'll need a few minutes to find the crèche and settle Bea in.'

'Fine, you have ten minutes.'

'Can't you delay the consultation for half an hour?'

'No.'

'No?' she repeated incredulously. 'Not, perhaps…or I'll see what I can do? Who made you the final decision maker? Oliver Darrington actually seconded me here, not you.'

'But I'm Georgina's OBGYN, so I make the final decision on this case. It's how we run it at Teddy's. Check with Oliver if you like, but he will without doubt defer to me.'

'I don't have time to chase down Mr Darrington.'

'Good because I'm already running behind.'

The doors of the lift opened into OBGYN. The waiting room was full and all eyes turned to them. Charlie considered compromise was in everyone's best interest. 'I'll give you twenty minutes to settle Bea into the crèche, Dr Turner. Then I'll begin the Abbiatis' consultation in Room Two-Thirteen.'

With that, Charlie disappeared down the corridor leaving Juliet and Bea standing opposite the nurses' station. Juliet realised immediately that the middle ground he had offered had more to do with circumstance than generosity of spirit. The patients were all looking in their direction and had clearly been the impetus for the change in tone. She was well aware that he had the potential to be a medical ogre when out of earshot of others.

'Dr Turner?'

Juliet looked up to see a very pretty willowy blonde nurse smiling back at her. 'Yes.'

'Hi, I'm Annabelle Ainsley. I'm the head neonatal

nurse,' the blue-eyed woman told her. 'We've been expecting you.'

Juliet guessed the nurse to be in her mid-thirties as she stepped out from behind the station with her hand extended.

'Juliet Turner,' she responded as she met her handshake.

'And who is this gorgeous young lady with the very pretty coloured cast?'

'My daughter, Bea.'

'Hello, Bea,' Annabelle said.

Bea gripped her mother's hand a little tighter as she looked up at the very tall nurse. Her long blonde hair was tied in quite a severe style atop her head that made her appear even taller.

'Pink's my favourite colour in the world,' Annabelle continued and bent down a little to come nearer to the little girl's height. 'I love it so much I even have pink towels and pink soap.'

Bea loosened her grip a little. 'Me too,' she replied with her toothy grin and then smiled up at her mother before she continued. 'I have a pink bed.'

'Yes, you do, and a pink quilt. In fact your room is a pink palace,' Juliet agreed.

'Wow, that's awfully special. I wish I had pink sheets and a pink quilt.'

Juliet was happy that Annabelle and Bea were engaging but she was becoming increasingly concerned about the timeframe she had to get to the consultation and she knew she was hiding the fact well.

'Is there something I can help you with?' Annabelle asked.

'Yes, actually there is. I need to find the crèche as soon as possible. Dr Warren and I'll be meeting with the Abbiatis shortly and I need to settle Bea in, and I haven't had a chance to look over the last two days' obs for Georgina as I've been travelling—'

'I can help with all of that,' Annabelle cut in.

'You can? That would be wonderful. Thank you so much.'

'Not at all,' Annabelle replied with a smile. 'I've just finished my shift and I have no plans so what if I take Bea to the crèche? It's on the ground floor, and I'll wait with her while you meet with Georgina and Leo. Bea and I can chat about all things pink.'

'That's so kind of you,' Juliet said as she turned back to the lift. 'We'll have to hurry though as I have less than fifteen minutes to get to the crèche and back here for the consultation.'

Annabelle took a few long steps and pressed the down button. 'If I may make a suggestion…what if you wait here and I take Bea to the crèche so you can read over Georgina's notes? I've just refreshed everything after the ward rounds, so you can sit at the nurses' station and read up for a few minutes. I'll ask one of the nurses to take you to Room Two-Thirteen when you're ready. It would be less rushed and you'll be up to speed on the babies and mother's condition in plenty of time for the appointment.'

Juliet was so grateful the world had given her a twenty-first-century Florence Nightingale but she also felt torn letting Bea go with a nurse she had known for less than five minutes. A brief internal battle prevailed, fuelled a little by Charlie's initial judging of her parenting, but common sense and her need to attend the consultation won out. 'I think Bea should be okay to go with you. She attends childcare two days a week.

'Is it all right with you, Bea, if the nurse takes you to the crèche? It's like Pennybrook back home when you go and play with the other children when Grandma and Grandpa don't have you. It's not far from here and I'll be there in about an hour once I've seen the very special patient we came all this way to help.'

'Are you going to help the lady with four babies in her tummy?'

'Yes, I am.'

'Okay, Mummy. I think you should go. Grandpa told me that you need to help the lady have the babies.'

Juliet smiled. Sometimes Bea was so wise and practical for a four-year-old. Spending quality time with her grandparents had brought an older perspective to her life and for that Juliet was grateful. She kissed the top of her daughter's head and watched her and Annabelle step closer to the opening doors of the elevator. Bea's fear, that was palpable in A&E, had all but disappeared. Annabelle did look a little similar to one of the pretty child-carers back at Pennybrook and that, Juliet surmised, went a long way to making Bea feel comfortable.

'And you can meet the other children at the crèche. They're all very nice,' Annabelle added as she reached for Bea's little hand and stepped inside the now fully open doors. 'And you can tell me about everything you have back in Australia that's pink. Do you have a pink kangaroo too?'

'No, that would be silly,' Bea said, giggling. 'But I have a pink bear and a pink….' The doors closed on Bea's chatter and Juliet felt herself smiling as she waved goodbye. Annabelle was a lovely addition to an otherwise dreadful day and she was so grateful for her assistance.

As Juliet took a moment to gather her thoughts she knew, with Bea under control, she could concentrate on the task at hand. Making sure that Charlie Warren was put in his place. She had not travelled halfway around the world, not to mention spent years qualifying in her field, to be contradicted by him without having an opportunity to deliver all of the facts. *In-utero* surgery was the quads' best hope and she would be damned if she would stand by and have Charlie convince the Abbiatis otherwise.

Juliet returned to the computer at the nurses' station and caught up with the Abbiatti quads' and their mother's observations before heading off in the direction of Georgina's room. She stood at the T-junction reading the room signs to ensure she had the right wing.

'So let's get you around to meet the parents of the infamous four,' Charlie said, startling Juliet and making her spin around. It was a voice that she would now recognise anywhere. 'I didn't want you to get lost on the way to the consult. I want the Abbiatis to hear your plan and make up their own minds. Despite what you may think, I do play fair.'

'Um…thank you,' she said with a little frown causing a furrow on her forehead. He wasn't playing fair in her books. He was on a mission and the way he looked, the way he spoke, his seemingly impeccable manners, none of it was playing fair.

He ushered her in the direction of the patient's room and she walked alongside him refusing to acknowledge to herself how he was unnerving and confusing her. Since Bea was born, Juliet felt confident in her appraisal of men and their intentions very quickly. No matter how cleverly they spun a story or expertly delivered a well-versed pick-up line. They were all the same and she knew not to trust them.

But Charlie, she had to silently admit, was the most difficult case to sum up that she had stumbled upon to date.

They walked in silence for a few steps, but as they neared the ward Charlie stopped and turned to face Juliet. 'There's something I've been wanting to say to you.'

Juliet's eyes widened and quizzically looked everywhere but at Charlie. She really didn't want to look into his eyes, not in such close proximity. Finally her gaze came back to him. His look was intense and she swallowed nervously.

'What is it?' she asked, not sure she wanted to know but equally puzzled. Even now, in his white consulting coat, he looked as dashing and irresistible as he did in his head-to-toe black leather motorcycle gear. His broad shoulders were not hidden underneath the shapeless clothing. A body like his could not be masked by anything. His boots very loudly announced bad boy even if the rest of him was temporarily dressed to indicate tame. There were definitely two sides to Charlie Warren.

'I've had time to reflect on my earlier behaviour and I wanted to apologise for jumping to a conclusion about you,' he told her.

Damn! Juliet swallowed again. How she wished with every fibre of her being she had refused the secondment and remained in Perth. Safely tucked away from what Charlie Warren could risk making her feel. It was scaring her. She had known him for less than two hours and he was confusing her more than she'd thought possible. All of her reservations and irritation about Charlie seemed to vanish, with the sound of his voice. It was a bedroom voice. Husky and innately masculine but with undertones of compassion….and tenderness.

Why did he have to apologise? Being angry was her best line of defence. Now what would protect her from herself…and whatever she might begin to feel about Dr Charlie Warren?

CHAPTER FIVE

'GEORGIE, LEO...' CHARLIE BEGAN as Juliet entered the room carrying some handwritten notes on a clipboard along with the printed obs. 'This is Dr Juliet Turner. She is the *in-utero* surgeon who has travelled from Australia to consult on your pregnancy. She will be providing another option with regards to the condition the boys have developed. I must say upfront that I'm not supportive of this option for reasons I have already explained. However, Dr Turner has flown a long way to explain the procedure and answer your questions so I will hand over to her.' He paused and turned his attention to a very stunned Juliet. 'Dr Turner, let me introduce Leo and Georgina Abbiati.'

Juliet couldn't believe that he had just put doubt in the Abbiatis' minds before she opened her mouth. Despite his apology and consideration in ensuring she made it to the consult, he was not giving her any other professional courtesies. She stepped forward with her hand outstretched. 'Very pleased to meet you.'

Juliet knew she was up against his bias. He was stubbornly conservative and not open to accepting proven progressive procedures just as her father had suggested. It was not what she would expect at face value from the motorcycle-riding doctor. The two seemed miles apart. She drew a deep breath hoping Charlie would leave any further opinions until they were alone in his office and show a mutual professional respect and, as he said, *hand over to her*. She was not about to back away from her belief that the *in-utero* surgery was the best and most logical option for the patient. In the limited time Charlie had given her, Juliet had read the last few days' patient notes and it was exactly as she had first thought: an open and shut case in favour of laser surgery. The twin-to-twin transfusion needed to be halted immediately.

'It's a long way to come just for our babies,' Leo said as he tenderly stroked his wife's arm. 'And we appreciate it. This is a huge decision for us to make. It's our babies' lives we're talking about.'

'Of course it is and I was more than happy to travel here so that you and your children have options to ensure for the best possible outcome,' she replied empathetically. 'The hospital board and the Assistant Head of Obstetrics believed it necessary for me to come and discuss the next management strategy that can be employed. Can you please tell me what you know about your babies' condition, so that I don't repeat anything that either Dr Warren or Mr Darrington have already covered?'

'We know that the two girls are okay and the two boys are sharing an artery or something so one of our boys is getting lots of blood and the other one not enough. Georgie's been having a special diet hoping to get all of them big enough in case they came early anyway. She's twenty-nine weeks tomorrow.'

'You certainly have an overall picture of what's happening. Twin-to-twin transfusion syndrome, or TTTS for short, is a condition of the placenta that affects identical twin pregnancies. The placenta itself is shared unequally by the twins so that one of your sons is receiving too little blood to provide the necessary nutrients to grow normally and the other too much and so his heart is being overworked. Your TTTS was diagnosed at stage three, which is already advanced, and unfortunately has progressed to stage four.' Juliet paused. She knew that she needed to be honest but what she had to say would be hard for the parents-to-be. 'I am not telling you this to add to your concerns but I need to tell it how it truly is and, while the recipient baby is coping at the moment, if we do not surgically intervene that can change quickly and he can suffer heart failure. If that happened, it would immediately cross to stage five and we cannot save him and you will only have three babies. And even then their survival will be compromised.'

The expressions on Leo's and Georgie's faces fell further. 'What do you think, Charlie?'

'I agree with Dr Turner that the boys' condition is serious but I feel the high-protein diet has assisted with the babies' gaining weight and if we continue on that path we may be able to deliver within the next two weeks if necessary.'

Juliet felt as if she were playing a polite game of medical ping-pong but she had to keep serving. 'I would like to commend Dr Warren for the exceptional care he has provided to you and your babies up to now, but unfortunately your boys' condition has worsened. I'm not convinced that without surgical intervention you'll be able to carry four healthy babies for long enough for a good outcome,' Juliet countered.

'But I don't understand why it happened,' Leo said, oblivious to the battle of medical opinion that was being waged very politely in his wife's room. 'We've asked everyone and everyone has told us we did nothing wrong, but you're the specialist. Be honest, was it something we did?'

'Not at all,' Juliet answered. 'It's something that the medical experts can't predict. The events in pregnancy that lead to TTTS are quite random events. The condition is not hereditary or genetic, nor is it caused by anything either of you did or didn't do. TTTS can literally happen to anyone having multiple births at any stage up until about thirty weeks.'

'So it's definitely not our fault?'

'Absolutely not,' Juliet responded again honestly and without hesitation.

'Charlie and Mr Darrington told us that but it's nice to hear it from you.'

Georgina's expression, on hearing confirmation about the cause of her babies' condition, was subdued but Juliet was happy that at least unwarranted guilt would not be another struggle for the quads' mother.

'We know the boys are in trouble but are there any risks to Georgie from the TTTS?' her husband asked as he looked at his wife with loving concern.

'That is something we have to consider, and another reason your wife is in Teddy's on bed rest,' Juliet continued. 'Carrying quads is in itself quite taxing on a woman's body and that stress has been increased by the TTTS. Her uterus is being stretched past what is normal for pregnancy—'

'Should you just wait then and take the babies in two weeks as Charlie says and not put Georgie at any risk?' Leo cut in.

Without giving Charlie time to interrupt, Juliet answered quickly. 'Actually no. That could've been a consideration if, since the diagnosis two days ago, the condition had not progressed, but it has and, for want of a better word, aggressively. I'm not convinced that the recipient baby would survive until thirty-one weeks. If the pregnancy was just twins, we could deliver at twenty-nine weeks. However, with quads the babies are still very small so if we can prolong the pregnancy another few weeks by having the laser surgery, the babies will be bigger when they're born and that will make their lives easier. At the moment they are all less than three pounds and we no longer have time on our side to observe their growth.'

'Like you said, Dr Turner,' Georgina responded, 'we agree that Charlie has taken such good care of me up until now we're really struggling to think about ignoring his advice. Perhaps we should have the needle and stay with bed rest.'

Charlie drew in a deep breath, plumped out his chest, and in Juliet's opinion looked like a pigeon about to mate. His polite interruptions made her believe their professional battle would lean towards a gentleman's sword fight, but a fight nonetheless, and she was right. But for the good of the mother and her babies, she would not hold back. There would be a level of professional courtesy, but she would not cower to him. Juliet was prepared to argue on the evidence-based merit of surgery and then leave the decision where it should lie. With the well-informed parents.

'While the needle you spoke of, an amniotic reduction, can work well in stage one patients, you have moved past this option very quickly. Teddy's brought me here to discuss laser surgery and the benefits and they would not have flown me halfway around the world if there was any doubt that surgery was a viable and preferable choice for you.' Juliet paused for a moment, then continued with a serious timbre in her voice. 'But I won't lie to you, there are risks in the surgical route as there are with any surgery, but the benefit far outweighs the risks. I also must let you know that if you choose to proceed with the laser surgery, then it would need to be this week. On Thursday or Friday at the latest as time is not on our side if we decide to help your sons surgically. If we leave it too long, your body will make the decision for us.'

Juliet watched Georgina's and Leo's expressions darken. It was a lot to process and, while she had not wanted to put additional pressure on either of them, she felt all the facts had to be stated. Time was unfortunately not on their side and that was the harsh realisation they all needed to accept. To deliver four living babies, something had to be done. She just prayed they chose surgery.

'Can you give us more details, like what the surgery involves and how long it will take?' Leo asked as he ceased stroking his wife's arm and reached down to hold her hand tightly.

Juliet stepped away from the bed to give the couple a little more space. Hearing news and making potential life-and-death decisions, she knew, was overwhelming and they needed to feel safe together in their own space. 'Of course,' she began and then noticed that Charlie had brought her a chair. She wasn't sure if he was being gallant and considerate or if he was trying to make her appear weary. She didn't waste time deciding which it was, instead choosing to graciously accept the chair and continue.

'The operation involves endoscopic surgery using a laser beam to cauterise the offending arteries and halt the exchange of blood between your boys. Each baby will remain connected to his primary source of blood and nutrition, the placenta, through the umbilical cord. The use of endoscopic instruments allows for short recovery time and no effect on the other babies and would be done only once during the pregnancy.'

'Dear God, we pray if we go ahead it's just one time,'

Leo interrupted as he looked into his wife's tear-filled eyes. 'Georgie's been through so much over the last eighteen months with the three rounds of IVF, and that was unsuccessful, and then finding out we're having four babies conceived naturally. And now this heartbreaking news about the transfusion while I was away.'

'Leo, you're suffering as much as me, and you had to make the trip to New York,' she told him as she mopped the tears that threatened to escape. Her eyes were reddened from too many nights of crying. 'We've *both* been through so much and we're doing our best to stay strong together.'

'And we will. No matter what, we'll get through all of this. And we'll take our babies home to where they belong. Their *nonni*, all four of them, are waiting to meet their grandchildren.'

Juliet nodded. 'That's my plan and I'm so pleased to hear your positive outlook. That's exactly what your babies need.'

'Ah, you know Italians, we're a strong race and our children will be fighters too.'

'Goodness, Leo,' Georgina said. 'You sound like my father!'

'Well, it's the truth,' Charlie added. 'You and Georgie have been strong and focused since the diagnosis and that's why you should not completely rule out continuing on the current conservative path.'

Juliet swung around on her chair with a look of indignation. She could not believe what she was hearing. Charlie clearly had not *handed over to her* as he'd promised. Fuming but unable to tell Charlie how she felt, Juliet regained her composure, turned back to the couple and continued. She would let Charlie know in no uncertain terms how she felt about his interference, after the consultation. But for the moment she intended to calmly give Georgina and Leo all the information so they understood it was their choice, and theirs alone.

'Minimally invasive fetoscopic surgery is the name of the procedure and it is aptly named because it's *minimally* invasive. It involves small incisions and I will be guided by both an endoscope and sonography. Essentially it's keyhole surgery so far lower risks than open foetal surgery, which is completely opening the uterus to operate on the foetus.'

'But there's still a chance it could go wrong?' Leo asked anxiously, looking from Juliet to Charlie.

'Yes, but not undertaking the surgery has equal if not greater risk,' Juliet said honestly and, armed with further facts, she elaborated. 'I do not want you to be under the misapprehension that the safer choice is doing nothing as that is quite incorrect. In the past the twin survival rate with severe TTTS was very low, around ten per cent before ultrasound made it possible for us to make an early diagnosis and the introduction of laser surgery. I think you should consider taking advantage of this medical advance. In years gone by women had no choice but to wait and pray they did not give birth to a stillborn baby. As I have mentioned excess amniotic fluid caused by the TTTS is causing your uterus to grow to an unsustainable size. It's a condition called polyhydramnios, and it can cause premature labour.'

'I have a fifty-four-inch waist now.'

'Yes, that's a combination of four babies and the fluid and it will continue to increase,' Charlie added. 'We're monitoring that and can continue to do so, and perform the amniotic reduction procedure.'

Juliet bit her lip again. Charlie was not allowing her much space to move.

'Georgina, you will be monitored in hospital until all four babies are born, no matter your decision. However, I'm suggesting surgery because there are four very tiny babies still growing inside you and they need optimum time to grow. The final decision rests with you.'

Georgina shifted on the bed and raised her feet again. Her rounded stomach was still covered by the sheet and lightweight blanket, but only just. Her pretty face was almost hidden by the mound that held her precious babies. Juliet knew the young woman's ribs would be excruciatingly tender from the pressure of four babies.

'So you can definitely separate the blood supply?' Georgina finally asked.

'The tiny telescope in your uterus will allow me to find and destroy all the connecting vessels. This is the only treatment that can *disconnect* the twins.'

'How common is it for parents to choose laser surgery?'

'Laser surgery is now performed all over the world as more and increasing numbers of progressively attuned doctors are convinced that this will lead to the best outcomes.' Juliet's words were directed at Charlie but she did not pause over the words or look in his direction. Two could play at the same game. 'Most physicians worldwide agree that placental laser surgery results in the highest numbers of healthy survivors.'

'Including those in the UK?' Leo enquired.

'Yes, particularly in a hospital like Teddy's.'

Georgina and Leo gave each other a knowing look. 'Would I be awake?'

'Yes, Georgie, you'd be awake. You would be under conscious sedation and local anaesthetic for this procedure. We need you and the babies to be relaxed and pain free during the procedure but there's no need for a general anaesthetic.'

Leo straightened his back, took a deep resonating breath and looked at Charlie. 'Charlie, by what we're hearing, and the urgency of everything, are we right in thinking we have to make the decision tonight? It's a lot to take in and not a decision we want to make in a hurry.'

Charlie cleared his throat and stepped a little closer. 'Not quite tonight but, yes, if you choose Dr Turner's surgical option you would only have a day or two to make that decision. However, my plan would not see you making any changes other than looking at prescribing heart medication as pills given to Georgie, or injected directly into the twin if he is showing signs of heart failure. We can also look at another therapy using medication to decrease the urine output in the recipient and lessen the amount of amniotic fluid that is causing Georgie's uterus to expand.'

Juliet bit her lip. She could counter but chose not to do so. She had said enough and if they chose the non-surgical option she would remain on staff at Teddy's to help in any way she could, including the delivery. But she hoped they would choose her way forward and she would be able to use her surgical skills to increase the babies' chances of survival and happy and healthy lives.

Georgina and Leo looked at each other with what Juliet knew would feel like the weight of the world on their shoulders but their love for each other still shone brightly in their eyes. Finally Leo spoke. 'Is it all right if we sleep on it?'

'Of course,' Charlie and Juliet said in unison then they too looked at each other. But it was not lovingly; their look was more of an aloof stare.

Juliet had felt as if she were on a roller coaster since

she'd touched down at Heathrow, and even before that with the last-minute packing. But now it was a different type of roller coaster. The emotional type. And for which she had not willingly purchased a ticket, nor even had any idea she would be experiencing. But in the few hours since Charlie had stepped into her life and lifted her tiny daughter into his arms, she had ridden highs and lows that she'd never imagined. He was opinionated and brash; considerate and caring; her old school colleague and stubborn opponent; and still, to her annoyance, attractive.

He was quite the package and she definitely didn't want to peel back too many layers or get too close. Charlie was confusing her and, working together for the next few weeks, she wondered how successfully she could avoid getting to know more about him. A conservative, bad-boy biker with attitude who seemed to adore children, or at least her child. Could he be any more complex? She doubted it.

And she wasn't convinced she wanted to understand Charlie Warren.

CHAPTER SIX

WITH LEO AND GEORGINA left alone to think everything over, Juliet had a chance to meet the rest of Teddy's nursing staff. Although Juliet had seen the Royal Cheltenham hospital emergency department up close and personal with Bea, Charlie knew that she had not seen Teddy's properly, so he took it upon himself to offer to show her around the centre dedicated to babies and birth. But not before setting the parameters of the working relationship in his mind.

'I think you would have to agree that we both behaved quite poorly in there,' he began, thinking that they should get everything out in the open and start afresh. 'Fortunately not that Georgina or Leo noticed.'

'I'm sorry, are you questioning *my* behaviour?'

'I'm just saying that we could have handled things a little more diplomatically.'

'So you're saying that we *both* behaved poorly and *we* could have handled things better?'

Charlie frowned. 'Yes, as I also said, it was done in a very polite manner so that the Abbiatis did not sense any professional tension, but you have to admit we were walking a fine line.'

Juliet's hands suddenly took pride of place on her hips as she began pacing, then drew to a halt in front of him.

'I can't believe what you're saying and I refuse to accept culpability for your, as you Englishmen say, *poor form*. I was seconded over here and you were clearly the one stirring doubt, if not confusion.'

Charlie studied Juliet's face. Even angry, she was very beautiful. And Juliet was clearly angry. She was riled up and ready to pounce on him for even suggesting that she had participated in the battle of wills. It was apparent when challenged Juliet was like a cat with an arched back. He wondered what made her so defensive. Had she been on the receiving end of too many challenges over her career? Or was it more than that? Was her attitude of fight or flight born from something outside work?

He suddenly stopped his line of thought mid-journey. What she did or did not do outside work was not his business. Whatever had caused, or was still causing, Juliet to fight back was not his concern. She was a grown woman, who had no doubt endured some heartache and some of life's lessons, but that did not excuse her from professional scrutiny.

Charlie eyed Juliet again. In fact he had barely taken his eyes away from her. All five feet four inches. But despite her petite appearance, he had quickly learnt that she was no shrinking violet. And he doubted she would tolerate fools either. He quickly realised that he wasn't about to win the argument. And suddenly, to his surprise, he was willing to accept the decision was where it needed to be, with the parents of the babies at risk. They had been given the facts. He couldn't do any more.

'Fair call, Dr Turner,' he offered. 'I'm sorry for the start we've had. Shall we begin again? Let's put the consultation behind us. One way or the other it looks as if we'll be spending time together so we should try and make this work.'

Charlie wasn't sure what had motivated him to call a professional truce but it seemed the right thing to do. He hoped she knew his words were genuine. He was calling a ceasefire. It was a masculine apology but sincere nonetheless. And one he hoped that she would accept.

She extended her hand. 'Truce accepted, Dr Warren. Let's agree to disagree and allow the Abbiatis to decide without further interference.'

As he met her handshake the warmth of her skin against his almost made him recant the apology so they could return to adversaries. He pulled his hand free as soon as he was able.

'We're both clearly passionate about what we do and that's a great thing so we will just have to respect our differing opinions and work alongside each other as best we can,' he said.

'Yes, and one of us will clearly be pleased with their decision and the other disappointed but we will simply wear it,' she added.

Charlie said nothing for a moment as he looked at the tiny powerhouse standing near him. She was without doubt one of the best in her field, and, despite not agreeing with that particular obstetric intervention, he had immeasurable respect for her skills. Her reputation had preceded her. But there was something other than respect simmering below the surface for him and it was making him uncomfortable. Very uncomfortable.

He walked in the direction of the large digital directory board in Reception. 'It might be a good idea if you took a look around and familiarised yourself with Teddy's. It would be best if you met everyone and knew where everything was in case you're needed.'

'You mean for *when* I'm needed?' she responded. 'Let's wait and see.'

The introductions soon became an induction. As she met each of the medical staff she learnt about the layout and workings of Teddy's. The nursing staff gave Juliet a message from Annabelle, letting her know that Bea had settled in well and that she was enjoying a light lunch with the other children while listening to a story. Knowing that, Juliet decided to keep on the tour and learn as much as she could about the hospital.

The reputation of Teddy's had been a driving force in Juliet's accepting the secondment. The opportunity to consult and operate in a hospital with facilities second to none in all of Europe was too good to refuse.

Juliet thanked Charlie for showing her the ropes.

'Not at all. It's been an eventful start for you and I hope Bea will be all right tonight. I know I don't have to mention it, but just give her a little oral analgesia if she has trouble sleeping and she should be fine by tomorrow.'

'I will.'

As Charlie watched Juliet walk away he realised that he hadn't wanted the tour to end. He had enjoyed his time with Juliet. She was challenging him and he felt the closest to alive that he had in a long time. They came from polar opposites. Both geographically and professionally. She was forging new ground surgically and he was of the belief that monitoring with minimal surgical intervention was the better method. But despite their differences, he admired her courage.

He had been an OBGYN for many years, and his conservative approach had always provided great outcomes for the mothers and the babies. Although as he walked back to his office he admitted to himself that he had not dealt with the complication of TTTS in quadruplets. As he sat down behind his desk, to stretch his legs out and read his emails before another ward round, he conceded they were on an even playing field with regard to experience. Neither had a track record that could negate the other. So neither one of them could say with any evidence that their treatment plan was better. It was purely subjective and tainted by preference.

Juliet for taking risks.

Charlie for avoiding them every day since he had taken a chance on the icy road and lost.

Juliet and a very tired Bea arrived back at their hotel late in the afternoon. Bea had enjoyed her time at the crèche and was not in a hurry to leave. Juliet suspected it was due to the fuss that Annabelle and the children had made of her. After lunch and the story, her mind had been distracted from the traumatic start to the day by the children all wanting to draw pictures on her cast and ask questions about koalas and kangaroos. She'd been the centre of attention and she'd managed that role well. When Juliet had popped up to collect her, she'd looked through the large glass window that was decorated with paper cut-outs of snowflakes to see Bea happily playing with the other children. Juliet had been convinced earlier in the day that bringing her daughter on the trip was a terrible idea, but as she'd witnessed her smiling and happily playing despite the cast the idea had left terrible territory.

A classic Georgian property, not too far from the hospital, had been restored and refurbished as an exclusive, eleven-room boutique hotel and it would be their accommodation for a day or so until Juliet could source something more practical for the two of them. Their room was toasty warm with a large bed covered in far too many oversized pillows and the softest mattress. The warmth was created by an antique radiator and the all-white decor, complete with heavy damask drapes and matching bedspread, was elegance in abundance. She felt very spoilt as the hospital board had insisted on covering the cost of the expensive room until she secured something else, in addition to her business-class flight and that of her daughter.

Back in Perth, she lived in a small home not too far from her parents and equally close to the hospital and Pennybrook childcare centre. When she'd purchased the three-bedroom house, it had been a very practical decision. It was a nice house but not ostentatious. Understated in its exterior appearance and equally in the interior. Juliet wasn't in love with her home but the location meant she could drop off Bea and collect her easily from childcare or her grandparents' home. Most decisions after Bea was born were practical. And never rushed. Up until this trip, Juliet had considered and reconsidered every move she made. Although Charlie clearly thought she was a risk-taker in suggesting the surgical intervention, she thought just the opposite. She carefully weighed up the risks, and never blindly jumped into anything. She had learnt the hard way by rushing into a relationship with Bea's father and she never planned on doing that again.

In fact, she swore on it.

The ambience of their hotel room was something Juliet loved almost immediately, along with the breathtaking scenery of the Cotswolds. It surprised Juliet that, while she had worried she would feel out of place, she quickly felt comfortable in the South Midlands of England. She was a long way from home but she didn't feel entirely lost.

As they sat at the small mahogany card table that doubled as a dining table for two, eating their room-service dinner of a hearty beef stew and finished off with a homemade apple pie, Juliet felt as if she had been transported back to another time. Bea managed to eat her children's size serving even with her sling in place and Juliet felt sure she would sleep well with a full tummy.

But no matter how stunning the room, Juliet had to admit the gorgeous antique bath positioned by the large bay window was completely impractical for a four-year-old with a cast. She felt so sorry for her tiny daughter as she stood her next to the porcelain wash basin and used the fluffy white washcloths to give her a freshen up. It would have been too awkward to place Bea into the free-standing and very deep bath. She needed to check the bathroom of the longer-term accommodation before she signed anything, she thought as she dried Bea and slipped her into snuggly warm pyjamas. Fortunately the pyjama top was made of a stretch knit and quite loose fitting so she could slip it over the cast. But working around her daughter's broken arm was not how she'd seen the first day ending.

With Bea snuggled in bed after some pain relief and drifting off to sleep, Juliet ran a bath for herself.

'Mummy,' Bea called out sleepily across the warm room.

'Yes, sweetie, what is it?' Juliet asked as she took a nightdress out of her suitcase, which was open and lying alongside Bea's. Juliet decided there was no point unpacking and using the ample white built-in wardrobe, which blended into the wall colour, or the ornately carved chest of drawers. They wouldn't be staying long enough.

'Why duth Grandpa call you honey and not Juliet?'

'He's just always called me honey since I was a little girl.'

'Ith that becauth he'th your daddy?'

'I guess so. It's his special name for me because I'm his daughter and everyone else calls me Juliet.'

'Charlie called me honey…'

Juliet stopped what she was doing. 'When?' she asked with a puzzled look.

'When I fell in the playground and he picked me up. Duth that mean Charlie could be my daddy?'

Juliet felt her stomach fall and her heart race as she dropped closed her suitcase. Her fallen stomach was the reaction to the unexpected daddy question and just thinking of Charlie in the role of Bea's father made her heart race. She swallowed a lump that had risen in her throat. Charlie's handsome face appeared in her mind. She no longer pictured Bea's father or even thought of him when she looked at Bea.

But now she suddenly pictured Charlie.

With legs shaking, Juliet walked back to her daughter and sat beside her, stroking her face and watching her tired eyes struggle to stay open. They were slowly closing as she kissed her gently. Juliet was trying to find the words to answer Bea. She was still too young to understand what had really happened and why she didn't have a daddy.

'No, my sweet, Charlie is not your daddy. But one day when you're much bigger we can talk about your daddy.' With that she pulled up the covers over her daughter.

'Okay.'

'Sweet dreams.'

As Juliet tiptoed back to the bath she heard her daughter mumble, 'Mummy?'

'Yes, sweetie.'

'I think Charlie would make a nice daddy.'

Juliet felt momentarily overwhelmed. It was obvious now that her daughter missed having a father. With a heavy heart, Juliet removed the last of her clothing in the soft light of the bedside lamp and climbed into the steaming bubbles, where she remained for a good half an hour thinking about her life and about Bea's. Her daughter's question was spinning along with all the others she had for herself. Her mind was on overload and Bea's innocent curiosity added another weight. While the travel was beginning to take its toll, the question of Bea's paternity was now an issue and one that she had no idea how exactly she would answer. Soon she would want more answers. And Juliet would have to answer each and every question as honestly as she could without letting her know that her father was a cad.

Juliet's eyes felt heavier and heavier as she reached for an oversized towel and stepped carefully from the bath. She was exhausted. Mentally and physically. It had been a whirlwind since she'd stepped off the final plane at Heathrow. Then she admitted silently the whirlwind had begun before she and Bea had even boarded the first aircraft. The push to hand over her patients at the Perth Women's and Children's Medical Centre in a matter of hours and packing their suitcases in temperatures hovering around one hundred degrees for freezing cold weather and all the while questioning the practicalities of travelling with a four-year-old. As she dried herself and slipped the nightdress over her head she heard the soft breathing of her sleeping daughter and knew that no matter what happened or what they faced they would do it together. And they would be just fine.

Barefoot, she tiptoed over to her side of the bed, slipped in between the brushed cotton sheets, turned down her mobile phone and turned off the bedside light. Sleep overtook her the moment her head rested on the softness of the duck-down pillows.

'Mummy, wake up! Someone'th here,' the lispy voice announced.

Juliet opened her eyes to see Bea standing beside the bed and looking in the direction of the hotel-room door. There was firm and unrelenting knocking. Not brash but loud enough to seem urgent. Juliet climbed from her bed, kissed the top of her daughter's head and grabbed her robe from the end of the bed where she had dropped it the night before.

'Who is it?'

'Charlie Warren,' came the response, but even without his self-identification his voice told her immediately that it was him.

Juliet's brow knitted. What on earth was he doing at her door? The heavy drapes stopped her seeing how dark or light it was outside but she imagined it was early; she felt as if she had barely been asleep.

'Is there something wrong? Has Georgina progressed to stage five?'

'No. Georgina's stable but they've made their decision and I thought I'd let you know first-hand.'

Juliet crossed to the door, running her fingers through the messy curls. She didn't care at that moment about her appearance. She just hoped the news was good and they had chosen surgery. She opened the door ready to ask that question when she came face to face with a vision head to toe in black leather. Suddenly she felt senses that had lain dormant for many years awaken without warning. Charlie stood before her, once again dressed in his leather riding gear, and holding his helmet in his leather-gloved hand. The same hand that had so tenderly applied Bea's cast the day before. This was the man that called Bea *honey* and made her think he might be her father. The look was intoxicating and took her breath and words away but allowing him into her life scared her too.

'Are you okay?'

'Yes,' she finally managed. 'You startled me. I was still asleep. I'm as keen as you to know the answer but it's still so early. Did the Abbiatis call you in the middle of the night?'

'No,' he replied. 'They spoke to me on my nine o'clock rounds.'

'Nine o'clock rounds?' she asked incredulously.

'I called your phone but it went straight to message bank and you didn't call back so here I am.'

'I never heard your call,' she told him with a slight frown. 'What time is it now?'

Charlie looked at his watch. 'Nearly ten-thirty.'

'Really? That means we slept for twelve hours.'

'I've been watching TV, Mummy.'

Juliet looked down at her daughter, who had cleverly managed to slip on her sling, and then turn on the cartoon channel on the television.

'I can't believe I slept in that long. You must be hungry, darling.'

'A little.'

Charlie smiled. Bea was adorable and he was beginning to feel that there might be a slim chance Juliet might be just as lovely if he got to know her better. He admired the fact she told him exactly how she felt. She didn't tiptoe around him like everyone else who *felt sorry for the widower*. He could see it in their faces and hear it in their voices. He had attended the hospital fundraiser in the hope the staff would see him as something other than a recluse. Charlie liked that Juliet was unaware of his wife's death and he assumed that was why she was able to stand up to him. She was the first person to do that in two years. Being around her made him realise he missed being challenged and being held accountable.

And her conviction in her treatment plan for Georgina Abbiati made him feel slightly less concerned about the surgical intervention although he still did not agree.

'What if I take you two ladies out for brunch?' He wanted to spend more time with the beautiful woman with the messy hair and the gorgeous smile who was still dressed in her robe. He couldn't explain it to himself— it was as if he had known Juliet and Bea for more than one day. His attraction was more than skin deep and it defied logic and his promise to himself that he would never get involved with anyone. But standing so close to Juliet, he felt that promise fading and the desire to know her increasing.

'Is this a brunch to break good news or bad?' she asked without a smile. 'Are you here to brag of your victory and tell me that the Abbiatis have chosen your conservative treatment option? Is that the reason you've come in person?'

Charlie was taken aback. He had not seen that reaction coming. His agenda had been very different. He just felt a pull to be with Juliet, to learn more about her away from the hospital, and against his better judgement he had decided to act upon it. Now he knew that was a stupid idea. Reckless in fact. He barely knew Juliet and, for some ridiculous reason, he wanted to spend his free time with her. And with Bea. Suddenly he was grateful she had given him the perspective he needed. He had no business being at her hotel. He should have left a message and waited until she had arrived at the hospital. He was better off alone.

It was the way he liked it.

And the way it should be.

'You're right, it was a bad idea,' he said as he stepped back and opened the hotel-room door. 'I'll leave you ladies to enjoy your late breakfast alone. And by the way, Juliet, the Abbiatis decided on the fetoscopic placental laser surgery. I guess I was just the gracious loser in a professional differing of opinion…offering to share a meal.'

With that he closed the door on Juliet.

And to stirrings he knew he had no right to act upon.

CHAPTER SEVEN

'CHARLIE, PLEASE WAIT,' Juliet called down the passageway. She couldn't follow him dressed in only her robe. 'I'm sorry, I was rude and ungracious.'

Charlie stopped long enough to turn and see her in the doorway. Her messy hair, the spattering of freckles across the bridge of her nose, and her pretty amber eyes that looked genuinely remorseful. He was grateful that she had sent him walking. It was for the best. She was too close to exactly what he didn't have room for in his life. And definitely didn't deserve. A pretty, intelligent woman with a fighting spirit. And a daughter who was cute as a button.

'Apology accepted. I'll see you at the hospital later, then. I've an opening at one-thirty if you would like to meet. We need to schedule in the surgery, brief the theatre team and then book another pre-op consultation as soon as possible.'

His tone was brusque and he didn't wait for a reply as Juliet watched him disappear out of sight. She closed her bedroom door and raced to the window with Bea in tow. Pulling back the heavy damask curtains to see him emerge from the building and climb onto the shiny black bike that he had parked in the small guest car park. He pulled down his helmet, and turned his head. Nervously she dropped the curtains before he saw her watching him. It appeared Dr Charlie Warren, intentionally or unintentionally, was going to make her second day in the Cotswolds as confusing as the first.

Charlie rode away but not before he noticed Juliet looking from her window. He saw in his rear-view mirror that she had closed the curtains as quickly as she had opened them. While he had accepted her apology he couldn't help but wonder as he headed along the leafy streets on his way to Teddy's what had made the Australian specialist so quickly think the worst of him.

Admittedly, the previous day he had been the one to jump to conclusions, and perhaps had not been his professional best at the consultation, but he had apologised for both. And to make amends and let her know that he would not challenge the Abbiatis' decision he had driven over to tell her in person. But once he'd known that neither Bea nor Juliet had eaten, it had felt natural to offer a shared brunch.

As he rounded the next corner, he told himself that it was his olive branch. But there was more to it and, as he righted himself on the large motorbike before the next curve, he silently accepted that Juliet had broken through his tough exterior shell. She had made him think of more than work. More than the mothers and the babies and the families he was helping to create. In twenty-four hours she and Bea had reminded him of all those things he'd wanted and dreamed of before the accident. Before the loss of his wife made him lose hope in the future.

But her reaction to his reaching out was unexpected. Shooting him down by questioning his motives.

Was it jet lag or was Juliet Turner always on the defensive? He wasn't sure but, with his hand on the throttle, he rode a little faster than usual. Although Charlie had grown up in the stunning Cotswolds countryside, he appreciated the architecture and landscape that defined the part of England he called home, but not that day. Instead of noticing the Regency town houses and their intricate ironwork balconies and painted stucco façades or the rolling green hills that were blanketed in pristine snow, he could only picture Juliet's face as he travelled back to work. Equally confused about what made Juliet so quick to judge…and what had really driven him to deliver the news in person.

Juliet knocked on the door. The brass plate read Dr Charlie Warren, OBGYN. She was in the right place.

'Come in.'

Juliet opened the door and entered with mixed emotions. She was thrilled that the surgery would take place and the quads would in her opinion have the best chance of survival, but her behaviour at the hotel a few hours earlier still bothered her. And underneath she knew that was because Charlie Warren was affecting her and she was confused and scared.

But despite those feelings unnerving her, the fact the obstinate but handsome OBGYN had reached out to her made her feel a little special. Perhaps that was why she took extra time to choose her outfit. A long black knitted dress that hugged her slim hips. It had a roll collar and she had added a silver necklace and a black patent boot with a medium height heel. It was her smart apology outfit, she told herself. The previous day's travelling clothes were for comfort and that morning he had seen her in her pyjamas so she wanted to show a level of professionalism in her dressing. There was no other reason for her to wear the figure-hugging dress.

The tight knit also kept her warm. Cheltenham was a cold place. That was all.

How could there be any other reason? It certainly wasn't to impress Charlie Warren the man.

'Hello, Juliet. Please take a seat. I won't be a moment. I'm just emailing through a medical report to a GP in London.'

'Thank you,' she said as she sat in the chair opposite him.

Juliet took the time to let her gaze wander around the office. But there was nothing telling about any of it. No personal belongings that jumped out and showed her a little about Charlie. No photos, just a couple of certificates that provided evidence of his qualifications. Without appearing nosey, she searched from her vantage point for something that would let her know more about him. There was nothing. No hint. It appeared that Dr Warren had no life outside his work…or if he did he was hiding it.

''I have taken the liberty of booking the operating theatre,' he began as he turned his attention to Juliet. 'And also confirming with the Abbiatis that the surgery will be on Friday.'

'Thank you.'

'Don't thank me, I'm just extending a professional courtesy on behalf of the board.'

Juliet frowned. His change in demeanour was extraordinary. But she knew she had been the cause. Her earlier reaction was cold and dismissive and just plain rude.

'Juliet, don't misread my actions for a change of mind. It isn't. I still don't think that surgery is the best option and, while I will not raise the issue again with the parents as they have made their decision, I still have grave concerns.'

'Well, I'm grateful that we can agree at least to provide a united front even if behind the scenes there is still a great divide.'

Juliet noticed a flick in his jaw. Finely covered with dark blond shadow, it was defined but tense.

'A very great divide.'

'May I ask why?'

'Because I know you have experience in TTTS and this procedure, your papers prove it, but you have never, according to my research, undertaken this with quads.'

'I have with triplets,' she argued.

'Once,' he returned. 'I read your notes.'

'Yes, once, but successfully and I am not operating on all four. Only two of the four are involved.'

'That's where you're wrong. You're exposing all four to a risk.'

'I agree but the benefits outweigh the risk—'

'I don't agree with that rationale. You're risking all four babies to save one and even success with that foetus is not guaranteed. It could take up to a month after the baby is born to know if there are any residual effects from the surgery. And even a year later in some cases long-term side effects have been diagnosed.'

'But the child may not live at all if we don't proceed.' Juliet slumped a little in her chair. Her apology meeting was turning sour quickly. Charlie's defensive stance was back again. She hoped she would have been more gracious if she had been the one assisting him with his treatment plan instead of the other way around. But she accepted that was easier said as the victor and her reaction a few hours earlier, suspecting he was delivering bad news, didn't show any sign of gracious defeat. Perhaps they were alike after all. But she would never know because she was the one who had won this battle.

'I've been performing this procedure for many years

and before proceeding the Abbiatis will be fully informed of the risk.'

'One additional baby complicates things ten-fold and I'm not sure that you'll be experienced enough to deal with those complications should they arise.'

Juliet decided to stand and signal the end of the meeting. It was going nowhere and it was pointless in her opinion. 'I don't see any value in going around in circles. The parents have agreed, Teddy's board flew me over and the theatre is booked thanks to you. It would appear the surgery is a fait accompli.'

'If it's not successful, I'll be noting my objections in a report to the board.'

'I would expect no less,' she replied as she crossed to the door. 'Will I have an office during my secondment? I think it would be a good idea so that I can have some time to look over the reports privately.' Her eyebrow was raised as she looked directly at Charlie. She hoped it was a look that didn't leave room for questions or second-guessing. It was a demand not a polite request that he could choose whether to approve. He had taken it back to adversarial colleagues. They were right back to where they started.

'I'll see what we can do.'

'Now that's settled, I'll be back tomorrow with my laptop ready to log on and begin the pre-op preparations.'

Juliet chatted with the nurses and asked to meet the midwife who was looking after Georgina.

'That's Ella O'Brien,' Annabelle offered. 'She's not on today but will be back tomorrow.'

Juliet thanked her and then left to visit Georgina.

'Leo's just gone home to get me some fresh clothes. I guess you heard we're going ahead with the surgery.'

'I did, and I must say I'm very pleased. I truly believe it's the best option.'

'So do we,' Georgina said with nerves and a little doubt still evident in her voice. 'We really like Charlie but we got to thinking if the board has flown you all the way here then they must believe in the surgery too. We didn't think they would go to that much trouble and expense if it wasn't something they believe worthwhile. We just don't know why Charlie doesn't feel the same way as them.'

'Dr Warren is a great doctor, and he has every right to have a different opinion. Medicine can be quite subjective at times and sometimes doctors differ but they both want the best for the patient. Dr Warren's taken the very best care of you up to now but the board do agree that the laser surgery will give you the best chance of taking four babies home with you.'

'We pray every day for them all. We've named them, you know.'

'That's wonderful. Are the names a secret?'

'We have told our family and Charlie, Ella and Mr Darrington. We like Graham and Rupert for the boys and Lily and Rose for the girls.'

'I feel very honoured to know, and they are the loveliest names,' Juliet said sincerely. She thought they were such sweet, old-fashioned names but they didn't sound very southern European at all.

'I guess you're wondering why they sound so English and not Italian.'

'You're a mind reader.'

'Not really, I think we're going to be asked that a lot but our families moved here from Italy many years ago. Leo and I met at Italian school so traditions are important but since we both come from huge families, I have five siblings and Leo has eight brothers and sisters, so the grandparents all have grandchildren named after them, and more than a few cousins share names too. We wanted our babies to be different. It's not that we don't love our culture, it's just we want them to have their own identity, which will be difficult enough with two sets of identical twins, let alone if they share names with their cousins. So we have our parents' blessings to give them very special names.'

'Were you born here, or in Italy?'

'Leo and I were both born in London. Leo's grandparents did very well producing rice and maize in the region of Abbiategrasso, in Lombardy in Italy, and that's where his surname originated. They sent his father to London for an education with the hopes he would return to his home, but instead he graduated from law, met a beautiful young Italian woman, married and settled in London raising Leo and his brothers and sisters. My grandparents' background was in grapes and olives in Umbria. My father was also sent to London for higher education and along with his international commerce degree came an English bride, my mother, who loved all things Italian including my father. And soon,' she said, looking down at her oversized belly, 'there will be another instant generation of Abbiatis a long way from Italy.'

'Well, I think the names are just gorgeous and I'm sure the children will make you very proud as they grow up.'

'So you're privy to the babies' names too?' came a deep and now familiar voice from the doorway. 'Well, I must say you've become a member of the Abbiati family more quickly than I did. It took me the best part of a month before that information was entrusted to me.'

Juliet turned to see Charlie in the doorway to the private hospital room.

'I feel quite special at this moment.'

'And so you should, for you know the names of the children you have been given the opportunity to save.'

Juliet suddenly felt the weight of the Abbiatis' decision fall squarely on her shoulders. She swallowed hard, unsure if unsettling her was Charlie's intention. If so he had succeeded.

'I will have a great surgical team, experienced—'

'And ready for the unexpected,' Charlie cut in.

Juliet was not impressed. She had hoped his doubts would not be voiced any more but apparently that was not the case. At least she was pleased his delivery was subtle enough not to cause any concern to Georgina. She was still unaware of the professional rivalry. For that Juliet was grateful.

'I would expect no less from any team, primed for success and prepared for the unexpected, but in this case I doubt there will be any surprises. We know there are four babies, and we know there's one problem to solve and then bed rest for you for another few weeks until they are all healthy and a good size for delivery. And on that note, Dr Warren and I need to discuss the procedure and have a scheduled meeting now.'

'We do?'

'We do.'

'Then, Georgie, I will see you later,' Charlie said as he followed Juliet from the room. Once they were out of earshot, Juliet did not hold back.

'You promised you would not try to unsettle my patient. She has made her decision and there is no point in you questioning them now.'

'Your patient? Georgina is my patient and has been for nineteen weeks since the quads were identified.'

'Well, she'll be your former patient unless you promise to cease this interference.'

'Since when does advice to my patient constitute interference?' he asked as he headed in the direction of his office.

'From where I'm standing that's exactly what it is and I won't stand for it. So please back off or I'll be forced to go to Oliver Darrington and ask to have you removed if he wants me to stay.' Juliet kept up with his fast pace.

'Is that a threat?'

'I'm not sure… I guess if you don't accept your behaviour to be tantamount to undue interference then I really don't have to acknowledge whether mine is a threat.'

'I said in front of Georgina that you have the opportunity to save her babies. They chose your procedure. It's now in your hands. A fact. And as for the team expecting the unexpected, that is my way of saying they are experienced and the Abbiatis have nothing to worry about. My words were designed to bring comfort to the quads' mother and by the look on her face they did just that. Did she look panicked?'

Juliet considered his words and began to think she might have overreacted again. 'Well, no.'

'That's because I know my patient, I've been treating her for almost three months now and I have built a good rapport with her.' He stopped outside his office.

At that moment, an orderly appeared wheeling a trolley laden with boxes. 'This is the last of the archived records, Dr Warren. A desk is being brought up from storage along with a chair and a sofa. Oh, and I've asked the cleaning crew to freshen up the office next door for the Aussie doctor as you requested and the flowers you ordered will be here first thing tomorrow. I'm sorry the office wasn't cleaned up this morning when you asked but we've been flat out. I wasn't sure if she'd arrived yet but it will be all done by lunchtime.'

'I guess your office will be ready for you to move in tomorrow, then, Juliet,' Charlie said as he left Juliet alone with another onslaught of thoughts.

Each one of them making her feel smaller by the minute. She had once again misjudged Charlie and in the process demanded something he had already planned on providing. Before he graciously asked her out to brunch to give her the good news. Suddenly she thought the ogre's shoes were more befitting her feet.

Juliet collected Bea without trying to find Charlie and offering to thank him. He had already organised an office for her before she'd made the demand earlier in the day. She felt foolish and thought better than trying to make amends yet again. She had made a habit of offending him that day just as he had of offending her the day before. He had made an effort to be courteous but the orderlies hadn't been able to deliver. The fact she did not have an office was not his fault.

And the flowers he ordered? What on earth did that mean? After the disastrous start to the day, and the terrible ending, he still wanted to make her feel at home with flowers. This man was more of a riddle by the minute. Just when she thought she had worked him out, he surprised her. Only this time it was a nice surprise and an extremely humbling one for Juliet.

Somehow she would make amends. But exactly how would take some time to figure out.

'Mummy!' came the little voice. 'I have a friend. Her name's Emma.' A little girl with flaming red hair and a toothy grin was holding Bea's hand. 'We played yesterday. And we played today. She'th such a good drawer. Her mummy'th a doctor too.'

'Hello, Emma.'

'Hello,' the little girl replied in the softest voice.

'Can Emma come home and play?'

'That would be lovely one day if her mummy says yes, but just not today, Bea, because we have to find another place to live. Somewhere with a nice bath and your own room.'

Bea studied her mother's face for a minute. 'Okay, Mummy,' she finally said with a smile. 'Bye Emma. See you tomorrow.'

'Bye, Bea,' the little girl replied before she ran back to the toys on the play mat in the centre of the room.

Juliet popped her daughter's woollen cape over her shoulders and led her to the car they had hired that morning. She was happy that Bea had made a new friend so quickly. She definitely had much better social skills than her mother, Juliet thought.

'I've found two houses that might be nice so we might just pop in and see them. A man with the keys is meeting us at the first one in half an hour. We can't stay in the hotel because it doesn't give us much room and the bath just won't do. It might be nice to have your own room—perhaps one day this week Emma might come over and play.'

'I hope so,' Bea said as she looked out of the window at the buildings as they drove down the main street of the town.

Juliet suddenly spotted a quaint tea room. 'Would you like something to eat?'

'Yeth, please.'

'Let's see if this little restaurant has Devonshire cream

tea,' she said as she checked her rear-vision mirror, then pulled the car over and parked.

'What'th that, Mummy?'

'Scones and jam and cream.'

'Yummy!'

Almost an hour later and quite full on the fluffy scones, homemade raspberry jam and freshly whipped cream, Juliet and Bea arrived at the first house. It was a fully furnished cottage only ten minutes from Teddy's. She pulled her small sedan into the lane beside the house, unsure of where else to park, and walked briskly around to the front gate. The lettings agent was already there. He looked about sixty years of age with a happy face with a ruddy complexion, strawberry-blond hair and wearing a tweed coat and a scarf.

'Good afternoon, Dr Turner. I'm Eugene Parry.'

'Hello, Eugene,' Juliet said as she approached him with her hand extended. 'Please call me Juliet.'

'Certainly, Juliet,' the man said as he unlocked the front door of the thatched-roof cottage. 'It's a lovely little place, this one. Just came back on the market for renting a week ago after the temporary bank manager left. They found a local to fill the role so the other one headed back to London leaving this vacant and you can have it on a monthly basis. No need for a long-term contract.'

Juliet stepped inside and was immediately taken by how cosy the home felt. It was small but very pretty inside.

'Two bedrooms, as I said, and an eat-in kitchen along with this sitting room,' Eugene said as they stood in the middle of the carpeted room. It was a little cold but Juliet knew with the flick of a switch the heating would change that quickly. 'There's a lovely garden room out the back, which is delightful in summer but not so nice in the chilly weather. Oh, and there's a bath and shower in the newly renovated bathroom.'

Juliet was happy to hear those words and took Bea by the hand to look around. The pretty tastefully wallpapered sitting room more than met her requirements with a large floral sofa and a big leather armchair, a coffee table and a large television. The master bedroom was very simply decorated in tones of blue, with a queen-sized bed and attractive blue-and-cream-striped curtains and a cream damask quilt cover. A free-standing dark wood wardrobe took up one corner of the room and the other corner held a matching large dresser with an oval mirror.

'Where'th my room?'

'Let's go and find out.'

And they did. And it was just perfect. It was painted in tones of peach and there were two twin single beds and a white dresser and robe. The curtains were peach floral with yellow window ties. And there was a four-foot fluffy yellow rabbit sitting under the window beside a toy box.

'The owners have two granddaughters and they used to come and stay but now they're all grown up so they've left it here for others to enjoy.'

'I like it, Mummy.'

'I like it too. We'll take it.'

Aware that the next few days would be hectic leading up to the surgery, Juliet decided, once she had signed the rental agreement, to leave the hotel and move into the cottage immediately. The estate agent was happy as the hospital provided a reference and a guarantee. So Juliet was approved instantly. He had given her the keys and explained how the heater and the stove worked and left.

'Well, Bea, it looks like we have our own little home

for the next few weeks. I've rented it for a month so we can stay here for Christmas and New Year's Eve.'

'Do we have milk and biscuits?'

Juliet smiled at Bea's funny random question and the look of worry on her daughter's face. 'We will get some milk and biscuits and a few other things. In fact, we should go now and stock the pantry before the shops close.'

Together they locked up, hopped back into the car and headed off to fill the cupboards and refrigerator with all they would need.

And as she drove into town Juliet realised she was no longer anxious about being so far from home. Despite her topsy-turvy relationship with Charlie Warren she was suddenly feeling quite at home in the Cotswolds.

Without warning she began to question if in fact it was because of him that she was feeling so at home.

CHAPTER EIGHT

IT WAS FIVE o'clock in the afternoon when they returned. Bea was napping on the sofa, with the heater warming the house, and dinner for two was cooking in the oven. Juliet had bought half a dozen small pork chops and decided to roast them with root vegetables. She thought they could have leftovers the next night. The house was quiet and the delicious aroma of the cooking made her think of home. She looked at her watch and did the mental arithmetic and quickly realised it was one in the morning back home. While she knew her parents loved her, one a.m. was not the time to test the depth of those feelings. She would wait until morning. She had called from the airport to tell them she was safe and since then they had each sent texts. There was nothing else to report. Nothing had happened. They hadn't really met anyone. As she put her feet up on the ottoman and leant back into the softness of the cushions, she realised that technically wasn't correct. Bea had met her new best friend, Emma.

And Juliet had met Charlie. Complicated, handsome, argumentative Charlie. She closed her eyes for a moment.

Who was he really?

And why was he making her think about him when he wasn't around? For almost five years, she had not given a man another romantic thought, until now.

Dinner was lovely and they both ate well, then Juliet washed the dishes before she gave Bea a nice warm bath, paying particular care to keep her cast dry. As she wrapped her daughter in a fluffy bath sheet before slipping her into her pyjamas, Juliet smiled at the little girl and thought how strong she had been. She couldn't have been more proud of her daughter. She didn't fuss or complain about it at all. Bea just worked around the cast and made the best of it. She was indeed a very special little girl. Despite having her own room, and thinking it was very pretty, that night she decided to sleep with her mother in the big bed. And after her favourite story, they both fell asleep around eight o'clock.

Bea dreamt about a princess who fought dragons and won…and Juliet's sleep began with a dream of Charlie.

It was close to ten when Charlie stood staring into the darkness from his kitchen window. The tap was running and steaming water was filling the sink where he had placed his dinner dishes but it was as if he were somewhere else. Somewhere other than in his home alone, the way it was every night that he didn't work late at the hospital. The silence made him feel even more solitary but that night he chose not to have the noise of the television. He didn't want white noise providing pretend company. He suddenly felt as if he wanted something more. The lightness of heart that he felt when he was near Juliet and Bea was something he had not expected. And something he could not fully understand nor thought he deserved. He lifted his gaze to see the haze of the full moon trying to break through the heavy clouds just as he was trying to step out from behind the guilt that was burying him. But he knew he had as much chance as the moon had.

* * *

The next morning was an early start. Along with meeting with Georgina and Leo, Juliet wanted to brief the surgical team to ensure there were no questions around the procedure. Bea needed help to dress in a stretch knit track suit and then after a hearty breakfast of porridge and honey the two set off for Teddy's.

'Ith the hothpital really called Teddy'th, Mummy?'

Juliet smiled as she drove. 'Yes, it is.'

'Like a teddy bear?'

'Yes, just like a teddy bear.'

'That'th silly. It'th a hospital for babies, not for teddy bears.'

Juliet laughed along with her daughter as she turned into the hospital car park. She loved that Bea could see the funny side of life at an early age. She had taken after her grandfather with that trait and clearly the ability to make friends quickly. After the uncomfortable situation with Charlie the day before, Juliet knew she was most definitely missing that skill.

But worrying about being friends with Dr Charlie Warren was not about to take precedence over what mattered and the reason she had travelled to the *teddy bear hospital*.

The day would be busy and she had a lot to accomplish. From a risk-management viewpoint, she needed to have contingency plans in place should the babies react poorly to the procedure. While she saw no reason for it not to proceed smoothly, guaranteed success was never a given and Juliet was always prepared for both the best and worst scenarios and everything in between. Should the laser surgery initiate early labour, she wanted Charlie on the team. She just had to ask him and then wait for the lecture about unnecessary risk she knew would follow. Despite this, she would not exclude him from the theatre as she valued his skills as an OBGYN. She just hoped and prayed she didn't need to call on it.

Her mind's focus was on ensuring that it went like clockwork. There were four babies, two parents and four grandparents who were stakeholders with a heartfelt interest in the surgery being successful. Not to mention Oliver Darrington and the board who had covered the cost of her temporary relocation. The surgery would not be lengthy but it would be intricate. She intended on spending time letting the theatre staff know exactly how she operated and what she needed. She knew this would not be the first laser surgery procedure at Teddy's, but she would not take any chances with miscommunication around the operation on these babies. The staff needed to be fully aware of her expectations. She wanted Lily and Rose to grow up with their brothers, Graham and Rupert. And she would do everything in her power to make sure that happened.

It was not until she saw the black motorbike parked outside the hospital that her thoughts returned to Charlie. At least that was what she told herself, when the butterflies returned to her stomach at the sight of the shiny black road machine. She knew it wasn't the truth because she had fallen asleep thinking of him, dreamt of him and then woken with his handsome face firmly etched in her mind. She hoped he had cancelled the flowers for her office after the words they had shared the previous day. She wanted him to be spiteful and give her reason to dislike him. She didn't want to believe that underneath the gruff exterior lay a good heart. She had told herself for too many years that a man like that didn't exist and she didn't want to doubt herself.

After dropping Bea at the crèche and watching her

daughter and her new best friend, Emma, hug each other excitedly, Juliet made her way to her office. She knew it was adjacent to Charlie's office. She walked past with her laptop computer under her arm ready to settle into her new workplace. As his door was ajar, against her better instincts she felt compelled to look inside. She crossed her fingers that he was not there and she did not have to address her poor behaviour first thing in the morning. This time her wish came true. Charlie was nowhere in sight. But she knew that she would have to face him. Soon. Avoiding him would only last for an hour or so as they needed to consult further on Georgina and the quads, but it would give her time to find the right words to say. An apology on her behalf was deserved. She just wasn't sure how to deliver it.

Her second wish was that the flowers were not in her office. Bracing herself, she opened the door. There was no floral arrangement in sight. Unexpectedly her heart fell. She had no idea why. It was her wish that he'd cancelled the order so she could hold that against him. But part of her had apparently, and unconsciously, hoped he wouldn't. She'd hoped he would be gallant and still have a beautiful bouquet waiting for her as a welcoming gesture. She hadn't expected it, until she'd heard about it. And at that moment she'd realised that deep inside Dr Charlie Warren was a gentleman. Despite her knowing they came from opposite sides of opinion, the fact that he had arranged an office for her and even thought of flowers made her believe in chivalry.

If only for a second.

But the lack of flowers, she knew, was fed by her own actions. She tried to remind herself it was only flowers, but the fact there were none still stung. For a few wonderful moments when she'd realised he had gone to the effort and trouble for her, she had felt special.

And she could not remember the last time a man had made her feel that way.

But it wasn't to be, Juliet decided as she dropped her oversized shoulder bag on the chair and her computer bag on the desk. Charlie had chosen to cancel the flowers, or perhaps give them to someone else. There would no doubt be a number of young women in the hospital who would be flattered to receive them. Perhaps he was even dating one of them. With his looks and position he would be quite the catch, she thought. But she wasn't fishing. She was very happy to live her life without a man who might disappoint her. She and Bea would be happy together.

And she didn't need any flowers.

She was glad she hadn't dressed in something as figure hugging as the previous day. There was no point. She was at the hospital to concentrate on the quads and nothing else. Juliet hung up her heavy overcoat on the coat stand near her desk, then smoothed down her black woollen skirt and checked her black-and-white-checked blouse was still properly tucked in. She did have very pretty black patent pumps with a kitten heel, so she hadn't entirely tried to hide her femininity. And she was also wearing her signature French fragrance. It was light and floral.

She remembered reading in one of her self-help books that she'd purchased when her trust in men had been broken four long years before that, *'When there isn't a man in your life to make you feel special, expensive perfume can.'*

She wasn't sure it would fill the void for ever, but it had worked up to that point.

Checking her emails, she noticed that Oliver had scheduled a meeting with the surgical team. She had sent a list of required staff for the procedure the day before. She'd wondered if she should consult with Charlie as the OBGYN about it, then decided it might become another debacle so decided to consult with Oliver. She was looking forward to getting to know the team and going over the procedure so that the babies had the optimum chance at leading normal, healthy lives. She couldn't see Charlie's name on the list and wondered if he had chosen to withdraw or if Oliver had made that decision for him.

Suddenly, there was a knock on her open door. She lifted her eyes to see the freshly shaven, impeccably groomed subject of her thoughts. His crisp white shirt highlighted his slightly olive complexion, and once again his blue eyes caught her attention. They appeared even more vivid from across the room.

'May I come in?'

'Of course,' she said, trying to keep the rhythm of her heart from racing and bringing a blush to her cheeks. She doubted she would be successful so she launched into the much-needed apology. 'I'm very sorry about yesterday. I behaved so poorly and I'm not sure how to make it up to you. It was professionally reprehensible, not to mention just plain awful, on my part to speak to you that way after you had made the effort to deliver the Abbiatis' decision in person.'

Charlie stood in silence for a moment and she was unsure how he would react.

'Apology accepted, Juliet,' he said, taking long purposeful steps across the room and very quickly closing the gap between them. His cologne filled those senses that his very being hadn't already claimed. 'You travelled a long way, it can't have been easy without much notice and I'm sure you have a lot on your mind. Let's just agree to disagree. I will not change my mind about the surgery and you, I can very clearly see, do not agree with the benefits of waiting.'

'You're right,' she returned. 'And it's very generous of you to accept my apology. I'm honestly not normally so rude—in fact I don't think I'm ever really rude at all. *Normally.*' Normally covered many different things for Juliet that day. Quite apart from not *normally* hopping on a plane with less than a day's notice, *normally* she didn't find herself fighting her attraction to a colleague.

'Let's call a truce,' he replied.

'Done,' she agreed, hoping that the heat she was feeling hadn't made her cheeks glow.

'I have something for you in my office. I'll be back, then we can discuss the Abbiatis.'

'Sure,' Juliet responded, not entirely sure at all what Charlie had for her but suspecting it was the update on the quads' condition. Juliet prayed it had not worsened during the night. She had intended on heading to Georgina's room as soon as she had read her emails. She wanted to speak in more depth with both Georgina and Leo about the surgery that was scheduled in two days. The risks needed to be explained again and the permission signed for surgery. Both parents had to accept that, while this was the best way forward, there would still be risks.

Juliet was deep in thought when she heard Charlie return. With a large arrangement of the most beautiful flowers.

'Oh, my goodness,' she said, getting to her feet as she watched Charlie place them on a small table by the window. 'They're gorgeous. You shouldn't have.' It was a lovely round arrangement, as if it had been picked from an English garden. Although she knew it wouldn't be from a garden in the snow-covered Cotswolds. She could see foxglove, hollyhock, snapdragon, sweet peas, roses and a few sprigs of lavender. It was the prettiest arrangement she had ever seen. And as she moved closer she could smell the delicate scent of the flowers' perfume.

'Glad you like them,' he returned. 'But I can't take the credit, since they're not from me. The board asked me to order them as a thank you for coming all this way on short notice.'

'Oh,' she mumbled, feeling silly and trying to mask the disappointment she was feeling.

'I thought I'd test the water before I brought them in case you were still upset and planned on throwing them at me. I know I didn't make it easy on you and we really did not get off to a good start.'

Juliet knew she had been crazy to think a man like Charlie Warren would buy flowers for her. She felt very foolish for thinking that he would.

'I agree we got off on the wrong foot,' she managed to reply. 'But…it's all sorted now.'

Little was truly sorted in Juliet's head. She had been entertaining romantic thoughts and even having dreams about a man who had just followed the instructions of a board and ordered flowers. At least she knew exactly where Charlie was coming from.

'Actually I haven't bought flowers since…' He paused, then stopped the conversation completely and walked to the door in silence.

Juliet thought Charlie was about to let her into something about him. The man who had an office devoid of photos or personal belongings. There was no visible history or connection to another person or persons. And no hint of a life outside the hospital. She didn't want the opportunity to know more about him to pass. 'Since?' she prompted before Charlie could leave.

Charlie drew a deep breath and turned to face her. 'Not since my wife died. There were so many flowers at the funeral that I couldn't face another flower again. Besides, there was no one to buy them for after that.'

Juliet's disappointment was quickly pushed aside by the shock of what he had said and the instinctive reaction to comfort him. She was momentarily speechless.

Her emotions were once again swinging like a pendulum.

And he was gone.

CHAPTER NINE

CHARLIE LEFT JULIET'S office before she had a chance to offer him any words of comfort or condolence. Juliet watched as he rushed out of the door, confirming matter-of-factly on the way out that they would meet with Georgina and Leo an hour later. There was no further reference to his wife or being a widower. He did not put a timeline of context to his statement. He apparently had another important appointment and one that oddly seemed to lift his spirits when he spoke about being needed elsewhere. He had quite literally dropped an emotional bombshell and run before she could say anything. The swing of the pendulum grew wider by the minute. Charlie mentioned he couldn't be late for his tough taskmaster. She couldn't think who would be harsher than himself but clearly there was someone in the hospital giving him orders. And he jumped. But jumped willingly. While the news was sad, Charlie seemed strangely upbeat as he left.

Juliet thought better than to try to learn more. He had said enough. He was a widower, and she was a single mother. Facts about each other that she had to remind herself had no relevance to their working relationship. But it was not news she had imagined hearing from him.

But it suddenly did make sense. And she could un-

derstand better why he appeared to not have a life outside Teddy's. He would have lost the life he knew when
he lost his wife.

Trying to push thoughts about Charlie from her mind,
she read the medical updates that had been emailed to her
and sent an email to her parents, informing them that she
would call in the next day or so once she had everything
under control. Although she wasn't sure exactly when that
would happen. She doubted while Charlie was around, or,
more accurately, while she was anywhere near Charlie,
that everything would be under control. He was complex
and perhaps even still grieving and she was confused.

She wasn't sure she would ever really know Charlie
Warren.

But she did still need to ask him to be in Theatre. She
had assumed he might have attended, but after seeing the
theatre staff listing and noticing his name was not there
she wanted to raise it with him. It had slipped her mind
in her office, but a lot did when he was around.

She had to put him back in context. He was Georgina's
OBGYN and having him there would make Juliet feel
more secure. She tried to tell herself it was purely from
a risk-management viewpoint, but it was more than that.

With half an hour until she had to be with Georgina,
Juliet decided to pop in and check on Bea. After step-
ping out of the elevator, she rounded the corner and saw
Bea and Emma happily helping the childcare assistant
to put Christmas decorations along the hallway window
ledges of the crèche. It was difficult with her arm in the
cast but she was managing to pass the sparkly tinsel to
the young woman and Bea beamed with delight as she
watched it being secured in place with tape. Juliet grew
prouder of her daughter by the minute. She had adjusted
to the move, albeit only for a few weeks, so well. She had

made friends, not dwelled on her broken arm and was loving the opportunity to do new things.

Juliet wished she were as resilient. She was still carrying around scars that should have long healed. It was as if she had her broken heart in a cast, and she had spent almost five years dwelling on it. She certainly needed to take a leaf out of her four-year-old daughter's book on how to cope with adversity and still enjoy life. She was still allowing Bea's father to affect her life's choices. To affect the way she saw other men. She was punishing all men for the mistakes of one and feeling sorry for herself in the unnecessary process. Her daughter was a better example to her than she was being in return.

And, she quite harshly reminded herself, she hadn't lost the person she had committed to spending her life with the way Charlie had. She had been seduced and dumped by a man she barely knew and it hurt. But she had the most wonderful daughter to love while Charlie had no one. He had lost the woman he loved. His scars would with good reason run deeper. She needed to put on her 'big girl' panties and stop letting the past rule her future.

Juliet decided to get in the Christmas spirit and offer to help with the decorations. But as she drew closer she discovered the three of them had a fourth helper.

'Charlie,' Bea called out sweetly. 'We need more tinthel.'

Juliet moved back out of sight and watched as Charlie stepped from inside the crèche and ruffled Bea's hair. 'Of course, boss. I'll get it for you now.' With that, he walked back inside the doorway and emerged carrying a large box with tinsel overflowing from the top. He placed it within Bea's little reach and then stepped back. 'Do you need any more help?'

'No, thank you, Charlie. You can go and meet my mummy about the babies but maybe you can come back and help.'

'I certainly will.'

Juliet realised the identity of the taskmaster that Charlie was meeting. She controlled the urge to laugh at the way Bea was throwing around orders and at the same time blink back tears as she watched a man who had lost his wife act almost like a father to her daughter.

Bea's banter with Charlie was so relaxed. Her orders were delivered in a cute voice, and with the best intention of getting the job done, but they were orders nonetheless. And she was only four. What made it more poignant was the fact that Charlie was taking them. She sincerely doubted anyone older than Bea could get away with being so forthright with a man like Charlie.

She suddenly worried that Bea might be auditioning him for the role of her daddy. Juliet felt torn as she walked away in silence. She and Bea would not be in the Cotswolds for ever and she didn't want her daughter to get too attached, but at the same time it was wonderful to see Bea so happy in Charlie's company. She bit her lip as she suspected with little effort it might be easy for her to become attached to Dr Warren herself. Particularly with what she now knew about him.

With her mind spinning, Juliet headed back to Georgina Abbiati's room. She needed to focus on the real reason for her travelling to Teddy's. And it was not to become involved with a complicated man. No matter how wonderfully he treated her daughter. And no matter how she felt herself warming to the handsome widower.

'So do you feel comfortable and understand fully everything I've told you about Friday's procedure?'

'I think so, Dr Turner. I mean, we've made our decision and we're not backing down now. Sorry, Charlie, but I think we've made the right decision,' Georgina said with a slight waver obvious in her voice.

Charlie nodded and, true to his word, said nothing.

'But I do have two more questions if you have time,' Georgina continued.

'Of course. I have all the time it takes to make you feel at ease and comfortable. Fire away,' Juliet said as she took one final glance at the morning's observations of her patient, including the results from the daily ultrasound she had requested. The boys' condition had remained stable and the girls were unaffected.

'I know I will have a local anaesthetic and sedation, but will I feel anything at all?'

Juliet had been asked the same question many times. 'There will be no pain, perhaps a small amount of dull tugging, but also there is a slight risk your uterus can react to any interference with contractions. Not sufficient in most cases to bring on labour but it may feel that way to you. There will be no pain, just tightness if a contraction occurs.'

'Will Charlie be in the theatre too?' Leo asked as he looked over towards Charlie. 'Just in case Georgina goes into labour.'

Juliet turned to Charlie and with equally baited breath awaited his response. She wasn't sure if Oliver Darrington was still to make the final decision on the attending OBGYN or attend himself.

'Of course,' he announced with conviction and keeping his focus on Georgina and Leo.

His words allowed Juliet to take the next breath and a smile spread over her face.

'I'm your OBGYN, and, while I have the utmost faith

in the skills of Dr Turner and the team, I'm your back-up plan. If the need arises, and I'm not pre-empting it, but should the laser surgery hasten labour, I will be bringing Rupert and his siblings into the world.'

Juliet was happy with his explanation. It had not been delivered in a manner that would elevate the Abbiatis' fears, in fact just the opposite, and for that she was grateful. Charlie was playing fair.

'And I'll be very happy to have Dr Warren in Theatre. No one knows you better than your OBGYN so his presence and skills are invaluable.'

Juliet could see from the corner of her eye that Charlie had turned his head in her direction. But she didn't reciprocate. It had the potential to be a moment that she was not ready to face. Mutual admiration and respect, coupled with what she had witnessed downstairs with Charlie helping Bea. It would have been an emotional overload that she could not afford at that time.

She was feeling more than a little vulnerable. To her feelings and to Charlie Warren.

Charlie was many things and increasingly she was seeing he might even have the potential to be wonderful, but she was not looking for a man. Wonderful or not. She doubted her heart would survive. Besides, she was not staying and she did not want to start something she could not finish.

'If that's all for the moment, and you know you can page me any time, I will head off to brief the theatre staff.'

'Georgie, Leo,' Charlie began as he edged closer to Juliet's direction, 'I'm in that meeting too, so we will see you later. Rest lots, try not to stress and write down any questions so you can ask either Dr Turner or myself when we call in.'

* * *

'That went well,' Juliet began as they walked down the corridor towards the elevators. She still did not make eye contact. 'I'm glad you'll be in Theatre. It wasn't articulated on the list.'

'I was waiting to be invited. You're the lead surgeon, so it was a professional consideration on my behalf to wait until I was asked.'

'I was going to do that today.'

Charlie eyed her suspiciously. 'Well, I guess I invited myself so, like the idea or not, I'll be scrubbing in with you on Friday.'

'I like the idea. Very much. Thank you,' she said as she pushed the button for the elevator with her pulse racing a little but a sense of contentment washing over her knowing Charlie would be there with her during the operation.

Twenty minutes later, Juliet was winding up her briefing to the theatre staff, a number of whom were pressed for time as they were due to scrub in for another procedure that afternoon. She had already gone over her theatre equipment requirements, spoken to the anaesthesia team and nursing staff. All of the medical team involved in Georgina's procedure, bar the one medical student and two interns on maternity rotation, were experienced with TTTS laser surgery, although none on more than two babies. Four was outside everyone's experience. Including Juliet's. And she did not hide that fact from the team.

'While I have performed fetoscopic laser surgery on triplets, I will not deny that on quadruplets it will be a slightly more challenging procedure. However, the direct visualisation through the fetoscope will allow us to successfully perform a targeted and focused laser termination of the vascular communications directly responsible for the TTTS and effectively separate the placenta into two components, one for each foetus. With each baby having its own placental mass, and the removal of this communication, there will be an interruption to the transfusion process and we should stabilise the situation so we can advance to a gestational age where the four babies in this situation all have a greater chance of survival. Does anyone have any further questions?'

'If the parents of the quads did not agree to the surgery, what would the risk be to the other three babies if the recipient baby went into stage five heart failure and died?'

Juliet could see the question came from one of the interns. 'That's a very good question. If one foetus was to become non-viable through cardiovascular complication arising from the TTTS, then it would put all three remaining babies at high risk of death, injury or disability. Essentially the fetoscopic laser procedure has taken what was until relatively recently a lethal placental disease and turned it into a manageable condition if detected early.'

The specialist team were all silent. Each nodded their understanding.

'Just one more question. If the outcome of moving forward with this intervention is pre-term delivery, are you certain that you're sufficiently prepared for the arrival of four twenty-nine-week gestational babies with a current average weight of less than three pounds?'

Even without hearing the voice or seeing the man, Juliet knew the question had to come from Charlie, who was standing with folded arms at the back of the room. She took a deep breath. But instead of feeling resentment or interference, she appreciated the question. It was fair and one he had every right to ask in that arena and one that others might have been wondering about.

'Yes, Dr Warren, that's why we have assembled a multidisciplinary team who can deal with all potential outcomes including pre-term delivery. In addition to Ella, who is Georgina's midwife, and two anaesthetists, Mr Darrington has already approved the four neonatal intensive care nurses and two neonatologists who are here with us today, and a senior paediatrician, paediatric resident and a paediatric cardiologist, all of whom I assume you will recognise on the day but can't be at this briefing. In all we will have sixteen in the medical team, three observing and four incubators in Theatre. All of which, God willing, will be under-utilised on the day.'

Surrounded by Theatre staff, many in scrubs, Juliet suspected the imminent laser surgery for his patient became more real in Charlie's mind, giving rise to his ongoing concerns.

'Good, I'm not surprised you have it under control, Dr Turner. Let's hope we don't need any of it,' he said, then turned and walked away leaving a tiny grain of doubt in Juliet's mind.

Juliet never operated with doubt over anything. She needed to manage it immediately.

CHAPTER TEN

'CHARLIE, MAY I see you for a minute?' Juliet asked at the same time as she knocked on his open door. She had excused herself from the pre-operative meeting with the medical team and followed him back to his office. 'I need to ask your advice with regard to a question hanging over Friday's procedure.'

'What would that be at the eleventh hour?'

'It's hardly the eleventh hour.'

Charlie rolled his eyes as Juliet stepped inside his office and closed the door behind her. Normally she would have shown professional courtesy by involving him in her plans earlier but his initial reservations had ensured that did not happen. She stepped closer to his desk and looked him directly in the eyes. 'I should have asked for your input around the team. I realise it may have come across as if I've gone behind your back and made arrangements with your Assistant Head of Obstetrics with no input from you as the quads' consulting OBGYN.'

'What's done is done,' he said as he continued rifling through the paperwork on his desk.

Juliet pulled out the chair opposite and sat down. 'I am sorry about the way I've handled this. I've been a bit like a bulldozer.'

His gaze lifted from the paperwork and met hers. 'Perhaps a mini dozer.'

She smiled. 'I really do appreciate you agreeing to be there in the surgery with me. Not for protocol…just because I need you there.' As the words slipped over her lips she surprised herself. Juliet never admitted needing anyone. And it wasn't just to make up for what she had done. She meant it. She actually needed Charlie.

He said nothing for the longest moment, leaving Juliet wondering what he was thinking.

'Let's just hope the procedure doesn't induce an early delivery because all four are too small for my liking.'

'I agree, that's why I need your advice around my contingency plan for that occurrence. Do I have everything in place? You've delivered more babies at this hospital than I've seen in my life and I'm not afraid to say that I feel a little like a fish out of water and I want your advice on how we can best prepare for the worst.'

Over the days since she had arrived, despite their disagreements, she knew Charlie was a great OBGYN. It was his passion for what he believed to be best for his patient that fuelled his stubbornness. Juliet knew he cared over and above and, while she conceded he was not one to take risks, perhaps that would make their collaboration perfect. He could temper her risks, mitigate the strategies and together they could find the best way forward.

'What is it you want to know?'

'I want to know if we have sufficient staff on board for starters. And if we don't, I need you to tell me who's missing. Oliver has left it up to me, and I would like your input.'

Finally he looked up and spoke earnestly. 'I think you're fine with the surgical team. Each and every one is the best that Teddy's has to offer and I don't think you want to further crowd the operating room. My concerns would be around the anaesthesia.'

'Why would that be?' she asked with her curiosity piqued as she shifted to the edge of her chair.

'If the laser procedure was to be the catalyst for pre-term delivery of the quads you would be looking at a Caesarean if the babies were to have any chance of surviving. They would be barely twenty-nine weeks' gestation, and babies that premature would not survive the birth canal. There would not be sufficient time for an epidural to be administered so you'd be forced to use a general.'

'So we'll have that option on hand?'

Charlie stood and walked around to the front of the desk, crossed his legs and looked directly at Juliet. 'I think you should try to avoid general anaesthesia.'

With a frown, Juliet continued the questions. 'How can we though? You just said yourself that our only option if labour was to commence as a result of the laser surgery was a GA.'

'No, I said that it would be the only option if we weren't fully prepared.'

'So you think we should have an epidural in place for the procedure rather than the local anaesthetic and conscious sedation?'

'Yes, that way we'll have both bases covered. It would meet your needs during the fetoscopic procedure, but allow a Caesarean to be performed immediately any signs of distress were detected from any of the babies.'

'It makes perfect sense.'

'Glad you agree.'

'Am I missing anything else?'

'No, I think we've covered it all now.'

They both felt the other trying to meet halfway. It was almost as if the slate had been wiped clean in a very short time by them trying to understand the other. It was starting to resemble a collaboration of minds and skills. And each of them was pleasantly surprised.

Juliet wondered fleetingly if there was a chance it could possibly become a collaboration in another sense. Then just as quickly she pushed that from her mind. She didn't need any complications in her life. And she knew Charlie Warren would be a very big complication. And if she fell for him, a very big heartache that she couldn't risk.

'I know we won't agree on the procedure,' she began with her mind back in appreciative colleague mode, 'but I value your advice. I'll meet with the anaesthetist tomorrow and brief him on the changes and then let the Abbiatis know. I'm glad we agree on this.'

'I'm glad too,' Charlie offered as he suddenly saw Juliet in a very different light. He had seen glimpses over the previous days but only in short bursts, before her need to bring home her opinion took over masking the woman he was seeing clearly again now. Suddenly he felt the defensive armour he had worn close to his chest for two years loosening a little. He had not meant to tell her about losing his wife but the words had just spilled out and he was not sorry. Letting Juliet know about his past seemed natural. In fact everything about being around Juliet suddenly seemed very natural.

'It's been a long morning,' he suddenly announced. 'And I'm quite hungry as I skipped breakfast. Would you like to join me for lunch?' He felt as if he was getting to know the real Juliet and it had been a long time since he had wanted to get to know anyone. Her interest in seeking his opinion, despite their opposing stands on the procedure, made him feel as if his advice meant something to her. And she had not pried into his personal life. He had told her about losing his wife and she had left it alone. He appreciated that respect of his unspoken boundaries.

'That would be lovely, Charlie, but I'm due to collect Bea. Would you mind if she joined us?'

'Not at all.'

Charlie was already smitten by Bea. She was a tiny version of her mother. Just as bossy, just as beautiful… and just as endearing. Her innocent joy of everything festive was making him see Christmas through her eyes instead of a man who had lost his wife at that same time of the year. The distaste he had held for anything close to celebrating was losing ground under the spell of the tiny decorator with a love of tinsel.

'Did you know that Charlie helped me with the tinthel on the windowth?'

'Did he indeed?' Juliet asked as she sipped her Earl Grey tea in the downstairs hospital tea room. Juliet did not want to let on she had witnessed Bea ordering Charlie around. It still brought a smile to her face as they sat together having a light lunch. Charlie had suggested they could head into town to have something to eat, but Juliet was well aware that he had a patient in labour and already beginning to dilate and thought better of taking him away. The roads were icy and she knew he would be taking his motorbike and the thought of him racing back in bad weather if the labour turned into a delivery without much notice did not sit well with her.

'Yeth. He was a very good helper. And he carried the boxthes.'

'Because you were a very good boss,' he said, with his eyes laughing. 'And you can't carry boxes of tinsel with a broken arm.'

Juliet laughed and looked over at Charlie. He was the

most complex man she had ever met. He had so many layers and she wasn't sure why but when he lowered his guard around Bea in particular she could see how very special he was. Juliet watched him smiling down at her daughter. His affection for her was palpable. And it made Juliet happier than she could have imagined. Not that she was looking for a father for her child, but if she had been Charlie would definitely have been a good choice.

Even Bea knew it.

'And how exactly did carting tinsel for a four-year-old became your role?' Juliet asked as she watched Bea happily sipping on her oversized chocolate milkshake. She felt certain the ladies in the tea room had found the largest cup and filled it to the brim. Bea's little legs were swinging back and forth as she gleefully watched the toy train, driven by a tiny Santa, circling a smaller Christmas tree in the corner of the tea room. Cotton wool covered the base of the tree like freshly fallen snow and it had been sprinkled with silver glitter. Juliet could see her daughter was in complete awe of it all. Juliet finally felt she could relax and exhale over her decision to bring Bea with her to the UK.

'I wanted to check on Bea's cast,' Charlie continued. 'I know you would have been keeping an eye on it, but I wanted see how my workmanship had stood up to the rigours of a four-year-old. Before I knew it I was recruited to decoration duty.'

'Be careful, knowing my daughter, she'll soon have grand plans of taking the tinsel to any part of the hospital that is not looking festive.'

'Oh, she's already scoped the entire floor and has plans of hospital-wide decorations!'

As they chatted over roast beef and mustard sandwiches all signs of animosity had abated, and for that Juliet was grateful. She could see that Charlie was a good man, a guarded, opinionated and stubborn one, with an overly cautious nature, but nevertheless a good man with a sad past. They spent a little while comparing the Australian landscape to the Cotswolds and then Charlie unexpectedly excused himself and made his way over to a very pregnant woman.

Juliet watched as he chatted with her for a moment and the two of them returned to the table.

The tall, ash-blonde woman was wearing a very tired smile and said, still chatting to Charlie, 'I can't join you but thank you for asking, Charlie. After they make my sandwich, I'll be heading home. I just finished up a long surgical repair of anomalous pulmonary veins on a newborn. It went well but I need a good sleep. I'm exhausted.'

'I'm not surprised. You're pregnant and insist on keeping up a fairly heavy surgical roster. You'll have to slow down soon,' he told her. 'But while you're waiting for your food, let me introduce you to Dr Juliet Turner and her daughter, Bea. Juliet's the *in-utero* specialist brought here from Australia to assist with the quadruplets.'

Sienna approached with her hand extended. 'Welcome aboard, Juliet. I hope you enjoy your time here.'

'Thank you,' Juliet said as she met Sienna's handshake, immediately liking the other woman.

'Sienna is Teddy's neonatal cardiothoracic surgeon,' Charlie explained. 'And one of the very best so we're fortunate to have her.'

'Said by Teddy's best OBGYN,' Charlie's very tired, very pregnant colleague told Juliet. 'But I should go... It's nice to meet you, Juliet. Perhaps we could meet up for coffee soon.'

'I'd like that, thanks, Sienna.'

'Mummy, ith that a printh?' Bea interrupted.

Juliet turned her attention to her daughter. 'Is what a prince, sweetie?'

'The man up there,' Bea said, pointing at the large television screen in the corner of the tea room. 'Ith he a printh?'

Juliet watched the news coverage and read the footnotes on the screen. 'Yes, he is a prince. It's Crown Prince Sebastian Falco of Montanari.'

'Does he have a printheth?'

'Not yet, sweetie, but he is engaged to be married and they're making quite the fuss of him. I suppose if you're a prince they will make a fuss of everything you do.'

'Will I ever be a printheth?'

'You're already *my* princess,' Juliet said as she kissed her cheek.

Sienna suddenly grabbed the seat that Charlie had offered. Juliet noticed she had also suddenly drained of colour.

'Is everything all right?' Juliet asked. 'Would you like some water? You look terribly pale.'

Charlie rushed to the cooler and, taking a bottle of water, undid the cap and passed it to Sienna. 'Get this into you.'

Juliet didn't understand what had happened as she watched the woman stare at the screen as if she had seen a ghost. She said nothing as she sipped her drink and then looked away from the screen and into the distance.

Charlie's pager abruptly beeped. 'I've been summoned. Looks like there's another baby about to enter the world. Will you be all right, Sienna? Should I get Oliver to take a look at you?'

Sienna shook her head. 'No, I'll be fine. I've suddenly lost my appetite. I really need to go home.'

Juliet walked Sienna to her car, and made sure the

other woman was safely on her way. She thought that Charlie was right, that Sienna needed to look at slowing down as her pregnancy progressed. It was obviously taking its toll on her.

The next day, Juliet managed to meet with the anaesthetist to discuss the change of plans. He agreed that the dual purpose epidural would be the better option and that information would be passed on to the rest of the team. She then headed to Georgina's room to let her know the change to the preferred anaesthetic and explain the benefits of Charlie's suggestion of an epidural. The results of the daily scans were emailed through to both Juliet and Charlie and thankfully there had been no change to the TTTS status and Juliet wanted to pass this information on as well.

She checked in at the nurses' station and was told that Leo had headed home to let the family know the latest update and have a good night's sleep at Georgina's insistence. He had spent a few nights at the hospital since his return from New York and she knew he would fuss over her if he stayed that night and not get any rest himself. Juliet knocked on the door and asked if Georgina would like company.

'If you have time that would be lovely,' the mother-to-be answered as she invited her to sit for a while. 'I've been here less than a week and I'm going a little stir crazy. I can't imagine how women confined to bed for months cope.'

'You do what you have to do, and, believe me, if you were told bed rest for nine months to have healthy babies, you would do it. It's just a mother's natural instinct.'

'I suppose I would,' Georgina agreed. 'But I would still be a little loopy by the end.'

Both women laughed before turning the subject to something a little more serious. Juliet wanted to know about the supports in place for when the babies finally went home. While it wasn't her role, she was interested to know how much assistance would be available as she reinforced the fact that four babies would be an enormous workload for the next few years.

'The babies' grandparents live very close to us, and I have a housekeeper, so I won't be struggling in terms of running the house,' Georgina answered. 'I'm very fortunate, and I know that Leo will be very hands-on too.'

'Leo's also running the family business, so he may not always be able to help, so please don't try to be brave if you feel overwhelmed at times. Let those around you know if you are struggling,' Juliet told her. 'Get extra help and take some time for yourself, even if it's just a ten-minute soak in a bubble bath. It will help you to re-energise, regroup and get right back to being a mother.'

'That sounds like you've been through it.'

'I have, believe me, but not with four babies. I only had one, she's four years old now, but it was a full-time job for me for the first few months.'

'Didn't your husband help at all?'

Juliet paused before she answered, thinking back for a moment to when Bea was a baby and then to even before that, to how scared she was as the delivery date drew closer. The fear that engulfed her some days knowing that she would be bringing up Bea alone. And how some nights she lay awake worried that she would not be enough for her daughter. That she wouldn't cope. But she did.

'I wasn't married. I'm a single mother.'

'And a surgeon,' Georgina responded. 'That's amazing. You're bringing up your daughter alone and hold-ing down a career.'

'It's not been that difficult. Bea's almost at school now.'

'But you've done it by yourself and flew all the way over here from Australia to help my babies. I think you're the one who should take time out and have a bubble bath!'

Ella stepped into the room as the women were still happily chatting. She was there to take Georgina's blood pressure.

'I think I will head off and leave you in Ella's care,' Juliet said as she stood up to go. She wanted to go back to her office and confirm that everything was on track. 'I will see you and Leo in the morning.'

With that Juliet walked back down to her office and as usual she looked into Charlie's office as she passed by. It was a habit that had formed quickly but she was grateful he wasn't always there or it might have seemed awkward. This time he was there, sitting on the sofa with his feet up reading. It looked like a report of sorts but she didn't stop.

Not until she heard him call her name and she turned back to see him standing in the doorway.

'How are Georgina and Leo holding up?'

'Georgina's doing very well and Leo's gone home. She wanted him to rest for tomorrow,' Juliet told him, still feeling warmed by the affection the parents-to-be shared. 'They would have to be the sweetest couple, so in love and looking out for each other. Truly beautiful.'

Charlie didn't comment and Juliet suddenly felt ter-rible for bringing up their marital happiness. She felt so insensitive and decided to change the subject rather than add to her verbal blunder.

'What about you?' she asked to break the uncomfortable silence. 'Did the baby have an uneventful entry into the world? It must've been a quick labour for you to be back here already.'

'It was her fourth,' Charlie said, clearly keen to move away from discussing Georgina and Leo's love story. 'She was a pro. Her baby boy was delivered in forty-five minutes and she has three more at home to match. There will be no shortage of men to mow the lawns in that household.'

Juliet assumed the conversation would end there and made a mental promise to herself to be more sensitive but Charlie continued the conversation. 'Is Georgina fine with the change to the anaesthesia, then?'

She paused mid step and turned back to him, elated that there was no damage from her inappropriate comment. 'Yes, she understood why you thought it would be best. And I'm sure, because the suggestion has come from you, she feels very comfortable. I think she's happy we're working closely together—it makes her feel better about everything.'

Charlie had heard the overall details the day before but wanted some clarification around a few of the finer details. He invited her back into his office and they talked through everything from the preoperative medication to the post-operative care. He was impressed that Juliet was thorough, focused and left little to chance. It was how he liked to operate. He wasn't one to ever take unnecessary risks.

They were winding up the conversation and Juliet mentioned heading down to collect Bea. 'You apparently said you could look at staying here longer if needed to one of the midwives.'

'That's right. I'll stay until the babies are born.'

'And after that?'

'I'm not sure. If there's a position here, and the need for my skills, I may look at my options. But my family and friends all live in Perth, quite close by, which is a great support for both of us and of course my mother and father still keep watchful eyes on both of us. I'm fortunate but some may find it odd that they still fuss over me at my age.'

'Helicopter parents?'

'You could say that, but with all good intentions.'

Charlie nodded. 'Well, they let you out of their sight to make this trip at least.'

Juliet laughed. 'They actually pushed me onto the plane. I wasn't convinced that I should come here but they insisted.'

'Then they can't be too overprotective. You and Bea have travelled a long way and you're definitely not under their watchful eyes now.'

Juliet smiled. 'What about you?' she enquired. 'Are your parents here in the Cotswolds?'

Charlie's smile seemed to drop instantly. The cheery disposition Juliet had been enjoying seemed to slip away and she wished she hadn't asked. She prayed they too hadn't died. That would be a heavy burden for someone to bear. She watched as he stood up slowly and walked to the window, looking out into the distance. He didn't appear to be focusing on anything in particular.

'It's none of my business, really you don't have to answer.'

Charlie stared ahead, still saying nothing for a few moments. 'No. My parents both passed while I was in medical school. They left me a sizable inheritance to ensure I could complete my studies but they left me alone. No brothers or sisters.'

'I'm so sorry.'

'It was a long time ago and it only hits home occa-
sionally. Usually around holidays like Christmas when
it's all about family time.' Charlie rested back into his
chair. 'On the subject of family, I overheard you tell the
nurse in A&E that Bea only has one parent. And tell me
if I'm overstepping the line but are you widowed like
me...or divorced?'

Juliet reached into her bag for her bottle of water and
took a large sip. She had known the subject could arise
but she wished it had not been that day. She had no intention of blurting out to him details around her irresponsible one-night stand. She was a doctor and she slept
with a man she didn't know and fell pregnant. Juliet accepted that it wasn't the eighteen-hundreds, as her father
had often said, but the circumstance of Bea's concep-
tion, in her eyes, still made her look fairly naive and irresponsible.

Charlie was so conservative in almost every way and
to announce that, *By the way I was reckless, slept with a
man I barely knew, trusted him when he said he'd handled the contraception and as a result became a single
mother, but the rest of the time I'm incredibly responsible...except of course for the day we met and Bea was
alone in the playground and fell...and last week when
I decided on a minute's notice to drag a four-year-old
halfway around the world.*

Any way she looked at the situation, she felt that Charlie might judge her.

But then why did she care? His opinion shouldn't matter. But it did. She had been silly enough to trust a man
who didn't deserve that trust the night Bea was conceived
and naive enough to think there would be more than one
night. Perhaps even forever.

She doubted that Charlie ever threw caution to the

wind and for that reason she felt anxious about confessing her stupidity. But just as Charlie had told her about his wife and his parents she felt she should give him the same level of honesty.

'Bea's never met her father but he is alive and living somewhere in Western Australia.' There it was said. Out in the open. And she knew the floodgates were also open to the barrage of questions that would follow. And she would answer all of them truthfully. Or not answer them at all.

'May I ask why?'

'It's for the best,' she mumbled. 'It's just that he's not a good person. To be frank, he's the worst type of bad.'

'Really?'

'Truly.'

'Do you want to talk about it?'

She momentarily closed her eyes and took a shallow breath. It was a risk to tell such a man about her stupid night, very stupid night with a serial womaniser. It made her appear as young and naive as she knew she looked.

'Then you don't have to…'

'No, I want to…' She swallowed pensively. 'The reason Bea's father has never met her…is because we haven't seen each other since I became pregnant.'

'So he left you when he discovered you were having his baby?'

'Not exactly. He left long before I knew.'

'How long before?' he asked.

'He left the morning after I became pregnant and he's married so there's no point going there.'

'Married?'

'He wasn't at the time…but he married a few weeks later. He was apparently engaged when we met but I had no idea. I discovered later, much later, he was a serial womaniser. He married before I had even known I was pregnant.'

'But he should have been held accountable. A man can't just walk away from the responsibility of his own child.'

That was what Juliet's father had said despite not knowing the identity of the man. No one knew the identity of the father, not even her parents. It was Juliet's secret. Perth was not a huge city and she did not want her father to confront Bea's father and tell him what he thought. It would have opened a Pandora's box and she thought that Bea might be the one to suffer the most.

'It wasn't long after the wedding I discovered he and his new bride were expecting triplets.'

'How did you discover that?'

'A cruel twist of fate had his wife's OBGYN reach out to me when a complication arose during the pregnancy. I couldn't bring myself to consult on the case so I deferred to another neonatal surgeon. How could I operate on the children of a man I despised so completely? If anything had gone wrong I feared that I'd have questioned myself for eternity and far more than anyone else ever would for sure, but it wasn't worth the risk.'

Charlie sat shaking his head. 'Still he should provide support for his daughter. It must be hard as a single mother, financially and emotionally.'

Juliet rested back into the generous padding on her high-backed chair. 'It is but I wouldn't change a thing. I adore Bea. She's my world.'

'She's adorable...despite her father. That must be because she's got more of you in her.'

Juliet smiled up at the man who was close to capturing her heart but she wasn't ready to let him. She still couldn't risk being hurt again.

'Thank you.'

'It's definitely his loss,' Charlie began before shifting the direction of the conversation slightly. 'Will you ever let Bea reach out to him?'

Juliet felt a warm feeling rush over her with his words. She would never have expected Charlie to say something like that. He wasn't judging her at all. He hadn't reacted the way she had feared.

'With three children under his belt and, from the gossip around Perth, more than a few post-honeymoon flings and another one or two since the birth of his children, I don't want him in her life. He's a real-estate developer with no conscience and both the means and opportunity to entertain other women and he's been doing that for a very long time. I will be thinking long and hard about allowing Bea to be the fourth, and unwanted, child of the man who enjoyed a pre-wedding fling with me despite having a fiancée at home waiting for him.'

'And if she asks about her father growing up?'

Juliet had not decided how she would respond when Bea asked about her daddy. And invariably she would one day.

'I'm not sure how I'll handle it. Despite my feelings about the man who fathered Bea, he's after all half of Bea and I want my daughter to grow up proud of who she is, not doubting herself because of her father's despicable behaviour. It's a dilemma I'll face later. Although I must admit recently I'm beginning to believe it will perhaps be sooner rather than later. Almost all of Bea's little friends at playgroup have fathers and Bea's beginning to talk about their *daddies*. She has a grandpa who had just retired but then… But that's another story. Anyway, he is more than thrilled to be the male role model but I know it's not the same as having a daddy.'

Charlie didn't reply. Bea was a wonderful little girl and didn't appear to be suffering from paternal neglect so obviously Juliet's father was a great surrogate. She was a sweetheart and many men would be proud to call her their daughter and watch her grow up under their watchful eye. Be there to unwrap Christmas presents together, buy her first bike and then her first car and of course scrutinise boyfriends who would never be good enough for his daughter.

Suddenly Charlie began to suspect if he wasn't careful he might just be one of those men. 'Look at the time— it's getting on and I have some paperwork to catch up on tonight at home,' he said abruptly, collected his leather briefcase, said goodnight and left his office.

Bea was happily playing in her room with cartoons on television and Juliet had just folded the last of the towels from the dryer, all the while thinking about Charlie. She could think of little else as she stacked the towels in the airing cupboard. With the empty basket in her arms, Juliet made her way into the sitting room. She could see the front porch through the lace-covered bay window.

Her jaw dropped and she almost dropped the basket when she saw who was standing on her doorstep.

CHAPTER ELEVEN

'OH, MY GOODNESS, what are you doing here?' Juliet squealed as she opened the door. She couldn't have been more surprised...or happier. 'Quickly come in from the cold!'

'It was your father's idea. He thought that we could help with Bea while you concentrate on the quads' surgery.' Her mother embraced Juliet, then stepped aside for her husband to do the same.

'It's a challenging surgery and we don't want you worrying about picking up Bea from the crèche,' her father chipped in as he carried one of the suitcases inside and then hugged his daughter warmly. He turned back for the other one still on the porch, then closed the door on the bitterly cold night air.

'Or worrying if she gets a sniffle with the sudden change in climate,' her mother added as she looked around the cosy sitting room of the cottage.

'Oh, my God, why didn't you tell me you were coming?'

'Because you would have said we were fussing—'

'Which you are...but I'm very glad you like to fuss.'

'And we missed you both terribly.'

'It's been less than a week.'

'See what an only child has to suffer. Two parents who

miss you after less than a week and follow you to the other side of the world,' her father continued as he placed the second suitcase down. 'So learn from us and give Bea some brothers or sisters in the future or she'll be doomed to having a helicopter parent hovering around like us!'

Juliet smiled. 'If I'm half as good a parent as you two, then Bea will be a lucky girl.'

'We are the lucky ones, Juliet. You make us both very proud.' Her father hugged Juliet again and then stepped away a little as his eyes filled with tears of happiness.

Juliet could see the emotion choking him and knew all three of them would be a mess if she didn't change the subject. 'So when did you decide to fly out? And how did you arrange it so quickly?'

'We had passports so we just rang the travel agent. We've booked into a hotel nearby for tomorrow but they didn't have a spare room tonight.'

'You'll do no such thing. There's plenty of room here.'

'We don't want to put you out. We'll just stay tonight if that's okay. We can sleep on the sofa.'

'Don't be ridiculous. You'll stay here…now how long are you able to stay?'

'Till you get sick of us,' her mother replied.

'Then you'll be here for a long time,' Juliet said. 'What about a nice cup of tea?'

'That would be lovely,' her father said.

'Well, actually, we've booked one of those river cruises through France and Spain,' her mother added. 'That's the week after Christmas.'

'I thought you had planned that for next July? You were going to enjoy summer in Europe. Leave the Australian winter behind and thaw out over here.'

'That was our plan but we brought it forward. No point flying out twice. It's a long way for two old people.'

Juliet laughed. 'Hardly old but you'll be missing the sunshine on your cruise.'

The three of them looked up as Bea came running down the hallway. 'Grandma! Grandpa!'

'Here comes all the sunshine we need,' her father said.

Juliet's parents both dropped to the ground, her father a little more slowly due to the arthritis that plagued his knees. A group hug ensued with lots of kisses.

'I knew Father Chrithmath was real,' the little girl said with a toothy grin.

'Of course Father Christmas is real, but why do you say that?' Juliet asked as she looked at the three of them nestled together on the rug on the floor.

''Coth I asked him to bring Grandma and Grandpa here to play in the snow with me and have Christmath food and everything.'

'How did the surgery go for Kelly Lester?' Juliet asked as they sat by the fire after settling into Bea's room. Bea was happy to move in to Juliet's room and sleep in the big bed and give her room to her grandparents. 'I got your email that the procedure was successful but how is Kelly progressing post-operatively?'

'Good, very good,' her father answered as he reached for a homemade cookie. 'She's a strong woman, lots of family support and, although there will still be hurdles as to be expected with spina bifida, the chances have been greatly improved of the child walking by about the thirty-month mark, which I know was your prognosis. And we both know without surgical intervention the little boy would never have walked or really enjoyed a quality of life.'

'Look at you two. Like peas in a pod,' her mother said as she finished her second cup of tea.

'You liked the tea, Grandma?'

'Yes, I did, Bea.'

'Would you like some more?'

'No, thank you, sweetie. But what I would like is to hear about how you got that cast. Mummy rang and told us how it happened but it did sound very scary.'

Momentarily distracted from her cup of hot chocolate, Bea looked at the cast intently. 'I fell from the slide and broke my arm.'

'Are you feeling better now?' her grandfather asked as he lovingly watched his granddaughter.

'Yeth, Charlie made my pink cast.'

'It's very pretty and has lots of beautiful drawings,' her grandmother replied.

'Yeth, my friendth drew them,' Bea told them, then, pointing at the image of a sunflower, she continued. 'Thith one is by Emma, my betht friend.'

'Well, she's very clever and I'm sure very nice.'

'Charlie ith very nice too, and very tall. Like a building,' Bea said as she jumped to her feet and stretched her hand up as high as possible. 'He'th Mummy'th friend and he'th going to get us a Chrithmath tree. A really, really big one.'

'Did Charlie offer to get a Christmas tree for the house?' Juliet asked with a curious frown. He had not mentioned it to her.

'Yeth, Mummy, he told me he would get a beautiful tree for uth.'

Juliet's parents looked at each other with a knowing smile.

'Don't go there,' Juliet said, shaking her head. Since the strange way he'd left off with Juliet, she wasn't sure about him. She felt that he was hiding something from her and she wasn't sure she wanted anyone that complex in her life. 'He's the OBGYN, and to be honest, most of the time, quite difficult to work with. It's taken almost all week to finally come close to understanding him. He's conservative and stubborn and fought me every inch of the way about the *in-utero* surgery.'

'Why did he attend to Bea? Since when do OBGYNs attend to paediatric fractures?'

Juliet drew a deep breath and put down her spoon. 'He's the doctor that rushed to Bea in the playground. The doctor I was waiting for inside and he was running late. He arrived at the hospital at the same time Bea fell.'

'Serendipity…'

'Mum, please, I said don't go there.'

'Is he handsome?'

'Mum…'

'It's a simple question, Juliet. Is the nice doctor who saved Bea, and is now, according to our granddaughter, *your friend*, who is going to buy you a Christmas tree, handsome?'

Juliet swallowed. 'Yes, he's handsome…and incredibly difficult at times—'

'And also with a very kind streak by the sound of it too,' her mother cut in.

Juliet's eyebrow was raised as she returned her attention to the last few crumbs of cookie on her own plate. She wasn't going to get into an argument. Her mother had said the truth. Charlie did have a chivalrous and kind side to him and she didn't want to think about that.

'He'th nice,' Bea added, completely oblivious to her mother's opinion of Charlie. 'We put up tinthel, and pretty thingth around the hothpital.'

'Really? Not what I would have thought was part of an OBGYN's job description?' her mother said without making eye contact with Juliet.

'Particularly not one who's difficult...' her father mused, looking at his wife.

'Let's not forget stubborn,' her mother commented with a wistful smile.

Juliet stood up. 'Have you finished?'

'With this conversation or the cookies?' her mother asked with a cheeky grin.

'Both!'

'Remember, if there are any issues or just for peace of mind, if you need or want to stay at the hospital and monitor the quads' mother, you know your mother and I are here to look after Bea.'

'I still can't believe you flew all that way just so I could focus on the babies,' Juliet said as she gathered the last of her things, wrapped her scarf around her neck over her heavy coat, pulled on her knitted cap, kissed Bea and headed for the door. They had all enjoyed a restful night's sleep and Juliet felt good about the impending surgery.

'If Bea needed you in the future, you would do exactly the same.'

Juliet knew that was the truth. She would indeed do anything for her daughter, at that time or any time in the future.

'Despite what you say, Juliet,' her mother added as she sipped her early morning cup of tea and prepared for the cold gust of air as her daughter opened the door, 'it's not easy being single and raising a daughter and having a career that makes you responsible for other people's lives. You have a lot on your very slender shoulders.'

'But I love it. It gives me purpose and I can't imagine doing anything else,' Juliet told them both as she stepped onto the porch and closed the door behind her.

'I know,' her mother replied as she looked over at her

husband, reading the local paper. 'The apple indeed did not fall too far from the tree.'

Georgina and Leo were waiting outside Theatre when Juliet arrived. With her hair tucked inside a disposable cap, and dressed in a hospital gown, Georgina had been prepped for the surgery. She was lying on the trolley with the sides up ready to be wheeled inside by the theatre staff. Leo was holding his wife's hand tightly and trying to put on a brave face but Juliet could sense the fear that was mounting by the minute.

'I will be scrubbing in for your procedure now,' she told them as she patted Georgina's arm. 'And, Leo, you can scrub in with me. I know that Georgie will want you right beside her during the procedure.'

'Sure.'

'Any questions?'

'Yes,' Leo said with a cheeky smirk. 'How hot does it get in Australia in summer?'

Juliet was surprised by the question. It was definitely left of centre. 'Quite hot in Perth, well over one hundred degrees on our hottest days. I left only a few days ago and we'd been through a heatwave—we had three days in a row that reached over one hundred and five degrees.'

'That's hot. Maybe spring would be nicer.'

Aware that time was ticking, and the medical team would be waiting, she quickly asked, 'For what, exactly?'

'Georgie and I have decided, should all of our babies come through this happy and healthy...' he paused for a moment and smiled lovingly at his wife '...that in honour of you we're going to take them all on a trip to Australia before they start school. We were planning on showing them Italy, but I think an adventure down under would be more fun for the six of us. Besides, Georgie and I have been back to Italy a few times but we've never seen a kangaroo up close and we can tell the girls how an Aussie doctor saved their brothers and, if you're home, perhaps we could call in and say hello.'

Juliet thought it was such a sweet sentiment and optimistic. It was what would pull them through whatever lay ahead. 'And I will put the barbie on for all of you.'

'I'll cook the pasta,' Georgina added from the trolley.

'And I'll bring the vino,' Leo chipped in as the theatre staff began to wheel his wife into surgery. Juliet couldn't help but see through his jovial façade that a tear trickled down his cheek. She patted his arm. 'Georgina is in good hands and so are your babies.'

Juliet then took Leo to scrub in.

'Heads up to the medical student and interns with us today, if you have questions about any of this procedure, ask. We will be using a laser to coagulate the shared blood supply between two of the four babies. This will be more complex with the four foetuses and will take considerable time to map the shared arteries and veins but it will be done. So we are all in here for the long haul.'

Charlie was pleased to hear the conviction in Juliet's voice.

'After this procedure I am hoping the two babies currently affected by the TTTS will be able to grow to their maximum size without complications.'

The epidural had taken effect and Leo was behind the blue surgical sheet holding his wife's hand. Everyone present in Theatre was wearing the protective goggles in preparation for the laser, including Georgina and Leo. Juliet carefully inserted the fetoscope and, guided by the screen, began the arduous task of locating Rupert, otherwise known as Baby A. Once this was done she traced his umbilical cord back to the placenta and began the process of identifying the offending arteries. Secure in the knowledge she had the first communication located, Juliet utilised the laser to cauterise the artery.

Charlie held his breath. That was only the first; he was well aware there were more to locate and sever. Juliet continued mapping the vascular placental linkages and painstakingly cauterising each one. The procedure was progressing slowly but successfully. Charlie was still cautious. Any disruption to the uterus he knew was risky. With only two veins to cauterise, Juliet announced they were on the home stretch and everyone in Theatre felt instant relief sweep over them.

'Well done, Juliet,' the anaesthetist announced. 'Great outcome.'

'I said home stretch, not completed,' she countered cautiously as she pushed down on the foot pedal for the laser and severed the second to last. 'We still have one to go.'

Charlie was impressed with her reply. She had every reason to gloat that close to seeing the end in sight but still she was hesitant to accept praise. He also realised that he had been wrong to judge the procedure. Perhaps, in fact, Juliet had made the right call with the quads. And if the babies all continued to grow, they would be able to prolong the pregnancy for at least a few more weeks until the uterus became too large, but by that time the babies would be all viable and have a good chance at a healthy life.

The final artery was the most difficult to locate due to Baby B's position. All eyes were on the monitor as Juliet carefully manoeuvred around the tiniest twin.

'We have a problem,' the neonatal cardiologist announced. 'Baby B's struggling, he's clearly in stress.'

Charlie stepped forward again to observe the screen. The invasive procedure had been delayed by the fact it was four babies, not two, and it had adversely affected the smallest quad.

'I'm ceasing laser now,' Juliet told the room, then quickly but delicately removed the fetoscope but it was too late. Without warning Georgina's water broke. The operating table was saturated with the amniotic fluid of the boys. The girls, in a separate sac, were unaffected but that would not mean they were safe. If the boys were to be born, so would the girls.

'I'll take over from here. We're in labour and delivering,' Charlie announced as he removed his protective laser glasses, switched them for clear glasses and stepped up to the operation table. He looked over the blue curtain to the Abbiatis. 'Georgie, Leo, your children are on their way,' he said, before turning his attention back to the immediate task. 'Nurses, please prepare for a Caesarean section—we have four twenty-nine-week foetuses that are neither large nor strong enough to pass through the birth canal.'

Immediately Juliet stepped back as she watched the surgical tray swing around in reach of Charlie. She approached Georgina and Leo, leaving the operation table free for Ella and the other midwife to approach and assist.

'The epidural was our safety net,' Juliet said softly. 'It won't be too long before your babies are born.'

'But…they're…too…tiny,' Georgina stated with fear paramount in each staggered word.

'They're small but, thanks to Dr Warren's suggestion of the epidural, we're more than adequately prepared. There'll be no delay in delivering all four babies and that is an important factor. They will be assessed by the neonatal team and then moved quicker to neonatal ICU.'

Carefully but with haste appropriate to the situation, Charlie made the first incision at the base of Georgina's engorged stomach, cutting through the outer layer of muscle. Then carefully he prised open the first incision to reveal the almost translucent uterus that had been stretched to capacity with the four babies. Once through to that layer, Charlie cut the unbroken amniotic sac of the girls, and, reaching in, he carefully pulled free the first of the tiny infants. Carefully he placed the baby in the first neonatal nurse's hands while he clamped the umbilical cord. One clamp for the first baby, who was named by the team, Baby C. The second girl followed a few minutes later; it was Baby D and she had two clamps. Baby D was slightly larger and began to cry immediately. Quickly she was taken by the second midwife. Then came Baby A and finally the smallest of them all, Baby B, who had been against his mother's spine. Removing him from the womb proved tricky as he was the smallest and the most fragile. She could see the concern in Charlie's eyes but along with it was sheer determination. Finally he was pulled free, blue and almost translucent, but alive.

Juliet watched in awe as Charlie tenderly held the tiny infant while the final cord was clamped. The paediatric team worked alongside the neonatal nurses to assess all of the babies. But it was Baby A that caused the greatest concern. He had been the recipient baby and, while not the smallest, his heart had been pumping furiously for the previous twelve hours as Georgina had teetered on the periphery of stage five.

Charlie's focus remained with Georgina. There were still two placentas that needed to be delivered and then the painstaking work of closing the Caesarean section. Juliet remained with Georgina and Leo. It was where she was most needed at that time. With a heartfelt admiration for Charlie, she watched as he expertly began to repair the opening that had allowed Lily, Rose, Rupert and Graham to enter the world.

'You're an incredibly skilled obstetrician and you have no idea how very grateful I am that you were in Theatre today,' Juliet commented as she removed the disposable gown over her scrubs. 'I'm just sorry you had to use your skills.' She was waiting for what she knew would follow. And what she knew would be a fair call. *I told you so.*

But it didn't. Instead, she received the most unexpected praise.

'I did okay, but your skills are second to none, Juliet. I observed you mapping the placenta's vascular pathways. Not an easy task with two babies, but with four it was a miracle and you managed to cauterise all but one artery. And if you'd been provided the time then the quads would still be happily tucked inside Georgina for another few weeks. But fate had another idea.'

Juliet pulled her surgical cap free. 'So you're not upset that I tried. I thought you would be…and justifiably so.'

Charlie turned to face her. 'The opposite, actually.'

'Now I'm confused.'

'If you hadn't pushed for the fetoscopic laser surgery, Juliet, then Rupert's heart would've remained overworked for another twelve hours and it might have been too late. We wouldn't have done another scan until tomorrow and there's every chance he would have gone into heart failure during the night. We would not have had the opportunity to save him.

'I'm very glad you came all the way from Australia to fight me on this. You saved at least one baby's life. If not all four.'

CHAPTER TWELVE

'THANK YOU, CHARLIE. That was an unexpected compliment.'

'Perhaps unexpected but not undeserved. I think you know me well enough after the last few days together to know that I don't hold back my opinion, whether others want to hear it or not. In this case I hope you want to hear it. And while I didn't initially agree, you proved me wrong and that rarely happens.'

'As I said, your compliment was unexpected but very much appreciated,' Juliet said as she removed her surgical gloves and dropped them in the designated bin along with her surgical cap and gown. 'There were a few scary moments in there and I must admit I felt a little out of my depth more than once.'

Charlie slipped his surgical cap free and ran his fingers through his hair. 'You seemed pretty poised and in control even when it all went south.'

'I may have looked composed but my mind was the duck's feet paddling underneath at a million miles an hour. You were the star today.'

Charlie smiled at her analogy and Juliet thought it was the most incredible smile.

'Seriously, you need to take credit where it's due. Teddy's are so fortunate to have you on staff. You could move permanently to anywhere in the world. There would be so many hospitals that would love to steal you, of that I'm sure.'

'What about you?' he answered quickly, still looking into her eyes with an intensity she had not experienced.

The deep blue pools were threatening to pierce the last barriers of resistance to him. Watching him so expertly and confidently lead the team and deliver the four babies safely had brought a new level of admiration for him that she knew few, if any, other doctors could surpass. But Juliet still wasn't sure what he meant. Was he asking if she wanted to steal him? The answer of course would be yes, if she could dull the alarm bells ringing in her head and bury her doubts.

'I'm not sure what you mean?' she asked nervously.

He crossed his arms across his impressive chest and stepped out his legs. It was a powerful stance not lost on Juliet.

'I mean, would you seriously consider living and working here? Would you let Teddy's perhaps steal you permanently from your base in Perth?'

'I'm not sure.'

Juliet felt the intensity of his gaze upon her. She wasn't sure if she was waiting for her to say anything as he stood looking at her without saying a word. She felt her pulse quicken and she became almost breathless with him standing so close to her. Her skin tingled and he had not touched her. She wondered for a moment if she would or could say no to him touching her if they were somewhere else alone…and he tried to pull her to him.

'Are you hungry?'

Juliet was taken aback by his question. *Hungry for what?* Her eyes widened and she felt excitement surge through her veins as she nodded.

'What if I cook us dinner at my place?'

'Your place?'

'Yes, my home's twenty minutes from here. You could follow my bike and I could whip us up something half edible and definitely better than the vending machine, which is your other choice if you stay here at this time of the night.'

'But what about Bea…?' she began to ask as her chest rose with a nervous intake of air.

'I don't think your parents will let her starve and they've more than likely eaten already. Bea may even be in bed asleep. It's almost eight o'clock.'

Juliet hadn't realised the time. It was true, it was late, and they all might have been asleep, not just Bea. She was trying to keep her emotions in check and remember it would be merely a dinner shared by two colleagues. She just had to keep remembering that fact and everything would be fine.

'Give me fifteen minutes to have a quick shower and change.'

'Of course. I could do with a hot shower to loosen my muscles as well. I'll meet you in your office in twenty minutes.'

Juliet walked away knowing she hadn't wanted anyone's company in a very long time. Not until that moment.

Juliet followed behind Charlie's bike along the winding road. The moon's halo lit his broad masculine silhouette as they travelled slowly through the darkened countryside. There was no other traffic, just the two of them on the road. Juliet felt herself mesmerised as he leaned into the turns and curves of the road. His was agile and strong and completely in control of the huge machine. He made it impossible for her not to stare in awe and a little bit of anticipation as he led her to his home.

Finally they pulled into the large estate and Juliet wondered if he had one of the cottages, but soon learned it was the stately mansion that was indeed his home. Even with just the moon lighting the grounds, she could see how magnificent the landscape and how grand his home.

'This is beautiful,' she said as she climbed from the car wearing jeans, a pullover and boots. Her hair was tied up in a makeshift ponytail and a thick scarf and coat rested on her shoulders. 'I've never seen anything quite like it.'

'It's a work in progress.'

'It looks wonderfully finished to me,' she replied as she followed him up the steps to the two-hundred-year-old home. 'It's simply glorious. Nothing quite like it in Perth.'

Charlie unlocked the door and held it open for Juliet to enter, before he stepped inside and closed the door. 'I'll put on a fire and start dinner then show you around, if you'd like.'

With her gaze scanning the furnishings and architecture of the beautiful interior, she nodded. 'I'd love that.'

The fire was roaring and the meat was ready whenever they were; it would take only a few minutes on the grill. Charlie reappeared in the doorway, aware that he was not in a hurry to cook or rush anything about the evening. The surgery, and everything that had happened over the last few days since meeting Juliet, had made him feel alive and made him hunger for more time alone with her, despite his better judgement. 'Would you like a glass of wine?'

'I do have to drive home.'

'Not for a while. Besides, you'll be eating and I'll give you only half a glass.'

'That sounds lovely. I won't head in until around one tomorrow so it might be nice to let my hair down.'

Charlie smiled. Seeing *Juliet* on the sofa, with her beautiful face lit by the fire, was a sight he had never imagined over the years of his self-imposed solitude. But it was a sight he was relishing. 'I'll be back.'

Juliet looked into the crackling fire and as another log was consumed by flames she thought how very different Charlie was from the man she'd first met. In five short days he had opened up and shown a compassionate, loving side completely at odds with the brusque exterior he had first displayed. Bea was smitten by him, and she felt sure if her parents met him they too would think he was very charming. An English gentleman with an English country manor. It was all very proper and lovely. A little like a fairy tale but she wasn't yet sure of the ending. Or indeed if fairy tales happened.

Charlie appeared with two glasses of red wine, Juliet's only a quarter filled.

'As I promised,' he said as he handed her the long-stemmed Waterford Crystal glass. Their hands touched as he gave her possession of the cold crystal and it instantly stirred an overwhelming desire to feel more than just her hand against his. His mouth immediately craved Juliet's full, inviting lips hovering only inches from his own. He let his gaze linger for a moment on her mouth, all the while wondering if it would taste as sweet as it looked. He pushed the cold rim of the glass against his mouth in a bid to control the mounting desire surging through his veins.

'Thank you,' she said as she climbed to her feet. 'Can I have the grand tour now? Do we have time?'

'All the time in the world,' he replied.

Charlie led Juliet around the ground floor. Leaving the generous sitting room, he showed her the kitchen with the butler's pantry, the dining room, which she noticed had been set for two, the utility room, a wonderfully inspiring floor-to-ceiling library, a study with a large oak desk and bookcase and a billiard room that housed an antique snooker table. As they entered each room he thought about kissing Juliet but then reasoning stepped in and made him keep a little distance. But each room was harder than the last.

'You said you were renovating but it all looks perfect to me.'

'I finished downstairs first then moved upstairs with the repairs and redecorating.'

'What's upstairs?' she asked, her curiosity driving her towards the staircase. She was fascinated by the house and couldn't wait to see more.

'The seven bedrooms,' he answered as he followed her lead and moved towards the grand staircase. 'Apparently all of them including the master bedroom are finished but I haven't seen them yet.'

Juliet thought the statement was odd and turned to him. She said nothing as she assumed he had been too busy to check it out, but she couldn't imagine not rushing home to see the progress every night, no matter what the time of day. He was very low-key.

'So where do you sleep?'

'Over there,' he said, pointing at the chesterfield. 'I'm accustomed to it now. I've been sleeping there for a few months while the work's been happening upstairs.' Charlie didn't tell her that he didn't feel any motivation to sleep in the new master bedroom alone.

'It's a very comfortable sofa, but if the master bedroom's finished then it's time you moved in. Let's take a peek.'

Charlie noticed everything about Juliet as she climbed the stairs ahead of him. Her slim hips swaying in her tight jeans with each enthusiastic step, the way her curls bounced when her head flicked from side to side as she looked at the antique framed paintings hanging on the wall, and the slender fingers of one hand gliding up the balustrade, the other hand encircling her glass. She was gorgeous, intelligent and sexy. And watching her, he suspected he was smitten. He wasn't sure if it could be more than that but it was still more than he had imagined ever feeling again.

By the time they had reached the large oak door of the master bedroom, Charlie knew he couldn't resist her any longer. He wanted to spend the night in the refurbished room. But not alone. He wanted to spend the night with Juliet. She had made him feel more alive than he had in years. She, and her little girl, had made him believe there could be life outside the hospital. He had been alone for so long, but now this sexy, desirable woman had stirred feelings that he'd never thought he would feel in his body and soul the way he did at that moment. And if all they had was that moment, he couldn't let it slip away without taking a chance.

Juliet tentatively opened the heavy door to the darkened room and Charlie brushed her shoulder gently as he reached around for the light. Her heart unexpectedly began to race with his touch. Nervously she swallowed and bit the inside of her cheek. She was at the entrance to Charlie's bedroom and she couldn't see anything. But she realised that she wasn't scared.

She couldn't see the future but suddenly that didn't matter either. She didn't need to have everything laid out. She felt safe. Safer than she could remember feeling before. The fleeting warmth of his body against hers caused butterflies to stir. As each second passed with him so close to her, she loosened her tether to fear. Pushing away the promises she had made to never trust again. With his warm breath on her neck, she felt herself feeling free to fall into whatever this could be. She didn't want to run away from her feelings.

As his fingers flicked on the light switch, Juliet found herself looking around at the elegant decor, in the soft lighting. But her focus was the imposing four-poster bed that dominated the room…and dominated her thoughts. It could be their bed for the night.

Suddenly everything felt right. The man standing so close to her was everything she could hope for and he was within her reach.

That bed would be theirs.

Her breathing became laboured with anticipation as she felt Charlie's strong hands on her hips. Gently but purposefully he swivelled her around to face him. Her mouth was only inches from his and it made the ache inside her almost overwhelming. With only the sound of their hearts beating, he searched her face for permission to kiss her and she smiled her consent as she reached up on her tiptoes to meet his lips. Taking her glass and placing it with his on the large oak dresser, Charlie scooped her up in his arms and carried her to the bed, where he laid her down and gently began to peel away her clothing. He slipped off her boots, tugged down her jeans and then slid her arms and body free of her jumper, revealing her white lace underwear.

Juliet watched and admired as he pulled free all of his own clothing, discarding each piece roughly to the floor. Finally, gloriously naked, he loosened her hair from its ponytail and then began to slowly remove the last remnants of clothing keeping them apart. With every part of his mouth and body he began to pleasure Juliet in ways she had not thought possible and ways she did not want to end. Willingly and wantonly, she gave into all of her desires for the man who had awakened the woman in her. And over the hours he loved her that night she gave a little part of her heart to him as they crossed the divide from colleagues to lovers.

Charlie looked over at Juliet still asleep. She was beautiful and loving and everything a man could desire. She had given herself to him willingly and, while it had been the most amazing night, in the soft light streaming from the hallway his actions hit home hard. He had taken the chance. For the first time in a very long time he hadn't denied his feelings but as he lay there looking out into the still of the darkness outside he knew he should have fought this harder. He should never have invited her to dinner, let alone to his bedroom. He regretted everything about the night. The sight of her peacefully sleeping tugged at his heart. A heart so damaged that it hadn't felt anything but pain for so long.

And now the pain returned two-fold. He had betrayed his resolve to live his life without love out of respect for Alice and now there was a second burden. He would be forced to hurt Juliet. A very special woman he did not want to hurt. A woman who did not deserve to be hurt. She was loving and trusting and she had given herself to him openly and honestly. He knew everything there was to know about her.

But she did not know everything about him. She had no idea that he could not let her into his life. Last night was all they would share. He could not accept happiness. He didn't deserve it. As he felt the warmth of her body against his he suddenly felt overwhelmed by the guilt that had been his constant companion for two years. Thoughts of Juliet and what might have been had their lives been different filled his mind. Her scent was on every part of his body and buried the guilt for those few hours but he knew it was only temporary. It wouldn't last and then he would bring her down too. She deserved better than to be with a man who would never be free to love her. He had to set her free.

'Good morning,' she softly said as she lifted herself up to meet his lips.

His mouth felt the warmth of hers but he ended the kiss before it deepened. The need for her was as strong in the morning as the night before but now he knew he had to fight it. It should never have gone that far.

'I'm sorry I fell asleep. I should have left a while ago. You invited me for dinner, not a sleepover.'

He sat bolt upright. If he held her close to him he would give in to his desire. He would take her again and feel her warm soft skin against his and that would make what he had to do more difficult. And more painful for both of them.

'That was my fault as much as yours. I guess we just got carried away by the heat of the moment. Yesterday was quite an intense day. But I'll get you some breakfast before you leave,' he told her as he lifted the covers, swung his legs down and found his boxer shorts and then a heavy winter robe lying on the chair beside the bed.

'I'm sure I can rustle up some toast for us. I'm going to head into the hospital and check on the quads and my other patients.'

'Is there something wrong?'

'No,' he lied. 'I just think we should get going. Last night was…well…special but I'm sure you agree not something we should repeat. It'd make working together difficult for the short time you still have here and neither of us would want that.'

Each word was carefully chosen to hide any level of emotion. What he wanted to do was to pull her into his arms and make love to her again, but he couldn't. He couldn't surrender to the emotions surging through him after they'd spent the night together. He feared his heart and soul were still in pieces and he needed to accept that in the harsh light of the morning. He was damaged and she needed a man who was still whole. Her tenderness and honesty made him feel worse. But he couldn't prolong what he knew he had to do. End it before it began. Not because he didn't care about her but because he feared caring too much.

'I'm really confused, Charlie. I won't lie,' she said as she pulled the covers up around her. 'After last night and…after what happened between us, why are you so distant to me this morning? You sound so cold and…just nothing like you were last night. Why are you in such a hurry for me to leave?'

'I'm not being cold. I'm being honest. Last night was great but we both need to see it for what it really is.'

'And what is that?'

'A great night together—'

'A one-night stand?' she cut in.

'Juliet, it was fantastic,' he said. 'But we're colleagues and I'm not looking for a relationship. I think the intensity of what we went through yesterday with the delivery of the quads heightened our emotions and we acted upon it.'

'So last night was just a fling after the surgery, a reaction to a successful outcome? Is that how you see it?'

Charlie used every ounce of his strength not to reach for her. Not to say how he really felt. Not to let her know that she was breaking through his defences and making him want more. That there was no one he wanted to be with more than her. But he couldn't.

'You can and will do far better than me. I was just for last night.'

'So in your mind it really was just a one-night stand?'

'That doesn't sum up what we shared...'

'But it's how you see it,' she spat back angrily.

'Well...'

'I can't believe this,' she said with anger and disappointment colouring her tone. 'You're no different from all the other men who want a quick roll in the sack with no strings attached—'

'That's not true.'

'Tell me how it isn't true. If this was only for one night then you should have let me in on that fact yesterday, before we fell into bed together. I thought we shared something more than that, or at least we could, given time.'

Charlie hated what he had to do and say. His heart wrenched. This woman was wonderful and loving but he could never be what Juliet needed.

'I didn't mislead you, Juliet. I don't think either of us thought too much about anything other than being with each other but now, in the light of day, we have to be practical. I need to be alone and you're not staying in the UK long term so let's not delay the inevitable.'

What he wanted, with all of his still unhealed heart, was to say that spending any more time with her and knowing he had to let her go would be unbearable. He was torn between the happiness that he felt around her and the guilt that he knew he deserved to carry.

The guilt that would ruin any chance for them having any sort of a future.

'Charlie, does this have something to do with your wife? Lots of people lose their partners but they go on to love again.'

'That has nothing to do with this,' he lied again. 'It doesn't matter why, it's just the way it is.' His voice was shaky as he tried to hold back what Juliet did not need to know.

'I'm not buying it. I think I know you almost better than you know yourself, even though that sounds ridiculous after a week but it's how I feel. So I need to know something. I need you to tell me what happened, Charlie,' she said. Her tone had softened. 'What happened to your wife? Because that has everything to do with your need to be alone. I know it has.'

Charlie's back stiffened and his jaw tensed. 'It won't change anything.'

'Perhaps not, but I want to know.'

He climbed from the bed and began to gather his clothes in silence. He did not want to open up old wounds.

'Charlie,' Juliet began as she leant against the bed head, the bedclothes wrapped around her still-naked body. 'I'll go. I know you want me to leave but you owe me an explanation for what is happening now. I need to know why you're rejecting us…and why you won't even try.'

'Fine,' he said as he inhaled and filled his tight chest with air and stood in the middle of the softly lit room staring back at Juliet. 'You know I'm a widower and you know my wife, Alice, died two years ago. It was a car accident that claimed her life on the road that leads out of town. She died in the Cotswolds only two miles from this house and I wish every day that I could change places with her but I can't. She died and I am forced to live on.'

Juliet sat for a moment in silence. 'Charlie, I'm sorry that you lost your wife so tragically, but you can't change what's happened or trade places with her. Do you think she would want you to be living with that much sadness? Don't you think you're being hard on yourself? You're still here and you can live your life…'

'After I took hers? I don't think so.'

'What do you mean, after you took hers? It was an accident.'

'I was driving.'

'Were you drunk?'

'No,' he spat angrily. 'I would never get behind the wheel if I'd been drinking.'

'Then it wasn't your fault.'

He stood rigidly. 'She was excited about going to the dinner. I couldn't have been further from excited. The weather had been the worst we'd seen in years, I'd been in surgery all day and wanted to stay home but I didn't want to refuse her. I didn't want to appear selfish so I gave in. When I should have said no, I said yes. Despite my reservations, we headed out on the snow-covered roads, I lost control and I killed her.'

'No, Charlie, you didn't kill her. The weather, the road, fate, that is what killed Alice. You can't take responsibility for that. Factors came together to take her life.'

He paced the room. His hands were clenched tightly. 'We shouldn't have been on the road, in the weather. I should have been more cautious. I should've protected her. I was her husband; that was my role.'

'I bet you had driven in that weather many times

without incident and you thought that night would be no different…'

'But it was different. I should've argued the point, and insisted we stayed in, out of the weather.'

'Even if you had done that, you know Alice could have been in an accident the next morning travelling to work. It could have happened any time. Or worse, she could have gone on her own and you wouldn't have been there for her. You tried to protect her. You were tired and yet you agreed and did your best to protect her by being with her.'

'But I failed and nothing you say can change this. I've felt this way since the day she died and I will feel this way until the day I die. And it's the reason I haven't driven in more than two years. I won't get behind the wheel of a car again. Ever. Please, Juliet, I think it's best that you leave.'

'Charlie, we can talk about this—'

'No.' He knew his coldness wasn't lost on Juliet and he wanted it that way. He had to push her away before he fell too hard and couldn't let her go. 'There's nothing else to say. I'm sorry if you were looking for more. But I'm not and never will be. You're a special woman, Juliet, but I can't… I suppose occasional lapses like last night will happen.'

Juliet stared back at him. He could see tears welling in her eyes. 'Lapses?'

'I'm sorry, you know what I mean.'

'If all of this is true, then you had no right to ask me back here last night.'

'I asked you here for dinner.'

'Then why didn't you leave it downstairs?' she demanded. 'Why did you show me the master bedroom?'

'I need to get dressed. There's no point discussing this further. We made a mistake last night. We shouldn't have overstepped the line. We work together and we should not have slept together. It won't happen again. I'll make sure of that.'

'You'll make sure of that?' she repeated solemnly. 'I'll make sure of it.'

'Juliet, I didn't mean to hurt you; you have to believe me.'

'I don't have to believe anything.' She climbed from the bed and began to gather her clothes. Angrily she pushed past him to the bathroom. She slammed the door shut and reappeared a few minutes later, dressed.

'There's just one more thing,' he said, determined to distance himself from Juliet and her tiny daughter. He knew it would sound heartless but it would ensure she stopped trying to help him.

'What?' she demanded.

'Would you mind telling Bea that the delivery she's expecting won't be arriving? The Christmas tree farm can't deliver. I'm truly sorry.'

CHAPTER THIRTEEN

JULIET ARRIVED HOME to see there were no missed calls from Charlie. He hadn't so much as sent her a text, let alone called to apologise or try to make it up to her. Her face was damp with tears she had shed but most of them had rolled down her cheeks on the short and painful drive home just before dawn. The road was dark and she felt more alone than she had ever done before.

It was her worst nightmare. A one-night stand with a man with whom she had thought she might possibly fall in love. If she wasn't already a little. With a heart heavier than she had dreamed possible, Juliet had run out of his home when he'd told her about the tree. She'd known she had to leave. Without saying another word.

She'd had to turn her back on Charlie Warren just the way he had turned his back on her.

But before he'd seen the tears she had promised herself all those years ago that she would never shed for a man.

She had pulled into her driveway and crept into the house before the sun came up and slipped into bed beside Bea, feeling stupid and filled with regret. She hoped her daughter would never make the same mistakes she had, twice. She wanted so much more for Bea. She wanted her to feel real love, the kind that lasted for ever with the bells and whistles and everything a man could give and that neither had given to Juliet.

She could hear her father snoring in the other room and knew her mother would be wearing the earplugs that had saved their marriage. Her father's snoring at times was like a long freight train rattling down the tracks, and, without the earplugs, she knew her mother would have gone mad from the sleep deprivation or divorced him. But she had found the solution in a pharmacy, popped them in her ears and had her happily ever after. For Juliet there was nothing in a pharmacy, no prescription or over-the-counter solution to her woes. She simply chose the wrong man and that was a problem that couldn't be cured.

In her lifetime Juliet had only chosen two men and both were wrong for her. And both were nothing more than one-night stands.

There would be no happily ever after.

She was, in her mind, the poster girl for stupid decisions with her one hundred per cent failure rate.

Bea had left the bed while Juliet lay with her eyes closed. Now she could hear her daughter giggling over the sound of the television in the other room. She could also smell fruit toast that she knew her mother or father had prepared for their granddaughter.

While her irresponsible mother slept in after a drive of shame home.

They had been careful, so at least she had no fear of another pregnancy. No, this time she had only gained a broken heart and damaged pride. Not to mention shattered dreams that what she had shared with Charlie in his four-poster bed would amount to more than a night. Climbing from the bed, she headed for the bathroom.

She needed to soak in the tub and try to wash the man out of her heart.

Only this time, she thought it would take longer and hurt more. Because this time she had believed in her heart it was real.

It was the weekend, and Juliet was not required at the hospital but she wanted to be there to see Georgina and Leo and also their babies. In general her role ended after the delivery, but the outcome of the Abbiatis' procedure was not what she had clearly hoped for and she wanted to check in with them. Despite what Charlie had said post-operatively, and what she knew to be true, she still felt responsible for the babies' pre-term arrival. It wasn't logical, it was heartfelt, and that was linked very closely to the outcome of becoming involved with Charlie.

Spending the night in his bed was illogical and…heart-breaking.

She left Bea playing cards on the floor with her grand-father. Snap was their game of choice. The house was lovely and warm and Juliet's mother was going to roast a chicken for lunch, then they thought they would all rug up in their winter best and head out for a walk through the town. Juliet wished she were in the mood to join them but decided to hide behind her work rather than pull them all down with her melancholy mood.

After parking in the hospital car park she made her way into the hospital. The chilly breeze seemed even colder that morning.

Juliet caught sight of Ella as she walked into Maternity. Worried that the midwife would sense immediately that she was upset, Juliet quickly realised that she had to avoid her. Ella had mentioned a few times how she was growing accustomed to Juliet's sunny personality and that day Juliet knew she was anything but sunny. With her head down, she waved and rushed past Ella, hoping she would assume she was in a hurry and not think anything of it. But she wasn't that lucky.

'Juliet,' Ella called to her. 'Do you know where I might find Charlie?'

Juliet shrugged her shoulders. She didn't want to be drawn into talking. She feared she might tell Ella that she hoped Charlie was rotting somewhere in hell. Or worse, burst into tears and confess how much she still felt for the man who had behaved so poorly. So she kept walking, offering Ella nothing. In Juliet's mind, it was best if she was the only person who knew about her foolish behaviour. No one else needed to know that she had actually believed, when he'd pressed his hard body against hers, that a man like Charlie wanted more than a fling.

With a deep breath to steady her emotions, she knocked on Georgina's door. There was another hurdle to face that day. Georgina and Leo and their questions about what went wrong.

'Come in,' came Leo's voice.

Juliet stepped into the room that was filled with flowers and family members. She suddenly realised she also had to face their family.

'Mum, Dad,' Leo began, then turned to the other set of parents and repeated himself. 'Mum, Dad, this is Dr Juliet Turner, the *in-utero* surgeon from Australia.'

Juliet attempted a smile. She was genuinely happy to finally meet Georgina and Leo's parents but it would have been a nicer meeting if it had occurred the previous day. Before the surgery had brought about the pre-term delivery of the four babies…and before she had stupidly slept with Charlie and hated herself.

Moving closer to Georgina, she did not attempt to

shake four sets of hands. The closest were folded, the next clasped, one set leaning on the window ledge and the final hands were arranging flowers. It was a little overwhelming and she suspected they were all making judgement calls on the laser surgery that had brought about the early arrival of the quads. And they had every right. While she'd known it was risky, she had forged ahead and in their eyes that was probably not the right decision.

'So you're the Australian doctor who performed Georgina's surgery?' one of the two older men said.

Juliet nodded and lifted her chin. The outcome was not perfect but Juliet still believed she had made the correct decision. The only correct decision she had made that day.

'Yes, I am. And I stand by my advice to operate. Despite the outcome, I believed then, and still believe now, that it was the best option, however—'

'Then we all owe you a huge debt of gratitude for saving our grandchildren.'

Juliet was taken aback. She'd thought both sets of parents, along with Georgina and Leo, would have been upset with her. Not grateful.

'Please take a seat. You must be exhausted after the day you had yesterday,' the taller of the two women said. 'We heard you stayed back to check on the babies. Have you seen them today? They're so tiny but the neonatologist is very hopeful they'll all pull through. They're tiny little Italian fighters.'

'You should have called Rupert Rocky instead!' Georgina's father suggested with a grin. 'It's not too late to change his name.'

'Rocky as in Rocky Balboa?' Leo asked, looking more than a little embarrassed.

'The greatest Italian fighter ever!' his father-in-law replied happily.

'Dad,' Georgina cut in, 'Rocky is a fictional character in a movie.'

'I know,' the older man replied. 'But Rupert's a fighter and the other three are just as strong. I know in my heart our grandchildren will pull through. And that's thanks to you, Dr Turner.'

'I'm not sure where this is all coming from,' Juliet admitted.

'Charlie was in early this morning to see me and check my stitches,' Georgina continued. 'He told me that, even though he was against the laser surgery, and despite it not going to plan yesterday, it saved Rupert's life because it brought on my labour early and he was born just before his heart stopped. A day longer and he would not have survived. You saved our baby's life, Dr Turner.'

'Charlie, is everything all right with Juliet?' Ella asked as she caught up with Charlie scrubbing in before visiting with the quads.

'Why? What makes you ask that?' His tone was defensive. He didn't want to be questioned by the midwife. They had been friends for a long time but he didn't want to feel forced to justify his behaviour to anyone. There was no other choice but to push Juliet away. He had to be cruel to be kind. While he regretted hurting Juliet, he knew if he led her on he would hurt her more. It would just take her longer to feel the hurt. She was looking for a happily ever after and he was not that man. He had a debt to pay. And it wouldn't allow him to love someone. Particularly the way he knew he wanted to love Juliet. With every fibre of his being.

But he wouldn't.

'She rushed past me this morning, and snubbed me. Well, almost, I mean she waved at me but it wasn't like her. And I asked about you and she just shrugged her shoulders. She and Bea are always so lovely and she seemed upset today.'

'Perhaps she's drained after yesterday,' he suggested to deflect from the real reason.

'No, she's a pro,' Ella responded. 'She wouldn't react that way.'

'Just leave it alone.'

'You know, Juliet would be perfect for you, Charlie. I know you may not have thought about her that way, but she's beautiful, sweet and intelligent. You're both single. I think she could be *the one*, Charlie.'

'I like it on my own. It's been that way for a long time. I had *the one*, and I lost her. I don't need to hurt another woman.' It was true that it had been a long time but it was a lie that he liked being alone. It was a penance he made himself pay for the accident.

'It's been over two years since the accident—that's long enough for someone as young as you to mourn. Your wife wouldn't want you to go on punishing yourself.'

'I guess we'll never know what she wanted, because I killed her.'

'It was an accident—a stupid accident that no one could have averted. It's lucky you lived through it.'

'I'm not so sure I'd call myself lucky. I lost Alice.'

Ella shook her head. 'It was a tragic accident that you survived. You are not the first person to lose their partner. It's awful, but it happens and people have to go on and rebuild their lives.'

'It was stupid and reckless. I've no right to a happy life when my wife died with my hands on the steering wheel. I'll never forgive myself for that.'

'Charlie, I hope you know from the way Juliet and little Bea look at you, you might just be punishing more than yourself by pushing them away.'

Juliet saw Charlie around the hospital when she popped in to check on the quads over the next couple of days but he said nothing to her. He had every opportunity to try to make amends. To apologise. But he didn't try. She felt as if the world were crashing in. A world she'd dreamed she might possibly begin to build with Charlie. She knew it was too soon to have been thinking for ever, but she had. For the first time in a very long time. They had shared his bed for one night and after she'd left, they did not even acknowledge each other.

She had no idea how he could be so cold but she made a promise to herself as she heard his office door close.

She would never trust her instincts where men were concerned.

And she would never speak to Charlie Warren again. Although she doubted she would ever stop thinking about him.

CHAPTER FOURTEEN

IT WAS EARLY Monday morning when Juliet awoke. The sky was overcast and threatening to rain down on the still-damp earth. While she knew she had so much to be grateful for, it still didn't lessen the pain in her heart. But just like the dismal weather, it too would subside in time, she reminded herself. But how much time that would take she didn't know. Sitting in bed with Bea still sound asleep beside her, she thought back over the week since they'd arrived. So much had happened. The rushed journey over was probably the least eventful.

Bea's pink cast took her attention and she remembered the sinking feeling when she saw her fall to the snow. Instinctively, sitting in the warmth of her bed, with her little girl safely beside her, she still dropped her head into her hands. That fleeting but very real fear that something had happened to her daughter had been the worst feeling in the world.

And how she felt as she thought about Charlie, she accepted, was the second to worst feeling.

Losing him, after only having him for one night, brought sadness to her every thought. She had been stupid to believe there could be more. She had fallen into bed with a man once again without thinking.

Then she shifted her shoulders and lifted her chin. It

wasn't quite like that, she had to admit to herself. Charlie was not just any man. He was different. Charlie never lied to her, like Brad. He didn't scheme, like Bea's father. He had never hidden the fact he liked his life the way it was. Alone. But Juliet had thought she could change that. And his clear affection for her daughter had convinced her that he was ready to open his heart to love.

But he wasn't.

Both of them were wrong.

She wasn't sure what she would do. Extending her contract with Teddy's was yet to be negotiated so she still had the option of returning home. Or perhaps going on a river cruise with her parents, she thought wryly.

In the jumble of thoughts, she decided to get up and make some tea and let Bea sleep in a little longer. She tiptoed down the passageway into the kitchen and put on the kettle. She couldn't let herself fall to pieces. Bea deserved better. She was too young to witness her mother's heartbreak. Juliet's tears would have to wait until the middle of the night, when she could cry alone and wish for what might have been.

Looking at the clock, she realised it was later than she had thought. It was almost nine. Jet lag, she assumed, had finally taken its toll on her parents. That was for the best, she thought as she sat in her pyjamas and robe, holding the steaming cup of tea at the kitchen table. Her socked feet were inside her slippers.

She thought she heard a car, but presumed it was the neighbours or local traffic passing by. It wasn't the motorbike she wanted to hear. Biting her lip, and trying to hold back the tears threatening to spill onto her cheeks, she accepted that she would never hear Charlie's motorbike in her driveway.

A rustling and thumping suddenly began. And it

seemed to get louder. Pulling back her kitchen curtains, to look out of her window into the neighbour's driveway, Juliet couldn't see anything. It was the oddest sound. Nothing she could really discern so she sat back down and sipped her tea. While some said tea solved everything, she doubted it would come close to resolving her problems.

The noise changed to heavy footsteps. And they were outside her house. She crossed the wooden floorboards to the front door expecting a deliveryman. She tugged her dressing gown up around her neck and braced herself for the inevitable gust of cold air as she opened the door.

But it wasn't a delivery man.

It was Charlie.

'What are you doing here?' Her voice was not welcoming. She was hurt and angry and disappointed and more confused than ever. And the reason for her tumultuous emotions was standing on her doorstep.

'I brought the Christmas tree I promised Bea.'

Juliet eyed him suspiciously as she looked to the side of the house where the six-foot tree was leaning against the wall. Snow was covering the deep green branches that had been tied up with rope.

'Why?'

'Because, as I said, I promised to do it. I won't let Bea down.'

But you would let me down, she thought. 'That's not what you told me,' she spat back. 'I'm heading off today with my father to collect one so you can take that one back. I don't want a tree or anything from you.'

Charlie didn't flinch. 'I know you're upset with me—'

'And does that surprise you?' she cut in angrily.

Charlie looked down at his snow-covered boots for a moment before he raised his gaze back to her. 'Not at all.

I deserve your anger. I behaved terribly. And I want to make it up to you. Bringing you the tree is just the start…'

'But how did it get here?' she interrupted. She hadn't heard his motorbike and there was no delivery van visible outside.

'I brought it here.'

Juliet stepped onto the freezing cold tiles of the front porch.

'How?'

Charlie paused for a moment before he turned and looked over his shoulder. 'On the roof of the car. I tied it to the roof rack.'

'But you don't drive. You haven't driven since the accident. I don't understand.'

Charlie, momentarily and in deep thought, closed his eyes. When he opened them seconds later he spoke. 'I had to drive. They couldn't deliver the tree.'

Juliet said nothing.

'I borrowed the car from the Christmas tree farm owner.'

'How long since you've driven?'

Charlie looked into Juliet's eyes in silence for a moment. 'I haven't climbed into a car…since the accident. Not to drive or be a passenger. This is the first time in two years I've been behind the wheel. I had no choice but to drive because I couldn't let Bea down.'

'Thank you for the tree. I'll get my father to help me in with it later,' she said as she stepped back inside and began to close the door.

Without warning, Charlie's boot stopped it closing. 'There's more. We need to talk.'

Juliet shook her head. 'No, Charlie, we've said everything there is to say. I know how you feel. I know you like living alone. I get it. I don't agree but I accept that it's your choice and not mine. So let's leave it at that. But thank you very much for the tree. Bea will love it.'

'Please, Juliet. Give me five minutes. This is not just about Bea. I won't ever let you down again, if you'll let me make it up to you.'

She looked at his handsome face, his stunning eyes that were pleading with her, but she couldn't let him stay. She needed space to heal and listening to his reasons, his justification for being so cold, would not help her to shut him out for ever. He needed to leave before she could not control her need to stroke the stubble on his chin with her fingers, before she reached up to kiss his tender lips with hers the way she had that night.

'I'm busy, Charlie.' Her voice was cold but her heart was still warm and she wished it were otherwise.

'It's nine in the morning and I know you don't start until one today.' He moved his foot free. She could shut the door but he hoped with all of his heart she wouldn't. 'Please don't close the door on us. Not without hearing me out.'

'Why, Charlie? We've said everything there is to say. You want to spend your life living in regret. Living something you can't change. You can't bring your wife back and I don't want to talk about it any more. I can't compete with the woman you lost. I'm alive and I wanted to be there for you but you threw me away. I have my pride and I have my daughter. And you can have your lonely existence.'

'I never threw you away. I wanted you to walk away before I hurt you.'

'Perhaps you should have thought about that before you invited me to stay the night,' she argued. 'You like being alone and I was just for one night. But that's not who I am. I want something more, something you can't offer. So just stay in your glorious house by yourself. It's how you like it.'

'It's not. But it took you coming into my life to make me realise that.'

Juliet frowned and began to shiver. The cold morning air had finally cut through her thick dressing gown and pyjamas and she felt chilled to the bone.

'Can we go inside?' he asked, aware that she was not coping in the cold.

'No,' she replied flatly. 'Everyone's sleeping and I don't want them to know about what happened between us. It's over and done and they do not need to be any the wiser that their daughter made another mistake.'

'It wasn't a mistake.'

'I disagree. I think me sleeping with you was a mammoth mistake. You were almost morose when we woke. I could see you didn't want me there with you.'

'I asked you to stay. I wanted you next to me.'

'Yes, maybe you did that night, but in your heart you knew it would be when the sun came up.' Juliet began to shake from the bitter cold…and her breaking heart. 'I just wish you'd never invited me over in the first place. I wish I'd never stayed.'

'So you regret making love to me? Do you think falling into my bed and into my arms was the biggest mistake you could have made? Because I don't. It's just taken me time to work it out in my head. And my heart.'

Juliet was angry but she couldn't lie. She didn't regret making love to Charlie. All she regretted was allowing herself to fall in love with him. 'I don't understand your question. Why are you wanting to torture me? I haven't wanted to sleep with anyone in more than four years and then I make this huge error in judgement and believe that you're different, that perhaps you're looking for something more, but I was wrong.'

'You weren't wrong.' He pulled off his heavy jacket and gently placed it on her shoulders.

'You'll freeze,' she said, attempting to give it back as he stood in a jumper and shirt. The air was misty and damp, the ground outside covered with a fresh layer of snow.

His strong hands remained resting lightly on her shoulders as he refused to take back the jacket. 'I'm warm-blooded enough to survive while you hear me out.'

Juliet hated the fact that she couldn't argue that fact. Charlie had been warm-blooded enough the night they'd spent together to keep her fire burning into the early hours. She also hated that while his coat was heavy it felt good to have it wrapped around her. His scent, the warmth of the lambswool lining that he had heated only moments before. It felt as if it were all she would ever need but she knew it wasn't hers to keep. Because he wasn't hers to keep.

'Just let me say a few things and then if you want me to go, I will.'

'Just go now—'

'I can't and I won't. Not without telling you how I feel. How I've felt since I first laid eyes on you.'

'When you told me off for being a bad mother.'

'I didn't say those words—'

'But you thought it,' she interrupted, trying to remind herself, as much as him, why they shouldn't be together.

'I admit, I've been judging everyone but mostly myself for as long as I can remember…'

'Since the accident?'

'Yes. I've been confused and carrying guilt with me

for so long that I felt lost without it. I was driven to punish myself since that day.' His voice was low and sombre.

'But it wasn't your fault.'

'You and everyone in this town have said that so many times,' he stated. 'But it was how I saw it.'

Juliet thought she heard something more in his words but she wasn't sure. 'How you *saw* it? So it's not how you *see* it now?'

Charlie looked at her and shook his head. 'It's not how I want to see it any more and being with you I know that's possible.'

'What's changed?' she asked, not daring to hope that he wanted her. And was ready to build a life with her. And with her daughter. The three of them as a family.

'I know that hurting you won't bring my wife back. Nothing can. I realised that as I've slept alone in my bed for the last two nights wanting you beside me. Wanting to feel your tenderness and love again. Being near you brought my spirit back and being with you and making love to you made me feel more alive than I thought possible. I won't let you go without a fight. I know that spending the rest of my life regretting the moment my wife and I climbed in that car two years ago won't change anything. I will still have a place in my heart for the woman I loved back then, but I don't want to lose the two special women who have come into my life now. I want to live in the present and build a future and I want to do it with you. I want you, Juliet, now and for ever if you'll have me, and I want to be the father that Bea needs. If you'll let me.'

'I never wanted to fight you on that. I just wanted to love you,' she told him with tears welling in her eyes.

'I know that, Juliet, and I'm sorry. The fight was never *with* you, the fight was *with* myself and my stupidity, my

need to carry the guilt like a cross and my need to punish myself to make amends. I don't want to do that any
more. In the week since we met, I have been questioning
everything that's been my life, my reality for the last two
years. You and Bea have made me want more. You've
made me want a life that's free of remorse and sad memories. You've brought a light back that I never thought I
would see again and warmth that I never thought I would
feel. I don't want to live in the cold or the dark any more.
I want to really live again. To have you by my side for
the rest of my life.'

'What are you saying?'

'Juliet,' he said, dropping to one knee and wrapping
her hand into the strength and warmth of his, 'I'm asking you to be my wife. To love me the way you did the
other night. To share your life and to bring life back into
my home and make me want to sleep in our four-poster
bed and make love to you every night. Will you? Will
you make me the man I want to be and the man I can be
if you'll allow me?'

'Yes,' she answered with tears freely flowing down her
face as she fell into his arms and kissed him as if there
would be no tomorrow. 'Yes, of course I'll marry you. I
love you, Charlie Warren.'

'And I will love you for ever, Juliet…and spend the
rest of my life decorating Christmas trees with Bea…
and the rest of our children.'

* * * * *

Look out for the final instalment of the
CHRISTMAS MIRACLES IN MATERNITY *quartet*

A ROYAL BABY FOR CHRISTMAS
by Scarlet Wilson

And, if you missed where it all started, check out

THE NURSE'S CHRISTMAS GIFT
by Tina Beckett
THE MIDWIFE'S PREGNANCY MIRACLE
by Kate Hardy

Available now!

A ROYAL BABY
FOR CHRISTMAS

BY
SCARLET WILSON

Published in Great Britain 2016
By Mills & Boon, an imprint of HarperCollins*Publishers*
1 London Bridge Street, London, SE1 9GF

© 2016 Harlequin Books S.A.

*Special thanks and acknowledgement are given to Scarlet Wilson
for her contribution to the* Christmas Miracles in Maternity *series*

ISBN: 978-0-263-91527-3

Printed and bound in Spain
by CPI, Barcelona

Dear Reader,

I always love writing Christmas stories—and what could be more fun than having a prince in your Christmas story?

This story is part of a series—Christmas Miracles in Maternity—set in the fictional Teddy's hospital in the Cotswolds. My heroine is feisty Scotswoman Sienna McDonald. She's always been focused completely on her career and is a dedicated neonatal cardiothoracic surgeon. Nothing gets between her and her babies!

Prince Sebastian meets Sienna unexpectedly and they spend two electrifying days together. He can't get her out of his head, even though he's expected to form an alliance by marrying a princess from another country. When he finds out Sienna is pregnant he's a man on a mission—to win the heart of the mother of his child!

I love to hear from readers. You can contact me via my website: scarlet-wilson.com.

Happy Christmas!

Scarlet

This book is dedicated to my fellow authors
Kate Hardy, Tina Beckett and Susanne Hampton.
It's been a pleasure working with you, ladies!

Scarlet Wilson wrote her first story aged eight and has never stopped. She's worked in the health service for twenty years, trained as a nurse and a health visitor. Scarlet now works in public health and lives on the West Coast of Scotland with her fiancé and their two sons. Writing medical romances and contemporary romances is a dream come true for her.

Books by Scarlet Wilson

Mills & Boon Medical Romance

Midwives On-Call at Christmas
A Touch of Christmas Magic

Christmas with the Maverick Millionaire
The Doctor She Left Behind
The Doctor's Baby Secret
One Kiss in Tokyo…

Mills & Boon Cherish

Tycoons in a Million
Holiday with the Millionaire
A Baby to Save Their Marriage

Visit the Author Profile page at
millsandboon.co.uk for more titles.

Praise for
Scarlet Wilson

'The book is filled with high-strung emotions, engaging dialogue, breathtaking descriptions and characters you just cannot help but love. With the magic of Christmas as a bonus, you won't be disappointed with this story!'

—*Goodreads* on
A Touch of Christmas Magic

PROLOGUE

May

HIS EYES SCANNED the bar as he ran his fingers through his hair. Six weeks, three countries, ten flights and thousands of miles. He'd been wined and dined by heads of state and consulate staff, negotiated trade agreements, arranged to be part of a water aid initiative, held babies, shaken hands for hours and had a number of tense diplomatic conversations.

All of this while avoiding dozens of calls from his mother about the upcoming royal announcement. His apparent betrothal to his lifelong friend.

All he wanted to do was find a seat, have a drink and clear a little head space. Il Palazzo di Cristallo was one of the few places he could do that. Set in the stunning mountains of Montanari, the exclusive boutique hotel only ever had a select few guests—most of whom were seeking sanctuary from the outside world. The press were banned. The staff were screened and well looked after to ensure all guests' privacy was well respected—including the Crown Prince of Montanari. For the first time in six weeks Sebastian might actually be able to relax.

Except someone was sitting in his favourite seat at the bar.

There. A figure with shoulders slumped and her head leaning on her hand. Her ash-blonde hair was escaping from its clasp and her blue dress was creased. Two empty glasses of wine sat on the bar in front of her.

The bartender sat down a third and gave Sebastian an almost indiscernible nod. The staff here knew he liked to keep his identity quiet.

Odd. He didn't recognise the figure. Sebastian knew all the movie stars and celebrities who usually stayed here. She wasn't a fellow royal or a visiting dignitary. His curiosity was piqued.

He strode across the room and slid onto the stool next to hers at the bar. She didn't even look up in acknowledgement.

Her fingers were running up and down the stem of the glass and her light brown eyes were unfocused. But it wasn't the drink. It was deep contemplation.

Sebastian sucked in a breath. Whoever she was, she was beautiful. Her skin was flawless. Her features finer than those of some of the movie starlets he'd been exposed to. Being Prince of Montanari meant that a whole host of women had managed to cross his path over the last few years. Not that he'd taken any of them seriously. He had a duty to his future kingdom. A duty to marry an acceptable neighbouring princess. There was no question about it—it had been instilled in him from a young age it was part of his preparations for finally becoming King. Marriage was a business transaction. It wasn't the huge love and undying happiness portrayed in fairy tales. There were no rainbows and flying unicorns. It came down to the most advantageous match for the country and his parents had found her. Theresa Mon Carte, his childhood friend and a princess from the neighbouring principality. They were to be married within the year.

Part of the reason he was here was to get some time to resign himself to his fate. Because that was what it felt like.

But right now, he couldn't think about that at all.

He was entirely distracted by the woman sitting next to him. She looked as if she had the weight of the world on her shoulders. There was no Botox here. Her brow was definitely furrowed and somehow he knew this woman would never be interested in cosmetic procedures.

'Want to tell me about them?'

'What?' She looked up, startled at the sound of his voice.

Light brown eyes that looked as if they'd once had a little dark eyeliner around them. It was smudged now. But that didn't stop the effect.

It was like being speared straight through the heart.

For a second neither of them spoke. It was the weirdest sensation—as if the air around them had just stilled.

He was drinking in everything about her. Her forgotten-about hair. Her crumpled clothes. Her dejected appearance.

But there was something else. Something that wouldn't let him break their gaze. A buzz. An air. He'd never felt something like this before. And she felt it too.

He could tell. Her pupils dilated just a little before his eyes. He didn't have any doubt that his were so big right now the Grand Canyon could fit in them.

There was something about her demeanour. This woman was a professional. She was educated. And she was, oh, so sexy.

He found his tongue. 'Your worries.' He couldn't help but let the corners of his mouth turn upwards.

She gave the briefest rise of her eyebrows and turned

back towards the waiting wine glass. Her shoulders straightened a little. He'd definitely caught her attention.

Just as she'd caught his.

He leaned a little closer and nudged her shoulder. 'You're sitting on my favourite bar stool.'

'Didn't have your name on it,' she quipped back.

Her accent. It was unmistakeable. The Scottish twang made the hairs on his arms stand on end. He could listen to that all day. Or all night.

She swung her legs around towards him and leaned one arm on the bar. 'Come to think of it, you must be kind of brave.' She took a sip of her wine. Her eyebrows lifted again. 'Or kind of stupid.'

He liked it. She was flirting back. He leaned his arm on the bar too, so they were closer than ever. 'What makes you think that?'

She licked her lips. 'Because you're trying to get between a Scots girl and the bar.' She smiled as she ran her eyes up and down the length of his body. It was almost as if she'd reached her fingers out and touched him. 'Haven't you heard about Scots girls?'

He smiled and leaned closer. 'I think I might need a little education.' He couldn't think of anything he wanted more.

Instant attraction. He'd never really experienced it before. Not like this. He'd wanted to come in here to hide and get away from things. Now, his sanctuary had become a whole lot more exciting.

A whole lot more distracting.

His stomach flipped over. What if he never felt like this again? Or even worse, what if he felt like this when he was King of Montanari and married?

Right now he was none of those things. The engagement hadn't been announced. He was about to step into a life of duty and constant scrutiny.

Theresa was a friend. Nothing more. Nothing less. They'd never even shared a kiss.

He hadn't come here to meet anyone. He hadn't come here to be attracted to someone.

But right now he was caught in a gaze he didn't want to escape from. The pull was just too strong.

Something flitted across her eyes. It was as if her confidence wavered for a second.

'What's wrong?' He couldn't help himself.

She sucked in a breath. 'Bad day at the office.'

'Anything to do with a man?' It was out before he thought.

She blinked and gave a little smile again, pausing for a second. 'No. Definitely nothing to do with a man.'

It was as if he'd just laid himself bare. Finding out the lie of the land. He couldn't ignore the warm feeling that spread straight through him.

He had no royal duties this weekend. There were no hands he needed to shake. No business he needed to attend to. He'd told Security he was coming here and to keep their distance.

If he lived to be a hundred he'd remember this. He'd remember this meeting and the way it made him feel. The buzz was so strong the air practically sparkled around her.

He was still single. He could do this. Right now he would cross burning coals to see what would happen next.

He leaned even closer. 'I came here to get some peace and quiet. I came here to get some head space.' He gave her a little smile and lowered his voice. 'But, all of a sudden, there's no space in my head at all.'

He took a chance. 'How about I stop searching for some peace and quiet, and you forget all about your bad day?'

She ran her fingers up the stem of her wine glass. He could tell she was thinking. She looked up from beneath heavy eyelids. 'You mean, like a distraction. An interlude?'

The warm glow in his body started to rapidly rise. He nodded. 'A distraction.'

She licked her lips again and he almost groaned out loud. 'I think a distraction might be just what I need,' she said carefully.

He tried to quieten the cheerleader squad currently yelling in his head.

'I've always wanted to meet a Scots girl. Will you teach me how to wear a kilt?' He waved to the barman. 'There are some killer cocktails in here. You look like a Lavender Fizz kind of girl.'

'I'll do better than that.' There was a hint of mischief in her voice. 'I'll teach you how to take it off.'

This wasn't her life. It couldn't be. Things like this didn't happen to Sienna McDonald. But it seemed that in the blink of an eye her miserable, lousy day had just got a whole lot better.

It was the worst kind of day. The kind of day she should have got used to in this line of work.

But a doctor who got used to a baby dying was in the wrong profession.

It had been little Marco's third op. He'd been failing all the time, born into the world too early with undeveloped lungs and a malformed heart; she'd known the odds were stacked against him.

Some people thought it was wrong to operate on premature babies unless there was a guarantee of a good outcome. But Sienna had seen babies who had next to no chance come through an operation, fight like a seasoned soldier and go on to thrive. One of her greatest successes was coming up on his fourth birthday and she couldn't be prouder.

Today had been draining. Telling the parents had been soul-destroying. She didn't usually drown her sorrows in alcohol, but tonight, in a strange country with only herself for company, it was the only thing that would do. She'd already made short work of the accompanying chocolate she'd bought to go with the wine. The empty wrappers were littered around her.

She sensed him as soon as he sat down next to her. There was a gentle waft of masculine cologne. Her eyes were lowered. It was easy to see the muscled thigh through the probably designer trousers. If he was staying in this hotel—he was probably a millionaire. She was just lucky the royal family were footing her bill.

When he spoke, his lilting Mediterranean accent washed over her. Thank goodness she was sitting down. There was something about the accent of the men of Montanari. It crossed between the Italian, French and Spanish of its surrounding neighbours. It was unmistakeable. Unique. And something she'd never forget.

She glanced sideways and once more sucked in her cheeks.

Nope. The guy who looked as if he'd just walked off some film set was still there. Any second now she'd have to pinch herself. This might actually be real.

Dark hair, killer green eyes with a little sparkle and perfect white teeth. She might not have X-ray vision but his lean and athletic build was clear beneath the perfectly tailored suit. If she were back in Scotland she'd tell him he might as well have *sex on legs* tattooed on his fore-head. Too bad she was in a posh kingdom where she had to be a whole lot more polite than that.

He hadn't responded to her cheeky comment. For a millisecond he looked a little stunned, and then his shoulders relaxed a little and he nodded slowly. He was getting comfortable. Did he think the game was over?

She was just settling in for the ride. She didn't do this. She didn't *ever* do this. Pick up a man in a bar? Her friends would think she'd gone crazy. But the palms of her hands were tingling. She wanted to touch him. She wanted to feel his skin against hers. She wanted to know exactly what those lips tasted like.

He was like every erotic dream she'd ever had just handed to her on a plate.

She leaned her head on one hand and turned to face him. 'Who says I'm a cocktail kind of girl?'

He blinked. Her accent did that to people. It took their ears a few seconds to adjust to the Scottish twang. He was no different from every other man she'd ever met. The edges of his mouth turned upwards at the sound of her voice. People just seemed to love the Scottish ac-cent—even if they couldn't understand a word she said.

'It's written all over you,' he shot back. He mirrored her stance, leaning his head on one hand and staring at her.

There was no mistaking the tingling of her skin. Part of her stomach turned over. There was a tiny wash of guilt.

Today wasn't meant to be a happy day. Today was a day to drown her sorrows and contemplate if she could have done anything different to save that little baby. But the truth was she'd already done that. Even if she went back in time she wouldn't do anything different. Clinically, her actions had been everything they should have been. Little Marco's body had just been too weak, too underdeveloped to fight any more.

The late evening sun was streaming in the windows behind him, bathing them both in a luminescence of peaches and purples. Distraction. That was what this was. And right now she could do with a distraction.

Something to help her forget. Something to help her think about something other than work. She was due to go home in a few days. She'd taught the surgeons at Montanari Royal General everything she could.

She let her shoulders relax a little. The first two glasses of wine were starting to kick in.

'I don't know that I'm a Lavender Fizz kind of girl.'

'Well, let's see what kind of girl you are.' The words hung in the air between them, with a hundred alternative meanings circulating in her mind. This guy was good. He was very good.

She half wished she'd changed after work. Or at least pulled a brush through her hair and applied some fresh make-up. This guy was impeccable, which made her wish she were too. He picked up the cocktail menu, pretending to peruse it, while giving her sideways glances. 'No,' he said decidedly. 'Not gin.' He paused a second. 'Hmm, raspberries, maybe. Wait, no, here it is. A peach melba cocktail.'

She couldn't help but smile as she raised her eyebrows. 'And what's in that one?'

He signalled the barman. 'Let's find out.'

Her smile remained fixed on her face. His confidence was tantalising. She sipped at her wine as she waited for the barman to mix the drinks.

'What's your name?' he asked as they waited. He held out his hand towards her. 'I'm Seb.'

Seb. A suitable billionaire-type name. Most of the men in this hotel had a whole host of aristocratic names. Louis. Alexander. Hugo. Augustus.

She reached out to take his hand. 'Sienna.'

His hand enveloped hers. What should have been a firm handshake was something else entirely. It was gentle. Almost like a caress. But there was a purpose to it. He didn't let go. He kept holding, letting the warmth of his hand permeate through her chilled skin. His voice was husky. 'You've been holding on to that wine glass too long.' Before she could reply he continued. 'Sienna. It doesn't seem a particularly Scottish name.'

A furrow appeared on his brow. As if he were trying to connect something. After a second, he shook his head and concentrated on her again.

She tried not to fixate on the fact her hand was still in his. She liked it. She liked the way this man was one of the most direct flirts she'd ever met. He could have scrawled his intentions towards her with her lipstick on the mirrored gantry behind the bar and she wouldn't have batted an eyelid because this was definitely a two-way street.

'It's not.' She let her thumb brush over the back of his hand. 'It's Italian.' She lifted her eyebrows. 'I was conceived there. By accident—of course,' she added.

A look of confusion swept his face as the barman set down the drinks, but he didn't call her on her comment.

Sienna had a wave of disappointment as she had to pull her hand free of his and she turned to the peach concoction on the bar with a glimpse of red near the bottom. She lifted the tiny straws and gave it a little stir. 'What is this, exactly?'

Those green eyes fixed on hers again. 'Peach nectar, raspberry puree, fresh raspberries and champagne.'

She took a sip. Nectar was right. It hit the spot perfectly. Just like something else.

'Are you here on business or pleasure, Sienna?'

She thought for a second. She was proud to be a surgeon. Most men she'd ever met had seemed impressed by her career. But tonight she didn't want to talk about being a surgeon. Tonight she wanted to concentrate on something else entirely.

'Business. But it's almost concluded. I go home in a few days.'

He nodded carefully. 'Have you enjoyed visiting Montanari?'

She couldn't lie. Even today's events hadn't taken the shine off the beautiful country that she'd spent the last few weeks in. The rolling green hills, the spectacular volcanic mountain peak that overlooked the capital city and coastline next to the Mediterranean Sea made the kingdom one of the prettiest places she'd ever visited. She took another sip of her cocktail. 'I have. It's a beautiful country. I'm only sorry I haven't seen enough of it.'

'You haven't?'

She shook her head. 'Business is business. I've been busy.' She stirred her drink. 'What about you?'

He had an air about him. Something she hadn't encountered before. An aura. She assumed he must be quite enigmatic as a businessman. He could probably charm the birds from the trees. At least, she was assuming he was a businessman. He looked the part and every other man she'd met in this exclusive hotel had been here to do one business deal or another.

But for a charmer, there was something else. An underlying sincerity in the back of his eyes. Somehow she felt if the volcanic peak overlooking the capital erupted right now she would be safe with this guy. Her instincts had always been good and it had been a long time since she'd felt like that.

'I've been abroad on business. I'm just back.'

'You stay here? In this hotel?'

He laughed and shook his head. 'Oh, no. I live…close by. But I conduct much of my business in this hotel.' He gave another gracious nod towards the barman. 'They have the best facilities. The most professional staff. I'm comfortable here.'

It was a slightly odd thing to say. But she forgot about it in seconds as the barman came back to top up their glasses.

She took a deep breath and stared at her glass. 'Maybe I should slow down a little.'

His gaze was steady. 'The drink? Or something else?'

There it was. The hidden question between them. She ran her finger around the rim of the glass. 'I came here to forget,' she said quietly, exposing more of herself than she meant.

Her other hand was on the bar. His slid over the top, intertwining his fingers with hers. 'And so did I. Maybe there are other ways to forget.'

She licked her lips, almost scared to look up and meet his gaze again. It would be like answering the unspoken question. The one she was sure that she wanted to answer.

His thumb slid under her palm, tracing little circles. In most circumstances it would be calming. But here, and now, it was anything but calming; it was almost erotic.

'Sienna, you have a few days left. Have you seen the mountains yet? How about I show you some of the hidden pleasures that we keep secret from the tourists?'

It was the way he said it. His voice was low and husky, sending a host of tiny shivers of expectation up her spine.

She could almost hear the voices of her friends in her

head. She was always the sensible one. Always cautious. If she told this tale a few months later and told them she'd made her excuses and walked away…

The cocktail glass was glistening in the warm sunset. The chandelier hanging above the bar sending a myriad of coloured prisms of light around the room.

The perfect setting. The perfect place. The perfect man.

A whole host of distraction.

Exactly what she'd been looking for.

She threw back her head and tried to remember if she was wearing matching underwear. Not that it mattered. But somehow she wanted all her memories about this to be perfect.

She met his green gaze. There should be rules about eyes like that. Eyes that pulled you in and held you there, while all the time giving a mischievous hint of exactly what he was thinking.

She stood up from her bar stool and moved closer. His hand dropped from the bar to her hip. She brushed her lips against his ear. 'How many of Montanari's pleasures are hidden?'

There it was. The intent.

It didn't matter that her perfect red dress was hanging in the cupboard upstairs. It didn't matter that her matching lipstick was at the bottom of her bag. It didn't matter that her most expensive perfume was in the bathroom in her room.

Mr Sex-on-Legs liked her just the way she was.

He closed his eyes for a second. This time his voice was almost a growl, as if he were bathing in what she'd just said. 'I could listen to your accent all day.'

She put her hand on his shoulder. 'How about you listen to it all night instead?'

And the deed was done.

CHAPTER ONE

SHE STARED AT the stick again.

Yep. The second line was still there.

It wasn't a figment of her imagination. Just as the missing period wasn't a dream and the tender breasts weren't a sign of an ill-fitting bra.

A baby. She was going to have a baby.

She stared out of her house window.

Her mortgage. She'd just moved in here. Her mortgage was huge. As soon as she'd seen the house she'd loved it. It was totally too big for one person—how ironic was that?—but she'd figured she'd have the rest of her life to pay for it. It was five minutes from Teddy's and had the most amazing garden with a pink cherry blossom tree at the bottom of it, and a little paved area at the back for sitting.

It was just like the house she'd dreamed of as a child. The house where she and her husband and children would stay and live happily ever after.

She sighed and put her head in her hands.

She was pregnant. Pregnant to Seb, the liar.

It made her insides twist and curl. She'd never quite worked out when he'd realised who she was, while she'd spent the weekend in blissful ignorance.

A weekend all the while holed up in the most beautiful mountain chalet-style house.

The days had been joyful. She'd never felt an attraction like it—immediate, powerful and totally irresistible. Seb had made her feel like the only woman in the world and for two days she'd relished it.

It was too good. Too perfect. She should have known. Because nobody could ever be *that* perfect. Not really.

She'd been surprised by his security outside the hotel. But then, lots of businessmen had bodyguards nowadays. It wasn't quite so unusual as it could have been.

And she hadn't seen any of the sights of Montanari. Once they'd reached his gorgeous house hidden in the mountains, the only thing she'd seen was his naked body.

For two whole days.

She squeezed her eyes closed for a second. It hurt to remember how much she'd loved it.

How many other woman had been given the same treatment?

She shook her head and shuddered. Finding out who he really was had ruined her memories of those two wonderful days.

Of those two wonderful nights…

She pressed her hand on her non-existent bump. *Oh, wow.* She was pregnant by a prince.

Prince Sebastian Falco of Montanari.

Some women might like that. Some women might think that was amazing. Right now she was wondering exactly why her contraceptive pill had failed. She'd taken it faithfully every day. She hadn't been sick. She hadn't forgotten. This wasn't deliberate. This absolutely wasn't a ploy to get pregnant by a prince. But what if he thought it was?

Her mind jumped back to her house. How much maternity leave would she get? How much maternity pay would she get—would it cover her mortgage? She'd used her savings as the deposit for the house—that, and the little extra she'd had left to update the bathroom and kitchen, meant her rainy-day fund was virtually empty.

She stood up and started pacing. Who would look after her baby when she returned to work? Would she be able to return to work? She had to. She was an independent woman. She loved her career. Having a baby didn't mean giving up the job she loved.

She rested her hand against the wall of her sitting room. Maybe someone at the hospital could give her a recommendation for a childminder? The crèche at the hospital wouldn't be able to cater for on-calls and late night emergency surgeries. She'd need someone ultra flexible. There was so much to think about. So much to organise.

She couldn't concentrate. Her mind kept jumping from one thing to the other. Oh, no—was this the pregnancy brain that women complained about?

She couldn't have that. She didn't have time for that. She was a neonatal cardiothoracic surgeon. She was responsible for tiny lives. She needed to be focused. She needed to have her mind on the job.

She walked through to the kitchen. The calendar was lying on the kitchen table. It was turned to April—showing when she'd had her last period. It had been left there when the realisation had hit her and she'd rushed to the pharmacy for a pregnancy test. She'd bought four.

She wouldn't need them. She flicked forward. Last date of period, twenty-third of April. Forty weeks from then? She turned the calendar over, counting the weeks on the back. January. Her baby was due on the twenty-eighth of January.

She pushed open her back door and walked outside. The previous owners had left a bench seat, carved from an original ancient tree that had been damaged in a lightning strike years ago. She sat down and took some deep breaths.

It was a beautiful day. The flowers in her garden had all started to emerge. Fragrant red, pink and orange freesias, blue cornflowers, purple delphinium and multi-coloured peonies blossomed in pretty colours all around her, their scents permeating the air.

She smiled. The deep breathing was beginning to calm her. A baby. She was going to have a baby.

She closed her eyes and pressed her lips together as a wave of determination washed over her. Baby McDonald might not have been planned. But Baby McDonald would certainly be wanted.

He or she would be loved. Be adored.

A familiar remembrance of disappointment and anger made her catch her breath. For as long as she could remember her parents had made it clear to her that she'd been a 'mistake'. They hadn't put it quite in as few words but the implication was always there. Two people who had never really wanted to be together but had done 'what was right'.

Except it wasn't right. It wasn't right at all. Anger and resentment had simmered from them both. The expression on her father's face when he had left on her eighteenth birthday had told her everything she'd ever needed to know—as had the relief on her mother's.

She'd been a burden. An unplanned-for presence.

Whether this baby was planned for or not, it would always feel loved, always feel wanted. She might not know about childcare, she might not know about maternity leave, she might not know about her mortgage—but of that one thing, she was absolutely sure.

Her brain skydived somewhere else. Folic acid. She hadn't been taking it. She'd have to get some. Her feet moved automatically. She could grab her bag; the nearest pharmacy was only a five-minute drive. She could pick some up and start taking it immediately. As she crossed the garden her eyes squeezed shut for a second. Darn it. Folic acid was essential for normal development in a baby. She racked her brains. What had she been eating these last few weeks? Had there been any spinach? Any broccoli? She'd had some, but she just wasn't sure how much. She'd had oranges and grapefruit. Lentils, avocados and peas.

She winced. She'd just remembered her intake of raspberries and strawberries. They'd been doused in champagne in Montanari. Alcohol. Another no-no in pregnancy.

At least she hadn't touched a drop since her return.

Her footsteps slowed as she entered the house again. Seb. She'd need to tell him. She'd need to tell him she was expecting his baby.

A gust of cool air blew in behind her, sending every hair on her arms standing on end. How on earth would she tell him? They hadn't exactly left things on good terms.

She sagged down onto her purple sofa for a few minutes. How did you contact a prince?

Oliver. Oliver Darrington would know. He was Seb's friend, the obstetrician who had arranged for her to go to Montanari and train the other paediatric surgeons. But how on earth could she ask him without giving the game away? Would she sound like some desperate stalker?

Oh, Olly, by the way...can I just phone your friend the Prince, please? Can you give me his number?

She sighed and rested her head backwards on the sofa watching the yellow ticker tape of the news channel stream past.

Her eyes glazed over. Last time she'd seen Seb she'd screamed at him. Hardly the most ladylike response.

It didn't matter that his lie had been by omission. That might even seem a tiny bit excusable now. But then, six weeks ago, rationality had left the luxurious chalet she'd found herself in.

It had been a simple mistake. The car driver—or, let's face it, he was probably a lot more than that—had given a nod and said *Your Highness* to something Seb had asked him.

The poor guy had realised his mistake right away and made a prompt exit. But it was too late. She'd heard it.

At first she'd almost laughed out loud. She'd been so relaxed, so happy, that the truth hadn't even occurred to her. 'Your Highness?' She'd smiled as she'd picked up her bags to go back in the house.

But the look of horror on Seb's face had caused her foot to stop in mid-air.

And just like today, the hairs on her arms had stood on end. Seb. Sebastian. The name of the Prince of Montanari. The person who'd requested she train the surgeons in his hospital. The mystery man that she'd never met—because he was doing business overseas.

Just like Seb.

She might as well have been plunged into a cold pool of glacier ice.

'Tell me you're joking?'

For the first time since she'd met him, his coolness

vanished. He started to babble. *Babble.* His eyes darting from side to side but never quite meeting her gaze.

She dropped her bags at her feet on the stony path. 'You're not, are you?' He kept talking but she stopped listening. Her brain trying to make sense of what was going on.

'You're Sebastian Falco? *You're* the Prince?' She walked right up under his nose.

It must have been the way she'd said it. As if it were almost impossible. As if he were the unlikeliest candidate in the world.

He let out a sigh and those forest-green eyes finally met hers. His head gave the barest shake. 'Is that so ridiculous?'

The prickling hairs on her arms spread. Like an infectious disease. Reaching parts of her body that definitely shouldn't feel like that.

Although the rage was building inside her, all that came out was a whisper. 'It's ridiculous to me.'

He blinked. She could see herself reflected in his eyes. Hurt was written all over her face. She hated feeling like that. She hated being emotionally vulnerable.

Her mother and father had lived a lie for eighteen years. She'd always promised herself that would never be her life. That would never be her relationship.

She'd thrown caution to the wind and lost. Big style.

He'd made a fool of her. And she'd let him.

'How could you?' she snapped. 'How could you lie to me? What kind of woman do you think I am?'

As she heard the words out loud she almost wanted to hide. She knew exactly what kind of woman she'd been these last two days. One that acted as though this was nothing. She'd experienced a true weekend of passion and abandon. She'd pushed aside all thoughts of consequences and lost herself totally in him.

Ultimate fail.

Now she was looking into the eyes of a man who'd misled her. Let her think that this was something it was not.

He pulled his gaze away from hers, having the good shame to look embarrassed, and ran his hand through his thick dark hair.

But even that annoyed her. She'd spent all weekend running her own fingers through the same hair and right now she knew she'd never do that again.

He reached up and touched her shoulder. 'Sienna, I'm sorry.'

She pulled back as if he'd stung her and his eyes widened.

'Don't touch me. Don't touch me again. Ever!' She spun around and walked back inside.

She ignored everything around her. Ignored the soft sofas they'd spent many an hour on. Ignored the thick wooden table that they'd eaten more than their dinner from. Ignored the tangled sheets in the white and gold bedroom that told their own story.

She grabbed the few things she'd brought with her—and the few other things she'd bought—and started throwing them into her bag.

Seb rushed in behind her. 'Sienna, slow down. Things weren't meant to happen like this. I'm sorry. I am. I came to the hotel to get away. I came to think about some things.' He ran his fingers through his hair again. 'And then, when I got there, there was just…' he held his hands up towards her '…you,' he said simply.

She spun back around.

'I didn't realise right away who you were. I'd asked

Oliver if he could send a surgeon to help with training. I'm the patron of the hospital and they only come to me when there are big issues. The hospital board were unhappy about all our neonates having to be transferred to France for cardiac surgeries. It was time to train our own surgeons—buy our own equipment. But once I'd made the arrangement with Oliver I hadn't really paid attention to all the details. Our hospital director took care of all those because I knew I wouldn't be here. I didn't even recognise your name straight away.'

She felt numb. 'You knew? You knew exactly who I was?'

He sighed heavily and his tanned face paled. 'Not until yesterday when you mentioned you were a surgeon.'

She gulped. She knew exactly what he wasn't saying. Not until after they'd slept together.

'Why didn't you tell me? Why didn't you tell me you knew Oliver yesterday?'

He shook his head. 'Because we'd already taken things further than either of us probably intended. We were in our own little bubble here. And I won't lie. I liked it, Sienna. I liked the fact it was just you and me and the outside world seemed as far away as possible.' He took a deep breath. 'I didn't want to spoil it.' He started pacing around. 'Do you know what it's like to have the eyes of the world constantly on you? Do you know what it's like when every time you even say hello to a woman it's splashed across the press the next day that she could be the next Queen?' The frustration was clearly spilling over.

'You expect me to feel sorry for you?'

He threw up his hands. 'The only time I've had a bit of a normal life was when I was at university. The press were banned from coming near me then. But every moment before that, and every second after it, I've constantly been on display. Life is never normal around me, Sienna. But here—' he indicated the room '—and in Il Palazzo di Cristallo I get a tiny bit of privacy. Do you know how good it felt to walk in somewhere, see a beautiful woman and be able to act on it? Be able to actually let myself feel something?'

Her throat was dry. Emotion and frustration was written all over his face. He couldn't stop pacing.

It was as if the weight of the world were currently sitting on his shoulders. She had no idea what his life was like. She'd no idea what was expected of him. Her insides squirmed. The thought of constantly being watched by the press? No, thanks.

But the anger still burned inside. The hurt at being deceived. How many other women had he brought here? Was she just another on his list?

She stepped up close to him again, ignoring his delicious aftershave that had wound its way around her over the last few days. 'So, everything was actually a lie?'

He winced. 'It wasn't a lie, Sienna.'

'It was to me.'

He shook his head and straightened his shoulders. 'You're overreacting. Even if I had introduced myself, what difference would it have made?' He moved closer, his chest just in front of her face. 'Are you telling me that this wouldn't have happened? That we wouldn't have been attracted to each other? We wouldn't have ended up together?'

She clouded out his words—focusing only on the first part. It had been enough to make the red mist descend. 'I'm overreacting?' She dropped the clothes she had clutched in her hands. 'I'm overreacting?' She let out an angry breath as her eyes swept the room.

She shook her head. 'Oh, no, Seb. I'm not overreacting.' She picked up the nearest lamp and flung it at the wall, shattering it into a million pieces. '*This*. This is overreacting. This is letting you know how I really feel about your deception.'

His chin practically hung open.

She stalked back to the bed and stuffed the remaining few items into her bag, zipping it with an over-zealous tug.

She marched right up under his nose. 'If I never see you again it will be too soon. Next time find someone else to train your surgeons. Preferably someone who doesn't mind being deceived and lied to.'

He drew himself up to his full height. On any other occasion she might have been impressed. But that day? Not a chance.

His mouth tightened. 'Have it your own way.'

'I will,' she'd shouted as she'd swept out of the chalet and back into the waiting car. 'Take me back to my hotel,' she'd growled at the driver.

Heavens. She hoped she hadn't got that poor man fired. He hadn't even blinked when she'd spoken. Just put the car into gear and set off down the mountain road. Her last view of Seb had been as he'd walked to the door and watched the car take off.

Now, it seemed all a bit melodramatic.

She'd never admit she'd cried on the plane on the way home. Not to a single person. And especially not to a person she'd now have to tell she was carrying his baby.

Her eyes came into focus sharply and she leaned forward.

The tickertape stream of news changed constantly. Something had made her focus again.

She waited a few seconds.

Prince Sebastian Falco of Montanari has an-
nounced his engagement to his childhood friend
Princess Theresa Mon Carte of Peruglea. Al-
though the date of their wedding has not yet been
announced it is expected to be in the next calendar
year. The royal wedding will unite the two neigh-
bouring kingdoms of Montanari and Peruglea.

Every single tiny bit of breath left her body. Her stomach plummeted as a tidal wave of emotions consumed
her.

It was as if the glacier ice pool she'd imagined on the
mountain of Montanari had followed her home. Nausea
made her bolt to the bathroom.

This wasn't morning sickness.

This was pure and utter shock.

He was engaged. Sebastian was engaged.

As she knelt on the bathroom floor she felt momentarily light-headed. Could this be any worse?

She squeezed her eyes closed. Trying to banish all
the memories of that weekend from her mind. Her body
responded automatically, curling into a ball on the
ground. If she didn't think about him, she couldn't hurt.
She couldn't let herself hurt like this. She had a baby. A
baby to think about.

She pressed her head against the cool tiles on the wall.

Pregnant by a prince. An *engaged* prince.

Funnily enough, no fairy tale she'd ever heard of
ended like this.

CHAPTER TWO

December

SHE WAS LATE. Again. And Sienna was never late. She
hated people being late. And now she was turning into
that person herself.

It was easy to shift the blame. Her obstetrician's clinic
was running nearly an hour behind. How ironic. Even
being friends with the Assistant Head of Obstetrics
around here didn't give her perks—but she could hardly
blame him. Oliver had been dealing with a particularly
difficult case. It just meant that now she wouldn't complete her rounds and finish when planned.

She hurried across the main entrance of the hospital
and tried not to be distracted by the surroundings. The
Royal Cheltenham hospital—or Teddy's, as they all affectionately called it—did Christmas with style.

A huge tree adorned the glass atrium. Red and gold
lights twinkled merrily against the already darkening
sky. The tea room near the front entrance—staffed by
volunteers—had its own display. A complete Santa sleigh
and carved wooden reindeers with red Christmas baubles
on their noses. Piped music surrounded her. Not loud
enough to be intrusive, but just enough to set the scene

for Christmas, as an array of traditional carols and favourite pop tunes permeated the air around her.

Sienna couldn't help but smile. Christmas was her absolute favourite time of year. The one time of year her parents actually stopped fighting. Her mother's sister, Aunt Margaret, had always visited at this time of year. Her warmth and love of Christmas had been infectious. As soon as she walked in the house, the frosty atmosphere just seemed to vanish. If Margaret sensed anything, she never acknowledged it. It seemed it wasn't the 'done thing' to fight and argue in front of Aunt Margaret and Sienna loved the fact that for four whole days she didn't have to worry at all.

Aunt Margaret's love of Christmas had continued—for Sienna, at least—long after she'd died. Sienna's own Christmas tree had gone up on the first of December. Multicoloured lights were decorating the now bare cherry blossom at the bottom of her garden. She wasn't even going to admit how they got there.

It seemed that Mother Nature was even trying to get in on the act. A light dusting of snow currently covered the glass atrium at Teddy's.

This time next year would be even more special. This time next year would be her baby's first Christmas. A smile spread across Sienna's face.

Thoughts like that made her forget about her aching back and sore feet. At thirty-four weeks pregnant she was due to start maternity leave some time soon. Oliver had arranged for some maternity cover, and he'd had the good sense to start her replacement early. Max Ainsley was proving more than capable.

He'd picked up the electronic systems and referral pathways of Teddy's easily. It meant that she'd be able to relax at home when the baby arrived instead of fretting over cancelled surgeries and babies and families having to travel for miles to get the same standard of care.

She hurried into the neonatal unit and stuffed her bag into the duty room. She looked up and took a deep breath. Every cot was full. An influx of winter virus had hit the unit a few weeks ago. That, along with delivery of a set of premature quads—one of whom needed surgery—meant that the staff were run off their feet.

Ruth, one of the neonatal nurses, shot her a sympathetic look. 'You doing okay, Sienna?'

Sienna straightened up and rubbed her back, then her protruding stomach. She was used to the sideways glances from members of staff. As she'd never dated anyone from the hospital and most of the staff knew she lived alone, speculation about her pregnancy had been rife.

The best rumour that she'd heard was that she'd decided she didn't need a man and had just used a sperm donor to have a baby on her own. If only it were true.

She'd stopped watching the news channel. Apart from weather reports and occasional badly behaved sportsmen, it seemed that her favourite news channel had developed an obsession with the upcoming royal wedding in Montanari early next year.

News was obviously slow. But if she saw one more shot of Seb with his arm around the cut-out perfect blonde she would scream. She didn't care that they looked a little awkward together. She just didn't want to see them at all.

She smiled at Ruth. 'I'm doing fine, thanks. Just had my check-up. Six weeks to go.' She waved her hand at the array of cots. 'I've got three babies to review. I'm hoping we can get at least two of them home for their first Christmas in the next few days. What do you think?'

As she said the words her Head Neonatal Nurse appeared behind Ruth. She'd worked with Annabelle Ainsley for the last year and had been more than a little surprised when it had been revealed that Annabelle was actually Max's estranged wife. She hadn't been surprised that it had only taken them a week to reconcile once he'd started working at Teddy's. For the last couple of weeks Annabelle hadn't stopped smiling, so she was surprised to see her looking so serious this afternoon.

'There's someone here to see you.' The normally unfazed Annabelle looked a little uncomfortable.

Sienna picked up the nearest tablet to check over one of her patients. 'Who is it? A rep? Tell them I don't have time, I'm sorry.' She gave Annabelle a smile. 'I think I should maybe hand all the reps over to Max now—what do you think?'

Annabelle glanced at Ruth. 'It's not a rep. I don't recognise him and didn't have time to ask his name. He's insisting that he'll only speak to you and…' she took a breath '…he won't be kept waiting.'

Sienna sat the tablet back down, satisfied with the recordings. Her post-surgery baby was doing well. She shook her head. 'Well, who does he think he is?' She looked around the unit and paused. 'Wait? Is it a parent of one of the babies? Or someone with a surgery scheduled for their child? You know that I'll speak to them.'

Annabelle shook her head firmly. 'No. None of those. No parents—or impending parents. It's something else entirely.' She handed a set of notes to Ruth. 'Can you check on little Maisy Allerton? She didn't take much at her last feed.'

Ruth nodded and disappeared. Annabelle pressed her lips together. 'This guy, he says it's personal.'

Sienna felt an uncomfortable prickle across her skin. 'Personal? Who would have something personal to talk to me about?'

The words were out before she even thought about them. Nothing like making herself sound sad and lonely. Did people at Teddy's even think she had a personal life?

Annabelle's eyes darted automatically to Sienna's protruding stomach, then she flushed as she realised Sienna had noticed.

Sienna straightened her shoulders. She'd never been a fan of anyone trying to push her around. She gave Annabelle a wide smile. 'Oh, he's insisting, is he?'

Annabelle nodded then her eyes narrowed and she folded her arms across her chest. She'd worked with Sienna long enough to sense trouble ahead.

Sienna kept smiling. 'Well, in that case, I'll review my three babies. Talk to all sets of parents. I might make a few phone calls to some parents with babies on my list between Christmas and New Year, and then…' she paused as she picked up the tablet again to start accessing a file '…then, as a heavily pregnant woman, I think I'll go and have something to eat. I missed lunch and—' she raised her eyebrows at Annabelle '—I have a feeling a colleague I work with might *insist* I don't faint at work.'

Annabelle smiled too and nodded knowingly. 'Not that I want to be any influence on you, but the kitchen staff made killer carrot cake today. I think it could count as one of your five a day.'

Sienna threw back her head and laughed. 'You're such a bad influence but I could definitely be persuaded.' Her eyes went straight back to the chart. 'Okay, so let's see Kendall first. Mr I-Insist is just going to have to find out how things work around here.'

Annabelle gave a smile and put an arm at Sienna's back. 'Don't worry. Somehow I think you'll be more than a match for him. Give me a signal when you come back. I can always page you after five minutes to give you an escape.'

Sienna nodded. She didn't really care who was waiting for her—her babies would always come first.

Seb was furious. He kept glancing at his watch. He'd been in this room for over an hour—his security detail waiting outside.

The sister of the neonatal ward had seemed surprised at first by his insistence at seeing Sienna. Then, she'd explained Sienna was at another appointment and would be back soon. What exactly meant *soon* at the Royal Cheltenham?

He'd paced the corridors a few times looking for her with no success. The doors to the neonatal unit had a coded lock, and, from the look of the anxious parents hurrying in and out, it really wasn't a place he wanted to be.

He'd been stunned when Oliver Darrington had phoned him to discuss his own difficult situation—after a one-night stand a colleague was pregnant. A colleague who he had feelings for. Oliver had been Sebastian's friend since they'd attended university together, even though they were destined for completely different lives.

He hadn't told Oliver a thing about his weekend with Sienna, so when Oliver had mentioned that Sienna too was pregnant, Sebastian had felt as if he couldn't breathe.

His tongue had stuck to the roof of his mouth and his brain had scrambled to ask the question he'd wanted to, without giving himself away. According to Oliver she was heavily pregnant—due to have her baby at the end of January.

For a few seconds Seb had felt panicked. The dates fitted perfectly. He didn't have a single doubt that her baby could be his.

He could hardly remember the rest of the conversation with Oliver. That made him cringe now. It was a complete disservice to his friend.

He'd had things to deal with.

Since Sienna had stormed out of his chalet retreat his life had turned upside down. He'd followed his parents' wishes and allowed the announcement of the engagement. Theresa had seemed indifferent. Uniting the kingdoms had been important to her too. But marrying someone she wasn't in love with didn't seem any more appealing to her than it was to him.

If Sienna hadn't happened, maybe, just maybe, he could have mustered some enthusiasm and tried to persuade Theresa their relationship could work.

But his nights had been haunted with dreams of being tangled in the sheets with a passionate woman with ash-blonde hair, caramel-coloured eyes and a firm, toned body.

She'd ignited a flame inside him. Something that had burned underneath the surface since she'd left. He'd been a fool. A fool to let his country think he would take part in a union he didn't think he could make work.

His parents had been beside themselves with anger at the broken engagement.

Theresa had been remarkably stoic about him breaking the engagement. She'd handed back the yellow diamond ring with a nod of her head. He suspected her heart lay somewhere else. Her voice had been tight. 'I hadn't got around to finalising the design for my wedding dress yet. The designer was furious with me. It's just as well really, isn't it?'

He'd felt bad as he bent to kiss her cheek. Theresa wasn't really upset with him. Not yet, anyway. She might be angrier when she found out about the baby. It could be embarrassing for her. He only hoped she would have moved on to wherever her heart truly lay.

The Head of his PR had nearly had a heart attack. He'd actually put his hand to his chest and turned an alarming shade of grey. And that had given Sebastian instant inspiration. In amongst breaking the news to both Theresa and his parents, Sebastian had spent the last two weeks doing something else—making arrangements to twin the Cheltenham hospital with the Montanari Royal General. He was already a patron of his own hospital; a sizeable donation would make him a patron of Teddy's too.

It was the perfect cover story. He could come to the Royal Cheltenham without people asking too many questions. Oliver had been surprised for around five minutes. Then, he'd made him an appointment with the board. In the meantime, Sebastian could come freely to the hospital with his security and press team in tow. The announcement was due to be made tomorrow. Seb was hoping he could also make an announcement of his own.

He glanced at his watch again as the anger built in his chest. Sienna hadn't even contacted him. Hadn't even let him know he was going to be a father. Was her intention to leave his child fatherless? For the heir of Montanari not to be acknowledged or have their rightful inheritance?

That could never happen. He wouldn't *allow* that to happen. Not in his lifetime.

He heard a familiar voice drifting down the corridor towards him. It sent every sense on fire. That familiar Scottish twang. The voice she'd invited him to listen to all night…

'No problem. I'll be along to review the chest X-ray in five minutes. Thanks, Max.'

The footsteps neared but he wasn't prepared for the sight. Last time he'd seen Sienna she'd been toned and athletic. This time the rounded belly appeared before she did.

Her footsteps stopped dead in the doorway, her eyes wide. It was clear he was the last person she'd been expecting to see.

She took his breath away. She didn't have on a traditional white coat. Instead she was dressed in what must be a maternity alternative to a suit. Black trousers with a matching black tunic over the top. It was still smart. Still professional. Her hair was gleaming, a bit longer than he remembered and tucked behind her ears. A red stethoscope hung around her neck, matching her bright red lipstick.

'Sebastian.' It was more a breath than a word.

Her hand went automatically to her stomach. His reply stuck in his throat. He hadn't been ready. He hadn't been ready for the sight of her ripe with his child. Even under her smart clothes he could see her lean body had changed totally. Her breasts were much bigger than before—and they suited her. Pregnancy suited her in a way he couldn't even have imagined.

But now he was here, he just didn't even know where to start.

This wasn't happening. Not here. Not now.

She'd planned things so carefully. All her surgeries were over. Any new patients had been seen jointly with Max. He would perform the neonatal surgeries and she would do later follow up once she was back from maternity leave.

But here he was. Right in front of her. The guy she'd spent the last six months half cursing, half pining for.

Those forest-green eyes practically swept up and down her body. Her palm itched. That thick dark hair. The hair she'd spent two days and two nights running her fingers through. Those broad shoulders, filling out the exquisitely cut suit. The pale lilac of the shirt and the shocking pink of his tie with his dark suit and good looks made him look like one of the models adorning the billboards above Times Square in New York. Imagine waking up with that staring in your hotel window every morning.

Her breath had left her lungs. It was unnatural. It was ridiculous. He was just a man. She sucked in a breath and narrowed her gaze. 'Congratulations on your engagement.'

He flinched. What had he expected? That she'd welcome him here with open arms?

Part of her felt a tiny twinge of regret. Her hand had picked up the phone more times than she could count. She'd tried to have that conversation with Oliver on a number of occasions. But it was clear that he'd never realised what was behind her tiny querying questions. The thought that his friend might have had a liaison with his colleague obviously hadn't even entered his mind.

Was it really such a stretch of the imagination?

Sebastian let out a sigh and stepped towards her. She held up her hand automatically to stop him getting too close—last thing she needed was to get a whiff of that familiar aftershave. She didn't need any more memories of the past than she already had. Baby was more than enough.

The royal persona she'd seen on the TV news seemed to be the man in the room with her now. This wasn't the cheeky, flirtatious, incredibly sexy guy that she'd spent two days and two nights with. Maybe her Seb didn't really exist at all?

There was something else. An air about him she hadn't noticed before. Or maybe she hadn't been paying attention. An assurance. A confidence. The kind of persona that actually fitted with being a prince.

He caught the hand she held in front of her.

The effect was instant, a rush of warmth and a pure overload of memories of the last time he'd touched her.

If she hadn't been standing so squarely she might have swayed. Her senses were alight. Now, his aftershave was reaching across the short space between them like a cowboy's rope pulling her in. Her hand tingled from where he held it. His grip initially had been firm but now it changed and his thumb moved under her palm, tracing circles—just as he'd done months ago.

Her breathing stalled. No. No, she wasn't going to go here again.

This was the man that had announced his engagement a few weeks after they'd met. An engagement to a childhood friend. Had he been seeing her the whole time? She'd checked. But the media wasn't sure. Had he been sleeping with them both at the same time?

She had no idea.

But no matter what her senses were doing, thoughts like that coloured her opinion of the man. He hadn't been honest with her. They hadn't promised each other anything, but that didn't matter.

She snatched her hand back.

'I'm not engaged, Sienna. I broke off my engagement when I heard the news you were pregnant.' His voice was as smooth as silk.

She felt herself bristle. 'And what am I supposed to feel—grateful?'

He didn't even blink. He just kept talking. 'I heard the news from Oliver. He called me about something else. A woman. Ella? Do you know her?'

Sienna frowned. 'Yes, yes, I know her. She's a midwife here.' She paused. Did Sebastian know the full story?

'They're engaged,' she said carefully, missing out the part that Ella was pregnant too. She wasn't sure just how much Oliver would have told Sebastian.

A wide smile broke across Sebastian's face. 'Perfect. I'll need to congratulate him.' His focus came back on Sienna. 'Maybe we could have a joint wedding?'

'A what?' Someone walking past the door turned their head at the rise of her voice. 'Are you crazy?'

Sebastian shook his head. 'Why would you think I'm crazy?'

He drew himself up in front of her. 'You're carrying the heir to the Montanari throne. We might still have things to sort out, but I'd prefer it if the heir to the throne was legitimate. Wouldn't you? If you come back with me now we can be married as soon as we get there. We can tell the world we met when you came to work in Montanari Royal General. Everything fits.'

He made it all sound so normal. So rational. So matter-of-fact.

She wasn't hearing this. She wasn't. It was some sick, delusional dream. She thought back to everything she'd eaten today. Maybe she'd been exposed to something weird.

He reached into his pocket and pulled out a ring. 'Here.'

She wasn't thinking straight and held out her hand. 'What is it?'

One of the ward clerks walked past and raised her eyebrows at the sight of the way-too-big diamond. Perfect. Just perfect. She was already the talk of the place and Polly was the world's biggest gossip. She just prayed that Polly hadn't recognised Sebastian.

She flinched and pulled her hand away. 'What am I supposed to do with that?'

'Put it on,' he said simply, glancing at her as if it were a stupid question. 'You need to wear an engagement ring.' He paused for a second and looked at her face. 'Don't you like it? It's a family heirloom.' His forehead wrinkled. 'I'm sure I can find you something else in the family vault.'

She shook her head and started pacing. 'It doesn't matter if I like it. I don't want it. I don't need it. I'm—' She stopped and placed her hand on her stomach. '*We're* going nowhere. I have a job here. A home. The very last place I'm going is Montanari. And the very last thing I'm doing...' she paused again and shook her head, trying to make sense of the craziness around her. She drew in a deep breath and stepped right up to him, poking her finger in her chest. 'The very last thing I'm doing is marrying you.'

Now Sebastian started shaking his head. He had the absolute gall to look surprised. 'Why on earth not? You're expecting our child. You're going to be the mother of the heir to Montanari. We should get married. And as soon as possible.' He said it as if it made perfect sense.

Sienna put her hands on her back and started pacing. 'No. No, we absolutely shouldn't.'

Sebastian held out his hands. 'Sienna, in a few years you get to be the Queen of Montanari. What woman wouldn't want that?'

She shuddered. She actually shuddered. 'Oh, no. Oh, no.'

Sebastian's brow creased. 'What on earth is wrong? We can have a state wedding in Montanari...' he glanced at her stomach and gave a little shrug '...but we'll need to be quick.'

Sienna took a step back. 'Okay, were you really this crazy when I met you in Montanari and I just didn't notice? Because this is nowhere near normal.' She put her hand on her stomach. 'Yes, I'm pregnant. Yes, I'm pregnant with your baby. But that's it, Sebastian. This isn't the Dark Ages. I don't want your help—or need it.' She ran her fingers through her hair, trying to contemplate all the things she hadn't even considered. 'Look at me, Sebastian. I live here. In the Cotswolds. I came here from Edinburgh. I purposely chose to come here. I've bought my dream house. I have a great job and colleagues that I like and admire. I've arranged a childcare for my baby and cover for my maternity leave.' She could feel herself getting agitated. Her voice was getting louder the longer that she spoke. 'I won't keep you from our baby. You can have as much—or as little—contact as you want. But don't expect to waltz in here and take over our lives.' She pressed her hand to her chest. 'This is my life, Sebastian. *My life.* I don't need your money and I don't need your help. I'm perfectly capable of raising this baby on my own.'

Polly walked past again. It was obviously deliberate. Not only was she spying, now she was eavesdropping too.

With a burst of pure frustration Sienna kicked the door closed.

Sebastian raised his eyebrows.

She took a deep breath. 'I need you to go. I need you to leave. I can't deal with this now.'

Her lips pressed tight together and resisted the temptation to say the words she was truly thinking.

Sebastian seemed to have frozen on the spot. The air of assurance had disappeared.

It was then she saw it. The look. The expression.

He'd actually expected her to say yes.

He hadn't expected her to reject him. He hadn't expected a no.

Sebastian Falco was hurt.

Now, it was her that was surprised. It struck her in a way she didn't expect. She could almost see a million things circulating around in his brain—as if he was trying to find a new way to persuade her to go with him.

She could see the little vein pulsing at the base of his throat.

Her mouth was dry.

If she were five years old—this would be her dream. Well, not the pregnancy, but the thought of a prince sweeping in and saying he would marry her, presenting her with a huge diamond ring and the chance to one day be Queen.

But it had been a long time since Sienna had been five.

And her ambitions and dreams had changed so much they could move mountains.

Sebastian folded his arms across his chest. 'Why didn't you call me, Sienna?' His voice was rigid. 'Why didn't you phone and tell me as soon as you knew you were pregnant?'

Oh. That.

She should have expected it to come up.

'I was going to. I meant to. But the day I did my pregnancy test was the day your engagement was announced on the national news.' She looked at him directly, trying to push away the tiny part of guilt curling in her stomach. 'Between that, and finding out I was pregnant, it kind of took the feet out from under me.'

He broke their gaze for a second, his words measured. 'Theresa was a friend. It wasn't going to be a marriage of love. It was going to be a union of kingdoms. Something my parents wanted very much.'

'How romantic.'

She couldn't help herself. She'd been a child of a love-less marriage. She knew the effects it had. She raised her eyes to the ceiling. 'Well, your parents must be delighted about me. I guess I'm going to be the national scandal.'

She'd been delusional. She'd thought she knew this man—even a little. But nothing about this fitted with the two days they'd spent together. The Sebastian she'd known then was a man who actually felt and thought. He'd laughed and joked and made her the coffee she craved. He'd cuddled up beside her in bed and taken her to places she'd never been before. He'd gently stroked the back of her neck as she'd fallen asleep. He was someone she'd loved being around.

Too bad all of it had been a lie.

The man in front of her now was the Sebastian that appeared on the news. The one with a fixed smile and his arm around someone else.

That was what it was. That was what she'd always no-ticed. Even though she'd tried not to watch him on the news—she'd tried to always switch channel—on the few occasions she had seen pictures of him, something had never seemed quite right.

She'd always tried not to look too closely. Her heart wouldn't let her go there. Not at all.

But little things were falling into place.

The smile had never reached his eyes.

Now, the look in his eyes seemed sincere. His tone much softer. 'You can be whatever you want to be, Si-enna. I'd just like you to do it as my wife.'

This look was familiar. She'd seen it so many times on the weekend they'd spent together. In between the flirting, fun and cheekiness there had been flashes of sincerity.

That had been the thing that made his untruthfulness so hard to take.

The room was starting to feel oh-so-small.

'Why didn't you call me later?'

It didn't matter that she'd just sipped some water. Her mouth felt dry. He wasn't going to let this go. He was calling her on it.

She licked her lips. 'I wanted to. I thought about it. But we didn't exactly exchange numbers. How easy is it to call a royal palace and ask to speak to the Prince?'

He shifted a little uncomfortably, then shook his head. 'You could have asked Oliver. You knew we were friends. He was the one who recommended you. He would have given you the number whenever you asked.'

'And how would that work out? "Oh, Oliver? Can you give me Seb's mobile number, please? I want to tell him that I'm going to ruin his engagement by letting him know I'm pregnant. You know, the engagement to his childhood sweetheart?" At least that's the way it sounded in the media.'

He smiled. He actually smiled.

'You think it's funny?'

'No. Not at all. But that's the first time you've called me Seb since I got here.' He stepped forward.

She sucked in a breath.

She hadn't even noticed.

Seb was too close again. She needed some space, some distance between them.

He touched her arm. Her bare skin almost caught fire. There was no opportunity to flinch or pull away. His palm surrounded her slim wrist. 'I've told you. It was never like that with Theresa. We just didn't think of each other that way. And we'd never been childhood sweethearts. We were friends. Just friends.'

'You've told her about the pregnancy?'

He gave a little grimace. 'Not exactly. Not yet anyway.' He ran his fingers through his hair. 'I wasn't quite sure how to put it.'

'You were sleeping with us both?'

She couldn't help it. It just came out.

'What? No.' Sebastian shook his head again. 'I've never slept with Theresa. I've told you. It wasn't that kind of relationship. I don't sleep with my friends.'

She hated the way that relief flooded through her. The sincerity was written all over his face. He might have lied by omission before but she was certain he wasn't lying now.

She met his gaze. 'How will she feel when she finds out? It will look to the world as if you've made a fool of her. As if *we've* made a fool of her. I hate that. I don't want anyone to think I'd have an affair with someone else's man.'

He sucked in a deep breath and reached up towards her face. 'But I wasn't in a relationship with Theresa. I was single. I was free when we were together. And if I'd known you were pregnant I would never have let my parents force me into announcing an engagement.' His hand brushed her cheek and his fingers tangled in her hair.

This was what he'd done when they'd been together. This was how he'd pulled her into *that* first kiss.

The touch should have been mesmerising. But his words left her cold.

Forced. He'd never really mentioned his parents in their short time together.

'They forced you? I didn't think you'd let anyone force you to do anything.' There was an air of challenge in her voice.

He recognised it and raised his eyebrows. He gave her a half-smile. 'You haven't met my parents—yet.'

It was her first truly uncomfortable feeling. The King and Queen of Montanari. They wouldn't like her. They wouldn't like her at all. She'd ruined the plan to unite the neighbouring kingdoms and was going to give Montanari an illegitimate heir. Her face was probably currently fixed to a dartboard or archery target in their throne room.

'And are they forcing you to do this too?' The words came out in a whisper. Every muscle in her body was tensed.

Duty. That was what she was sensing here.

He might be sincere. But there was no love—no compassion here. Tears threatened to fill her eyes. She licked her dry lips and stepped back, out of his hold. He hadn't answered her question and she couldn't quite believe how hurt she felt.

'I think you should go back to Montanari, Sebastian. I'll let you know when the baby arrives and we can sort things out from there.'

He looked surprised, his hand still in the air from where he'd touched her hair. He stared at it for a second, then shook his head. 'Who says I'm going back to Montanari?'

She concentrated on her shoes. It was easier than looking at him. 'Well, you will, won't you? You'll have—' she waved her hand '—princely duties or something to do. You can't stay here. There's been enough tittle-tattle about who the father of my baby is. The last thing I want is for someone to realise who you are and gossip about us. I'm the talk of the steamie already.'

He shook his head in bewilderment. 'The what?'

'The steamie. You know—the washhouse.'

He shook his head. 'I have no idea what you're talking

about. But you know what? Just keep talking. I'd forgotten how much I loved the sound of your voice.'

Ditto.

'The steamie. It's a Scottish term for an old washhouse—the place where people used to go and wash their clothes before everyone had washing machines. It was notorious. The women used to always gossip in there.'

'So, that's what we could be? The talk of the steamie?'

She nodded again. 'And I'd rather not be. It would be easier if you left. We can talk. We can make plans about access arrangements when the baby arrives. We have another six weeks to wait. There's enough time.'

'Oh, no, you don't,' he replied promptly.

She had a bad feeling about this. 'What do you mean?'

'I'm not going anywhere. I've already missed out on things. I'm not missing out on anything else.'

'What do you mean by that?' she asked again.

He leaned against the door jamb and folded his arms across his chest. There was a determined grin on his face. 'I've got work to do here.' He mimicked her hand wave. 'Princely duties. I need to sort out the twinning of our hospitals and iron out all the details. Get used to me being around.' He gave her a little nod. 'I'm your new best friend.'

CHAPTER THREE

IF HE DIDN'T love his friend so much he'd be annoyed by the permanent smile that seemed to have fixed itself to Oliver's face. Even sitting at a desk swamped with paperwork, Oliver still had the smile plastered on his face.

'Sebastian!' Oliver jumped to his feet, strode around the desk and engulfed Sebastian in a bear hug.

Sebastian returned the hug and leaned back. 'You're engaged? Do I get to meet the lucky lady?'

Oliver slapped his arm. 'You get to be my best man!' His smile wavered for a second. 'Are you here for the announcement tomorrow? I thought I would have heard from you.'

Sebastian gave a brief nod. He pushed his hands into his pockets and looked at Oliver. 'Not just that. It seems you and I are about to experience some changes together.'

Oliver's brow furrowed at the cryptic line. 'What do you mean?'

Sebastian glanced around. There was no one hovering near the door. Oliver's office seemed private enough. 'We're both about to be fathers.'

For a few seconds Oliver's expression was pure surprise. 'Theresa's pregnant? Congratulations. I had no idea—'

Sebastian held up his hand to stop him. Of course he

was surprised. He knew Sebastian's real feelings about that engagement.

He shook his head. 'It's not Theresa.'

Oliver paled. 'It's not?'

They were good friends. He'd experienced Sebastian's parents. He knew exactly how focused and overbearing they could be. They'd spent many hours and a number of cases of beer contemplating the pressures of being an heir, along with Sebastian's personal feelings and ambitions.

The grin that spread over Oliver's face took Sebastian by surprise. He let out a laugh and walked back around the desk, pushing his wheeled chair back, putting his feet on the desk and crossing his arms. 'Oh, this is going to be good. Tell me all about it.'

Sebastian shook his head and leaned on the chair opposite Oliver. 'You find this amusing?'

Oliver nodded. 'I find this very amusing. It's only taken you thirty-one years to cause a scandal. I hope it's a good one.'

Sebastian made a face. 'You might change your mind when you find out the rest of it.'

'What's that supposed to mean?'

Sebastian shook his head again. 'Is everything set for the board meeting tomorrow?'

Oliver nodded. 'It's just a formality. They've already agreed to twin the hospitals and develop the training programme. You realise as soon as it's announced there'll be around forty staff queued outside my door trying to get their name on the reciprocal swap programme?'

Sebastian took a deep breath. Was there even a chance in a million that Sienna might consider something like that?

He was still smarting about her reaction earlier. What

was wrong with making the heir to the Montanari throne legitimate? It made perfect sense to him.

Why was she so against it? He'd still felt the chemistry in the air between them—even if she wanted to deny it. He could admit that the timing wasn't great. But he'd dealt with things as best he could.

At the end of the day it was his duty to marry the mother of his baby. Maybe he could work on her, get her to reconsider?

'I plan on being around for the next few days—maybe longer.'

Oliver glanced at him. Sebastian's visits were usually only when he flew in and out of the UK on business and usually only lasted a couple of hours.

'Really, why?'

He'd picked up a pen and was scribbling notes.

Sebastian lowered his voice. 'Because I have to convince the mother of my child to marry me.'

The pen froze and oh-so-slowly one of Oliver's eyebrows rose. 'Say that again?'

Sebastian sat back in the chair and relaxed his arms back. He felt better after saying it out loud. It didn't seem quite so ridiculous a thought.

'Sienna—the mother of my child. I have to convince her to marry me.'

The pen flew past his ear. Oliver was on his feet. 'What? What do you mean, Sienna?' His head turned quickly from side to side. 'I mean, you? Her? The baby? It's yours?' It was almost as if he were trying to sort it all out in his mind. Then his eyes widened and he crumpled back down into his seat.

'Oh, no.' He looked as if he were going to be sick on the desk. 'How did you find out?' He didn't even wait for an answer. His head was already in his hands.

Sebastian gave a nod, reached over and clapped the side of one of Oliver's hands. 'Yep. It was you. You phoned about Ella and mentioned Sienna and how pregnant she was.'

Oliver's head shot back up. 'I thought you'd gone quiet when we spoke but I just assumed it was because you were surprised when I said Ella was pregnant.'

'It wasn't Ella's pregnancy that surprised me.'

Oliver ran his hand through his hair. 'Yeah, obviously.' He wrinkled his nose and a smile broke out on his face. 'You and Sienna, really?'

Sebastian was curious. 'What's so strange about me and Sienna?'

Oliver threw up his hands. 'It's just…it's just…she's so… *Sienna*.' He shook his head and laughed. 'Your parents will hate her. She'd be their ultimate nightmare for a queen.'

Sebastian felt a little flare of protective anger. 'What's that supposed to mean?'

Oliver shrugged. 'Where will I start? She's a surgeon. She's *always* going to be a surgeon. Sienna would never give up her job—she's just too good and too emotionally connected. Surgery is in her blood.' He was shaking his head. 'As for tactfulness and decorum? Sienna's one of the most straight-talking doctors I've ever known. She doesn't take any prisoners. She wouldn't spend hours trying to butter up some foreign dignitary. She'd tell them exactly what she expected of them and then move on to dessert.' He tapped his fingers on the table and stared up to the left for a second. 'It's almost like you picked the person least like your mother in the whole world. Except for looks, of course. Your mother was probably born knowing she'd one day be Queen. I bet even as a child Sienna never played dress-up princesses or looked for a prince. She'd have been too busy setting up her dolls' hospital.'

Sebastian had been about to interrupt, instead he took a breath. Oliver had absolutely nailed it.

Sienna was a career woman. His mother had always taken a back seat to his father in every way.

Sienna hadn't been scared to shout at him. He'd never heard his mother raise her voice in her life.

Sienna hadn't been afraid to be bold and take him up on his proposition. Her comment *How about you listen to it all night instead?* had haunted his dreams in every erotic way possible. His mother would have a heart attack if she ever knew.

Just as well Sienna was a doctor really.

The reality of his future life was starting to crash all around him. Sebastian didn't panic. He'd never panicked. But he felt wary. If he didn't handle things well this could be a disaster.

Could Sienna McDonald really be the future Queen of Montanari?

He leaned back and folded his arms. 'She's the mother of my child. Montanari needs an heir. It's my duty to marry her.'

Oliver raised his eyebrows. 'Please tell me you didn't just say that?'

When Sebastian didn't answer right away, Oliver shook his head. 'More importantly, please tell me you didn't say that to Sienna?'

Sebastian ignored the comment. 'Montanari needs change. Sienna will be just the breath of fresh air it needs. Who couldn't love her? She's a neonatal surgeon. She eats, breathes and sleeps her job. People will admire her intelligence. They'll admire her dedication. I know I do.'

Oliver started tapping his fingers on the table again. 'And what does Sienna have to say about all this?'

He was good. He was too good. He clearly knew Sienna well.

'Let's just say that Sienna and I are a work in progress.'

Oliver let out something resembling a snort. He stood up again. 'You're my oldest friend, Sebastian, but I'm telling you right now, I'm not choosing sides. She's one of my best doctors. Upset her and you'll upset me.' He gave a little shudder. 'She'll kill me when she finds out it was me that told you.' He leaned against the wall for a second. 'Why didn't she tell you herself?'

Sebastian shrugged slightly. 'Timing, she says. I'd just got engaged.'

Oliver rolled his eyes then narrowed them again. 'And why didn't you tell me that you'd got in a compromising position with one of my doctors?' He wagged his finger at Sebastian. 'Can't trust you for two minutes. I'll need to rethink this whole hospital-twinning thing. Can't have us sending all our doctors over there to get seduced by Montanari men—royal or not.'

Sebastian stood up. 'I have a baby on the way. My priorities have changed.' He headed to the door. 'I'll see you at the board meeting tomorrow—and for the press announcement.'

Oliver gave a nod. He tipped his head to one side. 'So, what's your next plan?'

Sebastian shot him a wide smile. 'Charm. Why else be a prince?'

Sienna stuck her head outside the doors to the paediatric ICU, then ducked back inside, keeping her nose pressed against the glass. The tinsel taped to the window tickled her nose and partially blocked her view.

'What are you doing?' asked an amused Charlie Warren, one of her OBGYN colleagues.

'I'd have thought that was clear. I'm hiding.' Her ever-expanding belly was stopping her from getting a clear view.

Charlie laughed. 'And who are you hiding from?'

'You know. Him.'

'Him, who?'

Sienna sighed and turned around, leaning back against the door.

'Sebastian.'

Charlie nodded slowly. 'Ah…now I see.'

Sienna brushed a lock of loose hair out of her eyes. 'I see the Teddy's super-speed grapevine is working as well as ever. He's been here less than twenty-four hours.'

Charlie leaned against the door with her and gave her a knowing smile.

'What are you grinning at?' she half snapped.

She'd always liked Charlie. They got on well. All her colleagues had been so supportive of her pregnancy. She stared at him again.

'There's something different about you.'

'There is? What?' He had a dopey kind of grin on his face.

She pointed. 'That. You've got the same look that Oliver is wearing.'

'I don't know what you mean.'

She poked her finger in his chest. 'Oh, yes, you do. What's her name?'

She was definitely curious. She'd spent the last week so wrapped up with preparations for Christmas and trying to keep her energy up that she'd obviously missed something important. Charlie was a widower. For as long as she'd known him there had been veiled shadows behind his eyes.

They were gone now. And it made her heart sing a little to see that.

He gave her a sheepish smile. 'It's Juliet.'

Sienna's mouth dropped open. 'No.' Then she couldn't help but grin. 'Really?' She got on well with the Aussie surgeon who'd performed *in-utero* surgery to save the life of a quad born at Teddy's last week.

His smile said it all. 'Really.'

She leaned against the door again. 'Oh, wow.' She flicked her hair back. It was really beginning to annoy her. 'First Oliver and now you. Lovesick people are falling all over the place.' She gave him a wicked glare. 'Better phone Public Health, it looks like we've got an infectious disease here.'

He nodded. 'Don't forget Max and Annabelle. This thing is spreading faster than that winter virus.' He gave her a cheeky wink. 'And from what I saw this morning at breakfast, others might eventually succumb.'

Heat rushed into her cheeks. She'd come in early this morning and walked along to the canteen for breakfast. She'd barely sat down before Sebastian had ambushed her and sat down at the other side of the table with coffee, toast and eggs.

It had been excruciating. She could sense every eye in the canteen on them both and it had been as quick as she could bolt down her porridge and hurry out of there.

Normally she loved breakfast in the canteen at Christmas time. Christmas pop tunes were always playing and the menu food got new names like Rudolph's raisin pancakes or Santa's scrumptious scrambled egg.

'I don't know what you mean,' she said defensively to Charlie, who was obviously trying to wind her up.

He laughed as he pulled open the door and looked

out for a second. 'He seems like a nice guy. Maybe you should give him a chance.'

She laid her hand on her large stomach. 'Oh, I think it's pretty obvious I've already given him a chance.'

He just kept laughing. 'Well, he's on the charm offensive. And he's winning. Everyone that's met him thinks he's one version of wonderful or another. Including Juliet's daughter.'

'He's met her daughter?'

Charlie nodded. 'She loves him already. He gave her some kind of doll that the little girls in Montanari love. A special Christmas one with a red and green dress. She was over the moon.'

Sienna wrinkled her nose. 'You shouldn't let her speak to strangers.'

Something flashed over Charlie's face. 'If I didn't know any better, Sienna, I'd think you were a woman reaching that crabby stage just before she delivers.'

She shook her head fiercely and patted her stomach. 'Oh, no. No way. I've got just under six weeks. This baby is not coming out before then.'

'If you say so.' Charlie stuck his head out of the door again. 'Okay, you can go. The coast is clear. Just remember to be on your best behaviour.' He held the door before her as she rushed outside. 'And just remember... I recognise the signs.'

The coast wasn't clear at all.

Sebastian was waiting outside the unit, leaning against the wall with his arms folded.

'I'm going to kill Charlie with my bare hands,' she muttered.

It didn't help that he was looking even sexier than before. When he'd joined her this morning at breakfast he'd been wearing a suit and tie. Something to do with a business meeting. She hadn't really been paying attention.

Now, he'd changed into jeans, a leather jacket and a slim-fitting black T-shirt. His hair was speckled with flecks of snow.

'What are you doing here?' she asked as she made her best attempt to sweep past.

Sebastian was having none of it. He fell into step beside her. 'Waiting for you.'

She stopped walking and turned to face him. She wanted to be angry with him. She wanted to be annoyed. But he had that look on his face, that hint of cheek. He was deliberately taunting her. They'd spent most of the weekend in Montanari batting smart comments back and forth. This felt more like sun-blessed Montanari than the snow-dusted Cotswolds.

She stifled her smile. 'This better not get to be a habit. I'm busy, Seb. I'm at work.'

His grin broadened and she realised her error. She'd called him Seb again.

'When do you finish work?'

'Why?'

'You know why. I'd like us to talk—have dinner maybe. Do something together.'

His phone buzzed in his pocket. He shifted a little on his feet but ignored it.

'Aren't you going to get that?'

He shook his head. 'I'm busy.'

'How long—exactly—have you been standing out here?'

He smiled. 'Around two hours.' He lifted one hand and shrugged. 'But it's fine. The people around here are very friendly. They all like to talk.'

'Talk is exactly what they'll do. You might be a public figure, Seb, but I'm not. I'm a pretty private person. I don't want anyone else knowing about our baby.'

The look on his face was so surprised that she realised he hadn't even considered that.

How far apart were they? Had he not even considered that might put her under stress? Not exactly ideal for a pregnant woman.

And it didn't help that wherever Seb was, men in black were permanently hovering in the background.

He'd already made the assumption that she would want to marry him. Maybe he also thought she would be fine about having their baby in the public eye?

Oh, no.

She gave a sway.

'Sienna? What's wrong? Are you okay?'

He moved right in front of her, catching both her arms with his firm hands. He was close enough for her to see the tiny lines around his eyes and the little flecks in his forest-green eyes.

'You're a prince,' she breathed slowly.

He blinked. There was a look of amusement on his face. 'I'm a prince,' he confirmed in a whisper.

'I slept with a prince.' It was almost as if she were talking to herself. She knew all this. None of it was a surprise. But all of a sudden things were sinking in fast.

Before, Sebastian Falco hadn't featured in her life. Apart from the telltale parting gift that he'd left her, there was really no sign of any connection between them. No one knew about their weekend together. No one knew that they'd even met.

When she'd come back, it was clear that even though Oliver was Sebastian's friend, he'd had no idea about their relationship.

That was the way things were supposed to be. Even

though, in her head, she'd known she should tell Seb about the baby, once the engagement was announced she'd pushed those thoughts away.

She'd pushed all memories of Sebastian and their time together—the touch of his hands on her skin, the taste of his lips on hers—away into that castle of his that she'd never seen.

A castle. The man lived in a castle. Not in the mountain retreat he'd taken her to. Her stomach gave a little flip as she wondered once more how many other women had been there.

'Sienna, honey? Are you okay? Do you want to sit down?'

Honey. He'd just called her honey as if it were the most natural thing in the world to do.

He wanted them to get married. A prince wanted to marry her.

Most women would be happy. Most women would be delighted.

Marry a prince. Live in a castle. Wasn't that the basis of every little girl's favourite fairy tale?

Not hers.

She wasn't a Cinderella kind of girl. Well, maybe just a little bit.

She definitely wasn't Rapunzel. She didn't need any guy to save her.

And she so wasn't Sleeping Beauty. She'd never spend her life lying about.

She looked around. They were three floors up. The glass atrium dome above them and the Christmas decorations directly underneath them. People flowed all around them. The Royal Cheltenham Hospital was world renowned. People begged to work here. Posts were fiercely contested. Three other surgeons she respected and admired had interviewed for the job that she'd been appointed to.

That had been the best call of her life.

She sucked in a breath. Teddy's was her life.

She loved her job, loved the kids, loved the surgeries and loved the people.

A gust of icy wind blew up through the open doors downstairs. The chill felt appropriate.

The kids' book character in front of her right now was threatening all that.

Would she really get any peace once people found out her child was the heir of Montanari?

Her hands went protectively to her stomach. 'What happens once he or she arrives?'

He looked confused. 'What do you mean?'

So much was spinning around in her head that the words stuck in her throat. After her childhood experiences she'd always vowed to be in charge of her own life, her own relationships and her own destiny.

Finding out she was pregnant had only made her sway for a second or two, then it had just put a new edge to her determination to get things right.

She'd made so many plans this Christmas—almost as if she were trying to keep herself busy. Carolling. Helping on the children's ward. Wrapping presents for army troops stationed away from home. Oh, her house was decorated as usual, and she opened the doors on her advent calendar every day. But she'd pictured spending this Christmas alone so was scheduled to be working over the holiday. She hadn't counted on Sebastian being around.

Seb was still standing straight in front of her, looking at her with concern in his eyes. He reached up and brushed her cheek with the gentlest of touches—the most tender of touches. It sent a whole host of memories flooding through her.

Seb. The man she'd shared a bed with. The man who kissed like no other. The man she'd thought was someone else entirely.

The man who'd thought he could walk in here and sweep her off her feet.

She shivered. She actually shivered.

'What are the rules in Montanari? Did you propose to me because an illegitimate child can't inherit the throne?'

He shook his head. 'No. No, of course I didn't. And no. There's no rules like that in Montanari. I'm the heir to the throne, and my firstborn son, or firstborn daughter, will be the heir to the throne once I'm King.' He gave an almost indiscernible shake of his head. 'But let's face it, it would be much better if we were married.'

'Better for who?'

He held up his hands, but she wasn't watching his hands, she was watching his face.

'Better for everyone. I have a duty—a duty to my people and my country. I want to introduce our son or daughter as the heir to the throne.' His gaze softened. 'And I'd like to introduce you as my wife.'

She had an instant dual flashback. One part caused by his word 'duty'. An instant memory of just exactly how both her parents had felt about their 'duty' and the look of absolute relief on her father's face as he'd packed his bags and left. The second part was caused by the first. A memory from months ago—those first few weeks when apparent morning sickness had struck at any second of the day or night. She wanted to be sick right here, right now. Right over his brown boots.

Duty. A word that seemed to have an absolute chilling effect that penetrated right down to her soul. Every time she heard people use the word in everyday life she had to try and hold back her instant response—an involuntary shudder.

Her insides were curled in knots. He'd just told her he wanted to marry her—again.

But not for the right reasons.

It didn't matter that her back had ached these last few days, she drew herself up to her full height and looked him straight in the eye.

It was almost like putting blinkers on. She wouldn't let those forest-green eyes affect her in the way they had before.

'I have a duty. To myself and to my child. We aren't your duty. We belong to ourselves. No one else. Not you. Not your parents. Not your people. I spent my childhood watching two people who should have never got together barely tolerate each other.' Fire was starting to burn inside her. 'What did you get for your eighteenth birthday present, Sebastian?'

The question caught him unawares. He stumbled around for the answer. 'A car, I think. Or a watch.'

'Well, good for you. Do you know what I got? I got my father packing his bags and leaving. But that didn't hurt nearly as much as the look of complete relief on his face. As for my mother? Two months later she moved to Portugal and found herself a toy boy. I can honestly say I've never seen her happier.' She pressed her hand to her chest. 'I did that to them, Sebastian. I made two people who shouldn't have been together spend eighteen years in what must have been purgatory for them.' She shook her head fiercely. 'I will never, *ever* do that to a child of mine.'

Sebastian pulled back. He actually pulled back a little. She'd done it again. Twice, in the space of two days, she'd raised her voice to Sebastian in a public place. Perfect. The talk of the steamie again.

But she couldn't help it. She wasn't finished.

There was no way Mr Fancy-Watches-For-His-Birthday could sweep in here and be part of her and her baby's life.

While she might have had a few little day dreams about the guy who was engaged to someone else, her reality plans had been way, way different.

This was why she'd negotiated new hours for the job she loved. This was why she'd visited four different nurseries and interviewed six potential childminders. This was why she'd spoken to her friend Bonnie—a fellow Scot who'd transported to Cambridge—on a number of occasions about how best to handle being a single mum.

This man was messing with her mind. Messing with her plans.

She didn't need this now. She really didn't.

She held up her hand. She knew exactly how to get rid of him. And not a single word would be a lie.

'I don't want this, Sebastian. This isn't my life. This isn't my dream. I will never, ever marry a man out of duty.' She almost spat out the word.

She lifted her hands towards the snow-topped atrium. 'When, and if, I ever get married, I'll get married to the man I love with all my heart. The man I couldn't bear to spend a single day without in my life. The man who would walk in front of a speeding train for me or my child without a single thought for himself—just like I would for him.' She took a few steps away from him. She was aware that a few people had stopped conversations around them to listen but she was past the point of caring.

'You don't know me, Sebastian. I want the whole hog. I want everything. And this, what you're offering? It doesn't even come close. I want a man who loves and adores me, who will walk by my side no matter what direction I take. I want a man who can take my breath away with a single look, a single touch.'

She could see him flinch. It didn't matter she was being unfair. Sebastian had taken more than her breath away with his looks and touches, but he didn't need to know that, not right now.

'I want a husband who will be proud of me and my career. Who won't care that I'm on call and he might need to reorganise his life around me. Who'll help around the house and not expect a wife who'll cook him dinner. Public Health may well have to do investigations into my cooking skills.'

She was enjoying herself now, taking it too far. But he had to know. He had to know just how fast to run.

'I will never accept anything less. I've been the child of a duty marriage. I would never, ever do that to my child. It's a form of torture. Growing up feeling guilty? It's awful.' She pressed her hands on her stomach again. '*My* child—' she emphasised the word '—is going to grow up feeling loved, blessed and, above all, wanted. By me, at least. There will be rules. There will be discipline. But most of all, there will be love.'

She walked back up to stand right in front of him. 'Whoever loves me will know how much I love Christmas, will want to celebrate it with me every year. Will know the songs I love, the crazy carols I love to sing. They won't care that I spend hours wrapping presents that are opened in seconds, they won't care that I buy more Christmas decorations than there is space for on the tree, they won't care that I have to have a special kind of cake every Christmas Eve and spend a fortune trying to find it. They'll know that I would only ever get married at Christmas. They would never even suggest anything else.'

She took a deep breath and finally looked at him—really looked at him.

Yip, she'd done it. He looked as if she'd just run over him with an Edinburgh tram. This time she lowered her voice. 'You might be a prince. You might have a castle. But I want the fairy tale. And you can't give it to me.'

And with that, she turned and walked away.

CHAPTER FOUR

'ARE YOU COMING down with something?' Oliver was staring at him in a way only a doctor could.

'What? No. Don't be ridiculous.'

Oliver gave a slow, careful nod. 'The board paper was excellent. They love the idea. It looks like the Falco charm has done its magic.'

'Except where it counts.'

'What's that supposed to mean?' Oliver rolled his eyes. 'No. Please. I'm not sure I want to know.' He walked around the desk and leaned against the wall.

Sebastian sighed loudly. He couldn't help it. 'I thought once I came here, Sienna might be happy to see me again. I didn't expect her to be quite…quite…'

'Quite so Sienna?' Oliver was looking far too amused for his liking.

Sebastian let out a wry laugh. 'Yeah, exactly. Quite so Sienna. I still can't believe she didn't let me know.'

Oliver shook his head. 'Doesn't sound like her. She's fierce. She's independent. She's stubborn—'

'You're not helping.'

Oliver laughed. 'But she's also one of the kindest-hearted women I know. She's always been professional but I can't tell you how many times I've caught her sobbing in a dark corner somewhere when things aren't going well with one of her patients. Working with neonates is the toughest area for any doctor. They're just getting started at life. They deserve a chance. And Sienna needs to be tough to get through it. She needs to be determined.' He paused for a second and his steady gaze met Sebastian's. 'Sienna puts up walls. She's honest. She's loyal. If she didn't let you know about the baby— she must have had a darn good reason.'

Sebastian bit the inside of his cheek. All of Oliver's words were striking chords with him. 'She said it was the engagement announcement. It put her off. She didn't want to destroy my engagement and cause a scandal.'

Oliver's brow creased. 'That's very considerate of her.' He stood up straight and took a few steps towards Sebastian. 'Quick question, Seb. Did you believe that?'

Sebastian was surprised. It hadn't occurred to him to doubt what Sienna told him. 'What do you mean?'

Oliver started shaking his head. 'I guess I just think it could be something else.'

'What do you mean?'

Oliver began walking around. 'It all sounds very noble. But would Sienna really deny you the chance to know your child? She could have spoken to me—she knows we are friends—I could have found a way to get a discreet message to you.' He gave Sebastian a careful look. 'I wonder if there was something else—a different kind of reason.'

Sebastian shifted in his chair. He couldn't get his head around what Oliver was saying. 'What do you mean? You think the baby might not be mine?'

Oliver held up his hand. 'Oh, no. Sienna wasn't seeing anyone. I couldn't even tell you when she had her last date. She's totally dedicated to her work. You don't need to worry about that.'

Thoughts started swirling around his head as relief flooded through him. Sienna had nailed exactly why he had come here. Duty. That was how he always lived his life.

It had been instilled in him from the youngest age.

He might not have loved Theresa. But she would have fulfilled the role of Queen with grace and dignity.

Sienna? Her personality type was completely different. She was intelligent. She was a brilliant surgeon. But she hadn't been brought up in a royal family. She didn't know traditions and protocols. He wasn't entirely sure she would ever follow them or want to.

He was pushing aside the way his heart skipped a beat when he saw her. The way his body reacted instantly. Passion like that would never last a lifetime no matter how pleasurable.

But that passion had created the baby currently residing inside Sienna. His baby. The heir to the throne of Montanari.

He stared back at Oliver. Knowing there were no other men in Sienna's life was exactly what he needed to hear. His press team were already wondering how to handle the imminent announcement about the baby.

'Then what on earth are you talking about?' He was getting increasingly frustrated by Oliver talking around in circles.

Oliver ran his hand through his hair. 'Let's just say I recognise the signs.'

'The signs of what? By the time you actually tell me what you mean this baby will be an adult.'

Oliver laughed again and started counting off on

his fingers. 'Do you know what I've noticed in the last day? Sienna's twitchy. She's on edge. She's different. Throughout this whole pregnancy she's been as cool as a cucumber.'

'You think I'm having a bad effect on her?'

Oliver put his hand on Sebastian's arm. 'I think you're having *some* kind of effect on her. I've never seen her like this.' He gave a little smile. 'If I didn't know any better—I'd say Sienna McDonald likes you a whole lot more than she admits to.'

Sebastian was stunned. 'Really?'

Oliver raised his eyebrows. 'It's such an alien concept to you?'

A warm feeling spread all over Sebastian's skin, as if the sun had penetrated through his shirt and annihilated the winter chill. When he'd proposed marriage the other day it had been an automatic reaction—something he'd planned on the flight over. But it had been precipitated by duty. Their baby would be the heir to the throne in Montanari.

Part of him was worried. She did actually like him? Was that why Sienna was acting the way she did?

He stood up and started pacing. 'She told me outright she'd never marry me. She told me she wanted everything. Love, romance, marriage, a husband who would love and adore her. She told me being a prince wasn't enough—not nearly enough.'

'And you thought it would be?' Oliver's face said it all. 'How come I've known you all these years and never realised how stupid you were?'

He stood up, stepped forward and poked his finger into Sebastian's chest. 'How do you feel about Sienna? How do you feel about her in here?'

His answer came out automatically. 'What does that matter? A marriage in Montanari is usually about a union. On this occasion, it's about a child. Feelings don't come into it.'

It was an uncomfortable question. Memories of Sienna McDonald had swirled around his head for months. The most obscure thing—a smell, a word—could conjure Sienna front and foremost in his mind again. The briefest thought could send blood rushing all around his body. His first sight of her—pregnant with his child—had affected him in ways he hadn't even contemplated.

From the second he'd met her Sienna had got under his skin.

The sight of her, the taste of her, the smell of her was irresistible. The way she responded to his teasing. He did care about her. He did care about this baby. But could it be more?

How would someone like him know what love was anyway? It wasn't as if he'd spent a life exposed to it. He'd had teenage crushes. A few passionate flings. But marrying for love had never really been on his radar. Sienna's words and expectations the other day had taken him by surprise.

Oliver folded his arms and raised his eyebrows. He knew Sebastian far too well to take his glib answer at face value.

'I… I… I…' He threw up his hands in frustration. 'I don't know. She confuses me. I never contemplated having emotional ties to the woman I'd marry. Sienna has just mixed everything up.'

Oliver shook his head. 'Then hurry up and decide. Hurry up and decide how you feel about the mother of your child. A beautiful, headstrong and highly intelligent member of my staff *and* a friend of mine.' He took a step closer and held up his finger and thumb almost pressed together. 'Do you want to know how much Sienna McDonald will care about you being a prince? Do you want to know how much a palace will impress her? This much.'

Oliver walked away and sat down behind his desk. He looked at Sebastian carefully. 'The trouble with you is that you've had too much help in this life.'

'What's that supposed to mean?'

Oliver waved his hand. 'Someone to do this for you, someone to do that. You didn't even do your own grocery shopping when we were students together.'

Sebastian looked embarrassed.

'Sienna doesn't have that. Sienna has never had that. Everything for this baby, she's worked out for herself. She's juggled her schedule. Worked out her maternity leave to the second. Put plans in place for every patient.' He put his elbows on the desk. 'Everything to do with her house—what we'd call a fixer-upper—she's sorted out herself too. She's spent years saving to get the house she really wants. It's not a house to her—it's a home. Do you know how crazy she is about Christmas? Do you know that she's a fabulous baker?' Oliver sighed.

Sebastian shook his head. 'All I know about Sienna is what I learned on that weekend back in Montanari, and what I've learned in the last few days. Everything's a mess. She's still angry with me—angry that I was engaged to someone else. She told me exactly what she wanted in this life and it was the whole fairy tale.' He dropped his voice slightly. 'She also told me I wasn't part of it. I have no idea how to connect with this woman, Oliver. I have no idea how I can manage to persuade her to give the thought of us a chance. Sometimes I think she doesn't even like me.'

Oliver frowned. 'Oh, she likes you—I can tell.'

'She does?' It was the first thing that gave him some hope.

Oliver leaned back again and looked his friend up and down as if he were assessing him. 'In the past she's been very selective. Guys who don't live up to her expectations?' He snapped his fingers and gave Sebastian a wicked grin. 'Gone. Just like that.'

Sebastian had started to feel uncomfortable. But Oliver was his friend—he couldn't keep up his serious face for long. It was obvious he cared about the welfare of Sienna. And Sebastian was glad about that, glad to know that people had her back.

He folded his arms across his chest and leaned against the wall. Some of the things that Oliver had said had struck a chord. There were so many things about Sienna that he didn't know. Things he wanted to know.

The bottom line was—could Sienna really be Queen material?

One weekend was not enough. It would never be enough. But he wasn't sure he wanted to say that out loud now. At least not to his friend.

'So, how do I get to know the real Sienna McDonald—the one behind the white coat?'

Oliver smiled. 'Eh, I think you've already achieved that.' He raised his eyebrow. 'There is evidence.'

Sebastian started pacing. Things were rushing around in his mind. 'Stop it. What about the other stuff? The Christmas stuff? What she takes in her tea?' His footsteps slowed. 'How she wants to raise our kid?' His voice got quieter. 'If she actually might more than like me...'

He stopped. Sienna. He needed to be around Sienna.

Oliver gave him a smile. 'I guess you should go and find out.'

It was an Aston Martin DB5. She'd seen one in a James Bond movie once. Even she could recognise it. A classic machine. She should have known he'd own something like this. He opened the door of the pale blue car revealing a red leather interior and she sucked in her breath.

She'd never been a show-me-your-money-and-I'll-be-impressed kind of girl. But this was a bit different. This was pure class. She'd watched enough car shows in her time to know that owning a car like this was a labour of pure love.

Just looking at it made her tingle.

The streets were dusted with snow. People were crossing the car park and staring, nudging each other and pointing at the car.

Christmas lights lit up the street opposite. Every shop had decorations in its windows. She could hear Christmas pop songs drifting out of the pub across the road. At the end of the road was a courtyard where a giant tree was lit with gold and red lights. It was paid for by the local council and the kids on the paediatric ward could see it from their windows. The lights twinkled all night long.

'What are you doing, Sebastian?'

He smiled. He was dressed for the British weather in a pair of jeans, black boots and his black leather jacket. She gave a little gulp as her insides did some weird little flip-flop.

He smiled. Oh, no. The flip-flop turned into a somersault. 'I came to pick you up. Someone told me you had car trouble. I thought I could drive you home.'

She bit her lip. Tempting. Oh, so tempting.

'I can call for roadside assistance. I really need to get my car sorted. It shouldn't take too long.'

He waved his hand. 'Albie, the porter, said if you leave your keys with him he'll get your car started later. It's too cold to hang around and wait for roadside assistance.' He stepped a little closer.

There it was. That familiar aroma. The one that took her back to Montanari, and sun, and cocktails, and...

'We could pick up a little dinner on the way home.'

Her stomach let out a loud growl. It was almost as if her body were conspiring against her. She scrambled to find a suitable excuse but her stubborn brain remained blank. 'Well, I... I...'

'Great. That's sorted, then.' He took her car keys from her hand and walked swiftly back to the hospital, leaving her to stare at the pale blue machine in front of her, gleaming as the sun dipped lower in the sky.

She was still staring a few seconds later when he returned. He stood alongside her and smiled. 'Like it?'

She couldn't help the smile as she met his proud gaze. 'I guess I'm just a little surprised.'

'By what?'

She waved her hand towards the car. 'I guess I thought you might be in something sleek, low-slung and bright red.'

He laughed out loud. 'You think I'm one of *those* kind of guys?'

She nearly laughed herself. He really didn't need to elaborate. But as she kept staring at the car she felt a wave of something else. 'I guess I don't really know, do I?'

She turned to look at him, her warm breath frosting the air between them. Those dark green eyes seemed even more intense in the darkening light. He held her gaze. She could see his chest rise and fall as he watched her, searching her face.

All of a sudden she felt a little self-conscious. Was there any make-up even left on her skin? When was the last time she'd combed her hair?

This time Sebastian wasn't smiling. He was looking at her in a way she couldn't really fathom. As if there were a thousand thoughts spinning around in his head.

He would be King one day. He would be King of his country. She'd tried not to think about any of this. It had been easy before. He was engaged. He was getting married. He was with someone else.

But now he was here.

Here, in the Cotswolds, to see her. Her, and their baby.

He leaned forward and she held her breath, wondering what would happen next.

His arm brushed against hers as he pulled open the car door. 'Then let's do something about that,' he said huskily.

Snowflakes started to fall around her. She looked up at the now dark purple streaked sky. She could almost swear that there was something sparkling in the air between them.

As she took a step towards the car he turned towards her again, his arm settling at the side of her waist.

'In case you haven't noticed, I'm not a flashy kind of guy. I like classics. Things that will last a lifetime. Something that every time you look at it, it makes your heart flutter just a little. Because you know it's a keeper. You know it was made just for you.'

She couldn't breathe. She couldn't actually breathe. Large snowflakes were landing on his head and shoulders. His warm breath touched her cheek as he spoke—he was that close. Her hand rose automatically, resting on his arm. They were face to face. Almost cheek to cheek. If she tilted her chin up just a little…

But she couldn't. Not yet. Maybe not ever. She needed her head to be clear around Sebastian. And right now it was anything but clear.

It was full of intense green eyes framed by dark lashes, a sexy smile and sun-kissed skin. She could smell the leather of his jacket mingling with the familiar scent of his aftershave. She could see the faint shadow along his jaw line. The palm of her hand itched to reach up and touch it.

She hadn't moved. And he hadn't moved either. Being this close was almost hypnotic.

But she had to. She had to look away. She broke his gaze and glanced back at the car. 'It's blue,' she said. 'I thought all these cars were silver.'

Cars. A safe topic. A neutral topic. Something that would stop the swell of emotion currently rising in her chest.

He blinked. His hand hadn't moved from her currently non-existent waist. He gave a nod. 'A lot of them were silver. James Bond's was silver. But mine? Mine is Caribbean blue. As soon as I saw it, and the red leather interior, I knew it was perfect. I had to have it.'

He held her gaze again and she licked her lips anxiously. *I had to have it* echoed in her head. Why did it feel as if he wasn't talking about the car?

There was a screech behind them. A bang. A huge shattering of glass. And they both jumped apart.

Two seconds later the air was filled by a blood-curdling scream.

Sebastian didn't hesitate. He ran instantly towards the scream.

The doctor's instinct in her surged forward. She

glanced towards the hospital doors. She could go and ask for help but Teddy's only took maternity and paediatric emergencies. It wasn't a district general and she didn't even know what was wrong yet.

She started running. Running wasn't easy at her current state of pregnancy. The ground was slippery beneath her feet as snow was just starting to settle on the ground.

As she reached the road that ran alongside the hospital she could see immediately what was wrong. One car had skidded and hit a lamp post. Another car had mounted the pavement and was now embedded in the dress shop's window. The Christmas decorations that had decorated the window were scattered across the street. She winced as her foot crunched on a red bauble. Sebastian was trying to talk to the woman who was screaming. He had his hands on both of her shoulders and was trying to calm her down.

Sienna's eyes swept over the scene, trying to make sense of the situation. An air bag had exploded in the car that had hit the lamp post. A young woman was currently slumped against it.

The other driver was slumped too. But there was no airbag. It was an older car and his head and shoulders were over the steering wheel of the car. The windscreen was shattered and shards of glass from the shop's window frame were directly above him.

The woman on the pavement was obviously in shock. She'd stopped screaming and was talking nonstop between sobs to Sebastian.

He turned towards her, his eyes wide. 'Her kid. Her kid is under the car.'

Another bystander stepped forward and put his arm around the woman, nodding towards Sebastian and Sienna. 'I've phoned an ambulance.'

Sienna gulped. She was familiar with obstetric emergencies. She was often called in for a consult if there could be an issue with the baby. Paediatric emergencies took up half of all her days. Neonates had a tendency to become very sick, very quickly and she needed to be available.

But regular emergencies?

She dropped to her knees and peered under the car. There was a mangled pushchair, and further away, out of her reach, a little figure.

Her heart leapt. Sebastian dropped down next to her, his head brushing against hers as he looked under the car.

He pressed his hand over hers. It was the quickest movement. The warmth of his hand barely had time to make an impact on her. 'I'll go.'

She hardly had time to speak before Sebastian was wriggling his way under the car. She opened her mouth to object just as baby gave her an almighty kick. Her hand went automatically to her belly. Of course. There was no way she could possibly fit under the body of the car—Sebastian was already struggling.

She edged around the front of the vehicle, watching the precarious shards of glass hanging above the car and staying on the ground as low as she could. The slush on the ground soaked her knees and legs, her cream winter coat attracting grime that would never be removed. She slid her arms out of the coat and pulled it over her head—at least she'd have some protection if glass fell.

'Can you try and feel for a pulse?' she said quietly to Sebastian, then added, 'Do you know what to do?'

There was a flicker of light. Sebastian had wriggled his phone from his pocket and turned on the torch, lying it on the ground next to him.

In amongst the darkness and wetness, Sienna thought

she could spot something else. The little boy was still tangled in part of the buggy and her view was still partially obscured.

She turned to the people behind her. 'Can someone find out the little boy's name for me, please?'

Sebastian's face was grim; he had a hand up next to the little boy's head. 'Yes, I've got a pulse. It's fast and it feels faint.'

Truth was, so did she.

She nodded. 'What position is he in?'

Right now she so wished she could be under there. Her frustration at not being able to get to the child was building by the second.

'He's on his back. Wait.'

She couldn't see what Sebastian was doing. He was moving his hand and holding up the torch to the little guy's face.

A voice in her ear nearly made her jump out of her skin. 'Gabriel. The little boy's name is Gabriel.'

She sucked in a breath. 'Sebastian, tell me what's wrong. What can you see? His name is Gabriel. Is he conscious?'

The wait must only have been a few seconds but it felt like so much longer.

Sebastian's face was serious. He held up one hand, palm facing towards her, and held his phone with the other so she could see. It was stained red.

'There's blood, Sienna. Lots of it. He's pale but there's something else—his lips are going a funny colour.'

Sienna turned to the crowd again, searching for the man's face she'd seen earlier. 'Any news about the ambulance?'

The man shook his head. 'Someone has run over to the hospital to try and get more help and some supplies.'

She nodded. 'I need swabs. Bandages. Oxygen. A finger monitor if they've got one.'

'I'll go,' said a young woman and ran off towards the hospital entrance.

Sienna felt in her pocket. All she had was an unopened packet of tissues. Not exactly the ideal product—but at least they were clean.

She threw them towards Sebastian. 'It's all I've got. Try and stem the flow of blood. Where is it coming from?'

Sebastian moved his body, blocking her view again, and she almost whimpered in frustration. She felt useless here. Absolutely useless. She couldn't check the child properly, assess any injuries or provide any care. It was the only time in her life she'd regretted being pregnant.

But Sebastian was calm. He wasn't panicking. He hadn't hesitated to slip under the car and help in any way that he could. As she watched he tore open the packet of tissues and tried to stem the flow of blood.

'It's coming from the side of his neck. I think he's been hit by some of the glass.' He paused for a second and she instantly knew something was wrong.

'What is it? Tell me?'

Sebastian kept his voice low. 'His lips are blue, Sienna.'

She hated this. She hated feeling helpless. 'Do you know what the recovery position is? Turn him on his side, Seb. Open his mouth and try and clear his airway. Check there's nothing inside his mouth. He's not getting enough oxygen into his lungs.'

The noise around them was increasing. There was a faint wail of sirens in the distance. The volume of the murmuring voices was increasing. People were always drawn to the scene of an accident. She could hear someone shouting instructions. A voice with some authority attached to it. She could only pray it was a member of the hospital staff dealing with one of the drivers.

The driver. She should really look at him too. But her first priority was this child. If Gabriel didn't breathe he would be dead. If his airway was obstructed he would be dead. She had no idea the extent of his other injuries but no oxygen would certainly kill him. If she had a team around her right now they would take time to stabilise the little guy's head and neck. But she didn't have a team—and there wasn't time.

All she had was Sebastian—the Prince from another country who was under there trying to be her right-hand man.

She could hear him talking to the little boy, coaxing him, trying to see if he could get any response. Shadows were shifting under the car; it was still difficult to see what was going on.

'Sebastian? Have you stopped the bleeding? What about his colour? Have you managed to put him in the recovery position yet?'

'Give me a minute.' The voice was firm and steady.

He doesn't have a minute. She had to bite her tongue to stop herself from saying it out loud. There was a clatter beside her. 'Sorry,' breathed a young woman. 'More help is coming.'

Sienna looked at the ground. There was a plastic tray loaded with supplies. She grabbed for the pulse oximeter. It was one of the simplest pieces of equipment they had—a simple little rubber pouch with a sensor that fitted over a finger and gave you an indication of someone's oxygen levels. She switched it on and reached as far under the car as she should, touching Sebastian's back.

'Here. Take this. Put it over his finger and tell me what the number is.'

Sebastian's position shifted. 'Come on, Gabriel,' he was saying encouragingly. He'd moved his torch. It was right at Gabriel's face, which was now facing away from her. For the briefest second she could see Sebastian's face reflected in the glass. He was focused. Concern and anxiety written all over his face.

She held her breath. His hand reached behind him to grab hold of the monitor. He'd heard her. He was just focusing on Gabriel.

She could almost swear her heart squeezed. If she were under the car right now, that was exactly how she'd be.

Focused on Gabriel. Not on any of the noise or circumstances around them.

'Watch out!' came the shout from her side.

There was a large crash and splinters of glass showered around her like an explosion of tiny hailstones. Her reaction was automatic: she ducked even lower, pulling the coat even further over her head. There were a few shrieks around her. Sebastian's head shot around. 'Sienna?'

His gaze met hers. He was worried. And he wasn't worried about himself. And for the tiniest second he wasn't thinking about Gabriel. He was thinking about her.

She didn't have time. She didn't have time to think about what that might mean. The cramped position was uncomfortable and baby wasn't hesitating to let her know it.

'His colour. How's his colour, Sebastian?'

Sebastian quickly looked back to Gabriel. 'It's better,' he said. 'He's still pale but the blueness is gone.'

Sienna breathed a sigh of relief. 'Put the monitor on his finger and tell me the reading.'

The sirens were getting much louder now; the ambulances must be almost there.

Sienna started grabbing some more of the supplies. Swabs, tape, some saline. She unwound the oxygen mask from the canister.

'Ninety-one. His reading is ninety-one. Is that good?' She could see the anxiety on his face. His steady resolve was starting to fade a little.

If she were in a hospital she'd say no. But since they were cramped under a car with a little boy bleeding and on his side she remained optimistic. Sebastian had done a good job. She was surprised at how good he'd been. He had no background in medicine. No training. But he hadn't hesitated to assist. And the weird thing was he'd been so in tune with her. He'd done everything she'd instructed. He'd been calm and competent, and somehow she knew inside that she wouldn't have expected Sebastian to act in any other way.

She took a deep sniff. No smell of petrol. No reason to deny Gabriel oxygen. She switched on the canister and unwound the tubing, pushing the mask towards Sebastian. 'Try and hold this in front of his mouth and nose. Let's see if we can get that level up a little.'

Something green flashed to her side. The knees of a paramedic as he bumped down beside her. He lifted the edge of her coat. 'Hey, Doc, it's you.'

She jerked at the familiar voice and felt a wave of relief. Sam, an experienced paramedic she'd met on a number of occasions, gave her a worried smile. He glanced upwards. 'I'm getting you out of here. Tell me what I need to know.'

She spoke quickly. 'There's a little boy trapped under

the car. He was in his buggy. He looks around three. His name is Gabriel. His mother is being cared for at the side by someone.' She almost stuck her head out from the coat to look around but Sam shook his head. She pointed under the car. 'He was blue. My friend had to move him into the recovery position and he's bleeding. His sats are ninety-one. There's oxygen under there too.'

Sam nodded solemnly. He didn't remark on the fact Gabriel had been moved. He just peered under the car. 'Who's your friend?'

She hesitated. 'Seb—Sebastian. He's just visiting.'

Sam had never been slow. 'Oh, the mystery Prince everyone's talking about. Is he a doctor?'

She pretended not to hear the first part of the conversation. 'No, he's not a doctor. He's just been doing what I told him to do.' She patted her stomach. 'I couldn't quite fit.'

Sam nodded and jerked his head. 'Right, move away and stay under that coat. Back away slowly. I'll get your friend to come out and I'll replace him.' Another siren came screaming up behind them. 'That'll be Fire and Rescue. They'll help with the car and the glass.' He gave her another look. 'Now move, pregnant lady, or I'll admit you with something or other.'

She gave a grateful smile. Sam wasn't joking. She backed away to let him do his job. She heard him give Sebastian a few instructions then, in the space of under a minute, Sebastian slid out from under the car and Sam replaced him. His colleague appeared with the Fire and Rescue crew and everything just seemed to move quickly.

Sebastian moved over to her and wrapped his arm around her shoulders. 'You okay?'

There was a tiny smudge of blood just above his eye. She felt in her pocket. No tissues. They'd used them.

She gave a nod. His jeans and jacket were muddy and dirty—as was her cream coat. Truth was, it would never recover. She shivered and pushed her arms into the damp coat. 'I'm fine. Give me a minute and I'll find something to clean your face.'

He shook his head, just as there was a shout and another shard of glass fell from the shattered shop window. Sebastian winced. But he didn't try and pull her away. He must have known she'd refuse. Instead they waited for another fifteen minutes as the Fire and Rescue crew worked alongside the paramedics and police to help all the victims of the accident.

Now she had time to take her breath she could survey just how bad things looked. The two drivers were quickly extricated from the cars, neck collars in place, one conscious and one still unconscious.

A policewoman was standing with Gabriel's mum. The poor woman looked terrified. Once the hanging shards of glass had been safely cleared from the shop window, the fire crew surrounded the car and, on instruction, just bodily lifted it to allow Sam to slide out from underneath with Gabriel on a sliding board. The buggy was still tangled around his legs.

Sienna drew in a sharp breath as her baby kicked in sympathy. Half of her wanted to rush back over and offer to help, but she knew that Sam and his colleague were more than qualified to do emergency care. Gabriel didn't need cardiac surgery—trauma wasn't exactly her field, and part of being a good physician was knowing when to step back.

Sebastian didn't rush her. He didn't try to hurry her away from the site of the crash. As they watched all the accident victims being loaded into the ambulances he just kept his arm wrapped firmly around her shoulders.

She was glad of it. The temperature seemed to have dropped around them and the underlying shiver hadn't left her body.

A few of her colleagues who'd also helped at the scene came over and spoke to her. One of the midwives gave a wry smile. 'Can't remember the last time I treated a seventy-year-old man.' She shook her head as she headed back towards the hospital main entrance.

Sienna turned to Sebastian. 'I think it's probably time for us to go.'

He nodded and glanced down at their clothes and smiled. 'Somehow I think dinner should wait.'

She put her hand to her mouth. 'We can't go in that gorgeous car while we're so mucky.'

As they walked towards the car he let out a laugh. 'That's the beauty of a leather interior—any dirt will wipe clean. Don't worry about it.'

Her stomach gave a growl. 'Let's pick up some take-out,' she said quickly.

Sebastian gave a little frown. She almost laughed out loud. He was a prince. The last time he'd eaten take-out he'd probably been a university student. She made a note to ask Oliver about that. For all she knew, Sebastian had arrived at university with his own chef. It was time to show him how the other half lived.

He held open the door for her again. She shot him a wicked smile. 'What will we have—Chinese? Indian? Pizza? Or fish and chips?'

He made something resembling a strangled sound and gave a sort of smile. 'You choose,' he said as he closed the door and walked around to the other side of the car.

She waited until he'd climbed in. 'Pizza it is, then. There's a place just five minutes from where I live. It does the best pizzas around here.'

She settled into the comfortable seat. Even the smell in the car sent little shivers down her spine. It was gorgeous. It was luxurious. It just felt...different from anything she'd been in before.

Sebastian started the engine. It was a smooth ride; even the engine noise was soothing.

She gestured to the sleek black car following behind them. 'Do they follow you everywhere?'

He gave a little shrug. 'It's their job. They've learned to be unobtrusive. I promise, you won't even know that they're around.'

She smiled. 'Do you have to buy them dinner too?'

He laughed and shook his head. 'Don't worry. They'll make their own arrangements.'

She gave him directions, pointing him to the pizza shop.

When they pulled up outside she went to open the door but he grabbed hold of her hand. 'No way. You stay where you are. I'll order. What would you like?'

Part of her wanted to refuse. But she'd spent so long outside in the freezing temperatures that her body was only just starting to heat up. She didn't answer straight away and he prompted again. 'What's your favourite pizza?'

'What's yours?'

Their voices almost came out in sync. 'Ham, onion and mushroom.'

Silence. Both of them stared at each other for a second and then both started laughing.

She shook her head. 'Seriously? Really?'

He nodded. 'Really.'

She held up her hand. 'Wait a minute. Deep pan or thin crust?'

He glanced outside at the thick snow that was falling around the car. 'Somehow, I think tonight has to be deep pan night.'

She gave a thoughtful nod. 'I think you could be right.'

She reached out and touched his hand, narrowing her eyes suspiciously. 'Seriously, when was the last time you ate pizza?'

He winked and climbed out of the car. 'That's for me to know and you to guess. Give me five minutes.' He slammed the door and ducked into the pizzeria.

She watched while he placed his order and talked away to the guys behind the counter. Within a few moments they were all laughing. She, in the meantime, was kind of fixated on the view from the back.

She was ignoring the grime and mud all down one side of his probably designer jeans and staring instead at the distinctive shape of his broad shoulders and muscled arms under his leather jacket. If she followed the gaze down to the jeans…

Her body gave an inadvertent shudder as baby decided to remind her of his or her presence. It felt odd having the same urge of sensations she'd felt the last time she'd been around Sebastian. It seemed like a lifetime ago now. And yet…it felt as if it had just happened yesterday.

But it hadn't been yesterday, it had been months ago.

And months ago she hadn't been this shape. Months ago, she hadn't needed to adjust her position every few minutes in an attempt to try and get comfortable. Months ago her breasts hadn't virtually taken over her body. Months ago she hadn't spent her days considering where the nearest loo was.

Months ago she'd been happy to toss her clothes across the bedroom floor and let the sun streaming through the windows drench her skin.

She sighed and settled back into the seat.

Then sat straight back up again.

Her house. She would be taking Sebastian to her house.

Now they weren't having dinner at some random neutral venue. They were both covered in mud. She'd need to invite him in, and to clean up.

Sebastian. In her home.

The place where she'd made plans. The nursery that was almost finished. The wooden crib that had arrived and was still in its flat-pack box as she was so disappointed by it.

The drawer with tiny white socks and Babygros.

Her stomach gave another leap as she saw Sebastian give the guys a wave and pick up the large pizza box. How would it feel to have Prince Sebastian Falco in her home?

It was almost as if the atmosphere in the car had changed in his absence. Sienna seemed a little tense as he handed her the pizza box. She gave him stilted directions to her house and one-word answers on the five-minute drive.

He had to admit the smell from the pizza box wasn't too bad. The last pizza he'd eaten had been prepared by a Michelin-starred chef. But somehow he knew that wasn't something he should share with Sienna right now.

Earlier, he'd felt the connection to her. It didn't matter he'd been completely out of his depth and—truth be told—a tiny bit terrified of doing something wrong under that car. But every ounce of his body had told him he had to help. There was no way he could leave an injured child under a car on his own, and, with Sienna's instructions, he'd felt confident to just do as she asked.

It didn't help that the whole time he'd been under there

he'd been thinking about the perilous glass dangling directly above the car and Sienna's body.

They turned onto a tree-lined street. Each house was slightly different from the one next to it. Most were painted white, and most were bungalows. A few had sprawling extensions and others had clearly extended into the roof of their property.

Sienna pointed to the left and he pulled up outside a white bungalow with large bay windows and a bright red door. It was covered in a dusting of snow and there were little white lights strung around one of the trees in the front garden.

It wasn't a castle. It wasn't a mansion house. It wasn't even a chalet in the mountains. But he could sense her air of pride. He could instantly tell how much she loved this place.

He gave her a smile. 'It's lovely.'

She let out a deep breath as her eyes fixed on her home. 'Thank you. I love it.'

He walked around quickly, holding the door open for her and lifting the pizza box from her hands. She opened the garden gate and they walked up the path to the front door.

Warmth hit them as soon as she opened the front door. She gave him a smile. 'I have a wood-burning stove. Costs next to nothing. I stack it full in the morning and it burns all day. I'd hate to come home to a cold house.'

A cold house. There was just something about the way she said those words. Almost as if cold didn't only refer to the room temperature.

She walked through to the kitchen and took the pizza, sliding it into her bright red Aga stove. She bit her lip as she turned towards him. 'I don't really have anything you can change into. You can clean up in my bathroom if you want. There are fresh towels in there if you want to use the shower.'

He could tell she was a little uncomfortable. He had no problem taking a shower in Sienna's home—it might actually help warm up his bones a little—but he didn't want to make her feel any more uncomfortable than she already did. He tried not to stare at his surroundings. There was tinsel looped over the fridge. An advent calendar with doors open hanging on the wall, and an array of little Santa ornaments lining the window ledge. Sienna really did love Christmas.

'Do you want me to leave?'

He almost held his breath.

'No. No, I don't.' She slid her dirty coat from her shoulders. 'Look, I'm going to put this in the wash. Leave your dirty clothes at the bathroom door and I'll wash them too. There's a white bathrobe on a hook behind the door. You can wear that while we eat dinner.'

He gave a little nod and walked down the corridor depositing his jeans and T-shirt outside the bathroom door. By the time he'd showered—and scoped out the bathroom for any non-existent male accessories—the pizza was back out of the oven and she had some glasses on the table.

He almost laughed out loud. The dressing gown covered him. But not entirely. His bare legs were on display and, although he'd managed to tie the waist, it gaped a little across his broad chest. It was clear Sienna was trying to avoid looking too closely.

He sat down at the table opposite her and adjusted it as best he could. 'It's not like you haven't seen it all before,' he half teased.

Colour flushed her cheeks. She lifted up the diet soda and started pouring it into glasses. 'Yeah, but I haven't seen it sitting at my kitchen table. Things that happen in Montanari tend to stay in Montanari.'

He tried not to flinch. It was a throwaway comment. He pointed towards her stomach as she served the pizza onto plates. 'It seems that what we did didn't want to stay in Montanari. It wanted to get right out there.'

He was doing his best to lead up to something. He'd had four phone calls today from the royal family's publicist. The British media knew he was here. The white-wash about twinning the two hospitals had quickly came unstuck. Any investigative journalist worth their salt wouldn't take too long to find out why he was really here. He expected to be headline news tomorrow.

She set down his plate with a clatter and before she could snatch her hand away he covered it with his own. 'Sienna, are you okay?'

She shot him an angry glance and walked around to the other side of the table and sat down, staring at him, then the pizza, then him again.

He folded his arms. 'Okay, hit me with it. It's time we were honest with each other.'

She pressed her lips together for a few seconds, then blurted out, 'Why are you here, Sebastian? What is it—exactly—that you want from me?'

He sighed. 'I'm here because of you, Sienna. Even if I hadn't heard about the baby I would never have gone through with the marriage to Theresa. I'm not my parents. I can't live that life. No matter how much they want me to.' He stared at the woman across the table from him.

She had little lines around her eyes. Her hands were spotless but there was one tiny mud splash on her cheek. Her pale skin was beautiful. Her light brown eyes looked tired. Her blonde hair had half escaped from the pony-tail band at the nape of her neck. Her cheeks were a little fuller than when they'd been together last; her whole body had blossomed and it kind of suited her.

In short, he'd never seen anyone look so beautiful.

'Baby or not, I would always have come back for you, Sienna,' he said quietly. 'I thought marriage was about a union between countries. I thought I could tolerate a marriage to a friend. But as soon as it was announced I felt as if the walls were closing in around me. It wasn't enough. I'm not built that way. I just hadn't realised it. A marriage to Theresa would have made her miserable, and me miserable. It could never have lasted.'

There was silence in the room. The only sounds from the ticking clock on the wall and the rumble from the washing machine in the next-door utility room.

She licked her lips. Those luscious pink lips that he ached to taste again. 'I don't believe you,' she whispered. 'You want the heir to your kingdom. You don't want me. I was just the stranger to have sex with.'

There was hurt—hurt written all over her face. A face he wanted to cradle in his hands.

He took his time to choose his words. 'It was sex. It was great sex. With a woman who managed to crawl under my skin and stay there. A woman who has haunted my dreams—day and night—ever since. The baby is a bonus, Sienna. A wonderful, beautiful bonus that I'm still getting my head around and I get a little more excited about every day.'

Part of what he'd said was true. She had got under his skin. He'd thought about her every single day. He'd just not ever considered making her his Queen.

But this baby? This baby was too important. In a way, it would be easier if it weren't Sienna that was having his baby. Theresa had been easy to put in a little box in his head. She was a friend. She would only ever be a friend.

But Sienna? She was spreading out of any little box like a new and interesting virus. One that had started reproducing the first second that he'd met her. He couldn't squash her into some box in his head.

Because he *felt* something for her.

He just wasn't entirely sure what that was—or what it could be.

Fear flashed across her eyes and her hands went protectively to her stomach. 'This is my baby, Sebastian. Mine. I get to choose. I get to say what happens. You haven't been here. You can't just show up for the grand finale and expect to be the ringmaster at the circus. This is my life. Mine.'

He couldn't help it. Emotions were building inside him. He hated that she felt this way. 'But I want it be ours. I want it to be *our* lives. You're writing me off before we've even started. You have to give me a chance. Look at tonight. Look at how we fitted together. Do you think I could have done that with anyone else?' He shook his head. 'Not for a second, Sienna. Only with you.'

He stopped. He had to force himself. He picked up a slice of pizza even though his appetite had left him. 'Let's try and relax a little. It's been a big night. We need some down time.'

He could see a dozen things flitting behind those caramel eyes of hers.

'Stuff it,' she said as she stood up quickly. She marched to the fridge and brought out a white box that came from a bakery. She lifted out the biggest chocolate éclair he'd ever seen and put it on a plate and shrugged. 'Figure you might as well see how I deal with stress. It might give you a hint for the future.'

He sat quietly, trying not to smile as she devoured the

chocolate éclair with a fork and sipped her diet soda. The atmosphere slowly settled.

From the table he could see outside into her snow-covered back garden, framed by the now black sky. It was bigger than he'd expected with an unusual style of seat and a large tree. Next to the seat was a little bush with a string of glowing multicoloured lights that twinkled every now and then.

He smiled. 'You really do like Christmas, don't you?'

She raised her eyebrows. 'Wait until you see the front room.' She sighed as she stared at her back garden. 'I've been here less than a year. I have visions of what my back garden should look like. Our local garden centre has a whole host of light-up reindeers and a family of penguins.' She pointed at the large tree. 'And I wanted lights for that tree too, and a light-up Santa to go underneath. But if I'd bought everything I wanted to, I would have bankrupted myself. So, I've decided to just buy one new thing every year. That way, I can build myself up to what I really imagine it should look like in my head.'

He watched her as she spoke and couldn't help but smile. The more she spoke, the more of a drifting-off expression appeared in her eyes, it was almost as if she were actually picturing what she wanted her garden to look like.

'Why do you like Christmas so much?'

She gave a throwaway shrug. 'I just like what it means.' She paused and bit her lip. 'It was the one time of year my parents didn't fight—probably because my Aunt Margaret came to stay.' She smiled. 'It was almost as if she brought the Christmas spirit with her. She had so much energy. So much joy. When I was little she made every Christmas special. She was obsessed by it. And I guess I caught a little of her bug.'

It was nice seeing her like this. He stood up and lifted his glass of diet soda. 'Okay, hit me with it. Show me the front room.'

She laughed and shook her head as she stood up. This time she didn't avert her eyes from the dressing gown that barely covered him. She waved her hand. 'Give me a second.' Then she walked along the corridor and bent down, flicking a few switches just inside the door. She smiled and stood back against the wall. 'I wanted to give you the full effect.'

He stopped walking. She was talking about her front room. He knew she was talking about her front room. But he was already getting the full effect. The full Sienna McDonald effect. Every time she spoke with that lilting Scottish accent it sent blood rushing around his body. Every time their gazes connected he felt a little buzz.

She looked excited. It was obvious she was proud of whatever he was about to see.

The main lights in her room weren't on. They weren't needed, because every part of the room seemed to twinkle with something or other.

He stepped inside. The tree took pride of place at the large bay window. The red berry lights twinkled alongside the red decorations. In the corner of the room were three lit-up white and red parcels of differing sizes. A backlit wooden nativity scene was set out on a wooden cabinet. The pale cream wall above her sofa was adorned with purple and white twinkling stars.

In the other corner of the room were a variety of Christmas village ornaments. All had little lights. He smiled as he noticed the school room, the bakery, the shop and Santa's Christmas workshop.

The one thing he noticed most about this place was the warmth. Nothing like his Christmases in the palace in Montanari. Oh, the decorations had been beautiful. But anonymous people had arrived and assembled them every year. There was no real connection to the family. Everything was impersonal. Most of the time he was told not to touch. Sienna's home had a depth that he hadn't experienced before.

He turned to face her. 'It's like a Christmas grotto in here. How long did this take you?'

She shrugged. 'Not long. Well…maybe a few days.'

He stepped a little closer. Close enough to feel her swollen stomach against his. The rest of the room was dark. He reached up and touched the smudge on her cheek. 'You didn't get a chance to clean up, did you? I wonder how little Gabriel is doing.'

She froze as soon as he touched her cheek. Maybe it was too familiar a gesture? Too forward of him. The tip of his finger tingled from where he'd come into contact with her skin. He couldn't help but touch her again. This time brushing her cheek as he tucked a wayward strand of hair behind her ear.

Her eyes looked darker in here. Or maybe it was just the fact her pupils had dilated so much, they were currently only rimmed with a tiny edge of brown.

'I'll phone the hospital later.' Her voice was husky, almost a whisper. If she objected to his closeness she hadn't said.

He took in a deep breath. A deep breath of her.

There it was. The raspberry scent of her shampoo, mixed with the light aroma of her subtle perfume and just the smell of her. For Sebastian it was intoxicating. Mesmerising. And sent back a rush of memories.

His fingers hesitated around her ear. He didn't want to pull them away. He didn't want to be out of contact with her.

This felt like something he'd never experienced before. Something worth waiting for.

She bit her bottom lip again and he couldn't stop himself. He pulled her closer and met her lips with his. Taste. He could taste her. The sweetness of the éclair. Now, he truly was having a rush of memories.

The memory of her kiss would be imprinted on his brain for ever. Her lips slowly parted and his fingers tangled through her hair, capturing the back of her head to keep her there for ever.

Her hands wound around his neck as she tilted her head even further to his. Somehow the fact that her swollen belly was next to his was even better than he could have imagined. Their child was in there. Their child was growing inside her. In a few weeks' time he'd be a father. And no matter what his parents might think, he couldn't wish for a better mother for his child.

His hand brushed down the side of her breast and settled on her waist.

He felt her tense. Slow their kiss. He let their lips part and she pressed her forehead against his. Her breathing was rapid.

He stayed like that for a second, letting them both catch their breath.

'Sebastian,' she breathed heavily.

'Yes?'

She lifted her heavy eyelids to meet his gaze. 'You have to give me a minute. Give me a few seconds. I need to go and change.'

He stepped back. 'Of course. No problem.'

He'd no idea what that meant. Change into what?

She disappeared into the corridor and he sank down into her comfortable red sofa for a few minutes, his heart thudding against his chest.

Maybe she wanted him to leave. Maybe she wanted him to stay.

He'd always been confident around women. He'd always felt in charge of a relationship. But things were different with Sienna.

Everything was at stake here.

Sebastian didn't do panic. But right now, if he said the wrong thing, he could mess up everything. And what was the right thing to say to a pregnant woman who'd already told you she wanted the fairy tale?

He looked around the room. The Christmas grotto. Sienna's own personal fairy tale. No castle. No prince. Just this. He tried to shift on the sofa but it was almost impossible. It was one of those sink-in-and-lose-yourself-for-ever kind of sofas.

Sienna had a good life here. She had a house that she loved. Loyal friends and the job of her dreams. The truth was, she didn't really need him. If Sebastian wanted to have a place in her life he was going to have to fight for it.

And he had to be sure what he was fighting for.

He'd meant it when he told her he'd always have come back for her. At first, it had just been words. He just hadn't said the next part—he just wasn't entirely sure what he was coming back *for*.

Someone to have a relationship with? An affair?

Or something else entirely?

It hadn't even been clear in his head until that moment. But as he'd watched her face he'd had a second of pure clarity—sitting across the table was exactly what he wanted. Tonight had given him a new perspective. If he hadn't been there he didn't doubt that Sienna would have put herself in harm's way to try and help that child. It was part of what he admired so much about her.

This might not be the way he had planned it. But Sebastian was always up for a challenge.

Sienna walked back into the room. She glanced at the gaping dressing gown and looked away. 'Your jeans are washed. I've put them in the dryer. They won't be long.'

He nodded. 'Thanks. Now, come and sit down. It's been a big day. Sit for a while.'

He could see her hesitation. See her weighing up what to do next. She'd washed her face, pulled her hair into some kind of knot and changed into what looked like pyjamas.

She walked over and sat down next to him, curling one leg up underneath her. He wrapped his arm back around her shoulder.

Sienna wanted things to be by her rules. He wanted to keep her happy.

'Tell me what you've organised for the baby. What would you like me to do?'

She looked at him in surprise. 'Well, I've pretty much organised everything. I've turned one room into a nursery. I just need to give it a lick of paint and some of the furniture has arrived. But I haven't built it yet.'

'Let me do that.'

She blinked. 'Which one?'

'Both. All of them. Do you know what colour you want for the nursery? I could start tomorrow.'

Had he ever painted anything in his life? What did he actually know about room decoration? It didn't matter. If that was what she needed for the baby, then he would find someone to do it. Money wasn't exactly an object for Sebastian. If he paid enough, he could get it done tomorrow.

She drew back a little. It was all he could do not to focus on those lips again. He was trying his best to keep her at arm's length. Even though it was the last thing he wanted to do. If he wanted a chance with Sienna and with his baby, he would have to play by her rules.

'Well, okay,' she said after what seemed like for ever. She pushed herself up from the sofa. 'Come and I'll show you the nursery.'

He tried to follow her and fumbled around on the impossible sofa. 'How on earth did you do that? This thing just swallows you up like one of those sand traps.'

She started laughing. 'It does, doesn't it? It was one of the first things I bought when I got my own flat. I love the colour and, even though it needs replacing, I've never found another sofa quite the colour that I love. So I keep it. The removal men just about killed themselves carrying it down three flights of stairs when I moved from my flat to here.'

He gave himself an almighty push and almost landed on top of her. 'Oh, sorry.' His hand fell automatically to her waist again. It hadn't been deliberate. Not at all. But not a single part of his body wanted to move.

This was his problem. His brain was screaming a thousand things at him. He was getting too attached. He was beginning to feel something for Sienna. Something other than the blood rushing through his body. The rational part of his brain told him she didn't really want him, she didn't want to be part of the monarchy in Montanari. She was probably the most unsuitable woman to be his wife.

But little question marks kept jumping into his thoughts. Was she really so unsuitable? She was brilliant. She had a career. She was a good person. Yes, she was probably a little unconventional. She certainly didn't hesitate to speak her mind. But, after spending his life around people who didn't say what they meant, it was actually kind of refreshing. Add that to the fact that even a glimpse of her sent his senses into overload…

She pulled back a little from him so he dropped a kiss on her forehead and stepped away. 'Blame the sofa.' He smiled.

She showed him across the hall to the nursery. So far he'd seen the bathroom, the main room, the kitchen and the utility. Two other doors in the corridor seemed to glow at him. One of them must be her bedroom.

He waved his hand casually. 'This is a nice house. What's down there?'

She looked over her shoulder. 'Just my bedroom and the third room, which is a dining room/bedroom. I hadn't quite decided what I wanted to do with it yet. There's another sitting room at the back, but the house layout is a little awkward. I think the people that built the house added it on at the last minute. It ended up being off the utility room.'

Sebastian gave a nod as she flicked the switch on the room she'd designated the nursery.

It was a good-sized room. There was a pin board on the wall covered in messages and cut-out pictures. Some were of prams, some of other nurseries, some of furniture and a few of treehouses and garden play sets.

He smiled as he looked at them all. She pointed to one of the pictures. 'That one. That's what I decided on.'

It was lovely. A pale yellow nursery, with a border with ducks and teddy bears and with pale wooden furniture.

She nodded towards the flat boxes leaning against one wall. 'It only arrived yesterday.' There was a kind of sad twang in her voice.

He walked towards it. 'What's wrong?'

She sighed. 'Nothing. It's just not quite what I'd hoped for. I'm sure it will look fine once it's all built. But there was no point in building it until I'd painted the room and put the border up.'

One of the ends of the flat-pack furniture box was open and he peered inside, reaching in with his hand to touch the contents. He got it. He got it straight away. The furniture on the picture on her pin board looked like solid oak with delicate carving and professional workmanship. Furniture bought from a store would never compare. He knew exactly what he could say right now, but he had to be careful of her feelings. She'd worked hard to make preparations for their child.

'Do you know what shade of yellow you want?'

She pointed to the corner of the room. There were around ten different little squares of varying shades of yellow. 'Yeah, I picked the one three from the end. I've bought the paint, I was planning on starting tomorrow.'

She walked over to a plastic bag. 'I have the border here, along with the matching light shade and bedding.'

He took a deep breath as he walked a little closer. 'I really want to help. I really want to be involved. Will you let me paint the room for you tomorrow? And hang the border? Once that's done I can build the furniture, and if you don't like it we can see if there's something more suitable.'

This was the point where she could step away. This was the point where he could end up flung out of the house. But she stayed silent. He could see her thinking things through. The reserve that she'd built around herself seemed to be slipping a little, revealing the Sienna that he'd connected with in Montanari.

His finger wanted to speed dial someone right now. There had to be someone around here that could help make good on his promises.

She nodded slowly then met his gaze with a gentle smile. 'Do you know what? That might actually be good…thanks.' She narrowed her gaze and wagged her finger at him. 'But you're not allowed to bring in someone else to do it. You have to do it yourself. I don't want anyone I don't know in my house.'

There was a tiny wave of unease. She could read him like a book. 'Of course. Of course, I'll do it myself. It will be my pleasure.' He looked around the room. It would be nice with the pale yellow colour on the walls.

He'd tell her things on a need-to-know basis.

He walked back to the pin board and pointed at the prams. 'Have you ordered one yet?'

The two on the board were both brightly coloured with modern designs. Nothing like the coach-built pram he'd been pictured in as a child. He gave a little smile, thinking about his room as a small child with its dark furniture and navy blue drapes.

She stepped up next to him. 'What are you smiling at?'

He gave a sigh. 'I know nothing about prams. But they both look kind of funky. I'm sure I won't have a clue how to put them together.'

Her gaze changed. It was thoughtful. Almost as if she'd finally realised that he planned on being around. Planned on being involved.

'You can buy a plain black one if you want,' she said softly. There was something sad in her voice.

His hand reached down and he intertwined his fingers with hers. 'I'll be proud to push whatever red or purple pram you choose. Why don't you let me buy you both? That's if you haven't ordered one yet.'

She paused. She hadn't pulled her hand away. He started tracing little circles in the palm of her hand with his thumb. 'Sienna, I'm here because I want to be here. I want to be here for you, and for our baby. But...' he turned to face her straight on '...this might all get a little pressured. I have to tell my parents that they're going to be grandparents.'

Her eyes widened. 'They don't know?'

'Not yet. I wanted to speak to you first. To give you a little time.' He reached and tangled his fingers through her hair. 'Once I tell them, the world will know. You won't just be Sienna McDonald, cardiothoracic neonatal surgeon any more. You'll be Sienna McDonald, mother of Prince Sebastian Falco's child. I want to protect you from that. You'll be bombarded with phone calls and emails. Everyone will want a little piece of you.' He shook his head. 'I don't want that.' He gave her a sorry smile. 'There's not enough of you to go round.'

For a moment she looked terrified. Surely, she must have expected this at some point. Surely she must have realised that the press would be interested in their baby?

Maybe his concerns about her had been right.

Her response was a little shaky. 'I don't want people interfering in my life. I'm a surgeon. I do a good job. I've made plans on how to raise this baby.'

Something twisted inside him. He wanted to say everything he shouldn't. He might only have known about this baby for a couple of weeks but every sleepless night had been full of plans for this child too.

Somehow he had to find a way to cement their plans together. There would need to be compromise on each side. How on earth would Sienna cope with his mother?

His mother's idea of compromise would be to sweep this baby from under Sienna's nose, transport the baby to the palace in Montanari and bring up the child with the same ideals she'd had for Sebastian.

For about ten seconds that had been his plan too. Had he really thought Sienna would be happy to marry him and leave her job and friends behind?

He could see himself having to spend the rest of his life having to prevent Sienna and his mother from being in the same room together.

It didn't even bear thinking about. There would be time enough for all that later. He had to start slowly.

He looked around the room. Then he glanced at Sienna's stomach. He let the wave of emotions that he'd tried to temper flood through him. That was his baby in there. *His.*

He didn't want to be a part-time parent. He wanted to see this child every day. He wanted to be involved in every decision.

And the truth was, he wanted to be around Sienna too.

He touched her cheek. 'I want to be part of those plans, Sienna. That's all I'm asking.'

She stared at him for the longest time. Her gaze unwavering.

'Let me do something to try and help. Once I've spoken to my parents, can I get one of the publicists from the palace to contact you? To try and take the pressure off any queries you might get from reporters?'

She gave the briefest of nods. At least it was something. It was a start. He hadn't even mentioned the fact that he would actually have to hire security to protect her.

'You can come tomorrow. You'll need to be up early before I go to work.'

He smiled. 'No problem. I like to be up early.' He pointed to the pin board again. 'What about the prams?'

The edges of her lips turned upwards and she gave a little shake of her head. 'You've no idea how hard this is for me.'

'What?' He couldn't keep the mock horror from his voice as he put one hand to his chest. 'You mean letting someone else help? Letting someone else be involved?'

She nodded. She waved at the photos on the board. 'I'm running out of time. I need to order the pram that I want this weekend if it's going to be here on time.' She pulled a face. 'Trouble is, I still can't choose. And the lie-down pram, buggy and car seat all go together. At this rate, if I don't choose soon, I won't even have a way to get my baby home from hospital, let alone out of the house.'

He nodded. She hadn't taken him up on the idea of getting both. 'How about we go this weekend and look again?'

She gave him the strangest look. 'Have you any idea what these places are like? The guys in the giant nursery stores always look like they've been dragged in there kicking and screaming and can't wait to get back out.'

He raised his eyebrows. 'Well, I will be different. I can't wait to spend hours of my life helping you choose between a red and a purple pram set.' He gave a hopeful smile. 'Is there coffee in these places?'

She nodded. 'Oh, yes. But you need to drink decaf in support of me. But there's also cake. So it might not be too bad.'

Finally, he was getting somewhere. Finally he felt as if he was starting to make inroads with Sienna. They'd made a connection today that felt like it had back in Montanari.

And this wasn't just about the baby—even though that was all they'd really talked about. This was about them too.

This would always be about them.

She walked back to the door of the nursery. 'Okay, thanks. Tomorrow it is. Now let me get your clothes. The dryer will be finished by now.'

His heart sank a little. It was time for him to go. It didn't matter how much he actually wanted to stay.

He followed Sienna down the hall as she pulled his clothes from the dryer. The jeans were still warm as he stepped into them and fastened them. He put the dressing gown on top of the dryer and turned to face her.

Her tongue was running along her top lip. She was watching him. Her eyes fixated on his bare chest. He took a step towards her.

'Sienna?'

He could act. He could pull her towards him and kiss her exactly the way he wanted to. But he'd already done that tonight. This time it was important for her to take the lead.

She put one hand flat on his chest and took a deep breath as she looked down at the floor. There was a tremble in her voice. 'You need to give me some time, Seb. It would be so easy just to fall into things again. To take up where we left off. But there's so much more at stake now.'

His heart gave a little jump. Seb. She'd just called him Seb again.

She lifted her head and met his gaze. 'I didn't expect to see you again. I didn't expect you to come.'

He placed his hand over hers. 'And now?'

'You asked me to give you a chance. I want to. I do. But I need to be sure about why we're both here. I've had more time to get used to the thought of our baby than you have. And the thought of being under the gaze of the whole world is something I hadn't even contemplated.'

He gave her hand a squeeze. Now he couldn't help himself. He stepped forward and put his arms around her.

'Let me help. Let me get you some advice. We could release a press statement together if you wanted.'

She pushed back and shook her head. 'Release a press statement? Those are words I never thought I'd hear. Just give me a bit of time, a bit of space. One step at a time,

Seb. If you want me to give you a chance, that's the way it's got to be.'

He was disappointed. He couldn't help it. He was rushing things. But being around Sienna and not *being* with her was more difficult than he could ever have imagined.

Now he felt a sense of panic. What about the press intrusion into Sienna's life? How would she cope? He was used to it. He'd been photographed since the day he was born. But, for Sienna, life was entirely different.

She loved her job. She'd trained long and hard to be a specialist surgeon. Would she be able to continue with the job she loved if she were his wife?

At first his only thought had been about duty. His duty to the mother of his child, and to his country. His proposal of marriage had only been about those things.

Now? Things were changing. Changing in a way he hadn't even contemplated. He gave a half-smile. Was this how Oliver felt around Ella?

He pulled his T-shirt over his head and reached for his leather jacket. She handed him a damp towel. 'Try and take some of the mud off it with this.'

She was so matter-of-fact. So practical. Ten seconds ago she'd been wearing her heart on her sleeve. He wiped the jacket as best he could and slid it on.

'My shoes are next to the door.' He paused; he really didn't want to leave.

She nodded. 'Okay, then. Be here early, around seven-thirty. I'll leave you a key to lock up when you're done.'

She followed him to the door and shivered as the icy blast hit as soon as he opened it. 'Stay inside,' he said quickly. 'Keep warm. I'll see you tomorrow.'

'Seb?'

He'd already gone down the first two steps and turned at the sound of her voice. 'Yeah?'

She closed her eyes for a second. 'Thank you,' she said softly, with one hand on her stomach.

He leaned forward and kissed her cheek. 'Any time. Any time at all.' Then he headed down the path back to his car.

CHAPTER FIVE

She didn't sleep a single wink—just tossed and turned all night.

Eventually, she got up and phoned to check on Gabriel. It was a relief to find out he was stable and had regained consciousness.

Seb arrived early with hot pancakes for breakfast and a hire car for her to use. He was in a good mood and only teased her a little when she gave him a list of instructions, including where he was allowed to wear his shoes.

In a lot of ways he was easy to be around. It was easy to forget he was a prince. It was easy to forget he had a whole host of other responsibilities. Ones that would ultimately keep him away from her and their baby.

The first time she knew something was off was when she arrived at work. There was a TV van in the car park and a reporter was shooting a story opposite the main entrance to the hospital.

As soon as she turned into the staff car park one of the porters gave her a nod of his head. He walked quickly to her car. 'You might want to keep your head down and go in the side door.'

She picked up her bag. 'Why? What's happening?'

'You haven't seen it?'

Her phone started ringing. She glanced at the number. Seb. She'd only just left him. Why was he ringing her already? She silenced it as Frank held out his mobile towards her.

There was a photo. A photo of her house. A photo of her and Sebastian in her doorway looking intimate.

The headline wasn't much better.

Montanari's Baby Secret

She put her hand up to her mouth. 'No. No way. Who took that photo? That was last night. Someone was outside my house?' She didn't care about her ratty hair, or the fact she was wearing pyjamas in the photo. It looked as if she'd just fallen out of bed to show Sebastian to the door—that implied a whole lot of other things. All she cared about was the fact someone had been hanging about outside her house, waiting to take a picture. Why hadn't Seb's security people seen them?

Frank glanced over at the crowd in the car park. 'What's with the different car—did you know they'd be here? Trying to throw them off the scent?' He was smiling. It was almost as if he were enjoying the fracas.

'No. My car wouldn't start last night. Sebastian gave me a lift home. This is a hire car. My car's still in the other car park.'

Frank was still watching. 'Pull your hood up and duck in the side door. I'll walk next to you.'

She glanced around the car park. It seemed to be getting busier by the second. She pulled up her hood on her cream coat and walked alongside Frank with her head down. It only took five minutes to reach her office, close the door and turn on the computer. Her phone buzzed again. Seb.

As the computer started to kick into life she sank into

her chair and put the phone to her ear. 'I've seen it. Reporters are all over the hospital. I've got a job to do. I don't need this.'

'I'll deal with it. I'll speak to Oliver and see what we can do. I'll phone you later once we have a press release ready.'

She put down the phone and watched as one headline after another appeared on screen. They had her name, her age, her qualifications. There was a report about the work she'd done in Montanari. There was speculation about how exactly she and Sebastian had met.

There was even more speculation about the timing. His sudden engagement and his wedding announcement, then his even quicker plans to cancel.

There was a camera shot of the King and Queen of Montanari from earlier on this morning. Sebastian's mother looked tight-lipped and quietly furious. He hadn't mentioned them at all. She could only imagine the kind of phone call that had been.

Oliver knocked on the door. 'Sienna? Can we talk?'

She sighed and rolled her eyes. 'Are the board complaining about the *femme fatale* on their staff?'

He snorted. 'Who cares? I'm worried about you. I've called Security. They'll keep an eye out for any reporters.'

'Thank you, Oliver.'

He paused for a second, hovering around the door as only a man who was struggling to find the words could.

She rolled her eyes again. 'What is it, Oliver?'

He pulled a face. 'I've no idea what happened between you before.' Then he shook his head and smiled. 'Well, actually the evidence is there. I've known him since we were at university. He was a few years younger than me but decided to join the same rowing club. We've been friends ever since. I just wanted you to know—I've never seen him like this.'

She frowned. 'Never seen him like what?'

Oliver hesitated again. 'Never seen him act like he's in love before,' he said as he retreated out of the door.

Her head started to swim. After a few seconds she actually put it down between her knees.

Last night had been overwhelming. Having Sebastian in her home, in a state of undress and then in the middle of their baby's nursery, had felt surreal.

She just hadn't pictured it happening in her head. It had seemed so far out of reach that she hadn't allowed her head room for it.

Now, it was a reality.

Now, the man that had haunted her dreams for months was finally only a fingertip away.

But how much was he actually offering?

When he'd told her he would always have come back for her, she'd really, really wanted to believe him. But words were easy. Everyone knew that.

And the fact was he'd left her warm bed and put an engagement ring on another woman's finger.

It didn't matter what the facts or circumstances were. It had still happened.

It had still hurt.

She would love to believe that one snowy day, out of the blue, Sebastian would have turned up on a white stallion to sweep her away from all this and declare his undying love.

But the word love had never been mentioned.

Maybe she was unrealistic. Maybe she was a fool to chase the fairy tale. But after being brought up by parents who clearly didn't love each other she could never do that to her child. Would it be even worse if she loved

Sebastian and he never quite loved her? How would their son or daughter feel about being brought up in an uneven relationship blighted by unrequited love?

It was too hard to even imagine.

So, what exactly had Oliver meant? He'd never seen Sebastian in love before?

Her stomach gave a little swirl. When she'd looked into those forest-green eyes last night all she'd been able to think about was how much this guy could hurt her. How much of her heart he'd already stolen despite the walls she'd tried to put up around it.

Self-protect mode seemed easiest.

He was being kind. He was being considerate. But could it really be love and not duty?

Her head wouldn't even let her go there.

There was a knock at her door and Juliet Turner, the neonatal specialist surgeon, walked in with contraband in her hands.

'Sienna? Are you okay?'

Sienna pulled her head up from between her knees and smiled. 'Yeah. Sorry, I'm fine.'

Juliet frowned. 'It seems like I'm just in time. I thought the road to your favourite coffee shop might be lined with reporters this morning, so decided to take the hit for you. Don't worry—it's caffeine-and-sugar-free.'

She set down the coffee and a mystery package in a paper bag. 'Anything I can do for you?'

Sienna shook her head and waved at the contraband. 'You've already done it. Have I told you lately that I love you?' Juliet laughed as Sienna continued, 'How are the quads?'

Juliet smiled. 'Things are looking good. They seem to get a little stronger every day.'

Juliet's pager beeped. She glanced at it and her smile

broadened. 'Charlie. Better go. Wedding plans are in the air.'

She practically danced out of the door as Sienna took a deep breath. It seemed that everyone else in this hospital had managed to find love just in time for Christmas. Max and Annabelle, Oliver and Ella and now Juliet and Charlie.

There was no way she could be that lucky too.

No way at all. The Christmas fairy dust had all been used up around here.

Her phone beeped. She opened the message. There was a photo attached that made her blink twice.

'Yuck,' she said out loud. It was from Sebastian. And it was apparently the colour she'd chosen for the baby's nursery. What she'd thought was pale yellow had actually morphed into something more neon-like. She smiled at the message.

Is this what you had in mind?

She glanced at her watch. Just over an hour and he'd already painted one wall. Too bad he'd need to paint it again.

She replied quickly.

Not quite.

Then she dabbed again.

Not at all!

Sienna jerked as her pager sounded. The caffeine-free skinny latte with sugar-free caramel toppled and some of the hot liquid spilled down her pale pink trousers.

She jumped up. 'Great.' She looked around her office. Of course. There was nothing to mop it from her trousers with—and by the time she found something the brand-new trousers would be stained for life.

She glared at the coffee Juliet had bought for her. 'That'll teach me,' she murmured.

The pager sounded again and she shook her head as she stared at the number. Labour ward. Something must be wrong.

She left the coffee and the tiny cake decorated with holly Juliet had bought to go with it lying on the table. Her appetite had abated already.

She walked quickly down the corridor to the labour ward. She could have phoned, but they usually only paged if they actually needed her.

Kirsty, one of the younger labour-ward midwives, was looking a bit frantic. 'You looking for me?' Sienna asked. This striding quickly was getting a bit more difficult.

'I need you to look at a baby. Labour went perfectly—no concerns. But since delivery the baby has been kind of flat. I called the Paeds and they told me to page you.'

Kirsty hadn't paused for breath, her words getting quicker and quicker. Sienna reached over and put her hand on her arm.

'Kirsty, tell me what I need to know.'

Her eyes widened with momentary panic, then her brain kicked into gear and she nodded. 'Caleb Reed, thirty-six plus three weeks, five pounds eleven ounces. Born two hours. He's pale, irritable and his breathing is quite raspy.'

Sienna walked to the nearest sink and washed her hands. She glanced down at her trousers. If she had a little more time she could put on some scrubs. But best not to keep the paediatrician waiting. 'Which room?'

'Number seven.'

Kirsty walked to the room and stood anxiously at the doorway while Sienna dried her hands.

Sienna gave a nod and walked inside. Lewis Connell, one of her paediatric colleagues, told her everything she needed to know with one glance.

She gave a wide smile to the two anxious parents and held out her hand towards the father, who was perched at the side of the bed. 'Hi, there. I'm Sienna McDonald.' She left her title out of the introduction. There was time enough for that later. The man warily shook her hand. 'John,' he said, and she held it out in turn to the mother. 'Dr Connell has asked me to come and take a look at your son. Congratulations. What have you called him?'

It didn't matter that she already knew. She was trying to get a feeling about the parents and how prepared they might be for what could come next.

The mother seemed a little calmer. 'Caleb. We've called him Caleb. And I'm Lucy.' She glanced at Sienna's stomach. 'When is your baby due?'

Sienna gave a little nod. 'Pleased to meet you, Lucy and John.' She patted her stomach. 'Not until the end of January. But if I follow your example I could have him or her any day.'

The mum gave an anxious laugh. 'My waters broke when I went to collect the Christmas turkey. Can you believe that?' She looked over to her baby with affection. 'I guess he couldn't wait for his first Christmas.'

Sienna nodded. 'I guess not. Do you mind if I examine Caleb?'

'No.' It came out as a little squeak.

Sienna smiled and walked to the sink and washed her hands again. Lewis had little Caleb lying in a baby warmer. He nodded to the chart next to him and she took a quick glance. Apgar scores at birth and five minutes later weren't too unreasonable. She was more concerned with the presentation of the baby in front of her now.

She unwound her stethoscope from her neck and warmed the end.

'Definitely cardiac,' murmured Lewis. 'But I'll let you decide.'

She trusted him. She'd worked with him for a long time. Lewis was one of the best paediatricians she'd ever worked with. His knowledge base was huge over a wide range of specialities.

Caleb was struggling. It was obvious. His skin was pale. His breathing laboured. She could see his accessory muscles fighting to keep oxygen pumping around his little body. His little face was creased into a frown and his whole body moving in little irritated twitches. The thing that she noticed most was the unusual amount of sweat glistening on his little body. Instinct told her it was nothing to do with the baby warmer. She lifted the chart and looked at the temperature. It was slightly lower than expected. The pulse oximetry readings were a little lower than expected too.

'Has he fed at all?'

She looked up to Lewis and both parents as she rested her stethoscope on the little chest. Lucy shook her head. 'The midwife tried to get him to latch on, but he didn't want to. He just didn't seem ready. She said we'd try again once the doctor had reviewed him.'

She gave a nod. 'No problem. Give me a moment while I listen to his heart.'

She scribbled a note to Lewis who nodded and disappeared out of the room to get what she'd just asked for.

She held her breath while she listened. There. Exactly what she expected. The whoosh of the heart mur-

mur confirming the disruption of the heart flow. She felt for the pulses around the little body—in the groin and in the legs, checking the temperature of the skin in Caleb's lower body.

Lewis backed into the room again, pulling the machine.

'What's that?' John stood up.

She walked towards them. 'It's called an echocardiogram. It will let me check the blood flow around and through Caleb's heart.'

'You think there's something wrong with Caleb's heart?' Lucy gasped and held her hands to her chest.

The words she chose right now were so important. She didn't want to distress the brand-new parents, but she wasn't going to tell any lies.

'I'm not sure. I think it's something we need to check out. He seems a little unsettled.'

John and Lucy shot anxious glances at each other. John moved over and put his arm around his wife.

Lewis had positioned the echocardiogram next to the baby warmer and was talking in a low voice to baby Caleb. Sienna gave the parents a little nod. 'Are you okay with me checking Caleb a little further?'

They both nodded. She could practically see the fear emanating from their pores. This was one of the worst parts of her job. In some cases, cardiac conditions were picked up during the antenatal scans, plans could be made in advance and parents prepared for what lay ahead. But in cases like these, there were no plans.

One minute parents were preparing for the exciting birth of their child—the next they were being told their brand-new tiny baby needed major surgery. She had a good idea that was what was about to happen for John and Lucy.

Lewis gave her the nod and she switched the machine on and spread some warmed gel on Caleb's chest. He was still grizzly. His colour hadn't improved and from the twitching of his arms and legs it was as if his little body knew something wasn't quite right.

While he'd been inside his mother and attached to the umbilical cord his cardiac system had had constant support. Now—outside? His little heart seemed to be struggling with the work.

'Hey, little guy.' She spoke quietly as she placed the transducer on his little chest wall and her gaze flickered between him and the screen. Her trained eyes didn't take long to see exactly as she suspected. She could see movement of the blood flow through the heart chambers and heart valves. She pressed a button to measure the direction and speed of the blood flow and then moved to the surrounding blood vessels.

There. Exactly as she expected. She took a deep breath and took her time. She had to be absolutely sure what she was seeing. The room was silent around her. But she'd dealt with this before. She had to make sure she had the whole picture before she spoke to the parents.

Finally, she gave a little nod to Lewis. 'Would you be able to contact Max and see if he is available?'

To his credit, Lewis barely blinked. He would know if she was looking for the other cardiac surgeon that she wanted to act promptly. He gave a brief nod and disappeared out of the room.

Sienna wiped Caleb's chest clean, talking to him the whole time, then lifted him from the baby warmer, wrapped him in a blanket and took him over to his parents. Once he was settled in his mother's arms she sat down on the bed next to them.

'Caleb has something called coarctation of the aorta.

The aorta is the big blood vessel that goes to the heart.'
She picked up Caleb's chart and drew a little picture on
some paper for them. 'Caleb's aorta is narrower than
it should be—like this. That means that his heart isn't
getting all the blood that it needs. His heart has to work
harder than it should to try and pump blood around his
body. And this is something we need to fix.'

She paused, giving the parents a few minutes to take
in her words.

'How...how do you fix it?' asked John.

She licked her lips. 'I need to do some surgery on him.'

Lucy let out a little whimper as she stared at her baby.
Sienna put her hand on Lucy's arm.

'Right now, Caleb is getting a very good blood supply
to the top half of his body. But his pulses are weaker in
the bottom half of his body—to his legs and feet. If we
don't do surgery to widen his aorta then his heart will be
affected by working too hard and he could suffer from
heart failure.'

Lucy was shaking her head. 'Why?' Her eyes were
filled with tears. 'Why has this happened to our baby?'

Sienna nodded. These were natural questions for parents to ask. She chose her words carefully. 'There are lots
of ideas around why some babies have problems with
their hearts, but the truth is—no one really knows. It
could be a family thing. It could be in your genes. The
type of condition that Caleb has is called a congenital
heart defect. Have you ever known anyone in either of
your families to have something like this?'

They exchanged glances and both of them shook their
heads. She gave a slow nod. 'Sometimes people think
congenital heart defects can be caused by things in the
environment, things around us. Other theories are it could
be caused by things that we eat and drink or medicines

a mum might take.' She gave Lucy's arm a squeeze. She had to be honest, but didn't want Lucy to blame herself for her baby's condition. It was important that they focused on Caleb right now.

'How often does this happen?' Lucy's voice had cracked already and tears had formed in her eyes.

This was always the hardest part—breaking the news to parents that something was wrong with the little person all their hopes and dreams were invested in.

She'd always found this bit hard. But not quite as hard as she was finding it today. She blinked quickly, stopped tears forming in her own eyes. It was hard not to empathise with them. In a few weeks' time she would be beside herself if something was wrong with her baby. It didn't matter how much she knew. It didn't matter what her skills were.

For the last few months she'd practically lived her life in a bubble. She'd been so focused on the plans. The plans about maternity leave, cover, nurseries, childminders, cribs, prams and car seats.

She hadn't really focused on the actual outcome.

The actual real live moment when she'd become a mother and her life would change for ever.

Sebastian had brought all that home to her.

Maybe it was having someone around who was so excited about their baby. She'd felt so alone before. So determined to make sure everything would be in place.

She hadn't let the excitement—or the terror—actually build.

But having Sebastian around had heightened every emotion she possessed in an immediate kind of way.

He talked about it so easily. Their baby being here. Their baby being loved. Their baby's future.

A horrible part of her thought that when he hadn't known it had actually been a little easier.

Because Sebastian wanted to be involved in *everything*.

And it was clear he had plans on going nowhere.

The door opened and Max came in. He didn't speak, just raised his eyebrows and walked over towards her.

She smiled gratefully. 'You asked how often this happens. It is rare. But not quite as rare as you might think. Around four out of every ten thousand babies born will have this condition. In some babies it's mild. For some people it's not picked up until they are an adult. Some children aren't picked up until their teenage years. John and Lucy, this is Max Ainsley. He's the cardiothoracic surgeon that is taking over from me while I go on maternity leave.'

Max didn't hesitate. He held out his hand, shaking both their hands but letting Sienna continue to take the lead.

'If you know about Caleb now, does that mean he's really bad?' John looked as though he might be sick.

Sienna moved her hand over to his arm. 'It means it's something that we need to fix, John. And we need to fix it now.' She scribbled something on Caleb's chart. 'I'm going to make arrangements to move Caleb up to the paediatric intensive care unit. You'll be able to go with him, but the staff will be able to monitor him better there. I'll arrange for him a have a few more tests—a chest X-ray and an ECG.'

Lucy's eyes widened. 'My dad had one of those when they thought he was having a heart attack.'

Sienna nodded. 'It gives us an accurate tracing of the heart without causing any problems for Caleb. Once we have all the test results Max and I will review them. The type of surgery we need to do is to widen the narrow part of Caleb's aorta. It's called a balloon angioplasty. We put a thin flexible tube called a catheter into the narrow area of the aorta, then we inflate a little balloon to expand the blood vessel. Sometimes we put a little piece of mesh-covered tube called a stent in place to keep the blood vessel open.' She paused for a second. 'If we think the angioplasty won't work, or it's not the right procedure for Caleb, then we sometimes have to do surgery where we remove the narrow part of the aorta and reconstruct the vessel to allow blood to flow normally through the aorta.'

She took a deep breath. 'I know all this is scary. I know all this can be terrifying. I understand, really, I do. But both Max and I have done this kind of surgery on lots of babies. It's a really specialised field and we have a lot of expertise.'

'Do some babies die?'

Lucy's question came out of the blue and Max glanced in her direction. It was clear he was happy to step in if she was finding this too difficult. And for the first time in her life, she was.

She gave a careful nod. 'There can always be complications from surgery. Caleb is a good weight. He isn't too tiny. The echocardiogram of his heart didn't show any other heart defects. Some babies with coarctation of the aorta have other heart conditions—but I don't see any further complications for Caleb.' She stood up from the bed; her back was beginning to ache.

'I have to warn you that surgery can take some time. We could be in Theatre for more than a few hours and I don't want you to panic. I'm going to bring you some information to read then we'll arrange to transfer Caleb upstairs for his tests. Both Max and I will come back and explain everything again, and answer any questions before you sign the consent form. Is there anything you want to ask me right now?'

Both John and Lucy shook their heads. They still looked stunned. Max put a gentle hand on her back. She'd done this kind of surgery on her own on more than thirty occasions but somehow, at this stage of her pregnancy, she was relieved she'd have a second pair of hands.

She gave a final smile at the doorway. 'Don't worry, we'll take good care of Caleb. I'll just go and make the arrangements.'

She ignored the stiffness in her back as she walked down the corridor. It was going to be a long day.

Sebastian was waiting at the end of the corridor. 'Hey,' she said. 'What are you doing here?'

He shrugged. 'I came to find you to see if we might actually make it to a restaurant tonight. I booked out a whole place so we might actually get some privacy. I thought we could try and make Christmas Eve special. But I just heard you're going into surgery.'

He made it all sound so normal and everything he'd said was true. But he was also worried about how she was, following the news story about them. Sienna seemed remarkably calm, however. She was focused. Her mind was on the job. And he admired her all the more for it.

She gave a little sigh. 'Christmas Eve is normally my favourite night of the year. I love the build-up. The expectation for Christmas the next day.' She squeezed her eyes shut for a second as Sebastian reached up and brushed his fingers against her cheek. She opened her eyes again and they met his. 'But this is the life of a surgeon,' she whispered. 'This is the life that I've chosen.'

She held her breath as he nodded slowly. Her heart thudding against her chest. He had to understand. He had to understand that this was her life. If he wanted to be part of it, he had to realise there were things she wouldn't give up—things she would never change.

He touched her cheek again and leaned forward, his lips brushing against her ear as he whispered back, 'I wouldn't have it any other way.'

Her heart gave a little swell as a few of the other staff walked past. She was jerked from their little private moment. She pointed to the elbow of his leather jacket. 'You touched the nursery wall, didn't you?' Then her mouth opened. 'You changed the colour, didn't you?'

He let out a laugh at the pale yellow stain on his jacket. A funny look passed over his face. 'Yip. I did. Those nursery walls have been painted with blood, sweat and even a few tears.' He grimaced. 'There might have been a bit of a problem with the border.'

'What do you mean?'

He made another face. 'Let's just say the painting I could just about handle. Border skills seem to have escaped me. I might need to buy you another.' He gave her a big smile. 'And I might have done something you won't be happy about.'

'What's that?' Her head was currently swimming with thoughts of the surgery she was about to perform. She didn't need distractions.

'I see what you mean about the furniture. I might have ordered a few alternatives.' He held up his hand quickly. 'But don't worry. If you don't like them, they can go back.'

His phone buzzed in his pocket. He pulled it out, silenced it and pushed it away again.

'Problem?'

He shook his head. 'Nothing I can't handle.'

'What is it?'

'Let's just say it's a mother-sized problem.'

Sienna's heart sank a little. 'How many calls have you had?'

He shifted from one foot to the other. 'I spoke to her this morning just as the press release went out. Since then, there's been another twenty calls.'

'And you haven't answered them?'

He shook his head firmly. 'I've already heard her opinion once. I don't need to hear it again.'

It was a horrible sensation. Like something pressing down heavily on her shoulders. 'Please don't fall out with your mother because of me.'

'Let me worry about my mother. You just worry about your surgery. Oliver said I can go into the viewing room and watch.'

'Oh.' She wasn't quite sure what to say. It was one thing inviting Sebastian into her home, but inviting him to watch her surgery was something else entirely. It seemed he was determined to be involved in both her personal and professional life. She wasn't sure quite how she felt about that.

He bent forward and kissed her on the cheek. 'Good luck. You'll be fantastic. They're lucky to have you.'

The doors swung open behind them and Max appeared in his scrubs. 'Let's go, Sienna. This could be a long one.'

She gave a quick nod and followed him to scrub. Right now she had a baby to focus on. Little Caleb deserved every second of her attention.

And he would get it.

The viewing gallery for the surgery was almost full. Sebastian had to squeeze his way between a couple of excited students.

Sienna appeared cool. She and Max had a long discussion with the staff around them to make sure everyone was on the same page. Then, she glanced up at the gallery as the anaesthetist put Caleb to sleep, and talked some of the students through the procedure they were about to perform. Even behind her mask he could see the brightness in her eyes—the love of her job shone out loud and clear. It made him wish he'd got to meet her while she'd been at the hospital in Montanari. 'Well, guys, I guess this isn't where any of us expected to be on Christmas Eve, but this is the life of a surgeon.' She pointed to the equipment next to her. 'We are lucky at Teddy's to have the best technology around. The whole time we perform this surgery cameras will record our every move. There are viewing screens in the gallery, which you'll be able to watch. You'll find that during surgery Max and I don't talk much. We like to concentrate on the intricacies of the operation—that's why we've explained things beforehand. We will, however, be available to answer any questions you have once surgery is over and we've spoken to Caleb's parents.'

There were a few approving nods around him.

Max walked to the opposite side of the operating table from Sienna. 'Ready?' he asked.

She nodded once and they began.

Sebastian had never seen anything like it in his life. He'd known exactly what her job was when he'd first met her, but he'd never actually seen her in action. He'd never realised just how tiny and intricate the procedures were that she and Max performed. The baby's vessels were tiny.

But Sienna was confident in her expertise. She and Max only exchanged a few words. They worked in perfect synchronisation. Little Caleb truly couldn't be in better hands.

Things started to swirl around in his head. Sienna had

a gift. A gift she'd perfected over years of sacrifice and training. No matter how much his mother's words had echoed in his head this morning about duty and expectations for the mother of the heir apparent, he could never expect Sienna to fulfil the role that his mother had for the last thirty years.

Sienna had a skill and talent he could never ask her to walk away from. Not if he really loved her. Not if he really wanted her to be happy.

It came over him like a tidal wave. The plans he'd spent today making. The guilt that had washed over him as the decorator he'd hired had painted the first wall that hideous colour. He'd paid the man more than promised and sent him on his way. The hours of rolling yellow paint onto the walls. The aching muscles and spoiled, crumpled border. The emergency phone calls. The special orders. All because he'd realised this was about trust. This was about him, doing something for their child. This wasn't about duty at all. This was so much more than that. So much more than he'd ever experienced before.

All because he wanted to win a place in this woman's heart.

It finally hit him. She was worth it. She was really, really worth it.

He didn't want to live a single day without this woman in his life.

And he'd be lucky if he could capture a heart like hers.

Caleb's tiny vessel was even more fragile than expected. It took absolute precision to try and widen the vessel and insert the stent to make it remain patent. Having Max next to her was an added bonus. Normally, she would have performed this procedure unassisted, but they both knew that Max was likely to do Caleb's immediate follow-up care so it made sense that they worked together.

Baby wasn't taking kindly to her being on her feet so long. Her back ached more than usual and her bladder was being well and truly kicked by some angry little feet.

'Sienna?'

Max's voice was much louder than usual. She glanced up sharply just as one of the instruments fell from her hand to the theatre floor.

She blinked. He was out of focus. A warm flush flooded her skin.

'Sienna? Catch her!' he shouted and it was the last thing she heard.

One second she was in the middle of an operation, the next second Sienna was in a crumpled heap on the floor. Sebastian was on his feet and racing down the stairs before he even had time to think. He banged on the theatre doors, which were protected by a code. A flurry of staff rushed past the inside of the doors towards the theatre she'd been operating in. A few seconds later two male scrub nurses were carrying her out of the theatre.

Sebastian banged the door again and one of the theatre nurses turned in surprise. She gave a little nod of her head, obviously realising who he was, and opened the door from the inside. 'I'm going to phone Oliver,' she said as she disappeared off to another room.

Sebastian rushed after the two male nurses. They were gently laying Sienna down on another theatre trolley. Their reactions automatic. One applied a BP cuff, the other stood next to her, talking quietly to her and trying to get a reaction.

It was all Sebastian could do not to elbow both of them out of the way. But they were better equipped to assist her than he was, and he had enough know-how to stand back and let them get on with it.

After a few seconds she started to come around. Groggy and—by the look of it—uncomfortable.

She took a few deep breaths, her hands going automatically to her stomach. One of the theatre nurses smiled at her. 'You decided to go on maternity leave, Sienna.'

She blinked and tried to sit up, but the other male nurse put his hand on her shoulder. 'Not yet. Give it another few minutes. Your BP was low. Let me get you some water to sip.'

Sienna groaned and put her hands to her head. 'Please tell me everything is okay with Caleb. Nothing else happened, did it? I can't believe I just stoated off the floor.'

'You what?'

Sebastian couldn't help it. Her accent seemed even thicker than normal.

The male nurse glanced at him with a smile. 'I think she means she fainted.' He moved out of the way to let Sebastian closer. 'And don't worry. Max is more worried about you than finishing off the surgery. I'll let him know you're okay. He just needs to close.'

Sienna turned to her side for a second, her face a peculiar shade of grey. 'I think I'm going to be sick.'

About ten arms made a grab for the sick bowls but they were all too late. Sienna tried to get up again. 'Don't anyone touch that. I'll clean it up myself.'

'No, you won't.' Oliver strode through the doors. 'Don't you dare move.'

Sebastian leaned across and touched her stomach to stop her getting up, just at the same second a little foot connected sharply with his hand.

'Oh,' he said suddenly, pulling his hand back.

'Try having it all day,' sighed Sienna. 'And all night.'

But Sebastian couldn't stop staring at his hand. That was his baby. *His* baby that had just kicked him.

Of course, he'd come over when he'd heard the news about Sienna—and her pregnancy bump was obvious. But he'd never actually touched it. Never actually felt his little baby moving beneath her skin.

Oliver walked around to the other side. 'I'll arrange for you to go upstairs and have a scan. We need to make sure that everything is fine—that there aren't any complications.'

Sienna sat up this time and took the plastic cup of water offered by one of the theatre nurses. 'Oliver, honestly, I'm fine. There's no need to fuss. I hadn't managed to eat before I got called into surgery. That, and my back is aching a little because I'm getting further on. I'm fine. Once I go and get something to eat, I'll be good as new.'

'You'll be on maternity leave. That's it. No more patients. No more surgeries.' Sebastian almost smiled. It was clear from the tone of Oliver's voice that there would be no arguments.

Max came through the swing doors tugging his theatre cap from his head. 'How are you? Is everything okay?'

Her voice wavered a little. 'I'm so sorry, Max. Is Caleb okay? Have you finished?'

He waved his hand easily. 'Of course, he's fine. Don't worry about Caleb. I'll look after him.' He pointed to her stomach. 'You just worry about yourself and that precious cargo in there.'

She swung her legs off the side of the trolley. 'Let me go and get changed.' She glanced at Sebastian. 'Sebastian can take me home. I'll get take-out on the way.'

She had that determined lift to her chin but Oliver had obviously seen it before. 'No way. Not until I say. Scan first.'

She opened her mouth to argue but Sebastian cut her off. 'That would be great, Oliver. Thanks for organising that. It's really important to us to make sure that everything is fine with the baby. Those operating theatre floors are harsh.' He met her simmering gaze. 'We both want to be reassured that the baby has come to no harm.'

He'd chosen his words deliberately. There was no way she could refuse. It would make her look as if she didn't care—and that would never be Sienna, no matter how argumentative and feisty she was feeling.

She turned towards him and whispered under her breath. 'Don't tell me what to do. And I can do this myself. You don't need to be there. Why don't you wait outside?'

He felt himself bristle. He pasted a smile on his face and spoke so low, only she could hear. 'How many scans have I already missed, Sienna? Let me assure you, I have no intention of missing this one.'

She met his gaze for a second, as if she wanted to argue. Then seemed to take a deep breath and gave a tiny nod of her head.

One of the other nurses appeared with something else in her hand. 'From my secret chocolate supply. You're only getting special treatment because I love you and I expect you to call the baby after me—even if it's a boy.'

Sienna let out a little laugh and held her hand out for the chocolate. 'Thanks, Mary, I know you guard this stuff with your life. I appreciate it.'

Sebastian was trying his best to be calm. Now that Sienna had woken up, the panic in the room seemed to have vanished.

A porter appeared with a wheelchair and, after another check of her blood pressure, she was wheeled down the corridor towards the scan room.

Christmas Eve. The staff in the maternity unit were buzzing. Placing bets on who would deliver the first Christmas baby. The canteen would be closed later tonight and as they walked past one of the rooms, Sebastian could see plates of food already prepared for the night-shift workers.

The scan room was dark, the sonographer waiting for them. 'Hi there, Sienna. I heard you took a tumble in Theatre. Slide up on the trolley and we'll get a quick check of baby.'

Sienna had just finished eating her chocolate bar and she moved over onto the trolley and pulled up her scrub top.

Sebastian gulped. There it was. A distinct sign of exactly how they'd spent that weekend together in Montanari. He watched the ripples on Sienna's skin. Their baby currently looked as if it were trying to fight its way out from under a blanket.

The sonographer put some gel on Sienna's stomach and lifted her scanner. She paused. 'Do you know what you're having?'

Sienna shook her head. 'Let's avoid those bits if you can. I don't really want to know.'

For the first time in a long time Sebastian felt strangely nervous. He'd never been in a scan room before. Like everyone else in the world, he'd seen it on TV shows and news clips. But this was entirely different.

This was his baby.

No, this was their baby.

He watched as the black and white picture appeared on the screen. The first thing he noticed was the flickering. The sonographer held things steady for a second as she smiled at Sienna. 'Look at that, a nice steady heart-rate.'

Ah...that was the heart.

His eyes started to adjust to what he was seeing on the screen. The sonographer chatted easily as she swept the scanner around. 'Just going to check the position of the placenta and the umbilical cord,' she said simply.

'Why are you doing that?' He couldn't help but ask.

Sienna's eyes were fixated on the screen. 'She's checking to make sure the cord isn't twisted or the placenta detached.'

Neither of those sounded good. 'What would happen if they were?'

This time when she met his gaze she looked nervous. 'Let's just say I wouldn't be getting home for Christmas.'

He moved closer, putting his hand on hers. He looked back at the sonographer. 'And is everything okay?'

The sonographer waited a few seconds before turning to nod reassuringly. 'Everything looks fine.' She pointed to a few things on the screen, 'Here's baby's head, face, spine, thigh bone and…*oops*…let's go back up. Here are the fingers. The placenta looks completely intact and the cord doesn't appear to have any knots in it.' She placed the scanner at the side of the machine again and picked up some tissues to wipe Sienna's stomach. 'Everything seems fine.'

As the picture disappeared from the screen he felt a little pang. He'd missed out on so much already. He didn't want to miss out on another thing. The baby kicked again and even though the room was quite dark he could practically pick out the little feet and fists behind the kicks.

Sienna let out a nervous laugh. 'I guess they're beginning to get impatient. There can't be much room left in there now.'

The sonographer packed away some of her equipment. 'Five weeks to go? That's when it starts to get really uncomfortable. Watch out for some sleepless nights.' She gave Sienna a wink. 'I'll go and let Oliver know that everything is fine while you two get ready.'

Sienna shook her head. 'Yeah, thanks for that, Dawn. More sleepless nights. Just what I need.'

'You haven't been sleeping?'

She'd swung her legs off the trolley and was about to pull her scrub top back down. She looked up at him. 'You might not remember, Sebastian, but I like to sleep on my stomach—' she stared down '—and the munchkin is making it a bit difficult.'

She went to pull her top down and he put his hand over hers. The baby was still kicking. *His* baby was still kicking. 'Can you wait a minute?'

He bent down, kneeling until his head was just opposite her stomach. He watched her skin closely for each tiny punch or kick. He couldn't stop the smile. 'It's totally random. You never know where the next one will be.' He looked up at her. 'What does it feel like?'

She didn't answer for a few seconds. She was watching him with a strange look in her eyes. Eventually she stretched forward and took his hand, pressing his palm to her stomach. 'Feel for yourself.'

Sienna's skin felt different than he remembered. It was stretched tight, slightly shiny. There were no visible stretch marks, nothing that made it anything but a beautiful sight.

There. A little kick beneath his hand again.

He laughed and pulled it back. The kicks kept coming so he put both hands on her stomach. He felt something else, something bigger beneath his hand, and Sienna gave a little groan. 'What was that?'

She shook her head. 'I think that might have been a somersault. It certainly felt like it.' She placed her hands next to his and leaned back a little. 'Here, I think this is one of the shoulders. The baby's head should be down by now and it looked that way in the scan. But they can still turn if they want to. It's just not that comfortable when they do.'

Her belly felt warm. And the life contained within it was just a wonder to him.

He hadn't known it would feel like this. He didn't know it *could* feel like this. And this wasn't just about the baby. He couldn't imagine ever feeling this way about Theresa if she'd carried his child. This was about Sienna too.

'Do you have a picture?'

She frowned. 'Of what?'

'Of our baby when you got the first scan. Most people get a picture, don't they?'

She looked surprised but gave a nod. 'Yes, of course I have. It's in my bag.'

'Can I see it?'

She looked around and then shook her head. 'It's in my bag. It's in the locker room. I'll get it as soon as we get the go-ahead to leave.'

He gave what looked like a resigned nod as he stood back up and lifted his hands from her stomach. It surprised her how much she wished he'd left them there. So many things were surprising her about Sebastian.

This was all about the baby. Not about her. She had to try and put her feelings and emotions in a box and keep them there. The irony of that at Christmas time almost killed her.

She could imagine the box, with all her hopes and dreams of a fairy-tale true-love romance for her, Sebastian and the baby all wrapped in glittering red paper and silver foil sitting under her beautiful Christmas tree just waiting to be opened.

Something sank deep inside her. Reality check time.

Sebastian was interested in the baby. Yes, he'd made a few gestures towards her. But no more than she would expect from a well-brought-up prince, looking after the mother-to-be of his child.

She almost laughed out loud. Exactly how many princes did she know?

She didn't even want to admit the security she felt when he was next to her. She didn't want to acknowledge the fact that, the more he hung around, the more she lost a little piece of her heart to him each day.

She couldn't admit that. She just couldn't.

She wouldn't be her mother. The woman who'd spent her whole life with a man that had never really loved her. That wasn't a life. That wasn't a relationship.

If she'd learned anything from her parents it was that sometimes it actually was better if parents didn't stay together. The tortured strain of living in that household had become unbearable.

And although she hated her father for his actions, with her adult brain she might actually understand, just a little.

Maybe if they'd separated much earlier, she might actually have enjoyed a different kind of relationship with her parents. One where they both had the life they wanted, and she fitted around it. But would that have been any fairer to a child than the life she'd had?

Sebastian pulled his phone from his pocket. 'What do you want to eat?'

She pulled her scrub top down quickly. 'Chinese. Hong-Kong-style chicken with noodles.'

He nodded towards the door. 'Give me a minute. I'll make the call and we'll pick it up on the way home.'

* * *

The room had felt claustrophobic for a few minutes there. Once he'd felt the kick from his baby, once he'd seen his baby's heartbeat on the screen, it had all become so real.

What had started from the first second he'd seen Sienna McDonald pregnant with his child, continued with her independence and snarkiness, been embodied by her vulnerability and the kiss they'd shared and culminated in feeling his baby kick after she'd collapsed, had just all built to the tornado of seeing that flickering heartbeat and touching the stomach of the woman who currently held all his dreams.

His head just couldn't sort out where he was. Oliver had hinted at signs of love. Did his friend even know what he was talking about? The guy was running around in a pink-tinged cloud.

The conversation with his mother this morning would have poured *Titanic*-icy waters over even the most embraced by love, soul and spirit.

Duty. The word sent prickles down his spine.

He hated it. But he actually agreed. It was his duty to marry Sienna and make this child the rightful heir to the kingdom of Montanari.

He'd been brought up to believe that duty was more important than anything. It was hard to shake that off.

But the feelings he was having deep inside about this baby and Sienna? Duty didn't even come near them. These feelings were entirely different.

They penetrated his heart, his soul, his very essence. They felt more essential than breathing.

He closed his eyes as the call connected and he placed the order in the calmest voice possible. A few people strolled past him in the corridor. As he opened his eyes

again it was clear they recognised him. The TV reporters outside meant that any chance of privacy he and Sienna had was gone for now.

Something else flashed into his head—the other secret arrangements he'd made today. He just had no idea
if they'd actually been pulled off. He made a quick call—
sighing with relief when it ended.

Sienna appeared at the doorway with a smiling Oliver.
Sebastian blinked. He hadn't even noticed him appearing. 'Take her home, feed her and don't let her come back
until she's ready to deliver this baby,' he said. 'Let's go
for the due date—twenty-eighth of January will be fine.'

Sienna looked a little more relaxed. 'Let me get
changed. I'll just be a few minutes,' she said as she disappeared into the locker room a few doors down the
corridor.

Sebastian looked at Oliver. He trusted his friend. He
trusted his expertise. 'Everything okay?'

Oliver nodded. 'Everything is fine. She's had a good
pregnancy. Her blood pressure is fine. But the truth is,
she's thirty-five weeks. She could deliver now, she could
deliver two weeks after her due date. We never know
these things.' He paused. 'Are you going to be around?'

He didn't hesitate. 'Count on it.'

Oliver held out his hand towards him. 'Good. I'll see
you soon.'

Sebastian shook his friend's hand. 'Can you tell Sienna I'll get the car and wait for her at the side door? It
might be easier than having to face the paparazzi when
we cross the car park.'

Five minutes later he was waiting right at the door in
his DB5. He'd always loved this car but it wasn't exactly
inconspicuous. They might be at the side of the hospital

right now, but as soon as he tried to pull out of the car park, they would be spotted.

Sienna came out of the door a few minutes later, her hood over her head. She climbed into the car and closed the door. 'Oh, well,' she sighed. 'That's two cars I've abandoned in the car park now. The broken-down one and the hire car from this morning.'

Sebastian shrugged. 'Leave me to deal with it. Don't worry. Let's just get you home.'

He wanted some privacy. He wanted a chance to get her away from all this and talk about the things they should be talking about.

He stopped at the Chinese restaurant—would his stomach ever recover from this take-away food?—and collected their meal, before turning ten minutes later into Sienna's street.

She let out a gasp.

If he'd known she was going to be unwell, he probably wouldn't have put all the plans in place that he had this morning. But it was too late now.

It was all done.

Her eyes widened as the car drew closer to her house. Everything was just as he'd asked for. A large Norway spruce had been transported to her garden and covered with multicoloured twinkling lights.

Icicle lights had been hung from the eaves of her house and stars around her two large bay windows.

She put her hand to her mouth as they pulled up directly outside. She still hadn't said a word but the expression on her face said it all. 'Wait until you see the back.' He smiled.

As they walked in the entrance hall he kept one hand around her waist, leading her straight past the nursery and down to the back door. He unlocked it and held it open.

It couldn't have been more perfect.

It didn't exactly look like a Santa's Grotto—more like a little Christmas paradise. He'd added lights to the rest of the trees and bushes. A heater next to her carved wooden seat.

The light-up reindeers and penguins from the nearby garden centre had been transported to her back garden. And to make it even more perfect the whole garden was dusted with snow, which was falling in large, thick flakes.

He kept his arm around her. 'Is it what you imagined?'

Her eyes were bright as she turned towards him. 'Oh, it's even better than I imagined. I thought it would be twenty years before it looked like this.' Her smile lit up her whole face.

He let out the breath he'd been holding, waiting to see what her reaction would be. He'd wanted to do something to make her happy. She'd already told him she loved Christmas and this was the first time they would be together at Christmas.

He was praying it wouldn't be the last.

Showering her with expensive gifts would have been easy. But he already knew that would make little impact on Sienna.

He had to know what was important to her. And this was part of the little bit of herself that she'd revealed to him.

He only hoped the rest would go down so well.

He steered her back inside. 'Let's get this Chinese food before it gets too cold. And I've something else to show you.'

The words were casual but obviously sparked a memory in her brain. 'Oh, the nursery. You've painted it, haven't you? Let me see what it looks like.'

She walked quickly back inside the house, striding

along the corridor enthusiastically. She flicked the switch at the doorway and stepped inside.

Now, he really did hold his breath again. Had he over-stepped the mark?

She must have already had a vision in her head for how she wanted the nursery to look—he only hoped he'd captured that invisible picture.

She made a little noise—a sort of strangled sound. Was that good? Or bad?

Then she walked straight over to the new, specially carved oak cot. Ducks and bunnies were carved on both the outside ends of the cot and along the bottom bar. She ran her hand along the grain of the wood.

He heard her intake of breath. He'd taken the step of making up the cot with the bed linen she'd already bought. But along with the pale yellow walls, and the curtains that had almost been the death of him, he thought the new furniture fitted well.

She opened the new matching wardrobe and chest of drawers.

He'd replaced all the furniture she'd bought with hand-carved pale oak furniture. It was all exactly the same style, just a different quality with a price tag that most people couldn't afford. That, plus the on-the-day delivery, would have made the average man wince. But Sebastian didn't care. He wanted the best for Sienna. The best for their baby.

She let out a little laugh at the crumpled border in the corner of the room. Darn it. He'd forgotten to throw it away.

He couldn't help himself. 'What do you think? Do you like it?'

She stood for a few minutes, her eyes taking in the contents of the room. He'd even added something extra, buying her a special cream nursing chair with a little table and lamp, and placed it in the corner of the room.

She walked back over to him, shaking her head slowly until she was just under his nose. Her eyes were glazed with tears when she looked up and his stomach constricted.

'I don't like it,' she said slowly, before opening her hands out and turning around. 'I love it! it's perfect. It just looks exactly as I'd imagined.'

'It is?'

'Yes!' She flung her arms around his neck. 'I can't believe you've done this all in one day. How did you manage?' Her hands were still around his neck but she pulled back a little. 'Did you have help?' She looked a little suspicious.

'The nursery was all me. The furniture came assembled. As for the outside decorations—I left very specific instructions.'

She raised her eyebrows. 'You can actually do some DIY?'

He laughed. 'Remember, I went to university with Oliver. The man that can barely wire a plug. So, yes, I can use a screwdriver and a paint roller.'

She was staring up at him with those light brown eyes. There was definite sparkle there.

'You did good,' she said simply.

'I did better than good,' he whispered. 'I found you.'

Her eyes widened and her lips parted a little. 'But you didn't mean to.' She glanced downwards. 'You didn't mean for this to happen.'

He shook his head. 'Neither did you. But this was always meant to happen, Sienna. I believe it. I was meant to meet you. You were meant to meet me. *We* were meant to be. This baby was meant to be. The more I see you every day, the more I can't imagine spending a single day without you.'

'But how can that be, Seb? How can that happen? I live here. You're part of a royal family in Montanari. You're the Prince, and one day you'll be the King. Somehow, I don't think I fit the job description.'

He shook his head. 'You don't get it, do you? It's up to me to think about the job description. And for me it's obvious. There's only one person I want by my side. Montanari needs to bring itself into the twenty-first century. A queen and royal mother that's a neonatal cardiothoracic surgeon? An independent, educated woman who is dedicated to her job? How can that be a bad thing? Why on earth would I ask you to give that up? I couldn't be more proud of the job that you do. I couldn't be more proud of the fact you came to Montanari to train our surgeons. I watched you in action today, Sienna. I don't think I've ever seen anything I admire more. You couldn't be more perfect if you tried.'

'I couldn't?' She looked stunned—as if it were the last thing she'd expected him to say. She looked as if she was about to say something else but he cut her off. He dropped a kiss on her perfect lips. Truth was, he'd thought about nothing else all day. She tasted sweet and as he kissed her and his fingers tangled through her blonde hair the fruity aroma from her shampoo swept around them. His hands went from her hair, to her shoulders and down her back.

He could feel their baby between them. It was stopping him getting as close as he'd like to. He intertwined his fingers with hers. 'Come here,' he whispered and pulled her through to the main lounge, sitting down on the swallow-you-up sofa and drawing her towards him.

She hesitated for the slightest second before moving forward and sitting astride him on the sofa. She looked at him for the longest time then finally lifted one hand and brushed her knuckles gently against the emerging shadow on his jawline. 'I don't know what to make of you, Seb,' she said in a throaty voice. 'I don't know what to make of any of this.'

He ran a finger down the bare skin on her arm. 'Tell me what you want.'

She shook her head. He saw the little shiver go up her spine as he ran his finger down her arm again. It was the gentlest of touches. The lightest of touches. They'd been intimate before. They'd been passionate before.

But not like this.

His hands settled on her stomach, feeling the baby lying under her skin. It seemed to be settled in one position. 'Do you think our baby is sleeping?' He smiled.

She arched her back, her stomach and breasts getting even closer. 'I hope so,' she murmured. 'But doubtless as soon as I go to bed they'll wake back up again. I think our baby is going to be a night owl and I have to warn you—' she leaned forward and whispered in his ear '—us Scots girls can get very crabbit when we have no sleep.'

He caught a strand of her hair and twisted it around one finger. 'Don't sell yourself short, Sienna. I seem to remember a couple of occasions when you managed quite well without sleep.' He released the strand of hair and let his hands brush against her full breasts then settle on her waist.

She closed her eyes and let out a little moan. Her hands pressed against his chest, her fingers coming into contact with the tiny hairs at the nape of his neck. He caught his breath. This was becoming more than he could have imagined. His body started to react.

Sienna smiled down at him. 'You like this? When I'm

tired? Have an aching back? And, even though I haven't checked yet, probably puffy feet?'

'I think you're perfect just the way you are,' he said simply. He put his hands on her stomach again. 'Pregnant. Not pregnant.' He lifted his hands higher. 'Big boobs. Small boobs. Swollen feet. Not swollen feet.'

'I'm not a queen-in-waiting, Seb.' She shook her head slowly. 'I've never wanted to be.'

'You want the fairy tale. I can give you that.'

She closed her eyes for a second. 'You can give me the palace, the lifestyle, the people.' She pressed her hand against her heart. 'But what's in here? You need someone who wants to live that life. I don't think that can ever be me.'

He put his hands on her thighs. 'But our baby will be the heir. That's written in the stars, Sienna. You can't wipe that away. I want our child to grow up loving the country that they will eventually rule. I want them to respect and appreciate the people that live there. I want the people of Montanari to love my family.'

He sucked in a deep breath. 'We should get married, Sienna. Think about it. We could make this work between us, and we could make this work as a family. Don't dismiss me out of hand like you did before. Take your time. Think about how we both want to bring our child up. Think about what's important to you.'

What was important to her? Right now her head was so muddled she couldn't think straight. Her breath had stalled somewhere in her throat. He had passion in his eyes when he spoke about Montanari. Just like the flicker she'd seen in his eyes a few moments earlier when they'd been locked in an embrace.

But when she'd pressed her hand against her heart,

he just hadn't picked up what she'd meant. She wanted to know what was in *there*. In that heart that was beating in his chest.

Because no matter how hard she'd tried to fight it, she'd developed feelings for Sebastian. Feelings that she just couldn't be sure were reciprocated.

He'd focused on part of her fairy tale—but not the most important part. The part that meant she and her Prince loved each other with their whole hearts. The part that she just couldn't live without.

Sebastian lit up her heart in a way she didn't want to admit. She couldn't put herself out there to find her love dismissed. The stakes were too high.

He was talking about Montanari. Making it sound as if that should be the place they have a future together. Lots of women might love that. A prince. A castle. A new baby.

But if he really knew her, he would know that a vital component was missing.

Something gripped her. Something tight, knocking her breath temporarily from her lungs. 'Oh.' She held out one hand towards Sebastian and gripped the other around her stomach.

'Sienna? Is everything okay?' He shifted position, moving her from his knees and onto the sofa.

She was stunned. 'I don't know. I've never felt anything like that before.'

His eyes widened. 'You don't think that…' His voice tailed off. His face paled.

She was still catching her breath, wondering where the sharp pain had come from and hoping against hope it was something else entirely.

She stood up and started pacing. Sebastian was right

by her side. This couldn't be happening. It was too early. She was only thirty-five weeks.

'You had that fall today—do you think it could be anything to do with that?'

Sweat started to break out on her skin. She looked from side to side. 'I'm not ready. I'm not ready for this. I should have another five weeks to think about this—to make plans.'

Tears prickled in her eyes. 'It's Christmas Eve. I was planning on watching some TV and wrapping some final presents.'

Sebastian glanced at the enormous pile under the tree. 'You have more?'

He slid his arm around her waist and she batted him on the chest. 'Stop it.'

He turned her around to face him.

One tear slid down her cheek. He brushed it away with his finger. 'Should I phone an ambulance? Oliver told me to phone if I was worried. Should I do that now?' He was babbling. The Prince was babbling.

It felt like an out-of-body experience. He'd always seemed so in control. Or at least he wanted the world to think that.

'Will our baby be okay? Will you be okay?'

Another tear slipped down her cheek. 'I'm thirty-five weeks today. They might give me some steroids to bring the baby's lungs on, and baby might be a little slow to feed. But there's nothing else we should worry about.' She slid her hands across her stomach. 'But, if I think I'm not ready, then I know for sure that you're *definitely* not ready.' Her heart started thudding in her chest. She'd operated on tiny babies. She'd been doing it for years and years. But she'd never actually *had* a baby before. And the truth was, she was scared.

Scared of what could lie ahead.

She broke out of his hold and started pacing again. 'I had everything planned. I knew what was happening. Then—' she turned to face him and held up her hand '—you come along with your kingdom and your press team, and your let's-twin-our-hospitals, and you've just confused me, stressed me—'

'You're saying all this is my fault?' She could see the pain and confusion written all over his face.

Then—*whoomph*. This time it was stronger. This time it made her bend double. *'Oohh.'*

'Sienna?'

Her hands went back to her stomach; she slid them under her loose top. This time there was no mistake. She could feel the tightening under the palms of her hands.

Sebastian strode towards her just as something else happened.

Something wet and warm. All over her living-room oak floor.

She closed her eyes.

'Is that what I think it is?'

She nodded and looked down at the darkening wet stain on her trousers. Thank goodness they were pale—otherwise she'd be panicking she couldn't tell the colour of the liquid. This liquid was clear.

'Start the car, Sebastian.'

'You don't want an ambulance?' There was an edge of desperation to his voice.

'On Christmas Eve? In the Cotswolds? We can get there much quicker on our own.'

In less than five minutes she'd changed and thrown some things into a bag; another contraction slowed her down. The front door was wide open, showing the snow-covered garden outside. Sebastian was standing with his jacket on, pacing at the front door. The car was running.

'Let's go. I'll lock up.'

She let him guide her out to the waiting car.

She groaned as he climbed in next to her. 'This wasn't what I imagined for Christmas Eve.'

He cleared his throat and shot her a nervous glance. 'Actually, I can't think of anything more perfect.'

'What?'

'We're having a baby.'

She took a deep breath and tried to clear her head. Focus. All she could focus on right now was the fact they were about to meet their child. She had to have some head space. She had to be in a good place.

'Truth is, I'm a tiny bit terrified,' she whispered, staring out at the snow-topped houses and glistening trees. Next time she came back here she'd have a baby with her.

His hand closed over hers. 'Then, let's be terrified together.'

CHAPTER SIX

'IT'S A GIRL!'

'It is?' Sienna and Sebastian spoke in unison.

Ella, the midwife in the labour suite and Oliver's new fiancée, smiled up at them as she lifted the baby up onto Sienna's chest. 'It certainly is. Congratulations, Mum and Dad, meet your beautiful new daughter.'

Sebastian couldn't speak. He was in awe. First with Sienna and her superwoman skills at pushing their baby out, and now with the first sight of his daughter.

She looked furious with her introduction to the world. Ella gave a little wipe of her face and body as she lay on her mother's chest and she let out an angry squeal. Ella laughed. 'Yip, she's here. Have you two thought of a name yet?'

A name.

His brain was a complete blank.

He still couldn't process a thought. He could have missed this. He could have missed this once-in-a-life-time magical moment. That couldn't even compute in his brain right now.

His daughter had a few fine blonde hairs on her head the same shade as her mother. He had no idea about her eyes as her face was still screwed up.

'She just looks so…so…big,' he said in wonder.

Sienna let out an exhausted laugh. 'Imagine if I'd reached forty weeks.' She looked in awe too as she ran her hand over her daughter's bare back. 'She's not big. She's not big at all. Ella will weigh her in a few minutes. But let's just wait.'

Sebastian shook his head as Ella busied herself around them. 'I have no idea about a name.'

He wanted to laugh out loud. For years in Montanari, the royal family were only allowed to pick from a specific list of approved names. His mother still thought that should be the case.

Sienna turned to him. 'I think we should cause a scandal. Let's call our daughter something wild—like Zebedee, or Thunder.'

Now he did laugh out loud. 'I think my mother would have a fit. It's almost worth it just to see the expression on her face.'

Sienna was still stroking their daughter's skin. 'Actually, I do have a name in mind.'

'You do?'

She nodded. 'I'd like to call my daughter after my aunt. She was fabulous with me when I was growing up and looked after me a lot when my mother and father were busy.'

She didn't say the other words that were circulating in her brain. *Or when my mother and father couldn't be bothered.*

It was an unfair thought and she knew that. But she was emotional and hormonal right now. She'd just done the single most important thing she would ever do in this life.

Her parents had never mistreated her. They just hadn't been that interested. Her aunt had been different. She'd always been good to her.

'What's your aunt called?'

Their daughter started to stir, squirming around her chest and making angry noises. 'Margaret,' she said quietly. 'My aunt was called Margaret.'

It was the last thing he'd really expected. A traditional name from an untraditional woman.

'Really?'

She looked up and met his gaze. Her hair was falling out of the clip she'd brought with her for the labour. Her pyjama top was open at the front to allow their baby on her skin.

He'd never seen anything more beautiful.

He'd never seen anything he could love more.

He blinked.

It was like a flash in the sky above him. He'd been trying to persuade Sienna to give him a chance for all the wrong reasons. He'd always liked her. The attraction had never waned.

But duty still ran through his veins. In his head he'd been trading one duty marriage for another. But Sienna had bucked against that.

She demanded more. She *deserved* more.

And it was crystal clear to him why.

He didn't want to have to persuade her to be with him. It was important to him that she wanted to be with him, as much as he wanted to be with her.

And she'd need to be prepared for the roller coaster that was his mother.

Sienna was more than a match for his mother—of that he had no doubt. But sparks could fly for a while in the palace.

His father—he was pretty sure he would love her as soon as she started talking in her Scottish accent and telling it exactly as it was.

Ella gave him a nudge. 'Do you want to hold your daughter? Sienna's work isn't quite finished yet.'

Sebastian gave an anxious nod as Ella first took their daughter from Sienna, weighed her, put a little nappy on her and supplied a pink blanket to wrap their daughter in. Two minutes later she gestured for him to sit in a comfortable seat she pulled out from the wall. 'Once she's delivered the placenta, we'll do another few checks. Oliver will arrive any minute. And I'll arrange for some food for you both. After all that hard work you'll both be exhausted. We have plenty to spare in the labour ward.'

He hardly heard a word. He was too focused on the squirming little bundle that had just been placed in his arms. The smile seemed to have permanently etched itself onto his face. It would be there for ever.

Her face was beautiful. He stroked her little cheek. The wrinkles on her forehead started to relax and her eyes blinked open a few times. He'd been told that all babies' eyes started as blue. His daughter's were dark blue; they could change to either green like his, or brown like her mother's. The blonde hair on her head was downy, it already had a fluff-like appearance and he could see the tiny little pulse throbbing at the soft centre in the top of her head.

He couldn't have imagined anything more wonderful. Less than twenty minutes ago this tiny little person had been inside Sienna, a product of their weekend of passion in Montanari. She might not have been planned but, without a doubt, it was the best thing that had ever happened to him.

They were the best thing that had ever happened to him.

Sebastian shook his head. 'Sienna did all the hard work. I was just lucky enough to be here.' He lifted one hand that had been thoroughly crushed for the last few hours. 'I might need a plaster cast, but I can take it.'

Ella smiled and went back to work.

By morning Sienna was back in a fresh bed with a few hours' sleep, showered and eating tea and toast. Margaret had finally opened her eyes and was watching him very suspiciously—as if she were still trying to work out what had happened.

Oliver came into the room to check Sienna over. 'Trust you not to hold on. You never did have any patience. I'm going to relish the fact that your daughter has obviously inherited your genes. Good luck with that, Sebastian,' he joked. He put his arm around Ella. 'Seriously, guys, congratulations. I'm delighted for you.'

He gave a nod towards the door. 'Word travels fast around here. There are a few more people who want to say hello.'

Ella looked to Sienna. 'How do you feel about that?'

Sienna glanced over at Sebastian, cradling their baby girl. 'Tell them to come in now. I want to try and give our daughter another feed. I think she'll get cranky quite soon.'

Ella gave a nod and Annabelle and Max, and Charlie and Juliet crowded into the room. Sebastian held his precious daughter while they all fawned over her, kissing Sienna and congratulating them both.

Charlie nodded at the clock on the wall. 'If you'd just held off for another few hours you could have had our first Christmas baby.'

Christmas. Of course. He'd almost forgotten this was Christmas Day now.

Sienna looked shocked for a second then threw back her head and laughed. 'Darn it! I completely forgot about that!' She looked suspicious for a second. 'Did any of you have a bet on me for the Christmas baby?'

Juliet shook her head. 'Not one of us. No one expected you to deliver this early.' She leaned over Sebastian's shoulder. 'But your girl looks a good weight for thirty-five weeks. What was she?'

'Five pounds, thirteen ounces,' answered Sebastian. Margaret's weight would be imprinted on his brain for ever.

Just as this moment would. Now he'd held his daughter, he didn't ever want to let her go.

Sienna's stomach grumbled loudly as she finished the toast. 'Sorry,' she laughed to her visitors.

She was trying to pay attention to them—she really was. But she couldn't help but be a little awed by the expression on Sebastian's face at the bottom of the bed. He was fascinated by their daughter. He could barely take his eyes off her.

She felt the same. She was sure she wouldn't sleep a wink tonight just watching the wonder of her little daughter's chest rising and falling.

'Here.' Annabelle thrust a little gift towards her. 'Something for your gorgeous girl.'

Sienna was amazed. 'Where on earth did you get a present on Christmas Day?'

Annabelle gave her a wink. 'I have friends in high places.'

Sienna felt her heart squeeze. Annabelle was the most gracious of friends. Sienna knew how hard she and Max had tried for a baby of their own; it had eventually broken down their marriage until their reconciliation a few weeks ago. And yet here they both were, celebrating with her and Sebastian over their unexpected arrival.

She opened the gift bag and pulled out the presents. A packet of pale pink vests, a tiny pink Babygro that had a pattern like a giant Christmas present wrapped with a bow, matching tiny pink socks and a pale pink knitted hat with a pom-pom bigger than Margaret's head. She laughed out loud.

She'd bought a few things for the baby's arrival but, with the rush, she'd forgotten to bring them from home. 'Oh, Annabelle, thank you, these are perfect. Now we have something to take our daughter home in.'

Sebastian looked up quickly, pulling the little bundle closer to his chest.

'We're going home?'

Oliver shook his head. 'No, sorry. Not tonight. The paediatrician wants to be sure that Margaret is feeding without any problems. I'm afraid you'll need to spend your daughter's first Christmas in hospital.' He glanced at Ella. 'Don't worry, the staff here are great. They'll make sure you're well looked after.'

Sienna sagged back against her pillows. 'I don't care. She's here, and she's healthy. That's all I care about. I might love Christmas. But it can wait.'

Max looked around the room. 'Let's say our good-byes, folks, and leave the new parents with their baby.' He rolled his eyes. 'Some of us have Christmas dinners to make.' Right on cue Margaret gave out a scream that made Sebastian jump.

Everyone laughed. They quickly gave Sienna and Sebastian hugs and left the room. Sienna pushed the table across the bed away and held out her hands. 'I think she must be hungry. Let's see if she's ready for a feed.'

Ella came back a few minutes later and helped Sienna position their daughter to feed. The first feed had been a little difficult. She gave Sienna a cautious smile. 'Sometimes babies that are born a little early take a bit longer to learn how to suck. They all get there eventually, but it can take a bit of perseverance.'

Sienna's eyes were on their daughter. 'It seems Margaret doesn't like to wait for anything. As a first-time mum I expected to have one of those twenty-hour labours.'

Ella shrugged. 'You might have done, if you'd reached forty weeks. You might be quite tall, but your pelvis is pretty neat.' She smiled up as Margaret latched on. 'Just remember that for baby number two.'

Almost in unison Sebastian and Sienna's heads turned to each other and their wide-eyed gazes met, followed by a burst of laughter.

Sienna waved her hand at Ella. 'Shame on you, Midwife O'Brien, mentioning another baby when the first one is barely out. You haven't even given me time yet to be exhausted!'

A warm feeling spread throughout Sebastian. His daughter's little jaw was moving furiously as she tried to feed. Sienna seemed calmer than he'd ever seen her, stroking her daughter's face and talking gently to her.

Ella looked up and met his contented gaze with a smile. 'I'll leave you folks alone for a while. Come and find me when you want some food, Sebastian. I take it you're staying all day?'

'Can I?' He hadn't even had a chance to discuss with Sienna what happened next.

Ella nodded. 'Of course. All new dads are welcome to stay with mum and baby. This is Teddy's. We're hardly going to throw you out on Christmas Day. This is a time for families.' She winked and left the room.

Sienna lifted her head and looked at the clock. 'I can't believe we had her on Christmas Eve. It all just seems so unreal. I thought I would spend today lying on my sofa, like a beached whale, watching TV and eating chocolates.'

A special smile spread across her face. 'I thought I wouldn't see you until next Christmas,' she whispered to their daughter. 'I'd planned to buy you one of those Christmas baubles for the tree with your name, date of birth and baby's first Christmas on it. I guess you've ruined that now, missy.'

Although she loved Christmas dearly, she'd been edgy about this year. Worried about what the future would hold for her and her baby. Sebastian showing up had brought everything to the forefront.

He was sitting in a chair at the end of the bed. Ever since her first labour pain he'd been great. After that first flicker of panic he'd been as solid as a rock. He'd rubbed her back, massaged her shoulders, and given her words of constant encouragement during the few short hours she'd been in labour. All without a single word of preparation. They hadn't even got around to the discussion about whether he would attend the labour or not.

He hadn't even blinked when she'd turned the air blue on a few occasions, and chances were he'd never regain the feeling in his right hand. She hadn't had time to think about whether he should be there or not. And the look on his face when he'd first set eyes on their daughter had seared right into her soul.

She'd never seen a look of love like it. Ever.

And that burned in ways she couldn't even have imagined.

'Seb?'

'Yes?' He stood up. 'Do you need something?'

She shook her head, trying to keep her wavering emotions out of her voice. 'I wouldn't ever have kept her from you. I would have told you about her as soon as she arrived,' she said quietly. She blinked back the tears.

She saw him swallow and press his lips together briefly. They were both realising he could have missed this moment. Missed the first sight of his daughter. Was it really fair that she'd even contemplated that?

She licked her lips. 'Your mother—what has she said about all this?'

For a few seconds he didn't meet her gaze. 'She's disappointed in me. That I didn't do things in a traditional way. She thinks I treated Theresa badly. She hasn't quite grasped the fact that Theresa was marrying me out of duty—not of love.' His eyes met hers and he gave a rueful smile. 'I think it's just as well I'm an only child. She would have tried to disown me at the beginning of the week because of the scandal I've caused.'

'But what does that mean? What does that mean for you, for me and for Margaret?'

Something washed over her, a wave of complete protectiveness towards her daughter. She wasn't going to let anyone treat Margaret as if she were a scandal—as if she weren't totally loved and wanted.

Sebastian sat down on the edge of the bed next to her and wrapped his arm around her shoulders. 'It means that I'll have to phone the Queen and tell her about her new granddaughter. She thought there would be a few weeks to try and manipulate the press. I guess our daughter had other ideas.'

The thought of the press almost chilled her. 'Can we keep her to ourselves for just a few more hours?' She hated the way that her voice sounded almost pleading. But this was their daughter, their special time. She wasn't ready to share it with the world just yet.

'Of course.' He smiled. His fingers threaded through

the hair at the nape of her neck. It was a movement of comfort, of reassurance.

Her hormones were on fire. Her heart felt as if it had swollen in her chest, first with the love for her daughter, and next for the rush of emotions she'd felt towards Seb in the last few hours.

Everything that had happened between them had crystallised for her. His sexy grin, twinkling eyes and smart comments. The way his gaze sometimes just meshed with hers. The tingling of her skin when he touched her.

The way that at times she just felt so connected to him.

All she felt right now was love. Maybe she was a fool to expect more than he already offered. She could live in Montanari. He had no expectations of her giving up work—she could work with the staff she'd trained in their specialist hospital.

Margaret could be brought up in a country she would ultimately one day rule. And although that completely terrified Sienna, it was a destiny that couldn't be ignored.

Did it matter if Sebastian didn't love her with his whole heart? He respected her—she knew that. And he would love their daughter.

This might be simpler if she didn't already know the truth.

She loved Sebastian. She'd probably loved him since that first weekend—she just hadn't allowed her brain to go there because of the betrayal that she'd felt. How hard would it be to live with a man, to stand by his side and know that he didn't reciprocate the love she felt for him?

Could she keep that hidden away? Would she be able to live with a neutral face in place in order to give their daughter the life she should have?

She pressed her lips together. Having just a little part of the man she loved might be enough. Having to look at those sexy smiles and twinkling eyes on a daily basis wouldn't exactly be a hardship.

And if he kept looking at her the way he did now, she could maybe hope for more. Another child might not be as far off the agenda as she'd initially thought.

She looked up at those forest-green eyes and her whole world tipped upside down. 'Your mother's name—it's Grace, isn't it?'

He nodded but looked confused.

She stared back down to her daughter's pale, smooth skin. 'I've had the name Margaret in my head for a while. But I had never even considered any middle names.' She looked up at him steadily. 'That seems a bit of a royal tradition, isn't it?'

He nodded again. She could see the calculations flying behind his eyes. 'What do you think about giving Margaret a middle name?'

The edges of his lips started to turn upwards. 'Seriously?'

She nodded, feeling surer than before. 'I chose our daughter's first name. We never even had that discussion. How do you feel about choosing a middle name?'

She'd already planted the seed. Maybe the Queen wouldn't hate her quite as much as she imagined.

He looked serious for a second. 'Our family has a tradition of more than one middle name—how do you feel about that?'

She frowned. 'You mean you're not just Sebastian?'

He laughed. 'Oh, no. I'm Sebastian Albert Louis Falco.'

She leaned back against him. 'Okay, tell me what you're thinking. Let's try some names for size.'

He took a few seconds. 'If you agree, I'd like to call our daughter Margaret Grace Sophia Falco.' He turned to face her. 'Unless, of course, you want to call her after your mother.'

Something panged inside her. But the tiny feelings of regret about her relationship with her parents had long since depleted over time. 'No. I'm happy with Margaret. I think it's safe to say that my mother will play her grandmother role from a distance.' She glanced at the clock. 'I'll let both my parents know in a while about their granddaughter. I doubt very much that either of them will visit.' She gave a sad kind of smile. 'I might get some very nice flowers, though.'

She looked down at Margaret again, who'd stopped feeding for now and seemed to have settled back to sleep. 'Who is Sophia?'

Seb smiled. 'My great-grandmother. In public, probably the most terrifying woman in the world. In private? The woman I always had the most fun with. She taught me how to cheat at every board and card game imaginable.'

Sienna couldn't help but smile. 'You mean that the Falco family actually had some rogues?'

He whispered in her ear. 'I'll show you the family archives. We had pirates, conquerors and knights. We even had a magician.' He leaned over her shoulder and touched their daughter's nose. 'Happy Christmas, Margaret, welcome to the Falco family.'

Sienna turned to face him just as his lips met hers. 'Thank you, Sienna. Thank you for the best Christmas present in the world.'

She reached up and touched the side of his face. Her head was spinning. He was looking at her in a way she couldn't quite interpret. Her heart wanted to believe that it was a look of love, a look of hope and admiration. He hadn't stopped smiling at her—and even though she knew she must look a mess, he was making her feel as if she were the most special woman on the planet.

'Thank you,' she whispered as her fingers ran across his short hair. 'We made something beautiful. We made something special. I couldn't be happier.'

'Me either,' he agreed as he pulled her closer and kissed her again.

CHAPTER SEVEN

HE'D HARDLY SLEPT. He hadn't wanted to leave the hospital last night, but both he and Sienna had been exhausted. She only ever cat-napped when he was in the room and he'd realised—even though he hadn't wanted to be apart from them—that it would be better if he let her spend the night with their daughter alone.

Not that she would have had much time. He'd left the hospital at midnight and was up again at six, pacing the floors in her house, itching to go and see her and Margaret again.

His mother's voice had been almost strangled when he'd phoned with the news. But after a few seconds of horror, she'd regained her composure and asked if Sienna and baby were healthy after the premature delivery. He'd assured her that they were.

When he'd told her the name of her new granddaughter there had first been a sigh of relief and then a little quiver in her voice. 'I'm surprised that such a modern woman picked such a traditional name. It's a lovely gesture, Sebastian. Thank you. When will we see the baby?'

He sent his mother some pictures of Margaret and told her he'd invited both Sienna and Margaret to join him in Montanari. He hoped and prayed that they would, but placated his mother with the easy opt out about travelling so soon after delivery and making sure that Margaret's little lungs would be fit to fly.

He stood in the middle of the yellow nursery that Sienna had dreamed of for her daughter. If she agreed to join him in Montanari he would recreate this room exactly the way it was—anything to keep her happy.

Things had been good yesterday. They'd been better than good. Sienna and Margaret were his family, and that was exactly how they felt to him. He couldn't imagine spending a single day without them. He'd had a special item shipped yesterday from the royal vault at Montanari. It was still dark outside but the twinkling lights from the Christmas tree across the hall glinted off the elegant ruby and diamond engagement ring in his hand. He hadn't mentioned this to his mother yet. But with Margaret's new middle names, it was only fitting that Sienna wear the engagement ring of his great-grandmother Sophia.

The two of them would have loved each other.

He'd meant to go back to his hotel last night but Sienna had asked him to collect the baby car seat from the house so they could be discharged today. Once he'd arrived back at her house he'd decided just to stay. It had seemed easier. He should have brought some of his clothes from the hotel, because this was where they would come back to in the first instance.

He hurried outside to his car. It didn't really matter what time it was—the hospital would let him in any time. He just wanted Sienna to have had a chance to rest.

As soon as he pulled up outside the hospital alarm bells started going off in his head. Every TV station with a van was parked near the entrance. Every reporter he'd ever met was talking into a camera.

Someone spotted his car. All he could hear was shrieks followed by the trampling of feet. He got out of the car in a hurry. One of the reporters thrust a newspaper towards him. 'Prince Sebastian. Tell us about your new arrival.'

'Congratulations. What have you called your daughter?'

They surrounded him. Security. He hadn't considered security for his daughter. He stared at the news headline in front of him.

A NEW PRINCESS FOR MONTANARI!

The questions came thick and fast.

His hand reached out and grabbed the paper. He hadn't agreed to a press release. He had discussed it with his team and they'd planned an announcement for later today, once he, Sienna and baby Margaret had left Teddy's.

How on earth did the press know about Margaret already? He looked a little closer and felt his ire rise. There was a picture of his daughter. *His daughter.* Wrapped in a pink blanket, clearly lying in her hospital cot. Who on earth had taken that?

He started to push his way through the crowd of reporters. He didn't manhandle anyone but he didn't leave them in any doubt that he would reach his destination.

'Prince Sebastian, what about Sienna McDonald, the baby's mother? Are you engaged? Are you planning a royal wedding?'

Right now, he wished he could answer yes. But it seemed premature. Even though things were good between them, he hadn't asked her again yet. But the enthusiasm being shown for the birth of the new Princess was more than a little infectious. These people would hang around all day. It would be smarter just to give them a quick comment—he could find out about that photo later.

He turned around and held up his hands. 'As you

know, my daughter was born a little earlier than expected on Christmas Eve. Both mother and baby are doing well and...' he paused for a second as he searched for the words '... I'm looking forward to us all being a family together very soon. Our daughter's name is Princess Margaret Grace Sophia Falco,' he finished with before turning around and walking through the main doors of the hospital.

The noise behind him reached a crescendo.

The length of his strides increased in his hurry to reach Sienna and his daughter. His hand slid into his pocket and he touched the ring again. The box had been too bulky to fit in the pocket of his jeans. But the ring was still safely there.

A few of the midwives gave him a nod as he walked towards Sienna's room. It was only Boxing Day so the decorations were still all in place and Christmas carols played in the background.

Hopefully, by the end of today, he could make things perfect for everyone.

Sienna felt cold. She had been ignoring the TV in the corner of the room and just concentrating on her baby. The midwives were great. Margaret had decided to have an episode of colic at three a.m. After half an hour, one of the midwives had told Sienna to get some sleep and she'd walk the corridor with Margaret. Sienna hadn't wanted to let her baby out of her sight, but she'd been exhausted. Two hours later she'd woken with a peaceful Margaret wrapped in her pink blanket and back in her crib.

By that time, she'd wanted to get back up. She'd had a bath to ease her aching back and legs, and fed and changed Margaret. Once Sebastian arrived she was hoping they would get the all-clear to take Margaret home.

Something caught her attention. A few words from the TV. Sebastian.

She looked up as the TV reporters camped outside the hospital all set off at a run to interview Sebastian on live TV.

She still couldn't understand how they knew about the baby. No one she worked with or trusted would speak to the press. Sebastian had said he would talk to her about a press release.

She smiled as she caught sight of him on camera. His hair was a little mussed up. He obviously hadn't taken time to fix it. His tanned skin sort of hid the tiredness she could see in his eyes. His leather jacket—still complete with yellow smudge—showed off his broad chest and his snug jeans caused her smile to broaden. Sebastian Falco. Was she really going to agree to what he'd suggested last night?

Sebastian was a seasoned pro when it came to paparazzi. He wouldn't speak to them.

But actually, he stopped.

Just like Sienna's heart.

They were all firing questions to him about Margaret. Asking him to confirm the birth and her name. Someone thrust a newspaper towards him and she saw the tic in the side of his jawline. Whatever was in that newspaper had made him angry.

Another voice cut above the rest. 'Prince Sebastian, what about Sienna McDonald, the baby's mother? Are you engaged? Are you planning a royal wedding?'

A prickle ran down her spine. How could he answer that? They hadn't even finished that discussion.

Something flickered across his face, the edges of his lips turned upwards. 'As you know, my daughter was born a little earlier than expected on Christmas Eve. Both mother and baby are doing well and...' he paused for a second as a smile spread across his face '... I'm looking forward to us all being a family together very soon. Our daughter's name is Princess Margaret Grace Sophia Falco.'

Her heart plummeted.

Oh, no. Oh, no. Did he realise how that looked?

Sure enough the reporters had a field day. A woman in a bright red coat swung around and announced straight into the camera. 'We have a royal engagement *and* a royal wedding! It seems that Dr Sienna McDonald is about to become the wife of Prince Sebastian and the future of Queen of Montanari.'

The woman's bright red lips seemed to move in synchrony with the other reporters all around her, talking into their respective cameras.

A chill swept across her skin. The woman seemed to think she'd got the scoop of the century. She held her hand up to the sign of the Royal Cheltenham hospital. 'Looks like Teddy's is going to have to find another cardiac baby surgeon.' She said the words with glee. 'Once Sienna gets to Montanari she will have no time to worry about being a doctor.'

Fury swept around her. How dared they? How dared any of them assume that she would give up her job, her house, her life?

The door swung open and Sebastian strode in with a smile. 'You're up? You're awake?' He was still carrying the newspaper that had been thrust at him in his hand. 'Great. We need to talk. We need to make decisions.'

'Haven't you already just made all those for me?' She walked right up to him. 'Who on earth do you think you are?'

He pulled back and glanced towards their sleeping bundle in the corner. 'What on earth are you talking about?'

She flung her hands up in the air. 'Oh, come on, Sebastian. You're not naïve. You've been doing this all your life. You know better than to get pulled into things.' She couldn't stop the build of fury in her chest.

He'd tricked her. He'd sweet-talked her. He'd used all that princely charm. All to get exactly what he wanted.

All to get his daughter back to Montanari.

Sebastian shook his head. 'What do you mean?' He tried to step around her—to get to Margaret.

Sienna stepped sideways—stopping his path. 'You practically just announced to the world that we were getting married.'

His tanned face blanched. 'I didn't.' It sounded sort of strangled.

She pointed to the yellow tickertape-style news headline that had now appeared along the bottom of the TV screen.

Prince Sebastian to marry Dr Sienna McDonald, mother of their daughter.

He flinched. Then something else happened. The expression on his face changed. He reached down into his pocket. 'Sienna, I didn't say we were getting married.'

'No. But with a smile on your face you just said that we were all going to be a family together soon. You practically told them we'd be moving to Montanari with you!'

He put his hands on her shoulders. 'What's wrong with you? Calm down. After last night, I thought things were good between us. I thought that maybe we were ready to take the next step.' He glanced over her shoulder. 'The right step for us—and our baby.'

She shivered. She felt as if she were in a bad movie with the villain in front of her. 'You did this,' she croaked as she looked frantically back to Margaret.

'What?' Confusion reigned over his face.

'The leak. It was you.' She pushed him away from her, forgetting for a second about Margaret as she strode forward and lifted the discarded newspaper. The picture of their baby brought tears to her eyes. 'You did this?' She couldn't actually believe it. 'To get what you wanted, you actually gave them a picture of my daughter without my permission?'

She couldn't think straight at all. She was just overwhelmed with emotions and a huge distinctive mothering urge. She'd been tricked. Manipulated. By a man she'd let steal her heart.

He'd left last night after telling her things could work. He'd introduce her to the family. Margaret could be brought up in Montanari and they could all live together as a family. He'd let her think they'd embrace a new-style queen—even though it wasn't a title she'd wanted. She could continue with the job she loved.

Sebastian looked utterly confused and shook his head again. 'What on earth are you talking about?' He took the paper from her hand. 'You think I did this? Really? Why on earth would I do that? We talked about this last night.'

'Yes. You said you'd wait. You said we'd agree to a statement. But that obviously wasn't good enough for you. You're used to getting your own way, Sebastian. You're used to being in charge. You lied to me last night. I was wrong to trust you. You made me think you would consider my feelings in all this.' She swung her hand to the side. 'Instead, you let the world know about our baby.' Tears sprang to her eyes. 'This is my time with my baby, mine. I don't want to share her with the world.

I'm not ready.' She shook her head as everything started to overwhelm her. He was just standing there, standing there looking stunned.

She kept shaking her head. Now that they'd started, the tears just kept on coming. She was angry at herself for crying. Angry that she was standing here in her ratty pyjamas, hair in a ponytail and pale skin telling the Prince she wouldn't stand for this behaviour. She wouldn't be manipulated into more or less giving up her life and her daughter.

She'd thought there might just actually be some hope for them both. They could reconnect the way they had in Montanari. The memories that she had of the place would stay with her for ever.

There had been moments—fragments—when they'd captured that spark again. But she'd been a fool. She'd been living the fairy tale in her head. Why? Why would a prince ever love her?

Things shouldn't be like this. If she were telling him to leave, she should be doing it in some magnificent building, wearing an elegant dress, perfect make-up and her hair all coiffured. She should be looking a million dollars as she told the fairy-tale Prince he couldn't manipulate her or deceive her. That she would bring their daughter up here, rather than be promised a lifetime without love.

Because that was what it really came down to.

That was what she wanted. What she'd always wanted.

For Sebastian to love her, the way her heart told her she loved him.

The clarity in her brain made her turn on him.

'You've deceived me. You've deceived me right from the start. You've spent the last few days trying to sweet-talk me. Trying to persuade me to bring our daughter to Montanari. And now? You think if you just leak the story to the press, then give them some kind of coy smile, and tell them we're about to be a family—then that's it. A fait accompli.' She flung her hands in the air again. 'Well, no, Sebastian. No. I won't have it. I won't get trapped into a life I don't want. I won't bring Margaret up in a marriage with no love in it.'

If Sebastian had looked stunned before, now his mouth fell open. He stepped forward then froze as she continued to rant.

She pressed her hand to her heart as the tears streamed freely. 'I won't do it. I just won't. I've been there. I've already spent eighteen years in a relationship like that. A relationship where I was tolerated and not really loved.' She shook her head. 'Do you know what that feels like? Really? Do you honestly think I'd bring my daughter up in a relationship like that? It's not enough. Not nearly enough. I love you. You love her. But you don't love me. I don't want a loveless marriage. I want a husband that will love and adore me.' She looked off into the corner as she tried to catch her breath.

'A husband that will look at me as though I'm the most important person in the world. A husband that will trust me enough to always talk to me. To always be truthful with me. To support me in the job that I've trained to do since I was eighteen.' She took a step towards Sebastian. Looking into the face of the man that she'd thought would love her as much as she loved him. Being here in front of him made her stomach feel as if it were twisting inside out. It was hurting like a physical pain. That was how much she wanted this dream to come true. That was how much she wanted to be loved by him. It felt like the ultimate betrayal.

'You lied to me,' she said with a shaking voice. 'You said Montanari was ready for a new kind of queen. A queen who had a career. A queen who worked. You said that could happen. But according to the world outside, the expectation is that I give it all up. My years and years of training don't count. They don't matter. Well, they matter to me. And the environment I bring my daughter up in matters to me. I want Margaret to feel respected. To know she should work hard. To know that money doesn't grow on trees and you have to earn a living.'

She kept her voice as strong as she could. 'Your plan didn't work, Sebastian. I won't marry you. We won't be coming to Montanari.'

Sebastian felt as if he'd been pulled up in a tornado and dumped out of the funnel into a foreign land. He couldn't believe what she was saying. He couldn't believe what he was being accused of.

Worst of all were her words about being trapped inside a loveless marriage. Did she really hate him that much? She could never grow to love him even a little?

The ring felt as if it burned in his pocket. His plan had been to come in here this morning, tell her he loved her and would make this work, and propose. He'd felt almost sure she would grow to love him just as much as he loved her.

But her words of a loveless marriage were like a dagger to the heart. No matter what he promised her it seemed she couldn't ever imagine a life with him. A life with them, together as a family.

Had he really been so blind that he thought they were almost there?

Margaret gave a whimper from the crib. Twice, Sienna had stopped him walking towards her. Twice, she'd stopped him from seeing his daughter.

Sebastian felt numb.

'I'm done trying to force what isn't there. I'm done trying to be anything other than I am. You should have told me as soon as you found out you were pregnant. You should have let me know that I was going to be a father. The news blindsided me. You had months to get used to the idea. I had two weeks.'

He looked furious now.

He put his hand on his chest. 'And I wanted it, Sienna. I wanted it more than you could ever have imagined. I can't believe you're being so judgemental.' He shook his head. 'What did I say? I said I was looking forward to us all being a family together very soon. That's it. What's so wrong with that? They asked me if we were engaged and if we would get married and what did I do? I smiled. Because a tiny little part of me actually wanted that to happen.'

He started pacing.

'Do you know why? Because I was a fool. I was a fool to think we actually could have a life together. I was a fool to think you might grant me a scrap of that affection and passion you keep so tightly locked up inside you.'

He spun around towards her again.

'Well, I'm done. I'm done trying to force this. You clearly don't know how to love someone. Or if you do, it's clear that person will never be me. I won't spend my life tiptoeing around you. Margaret is my daughter, as much as yours. I'm not going to fight with you, Sienna. I will not have my daughter witnessing her parents rowing over her. If you're incapable of talking to me about her—if you're incapable of compromise—then we can talk via lawyers. You don't get the ownership on loving Margaret. She has the right to be loved by both her parents. I want to see her. I want to spend time with her.

And, even though you clearly hate me, I won't let you stop me seeing her.'

He couldn't stop the words from coming out of his mouth. This woman, Sienna, who he'd hoped would make his heart sing, had just turned his world upside down. He loved her with his whole heart. He loved his daughter with his whole heart.

This morning, he'd thought he could turn this into something wonderful. He'd had the audacity to think that he and Sienna could love each other and it could last a lifetime.

Now…?

He just didn't know.

Sienna couldn't find any more words. Sebastian turned on his heel and walked outside.

She sagged on the bed out of pure exhaustion. What had happened? The tears continued to fall and her only comfort was lifting Margaret to her chest and holding the little warm body next to hers.

Her precious daughter. *Hers.* That was what she'd said to Sebastian. It didn't matter that it had been in the heat of the moment. She'd said it deliberately to exclude him. But Margaret wouldn't be here without Seb. The facts of life were simple.

The reporter in the red coat was still talking incessantly on the TV. Now, she was talking about how delighted Queen Grace was, how angry Princess Theresa was, how the people in Montanari were waiting for a formal announcement about their new heir, and how the Prince was clearly enthralled by his new daughter and fiancée since there had been no sign of him.

All she could think about was the expression on Sebastian's face. The hurt. The shock. The surprise. The words, 'I said I was looking forward to us all being a family together.'

She screwed her eyes closed for a second. When she'd challenged him on that he'd said he'd smiled because he'd hoped they could have a life together. They would get engaged. They would get married. Something tugged at her heart. The tone of his voice. The pain in his eyes. What did that mean? Did that mean he did care about her? He might actually love her?

There was a knock at the door and one of the midwives entered. She looked uncomfortable and pale-faced. She hesitated before talking. 'Seb... The Prince. He's down at the nursery. He asked if he could see Margaret before he leaves.'

'He leaves?' She felt sick. She stared down at her daughter's face. Margaret stared back and blinked. It was as if she was trying to focus. Already her eyes looked as if they would change colour. Change colour to the same as her father's forest green.

The midwife hesitated again. 'He asked if he could see her before he returns to Montanari.'

There.

She had what she wanted.

Sebastian was going to go.

It was like being rolled over by a giant tidal wave. The isolation. The devastation.

She started to shake as she gazed at Margaret. How would she feel if the shoe were on the other foot? How would she feel if someone stood between her and her daughter?

She'd chased him away. She'd said everything she probably shouldn't have said. But she couldn't think straight right now. Her heart was already wrung out by the birth of her baby.

When Sebastian had given that smile to the reporter she had instantly judged. She'd assumed he was being smug. She'd assumed he was calculating. But what if it had been none of those things? What if he'd been entirely truthful with her?

What if…what if he'd actually meant what he'd said? He'd believed they could have a life together. But did that life include love?

She started sobbing again. She didn't want him without love. She wanted everything. She couldn't let herself settle for anything less.

The midwife pulled tissues from a box that had miraculously appeared and handed her a few. She didn't say anything, just put a gentle hand on Sienna's shoulder.

She stared at her little daughter's face. He'd accused her of being incapable of love. She felt like just the opposite. As if she loved too much. She loved Margaret so much already. And right now? Her heart was breaking in two about Sebastian. She wasn't a woman incapable of love.

Far from it.

'What do you want me to tell him?' came the gentle voice of the midwife.

She nodded as a tear dripped from her face and onto Margaret's blanket. 'Yes. Tell him, yes. He can see Margaret.'

She handed her baby over with shaking hands.

She'd ruined everything and there was no way back.

The midwife took tentative steps down the corridor towards him, holding Margaret still wrapped in the pink blanket. His heart gave a little surge of relief. He turned back to the window of the nursery. The quads he'd heard everyone talking about looked tiny compared to Margaret. But he could see each of them kicking their legs and punching their tiny hands. Each fighting indignantly against their entry into the world. Their names were emblazoned over their plastic cribs. Graham, Lily, Rupert and Rose. He smiled. Traditional names, like Margaret. Maybe it was a new trend?

The midwife gestured with her head to the next room. 'Would you like to sit in here with your daughter?' He nodded and followed her inside, sitting in a large chair next to the window as she handed Margaret over. 'I'll wait outside,' she said quietly, then paused at the doorway. 'Sienna. She's very upset.' She sighed. 'I think you both need to take a deep breath.' She waved her hand. 'It's none of my business. I'd just hate you both to lose something that you love.' She turned and walked outside.

Sebastian stared at his daughter in his arms. His heart should be soaring. He should be celebrating. He should be rejoicing. But he'd never felt quite this sad.

This hadn't been the day he'd planned for.

This hadn't been the day he'd expected. In fact, it was so far away from what he'd thought would happen that he could barely even believe this was how things had turned out.

It was never meant to be like this between them. Never.

Of that—he was sure.

But how on earth did they come back from this? He'd said some things he regretted. He'd said a lot of things he regretted.

He'd never been a man for emotional outbursts. He'd spent a life of control, of restraint. But Sienna brought out a side of him he'd never thought he had.

Around her, his feelings ran stronger than he thought possible.

So, it was true.

Love could cause the greatest happiness.

And love could cause the greatest misery.

Margaret grumbled in his arms. Her little head turned from side to side, probably rooting for her mother.

Could he really go home? Could he really bear to leave them and not see them for how long—a few days, a week, a month?

He shuddered. He couldn't bear that. Not at all.

Life was precious. Life was fragile. Life wasn't supposed to be like this.

What would he do if he returned to Montanari? Probably fight with his parents. Probably take his frustrations out on those around him. All because he'd messed up the most important relationship of his life.

The relationship with the woman he loved with his whole heart.

He'd tried to forget about Sienna. He'd tried to follow his parents' wishes and get engaged to someone else.

In the end, it hadn't worked. It would *never* have worked. His heart belonged to Sienna.

And he had to believe, he *had* to believe that part of her heart belonged to him too.

Margaret was important. Margaret would always be one of his priorities. But his other priority would be the woman he wanted as his wife.

Life ahead for him was formidable. Ruling Montanari would only be possible with a strong woman by his side. A woman whom he loved and respected. A woman who could help to lead Montanari into the modern world.

Everything about Sienna had captured his heart. Her wit. Her intelligence. Her stubbornness. Her determination. The look in her eyes when she'd first seen their daughter...

He had to win her. He had to win her back.

He'd never actually told her how he felt about her. He'd never actually put his heart on the line.

He'd been scared his feelings wouldn't be reciprocated. And that could still happen.

But he wasn't leaving her until he tried.

He stood up and walked to the door. The midwife stepped forward to take Margaret. 'No.' He shook his head. 'I'll take Margaret back to her mother.' He took a calm breath. 'I won't leave without talking to her.' He added quietly, 'I won't leave without putting up a fight for them both.'

The midwife gave a little nod of her head. 'Good luck,' she said quietly as he started down the corridor.

She'd finally managed to stop crying, wash her face and change out of the pyjamas into the clothes that Sebastian had set down in the corner for her earlier. She'd be going home soon.

Home with her daughter.

Right from when she'd started making her plans, she'd always expected to take Margaret home on her own.

But this last week, those steadfast plans had started to wobble.

Sebastian had slowly but surely started to creep his way around the edges and somehow into the middle of them all.

The night before last, when she'd seen the beautiful job he'd made of the nursery she'd been overwhelmed. It was almost as if Sebastian had climbed into her brain and seen the picture that she had stored in there.

He'd made the dream a reality.

His face when he'd looked at their daughter had taken her breath away. And when he'd then turned and met her gaze? She'd never felt so special. She'd never felt so connected or loved.

How could she go from that point to this?

She finished rubbing some make-up onto her face. Right now, she was paler than she'd ever been. She needed something—anything—to make her look a little alive again. She couldn't find her mascara, or any blusher, and there was only one colour of lipstick in her make-up bag, so she rubbed a little furiously into her cheeks and put some on her lips.

The door swung open behind her and she stepped out of the bathroom to get Margaret from the midwife. Her boobs were already starting to ache and Margaret was probably hungry again.

But it wasn't the midwife.

It was Seb.

For a second, neither of them spoke. They just stared. Finally Seb drew in a breath. 'You look…good.'

'That good, really?' It came out of nowhere. The kind of smart retort she'd got used to saying around him. Her eyes instantly started to fill with tears again—it was just as well she hadn't found mascara.

Margaret gave a little yelp and she held out her arms. 'Give me her. She needs to feed.'

He hesitated. And instead of handing Margaret over, he put her up on his shoulder. 'We need to talk.'

Sienna shook her head. 'We're done talking. We've said enough. We both need some space.'

He nodded. 'You're right. But just exactly how much space do you need?'

She frowned. 'What do you mean?'

He met her gaze. 'I mean, I don't want to leave. I don't want to go back to Montanari without the two people I love.'

She froze. Part of her wanted to believe. But part of her questioned everything.

'You just want Margaret. You don't want me. Don't panic, Seb. We'll work something out. You can see her.'

He stepped closer. Margaret seemed to be sucking at his neck. It wouldn't take her long to realise there was no milk there. He touched her arm. 'You're wrong. I do want you. I've always wanted you, Sienna—even when I didn't really know it myself. I would have come back. I would have always come back for you.'

She could hear what he was saying. He'd tried to say it before. But she just couldn't let herself believe it.

'But you didn't,' she whispered. 'You only came because of Margaret.'

He closed his eyes for a second. 'Sienna, you have to believe that even if Margaret wasn't here, I still would be.'

It was painful when she sucked in a breath. She shook her head. 'Words are easy. I'd like to believe you but, for all I know, you might just be saying this to persuade us both to come back to Montanari with you. This might all just be a trick to get Margaret back to your country.'

He reached over and touched her face. It was the gentlest of touches. 'Sienna, don't. Don't think like that of me. Is that really how you feel about me? I'm a liar? A manipulator?' He looked genuinely upset. His forest-green gaze held hers. 'Is that how the woman I love really feels about me?'

Her heart squeezed tightly in her chest. Her mouth was so dry she could barely speak. 'You love me?'

He stepped even closer. Margaret let out a few grumbles. His hand brushed back across Sienna's cheek and this time across her long eyelashes too.

'I love you so much I sometimes can't breathe when I think about you. I love you so much that the face I see when I close my eyes is yours. I can't let you slip through my fingers. I can't let the chance for this to become real get away because I'm emotional. You're emotional. And I'm a fool.'

She smiled. He knew how to charm a lady.

His fingers moved around her ear, tucking some stray strands of hair behind it. 'But I will, Sienna, if that's what you want. If you want me to leave—to give you space—I will. But know that I'll do it because I love you. Because you are the most important thing to me on this planet. Because I will always put what you want before what I want.'

Tears pooled in her eyes again and she took a step towards him. 'How can you do that, silly? You have a kingdom to look after. All those people. How on earth can I matter?'

He bent his head towards her. 'You matter because I say you matter. You and Margaret will always come first for me.'

This wasn't charm. This wasn't manipulation. This wasn't lies.

This was real.

'Oh, Seb,' she whispered. 'Can this really work?'

He took a deep breath. He was shaking. He was actually shaking. 'Only if you love me. Do you love me, Sienna?'

A tear dripped down her face. She reached up and touched the stubble on his jawline. Her lips trembled as she smiled. 'I do,' she whispered as she pulled his forehead towards hers.

His smile spread across his face. His eyelashes tickled her forehead. 'I think you've said that a little too early.'

She laughed as he fumbled in his pocket. 'Give me a second.'

She held her breath as he pulled out a glittering ruby and diamond ring—bigger than she could ever have imagined. He smiled at the ring. 'This is a family heirloom. It belonged to my great-grandmother, Sophia, one of the most spirited women I've ever had the pleasure to know.' He gave her a special smile. 'She would have loved you, you know. She told me to give it to the woman that captured my heart and my soul. That's you. Will you marry me, Sienna?'

She lifted Margaret from his shoulder and tilted her lips up to his.

'A princess and a surgeon? Do you think you can cope?'

He slid his arms around her as his lips met hers. 'I can't wait to spend my life finding out.'

EPILOGUE

Montanari was covered in snow for the first time in twenty years. It was almost as if every weather system had aligned especially for the royal wedding.

Sienna looked at the snow-covered palace lawn, trying to hide the butterflies in her stomach. She kissed her ruby and diamond engagement ring and closed her eyes for a second.

This was it. This was when she married the man who had captured her heart, her soul and the very breath in her body. Sophia's engagement ring had been a lucky talisman for her. So much so that, when she couldn't decide on her wedding gown, late one night she'd trawled through the palace archives and found a picture of Sophia on her wedding day.

It had been perfect. A traditional gown covered in heavy lace was the last thing she would ever have contemplated. But somehow, the style reached out and grabbed her. The long-sleeve lace arms and shoulders were perfect for a winter wedding, as was the lace that covered the satin bodice and skirt. She'd taken the picture and asked the wedding designer to replicate the dress for her.

The door opened behind her and Juliet and her daughter Bea walked in. Both were wearing red gowns

that matched their bouquets. Juliet gave her a smile.
'Ready, Princess?'

Sienna shook her head. 'Don't. I might just be sick all
down this gown before anyone has had a chance to see it.'

Juliet walked over, her pregnancy bump clearly visible in her gown. Babies were in the air around here. She
pulled at a strand of Sienna's curled hair. 'I spotted Sebastian earlier. He couldn't wipe the smile off his face.
And you needn't worry about sickness. Margaret has just
been sick on the Queen's outfit. I thought she was going
to pass out with shock!'

Sienna threw back her head and laughed. 'Really?
You mean, she'll actually have to change her outfit? Oh,
I love that girl of mine. She knows exactly how to make
her mother proud.'

There was a knock at the door and Oliver stuck his
head inside. 'Sebastian asked me to give you a message.'

Her heart gave a little flutter. 'What is it?'

Oliver laughed. 'Hurry up and get down the aisle. He's
done waiting. It's Christmas Eve tomorrow and Margaret's birthday. You have presents to wrap!'

Sienna gave a nervous nod. 'I'm ready. Tell him, I'm
ready.'

Oliver walked across the room and gave her a kiss on
the cheek. 'Ella and I couldn't be happier for you.'

She smiled as he left. Ella and Oliver had got married
a few months before the birth of their baby, Harry. She'd
never seen him happier.

Music drifted up the stairs towards them. Juliet gave
her a nod and walked around, picking up the skirts of
her dress.

The wedding was being held in the royal chapel, with
the reception in the palace. She'd tried to memorise all
the visiting dignitaries in the hope she wouldn't make

some faux pas. Queen Grace had only thawed a little in the last year. She seemed a little interested in Margaret, and when she'd made a few barbed comments about the wedding plans Sienna had happily handed over the guest list and seating plan and told her to take charge, in case she seated some feuding families next to each other.

She was learning how to manage her mother-in-law and Sebastian was entirely grateful.

They reached the entrance to the chapel and Sienna sucked in her breath. The entire chapel was lit by candles, creating a beautiful ethereal glow. Juliet rearranged her skirts then set off down the aisle with Bea. Charlie watched them the whole way, his face beaming with pride. Their wedding plans had been put on temporary hold due to Juliet's pregnancy, but Sienna couldn't wait to attend the ceremony in the Cotswolds next summer.

Oliver held out his elbow. 'Two jobs for the price of one. Do I get double the salary for this?'

She bent over and kissed his cheek. 'You get my eternal thanks for being such a good friend. I couldn't have picked anyone more perfect to give me away, or to be Sebastian's best man.' She winked as the wedding march started. 'Just remember, the wedding speech will be watched the world over. I love you, but tell any Sienna-got-drunk stories and I will lace your dinner with arsenic.'

He laughed and patted her arm. 'I'll keep that in mind. Ready?'

She licked her dry lips and nodded.

As soon as they started down the aisle, Margaret started to call to her. 'Mama, Mama.' She was being held by Annabelle while Max held their daughter, Hope. Max and Annabelle had renewed their wedding vows and, after adopting Hope, were hoping to adopt two boys who were in foster care in North Africa.

Margaret was tugging at Annabelle's hair with one hand and waving at Sienna with the other. Her cream dress was rumpled—she crawled everywhere—and her headband was almost off her head. Margaret was destined to be the biggest tomboy in the world.

Sienna stopped to kiss her little hand, then carried on the last few steps to Sebastian.

He didn't hesitate. He took her hand immediately. 'You look stunning,' he said simply.

'You don't look too bad yourself.' She smiled. His athletic frame filled the royal dress uniform well, the dark green jacket making his eyes even more intense. Her heart skipped a few beats.

They fought regularly and made up even more passionately. He'd helped prepare her for the new role she'd have in Montanari and supported her in every decision she'd made. She'd started working between both hospitals but, to Oliver's disappointment, had made some plans recently to work permanently in Montanari. Sebastian didn't know that yet.

The music started to play around them for the first hymn and he leaned over and whispered in her ear. 'I didn't think it was possible, but I love you even more each day.' His thumb traced a circle in her palm. 'Ready for two to become one?'

She smiled at him with twinkling eyes. 'Actually, it's three becomes four.'

He blinked. Then his eyes widened and his smile spread from ear to ear as Sienna started to laugh.

And that was the picture that made the front page of every newspaper around the world.

* * * * *

We hope you enjoyed the final story in the
CHRISTMAS MIRACLES IN MATERNITY *quartet*

And, if you missed where it all started, check out

THE NURSE'S CHRISTMAS GIFT
by Tina Beckett
THE MIDWIFE'S PREGNANCY MIRACLE
by Kate Hardy
WHITE CHRISTMAS FOR THE SINGLE MUM
by Susanne Hampton

All available now!

MILLS & BOON®

MEDICAL ROMANCE

THE ULTIMATE IN ROMANTIC MEDICAL DRAMA

6/03

MILLS & BOON®

EXCLUSIVE EXTRACT

Saoirse Murphy's proposal of a 'convenient'
arrangement with paramedic Santiago Valentino
soon ignites a very inconvenient passion...

Read on for a sneak preview of
SANTIAGO'S CONVENIENT FIANCÉE
by Annie O'Neil

Saoirse went up on tiptoe and kissed him.

From the moment her lips touched Santiago's she
didn't have a single lucid thought. Her brain all but
exploded in a vain attempt to unravel the quick-fire
sensations. Heat, passion, need, longing, sweet and tangy
all jumbled together in one beautiful confirmation that
his lips were every bit as kissable as she'd thought they
might be.

Snippets of what was actually happening were hitting
her in blips of delayed replay.

Her fingers tangled in his silky, soft hair. Santi's wide
hands tugged her in tight, right at the small of her back.
There was no doubting his body's response to her now.
The heated pleasure she felt when one of his hands
slipped under her T-shirt elicited an undiluted moan of
pleasure. He matched her move for move as if they had
been made for one another. Her body's reaction to his
felt akin to hitting all hundred watts her body was capable
of for the very first time.

She wanted more.

No.

She wanted it *all*. The whole package. The feelings. The pitter-patter of her heart. Knowing it was reciprocated. Being part of a shared love. Not some sham wedding so she wouldn't have to live in a country where her soul had all but shriveled up and died.

She felt Santi's kisses deepen and her will-power to shore up some sort of resistance to what was happening plummeted. This felt so *real*. And a little too close to everything she'd hoped for wrapped up in a too-good-to-be-true package. That sort of thing didn't happen to her. And it wasn't. She'd started it, Santi was just responding. She heard herself moan and with its escape her resolve to resist abandoned her completely.

Don't miss
SANTIAGO'S CONVENIENT FIANCÉE
by Annie O'Neill

Available January 2017
www.millsandboon.co.uk